KU-272-152

Shirley Mann is a Derbyshire-based journalist who spent most of her career at the BBC. She then went on to make short films for organisations such as the Heritage Lottery Fund. Her first novel, *Lily's War*, was inspired by Shirley's mother, who was a WAAF and her father who was in the Eighth Army. Her second book, *Bobby's War* is about a young ATA pilot. *Hannah's War* is her third novel.

Hannah's WAR

Shirley Mann

ZAFFRE

First published in the UK in ebook in 2021
This paperback edition published in 2022 by
ZAFFRE
An imprint of Bonnier Books UK
4th Floor, Victoria House, Bloomsbury Square, London, England, WC1B 4DA
Owned by Bonnier Books
Sveavägen 56, Stockholm, Sweden

Copyright © Shirley Mann, 2021

All rights reserved.
No part of this publication may be reproduced,
stored or transmitted in any form by any means, electronic,
mechanical, photocopying or otherwise, without the
prior written permission of the publisher.

The right of Shirley Mann to be identified as Author of this
work has been asserted by her in accordance with the
Copyright, Designs and Patents Act, 1988.

This is a work of fiction. Names, places, events and
incidents are either the products of the author's
imagination or used fictitiously. Any resemblance to
actual persons, living or dead, or actual
events is purely coincidental.

A CIP catalogue record for this book is
available from the British Library.

ISBN: 978-1-83877-445-5

Also available as an ebook and an audiobook

1 3 5 7 9 10 8 6 4 2

Typeset by IDSUK (Data Connection) Ltd
Printed and bound in Great Britain by Clays Ltd, Elcograf S.p.A.

MIX
Paper from
responsible sources
FSC www.fsc.org **FSC® C018072**

Zaffre is an imprint of Bonnier Books UK
www.bonnierbooks.co.uk

For Kevin, my husband and an original 'farm boy.'
Your support means the world to me. Thank you
from the bottom of my heart.

Chapter 1

January 1943

Hannah flung herself back against the wooden struts of the stall. In front of her, a huge black shire horse was rearing up on its back legs, its eyes wide with fear. Hannah, a new recruit to the Land Army, brought her hands up to protect her head, but that seemed to make the horse worse. The bucket of hay she was trying to feed it had already been knocked to the stone floor, its contents scattering in all directions. The light from the doorway was blocked by the massive flank of the stallion and Hannah knew she was trapped. She looked around frantically to see whether there was anything she could use to protect herself, but there was nothing. The animal was completely out of control, and she had no idea how to calm it down.

'Shhhh, it's all right, it's all right,' she said as reassuringly as she could, but the horse was blowing out through its huge nostrils and stamping its feet so loudly that her voice was lost in the commotion. She tried to reach up to get hold of its head-collar, but it reared up again, banging its hooves against the wooden edges of the stall and trying to turn around in the limited space. Hannah was pinned to the wall.

At that moment, the horse seemed to register that she was there. Its eyes, wide with panic, looked down from its great height, straight into hers as if she were the enemy it had been trying to wreak revenge on all its life.

'I'm going to die, I'm going to die,' Hannah whispered out loud. She had only been at Salhouse Farm in Norfolk for twenty-four hours and already she had done something terribly wrong, but she did not know what. She cowered, sank to her knees and put her hands over her head to try to protect herself. She started to cry as the horse came towards her. *This is going to be the last moment of my life,* she thought.

A gentle voice came from behind the horse.

'*Das ist gut, das ist gut, mein Lieber, komm mit mir, schön ruhig. Ja, das ist gut, das ist gut.*'

Hannah peered out from between her fingers. A tall, young man with blond hair was taking hold of the leather strap on one side of the horse's mouth while avoiding any direct eye contact with the animal. He turned sideways to carefully manoeuvre the horse towards the door of the stable.

'Put down your hand, your watch is catching the sun in his eyes,' he said out of the corner of his mouth. His voice was soft, but the German accent made the hairs on her neck stand on end. The young man then gently started to stroke the beast's nose, turning its head so it could see the doorway. Lulled by the rhythmical movement and, sighting a way out, the horse calmed slightly and gradually allowed itself to be led out of the stall. Hannah put her head down, hugged her knees and rocked backwards and forwards, making whimpering noises.

After about five minutes, through the gap in her knees, she saw heavy boots walk along the floor towards her. She peered up slowly.

'It is all right,' the German told her. 'You are safe now.'

Hannah jumped to her feet, glared at the man in front of her and started yelling.

'Safe, safe? You think I'm safe. You're a German. The bloody enemy. How in hell's name can I be safe?'

And with that, she ran, sobbing, out of the barn.

Hannah ran across the yard, past one-legged Jed, the creepy under-foreman who was essentially her boss, past the young lad who always blushed with embarrassment every time he had to deal with one of the Land Army girls and past Andrew Hollis, who may have been the owner of Salhouse Farm, but who walked around the place with his shoulders bowed as if he was carrying an enormous sack of grain.

They all stared after the young girl. Jed was about to shout after her when Andrew Hollis put his arm out to stop him. The girl was out of danger and he had seen the terrified horse being led to the field to safety. He wanted no more fuss and it was almost the end of the day anyway. He was already angry enough that one of the German prisoners of war had been allowed out of the compound to help. Having not even acknowledged the presence of these Germans that it seemed were going to be forced upon him by the government, he was certainly not going to appear grateful or even interested.

Jed Roberts shook his head in frustration. How was he supposed to work this farm with a couple of Land Army girls who knew nothing, some lads too young to shave or men too old to climb a stile and a boss who was a closed book that only Archie, the head foreman, could read. And now, he had to deal with the bloody Krauts as well. He shuffled off, dragging his false leg behind him, surreptitiously taking out an aluminium flask from his filthy gaberdine pocket and swigging its contents.

Hannah ran into the brick barn where she was billeted, through the dark dining room and up the wooden stairs in the corner. She hurled herself onto her side of the bed she shared with the other Land Army girl, Dotty, and cried non-stop for twenty minutes.

She hated this life, she hated the farm, she hated sharing a double bed with a stranger and she wanted to go home.

Chapter 2

'What happened to you?' Dotty said, roughly pushing the bedroom door open a while later. 'Are you all right? I heard you had a set to with Hercules. He's a tough one, you should never turn your back on him.'

She sat on the bed and looked keenly at Hannah, noting the tear-stained cheeks and defeated expression. Dotty reached out her hand to cover Hannah's cold one.

'Seriously, Hannah, are you OK? I heard from that young lad,' she said, 'you know, the timid one, well, anyway, he told me you'd met one of the POWs. The boss has said he doesn't want them back on the farm but who knows what'll happen. Anyway, what was he like? Was he a monster? Are we all to be murdered in our beds? They're the enemy, I hate them all.'

The memory of Hannah's saviour was coloured by her anger at having to speak to a German, but she did have a vague disquieting thought that he seemed kind, which challenged all her preconceptions. She gave a non-committal answer to Dotty, unsure of what to say.

She tried to pull herself together, furious, as always, that she could not get the words out that were forming in her head. Hannah sometimes looked in the mirror and wondered at the scared girl who looked back at her. Inside, she had so much to say and abilities no one would ever give her credit for. The problem was that by the time she opened her mouth, all those things had evaporated and she was just shy Hannah. She wearily acknowledged that her new younger room-mate, Dotty, was already behaving like an older sister to her; it seemed she was destined to be surrounded by people who appeared more mature and wiser than she was. Hannah tried to think of the future like her school friend, Lily Mullins, did – as an exciting journey. But thanks to her mother's anxiety, Hannah had always been taught that adventure was not for her. She had joined the Land Army determined to change that.

Hannah Compton was nineteen years of age. Tall with dark, curly short hair and blue eyes that rarely flashed with anger, she was an only child, used to being ignored by her father and suffocated by her mother. Only her grandfather listened to anything she said and joining the Land Army had been a rebellion against the invisibility that threatened to define her life.

It had been such a short time since she had put on her new uniform, worth a whole thirty shillings, pulled her khaki jacket over the green jumper and brown breeches and proudly placed her brown hat on her head. Walking away from her terraced house in Colley Street, Stretford, she had glanced back at her mother, who was clutching a handkerchief, and her father, who was staring into space as usual. As soon as she was out of sight, Hannah actually skipped along the pavement, feeling the apron strings of her mother stretch and break as she neared the bus stop. The determination that this was going to be the turning point she had promised herself for years gave her footsteps a firm tread.

It was a taller, straighter Hannah who had arrived at Norwich Station ready to take up her posting at Salhouse Farm, just seven miles out of the city. The young girl had pushed her way along the platform, carrying her battered leather suitcase in front of her like a defence shield. To celebrate her arrival, she had bought a postcard at the kiosk near the entrance to the station, which she wrote and stamped to send to her mother as proof that she was strangely capable of finding her way without getting lost, being raped, murdered or arrested en route. She could not resist a smug smile as she popped it in the letterbox, delighted that all her mother's dire warnings had been in vain and headed for the bus.

Her satisfaction did not last very long. No sooner had she entered the gates of the long gravel drive at Salhouse Farm, than a loud horn was sounded by a vehicle coming towards her, forcing her to jump to the side, almost colliding with the huge stone pillars that guarded the entrance. A large grey truck swung out of the drive, and as it passed her, she gasped. In the back, peering out from the tailgate, were a group of German soldiers wearing the uniforms sewn with black patches that she'd seen on the Pathé Newsreels shown at her local cinema. The morale-boosting films explained how prisoners of war were being used to help beleaguered farmers feed a nation beset by the constant bombardment of supply convoys. The flickering images had been greeted with shouts of: 'Too right, give them the muckiest jobs' or 'They should be shot instead.' It had never occurred to Hannah that she would come across any prisoners of war in her new job. The uniforms that the men in the back of the truck were wearing were a far cry from the neat, pristine ones that she had seen in the films, and these men looked as grey and defeated as every British person in January 1943 could ever have wished, but that hadn't helped Hannah, who had clung to the gatepost, feeling sick.

Hannah was too intent on processing the last twenty-four hours to realise that Dotty was still waiting for an answer to her questions about the German rescuer. An impatient cough made her focus on the room again.

'Come on, Hannah, you'll have to do better than this,' Dotty told her, sternly. Although only seventeen, she had been in service for three years before this posting and had so much more experience than her new room-mate.

'I don't think I can do this, Dotty, I just can't.'

Dotty brushed her dark-brown hair out of her eyes and looked surreptitiously at her watch. Time was ticking on and the cows would not wait.

'OK, we're going to have a talk about this, but not now.' She leaned over and gave Hannah a quick hug and went over to the door. She sighed with exasperation as she glanced back at the dejected figure on the bed and went downstairs. All Dotty's optimism when she had been told she was going to be joined by one, maybe two more Land Army girls was vanishing. She had been waiting for another girl to join her for a month now but this one was already infuriating the hell out of her.

Hannah leaned back against the pillow and stared up at the ceiling. The room was in the attic and had peeling plaster and one metal skylight. The window in the roof had an iron bar down the middle and a blackout curtain pushed to one side, held in place by an elastic band. Originally, the room had been painted a mustard colour, but the walls had faded to a dirty brown and although it was quite large, it was sparsely furnished, suggesting only the bare essentials in life were really necessary. In the dim lamplight, an oval tarnished mirror reflected a couple of small side tables, three stools, a jug, a china bowl and some wall hooks, and a very dejected young woman.

She turned over on the bed and pulled the bolster in towards her, curling her knees up. From the first moment she'd peered around the stone gateposts, everything about this farm seemed huge and foreboding and, once she had seen the German POWs, all she had wanted to do was turn tail and run. She was cross with herself because, for so many years, she had planned her escape from the stifling atmosphere at her home. There, she'd felt the green tendrils of the flowers on the wallpaper threatening to curl around her throat and choke the life out of her, a sensation worsened by her mother's dependence on her. Her father, in contrast, spent so much time just staring at the wall that she wondered whether he would even notice she had gone.

Then she'd met Dotty. The small but terrifyingly capable young woman had immediately launched into a list of instructions on the most efficient way to fit twenty-four hours work into twelve, how to deal with scorn of the men and finally, how to wash at the cold-water pump in the yard without losing her modesty. Chatty to the point of garrulous, Dotty hadn't noticed that Hannah's eyes were widening with increasing dread and didn't even hear the gasp when the new girl realised she was actually supposed to share a bed with this talkative stranger in front of her.

Hannah was an only child and to share a bed with anyone but her old, one-eyed teddy seemed a terrible invasion of her privacy. Making a rapid scan of the room, Hannah had looked hopefully at the bolster as a possible barrier to place between them but then Dotty leaped, fully clothed into the right-side of the bed, reaching down to start taking off her socks before, one by one, flinging every item of clothing she was wearing onto the floor next to the bed and pulling a winceyette nightie over her head. In a matter-of-fact manner, she had then advised Hannah to do the same thing if she wanted to avoid freezing to death and, with that pronouncement, she hugged the warm brick to herself, turned over and immediately went to sleep.

Hannah rocked backwards and forwards to shut out the memory of her first sleepless night in that bedroom when she had curled up her body on the edge so as not to touch the warm skin of Dotty. Her mother's fears were right, she thought. She wouldn't be able to deal with life in the Land Army and would have been much better staying at home to look after her parents.

Then she heard Lily's voice. Friends from the age of five, Hannah and Lily, along with the ever-practical Ros, had been through primary school first and then on to Loreto Convent. Somehow – Hannah never knew how it happened – she had stepped back and let the other two take the lead. As time went on, and things at home became more difficult, she became quieter and quieter, until not talking or standing up for herself became a habit.

As usual, Lily was characteristically blunt, even in her head.

You joined the Land Army to escape that oppressive house, you know you did, the voice told her. *The reality is you're terrified of stepping away and being your own person. But now is the time for us girls to really find out what we're made of and you may find you're made of tougher stuff than you think.*

Hannah grumbled into the bolster. She hated it when Lily was right.

Chapter 3

By the time Dotty came back from milking, Hannah had reluctantly washed her face and brushed her hair to join her room-mate downstairs in the large, cavernous space that was their dining room and sitting room. The previous night, she had been so tired and overcome with homesickness, she'd retired without supper to the bedroom, and then she'd overslept and had missed breakfast, so this was her first opportunity to take in the rest of the house. With its brick walls, the dining room was freezing, but it had a few old armchairs with faded fabric and occasional tables dotted around the sides and in the middle there was a long wooden table surrounded by a variety of hard-backed chairs. At the far end, a trestle table along the wall held plates, a jug containing cutlery and some water glasses tipped upside down in neat rows. There was a polished metal urn fronted by pale green cups and saucers.

Their meals were brought across from the farmhouse by a girl of about sixteen. Rachel's hair was pulled back into a ponytail and she walked with a limp, the result of childhood polio. She put an enamel dish covered in pastry in the middle of the table and gave Hannah a warm smile. The meal was a vegetable pie, and taking a first taste, Hannah realised how hungry she was. The hot food and Dotty's relentless chatter took Hannah's mind off the drama of the day and, finally, she felt her shoulders relax slightly.

'So you've survived your first couple of days,' Dotty said, ignoring Hannah's sceptical look and grabbing some bread from the plate in the middle of the table. 'Let's think, what little gems of information have I got that'll make life more bearable here?' 'Oh, I know. Well, you have to steam your hat; it's the only way to make it wearable. Then you'll need olive oil and beeswax for your hands, otherwise they'll be like sandpaper.

'Oh, and for chilblains you'll need that olive oil again, but it needs mixing with menthol. And you need to put sheep's wool in your boots, the oil in it will soften them.'

Hannah looked with renewed awe at the girl in front of her and was about to speak, but Dotty waved away her admiration and leaned forward conspiratorially.

'You know, we're really lucky, Hannah. I've been here a few weeks now, and on your first day off, I think we should go and have a look at the Broad. It's only just down the road. It's really pretty and we can take a flask and sit on the fallen tree. Oh, and we can feed the ducks!'

Dotty sounded so excited but Hannah was too traumatised by her introduction to Salhouse Farm to feel anything but a heaviness in the pit of her stomach.

Dotty hadn't finished, however. 'And this—' she waved her arms expansively '—well, it's a huge farm and that means they have three tractors and four horses, including the lovely Hercules. That makes life easier for us and they treat us well – a lot better than other places I've heard about. And after where I've been, I can't tell you how relieved I was when I arrived here.'

She went on to describe her life before Salhouse Farm, which included being a skivvy in a large, freezing cold house outside Stratford-on-Avon. She talked in factual terms, but her words gave Hannah a chill at the back of her neck.

'I hardly got much to eat,' she said, lifting her fork to her mouth with relish, 'I was always starving and oh, Hannah, the garret I was in was absolutely perishing. I only had one thin blanket *and*,' she stressed, 'we had to work fourteen hours a day.'

She sat back, satisfied that Hannah's mind had finally been distracted.

For the first time, Hannah focused her gaze, really seeing the young girl in front of her. She had been so wound up with her own thoughts, it had never occurred to her that there were any other stories to be told.

Dotty waved an enthusiastic arm around the cold, empty room. 'This, I'll have you know,' she said with a grin, 'is pure luxury.'

Hannah looked dubiously around her and tried to see her surroundings through Dotty's eyes. To her, it was still a room devoid of any warmth, character or homeliness, but, listening to Dotty, she made a real attempt to see it differently.

'My home,' Dotty scoffed at the word, 'is a back-to-back in Birmingham. There's five of us, I'm the oldest. I shared a bed with two of my sisters and our two brothers slept on the floor. My mum just works herself to death doing people's washing, and my dad . . .' Her voice faded, she was not ready to share her whole life with Hannah yet. 'Anyway, I've been in service since I was fourteen.'

Her sallow complexion, pinched cheeks and red raw hands bore testimony to the hours of hard graft she had put in at a previous position as the lowliest member of a well-off household. As soon as she could, she had volunteered for the Land Army, the only wartime occupation she could join at the age of just seventeen, and she was excited about the skills she was going to learn, believing they might prevent her from ever having to go back into a scullery. She had worked briefly at another farm in Lincolnshire before being sent to Norfolk and told Hannah that the family at Salhouse Farm seemed a sad bunch but she did not know why. She then said with a grin: 'Anyway, don't you worry, I've been dying for another LA girl to turn up and now you're here! We're going to have such fun. By the way, I've checked out the locals for you, although, I warn you, it doesn't look too promising. Most of them are so old I'm not sure the last war wanted them, never mind this one.

'And then here on the farm, there's Jed, as you know,' she said, pausing for a moment, 'just watch him, Hannah. I'm too scrawny for him but I know his type, he reminds me of . . .' she paused but then carried on in a rush '. . . one of the footmen when I was in service. I always had to make sure I was never alone with him in the boot room; you make sure you're never alone when Jed's around either.'

Hannah was absorbing Dotty's words when the door to the yard opened and the blackout curtain fluttered in the icy blast of air as the regular farmhands walked in. There were three men, much older than the girls and a younger, fresh-faced youth. Other than a quick nod when they had been introduced to Hannah, they had not spoken to either of the girls all day and their whispers made it clear that women were not wanted. The older ones looked with disdain at the two young women, too experienced in farming to ever believe that young slips of girls could do the hard, physical work a farm demanded. One of them tossed his head back and made a dismissive snorting noise.

Dotty immediately spoke up. 'You mind your own, William Handforth. I'm doing as well as any of you and don't you suggest for one minute that I'm not. And Hannah here'll work hard too.'

The group of experienced farmhands muttered their disapproval and moved along the table to the other end where they sat down waiting for Rachel to come back with their meals. They glared at Hannah and Dotty until Dotty poked out her tongue at them.

'Less of your lip,' a man with pockmarked skin called Albert said to her. 'I've told you; we don't want you here, you're no bloody use and you'll just make more work for us. Girls . . . Land *Army* . . . God help us if you lot are an army. Hah!'

'Ignore them,' Dotty whispered to Hannah, who was looking at the men with horror. She had never come across so much ill-feeling from strangers. She felt a sudden renewed wave of homesickness and swallowed hard.

As soon as supper was finished, the girls went up to their room. Hannah was too exhausted to talk and flopped onto her side of the bed.

It occurred to her she had just experienced the worst two days of her life.

Chapter 4

In the outhouse on the farm, where the German prisoners of war stopped work to have their sandwiches, Karl Schneider was trying to pummel a sack full of straw into shape so as to make a cushion for the bales they were allowed to sit on. The POWs had been sent to Salhouse Farm to help out on a temporary basis, but he knew the owner of the farm was fighting the authorities' insistence that he should take some of them on for a longer period of time. Karl didn't care whether the man wanted them or not, he was too engrossed in striking the sack with an anger that seemed to be engulfing him these days. He almost didn't recognise the young trainee doctor who had started his course with so much enthusiasm at the University of Stuttgart.

At the age of twenty-five, he was beginning to feel he had already lived two separate lives. One encompassed an innocent childhood on his beloved family farm near Tübingen, playing with his two older brothers, Horst and Werner, and his older sister, Greta. Even then, he had been the one who wanted to cure birds with damaged wings or a farm cat with a thorn in its paw. That passion to mend what was broken had led to excellent grades at school and a place at Stuttgart to study medicine. He had been almost at the end of his course, too absorbed in his studies to really notice the changes taking place in his own country, when an administrative error led to him being called up. That's when his second life began – the one that had left him bewildered, injured, and now, a prisoner of war. His medical training was going to be of benefit to the Fatherland, he was told, as they handed him his Luftwaffe uniform. As soon as he put it on, he had become part of a huge machine that seemed to be taking over the Germany he knew and loved, and for the first time, he started to question where his country was taking him.

'You,' a voice called from the doorway. 'Come here.'

It was the military guard and, from the expression on his face, he was not happy.

'You think you can just wander around the farm whenever you feel like it?'

Karl dropped his head in submission, a ploy he had learned early on in his new career.

'You're not allowed out without me, capeesh?' the guard asked angrily. Stanley Parish had been hauled up by the owner of the farm for not keeping the prisoners under close guard after Karl had saved that young Land Army girl from the horse. Andrew Hollis's furious red face had mirrored his auburn hair and the conversation had been extremely uncomfortable.

Another German airman came up behind Karl. In broken English, he said: 'But he save the *Mädchen*. The horse, it would kill her.'

The guard looked at both of the men with distaste and moved his rifle from one shoulder to the other. Conscripted in 1939 at nineteen, he felt superior to the wet-behind-the-ears youngsters in his regiment, who had hardly learned to shave, and was sure his daring achievements would make him stand out from the crowd. But everyone else knew that the only thing that distinguished Stanley Parish from the others was the amount he could drink in the Mess and how many girls he could flirt with. Under threats of serious charges, he had been sidelined to look after the German prisoners of war and he hated it. He was convinced that his superiors had overlooked his excellent qualifications and abilities when they made him taxi driver and guardian of a bunch of Jerries. His main responsibility was getting them to the farm and back to the POW camp at Mousehold Heath every day. He was not going to be mollified. 'Special duties for you for three days when we get back to camp. That's peeling spuds, and if you don't know what that is, then ask that smart-arse commandant of yours. He seems to know everything.'

Karl tried not to smile. Many of the Germans felt the same way about their commandant, who was an officious type, but then he raised his head and looked the guard in the eye.

'I am an officer and under the Geneva Convention, it is not in order that I do that.'

'Yeah, yeah . . . You can always complain to Mr Churchill, I'm sure he's got lots of time to listen to the pathetic complaints of a German prisoner of war.' The guard spat out the words sarcastically. He hated the way these prisoners were mollycoddled just because everyone was so frightened in case the Germans saw it as an excuse to mistreat their British prisoners over on the continent.

'But perhaps you will also understand,' Karl continued, calmly, 'that it was a good thing I was "wandering" the farm as you say, or the girl would, I think, as my friend here says, be dead.'

'Well, that's beside the point,' the guard conceded. 'You're still doing the spuds.' And with that he went to march out of the outhouse.

Karl smiled wearily at the airman who had come to his aid.

'*Danke. Das war . . .*'

'AND SPEAK ENGLISH,' the guard called from the doorway. 'ALL THE TIME, you hear me? That's the rule for you two and don't you forget it.' The discovery that these two prisoners spoke English had given Stanley an extra power he loved to exercise.

Karl and the bombardier, whose name was Peter, burst out laughing once Stanley had left. The two men had met on the transport truck to their camp at Mousehold Heath just outside Norwich, discovering in a very short time that they both had an agricultural background – Karl as the son of a farmer and Peter as a labourer on a farm in the Austrian Alps. Peter's Dornier Do 17 had been shot down near the north coast of Norfolk and Karl had been on a reconnaissance flight in a Junkers Ju 86 which had been hit over Dover. He was not even supposed to have been on the flight, he ruefully remembered.

As a trainee doctor in his final year, Karl had been exempted from conscription, but as the hostilities heightened, he had received a letter telling him his application had been accepted. A man dedicated to saving lives, he had been horrified as well as mystified until he discovered that there had been a mix-up between himself and another Karl Schneider, but by then it was too late; he was in the Luftwaffe. Arguing against the mistake, he managed to convince the Luftwaffe that he had enough training to be allowed to help as a junior medic and was accepted into the Luftwaffe section of the joint medical service, the *Sanitätsdienst*, but one day, he heard there was a reconnaissance flight leaving and he begged to be allowed to join the crew.

'I really wanted to see the country my sister had chosen to live in,' he told Peter in German with a wry smile. 'Otherwise, I would not have been on that plane. That is a lesson I will remember.'

His sister, Greta, had left Germany in 1930 to work as a baker's assistant in King's Lynn and had fallen in love with an Englishman. She had sent regular letters about the pretty villages and wonderful North Norfolk coast-line and Norfolk Broads, making the English countryside sound so appealing that Karl had longed to see it and a view from an aircraft seemed the perfect opportunity. It was scheduled to be an uneventful flight and the air-craft was thought to be unassailable, capable of climbing to an altitude of 41,000 feet to put it out of harm's way, so the pilot finally agreed, telling Karl to wedge himself into the corner of the empty gun turret at the front where he would get a good vantage point. As they approached the famous white cliffs, the clouds were thickening and the aircraft was forced to fly lower than the pilot had intended. The four automatic cameras were clicking away, recording vital information, when a Spitfire came up from behind. The pilot was in the process of cursing the Luftwaffe's arrogance that the plane was invincible and therefore had no need of defence armaments when one of their engines was hit, causing the aircraft to veer to one side. With extreme skill learned during the Battle of Britain, the pilot managed to steer the aircraft with its crew down to some farmland just a few miles inland from the iconic cliffs.

Karl's first reaction was one of surprise when he realised the whole crew had survived; the second was one of aston-ishment when two ladies in paisley-patterned pinnies raced over the field to them.

'Are you going to shoot us?' Karl had asked in alarm, rubbing the huge bump on his head. He felt dizzy.

'No, this is England,' one of the women said proudly, 'we don't do that. But we could make you a cup of tea.'

With that, Karl had passed out and it fell to his two less-injured crewmates to carry him to the nearby village, where the women contacted the Red Cross. Karl did not remember much after that – just a vague memory of being transported in an ambulance and waking up in a hospital somewhere, surrounded by white coats and white sheets. The crash had damaged his cognitive functions, which the doctors believed would improve over time, but the problem he had was that he would sometimes find himself somewhere he shouldn't be, like the stables, and have no recollection as to how he got there.

'That guard, Stanley, he is as bad as the men at the London Cage,' Peter confided.

Karl nodded. After several weeks in hospital, he'd been deemed well enough to be moved to a Kensington Palace Gardens building where captured Germans were taken for questioning. He was shown into a bare room by a man in Russian uniform, which surprised him. He suspected it was as a determined attempt to intimidate the German prisoners, knowing how frightened his countrymen were of the Russians. Once in the room, he faced three stern-faced men, who systematically subjected him to relentless questioning to gauge his views on the Nazi regime. One, who he believed was Norwegian, spoke fluent German. They were surprised to discover the prisoner spoke excellent English and the panel were torn between thinking he might be a spy or that he really was a British sympathiser and the probing intensified. Karl's special interest in psychiatry helped him recognise the techniques used to try to wheedle out as much from him as they could about his own loyalties, his family's opinions on how the war was going and even how German people in general were thinking. Karl's memory was still patchy from his head injury and his thought processes muddled, but his responses were emphatically anti-fascist. As a result, he was categorised as a Grade A 'white' prisoner – an Anti-Nazi – which meant he avoided being sent to Canada like many of his captured compatriots. Once the authorities knew he had experience of agriculture, he was told he would be sent to a farm in Norfolk to help produce food for a nation beset with food shortages. Every day, when he arrived at the farm to the familiar sight of fields of crops, he breathed a sigh of relief that he was at least able to do one of the two things in life he loved.

Chapter 5

It had been during a trip to her beloved grandparents' house in Old Colwyn that Hannah's grandad had suggested she should join the Land Army. From when she was a little girl, she had loved spending time with him in his small shed on the market garden behind their house, weighing out potatoes, carrots and apples on the old Salter scales.

Ted Lloyd noticed the bowed shoulders of his beloved granddaughter and the constant expression of anxiety that clouded her face. He knew the war had hit Manchester so much worse than the coastal region of North Wales, but he was worried by how quiet Hannah had become. He remembered her as a joyful child, prancing through the Fairy Glen as it meandered behind their house in Coed Coch Road. There she had created a magical world where old tree stumps were the villages for the little folk, the bushes were where the goblins lived and the nymphs frolicked in the sparkling water of the stream. This had been the solitary little girl's playground and she had been completely absorbed by it. Stood inside the little wooden hut at the top of the hill on the other side of the glen, he wondered when it had all changed and watched as Hannah closed her eyes, taking in the smells of the creosote, the earthy potatoes and the mustiness of last season's apples.

'Oh, I've so missed this,' she said, giving him a hug. 'I love Manchester but here you can breathe.'

'That's not just the fresh air,' he said quietly.

She glanced at him.

'What do you mean?'

'That daughter of mine is enough to suck the air out of anyone,' he said.

Hannah looked sideways at him. He was naturally a taciturn man, but every now and again, he would make a short, pithy comment that seemed to see into Hannah's soul. Ted Lloyd turned towards his beloved granddaughter.

'I've been wanting to talk to you since you arrived,' he said finally, coming out with the words he and his wife, Florrie, had discussed the previous night. 'You have to escape, lass. Your mum's a wonderful woman, but since your dad came home from the Great War, she's not been coping too well, and as long as you're there, you'll be a crutch to her.'

Hannah started to weigh out the potatoes on the green metal scales. At the same time, she weighed up his words.

'But what can I do? She'd never manage without me,' she said vaguely.

'You're nineteen, but next year, there'll be conscription anyway. Then she'll have to.'

He reached over and took the potatoes from the tarnished brass bowl and put them into a paper bag. Every week, he had a quota of vegetables he had to supply to the Ministry of Food, leaving just the slightly rotting ones for his own household

The two worked companionably together, as they had done since Hannah was eight years old.

She knew her grandfather had put into words the thoughts that had been going around her head since her school friend, Lily, had volunteered. Her letters talked of an exciting life in Blackpool being trained to be a wireless operator and Hannah read them with a pang of envy, but every time she walked into the back kitchen in the little terraced house in Stretford, she felt she was gasping for breath.

'Dad needs me,' she finally said, in a flat voice.

'No, he doesn't. He needs to get out of that chair and be the man of the house again,' was the unsympathetic reply. 'Your mother panders to him. If you leave them to it, they'll have to cope, and it'll do them both the world of good. You could join the Land Army. You'd like that.'

With that pronouncement, Ted Lloyd turned away to concentrate on sorting his carrots and Hannah knew the discussion was at an end.

Hannah went back to sorting the vegetables out, but her mind was assessing her future. Until now, it had never occurred to her that she might have one. She had started to feel she was the weak bridge that held her father to the mainland of life, and that without her, he would crumble and fall into the deep ocean below. Her role at home had become one where she felt indispensable and her mother's reliance on her had started to make her feel stifled. When the Blitz came, her mother had clung to Hannah in the cupboard under the stairs while her father had sat curled up in the other corner, next to the brown Bex Bissell cleaner, his face blank, showing no outward sign of the horrors from the Great War that were being replayed in his head. From that night on, Hannah always felt she needed to be the one to save her parents from both their own fears and the German bombers above. The responsibility was enormous.

* * *

Just a few months later, here she was, a member of the Land Army and hating every minute of it. She wondered how on earth she could ever have thought that weighing out a few vegetables would qualify her for the life she had now chosen. After a freezing cold night, spent silently weeping, thinking of her warm, cosy bed at home, Hannah felt her spirits rise slightly when Dotty told her the shire horses were being shod by the farrier and had been fed early, meaning Hannah didn't have to go near Hercules for today at least.

She rubbed her hands together to get some feeling in them and meekly followed an unremittingly chirpy Dotty out to the north field, where they faced a back-breaking morning picking sprouts. Dotty was enjoying being the one to show the new girl the ropes and demonstrated how to bang two stalks together to remove the mud, sending sprays of wet soil splattering over the sack that Dotty had tied around Hannah's waist to protect her breeches, confirming Hannah's suspicion that she would never feel clean again. The landscape around the farm varied but this part consisted of large, flat fields and to Hannah, who had always been able to see the Pennines from her home city of Manchester, seemed far too big and uninteresting. This morning, however, the mist was gradually lifting to reveal a blue sky that seemed to go on forever. The air was still icy cold though and the ground beneath their feet was completely frozen, making pulling the stems out of the soil like extracting teeth. Dotty sang happily to herself, her breath circling around her nose in the wintry January air, while Hannah tried not to think of her mother's warm back kitchen where she would have been, perhaps, making a cake.

'You can watch me tonight when I milk the cows,' Dotty told Hannah, piling some stalks of plump, green sprouts into a basket, 'you'll soon have to do it yourself.'

Hannah felt a quiver of fear; after her altercation with Hercules, the thought of dealing with any animal bigger than a chicken filled her with dismay and she looked down at the horizon of row after row of sprouts, surprised at how appealing they suddenly looked. 'I'd rather stay here,' she said, blowing hot breath onto her hands.

'Don't be daft,' Dotty told her, handing her another basket. 'You won't be saying that when you've filled a hundred of those.'

So, later, Hannah reluctantly followed Dottie to the milking parlour, where the young girl immediately lit the boiler, explaining that the hot water was needed so that the buckets and churns could be sterilised. Dotty put on a white coat, washed her hands thoroughly in some of the water left and went to sit on a three-legged stool to gently wash the cow's udder which were encrusted with dirt. 'It's vital everything is squeaky clean,' Dotty told her. 'If the milk's tainted, there'll be hell to pay.'

The milk started off by making a clinking sound as it hit the galvanised bucket but this became a rich, whooshing sound as the bucket filled up.

'You're looking for a good froth on the top,' Dotty said, and then she grinned. 'Watch this.'

She aimed the teat at a hay bale where two of the farm cats were sitting, waiting to pounce on any drops that fell to the floor, but when a stream of warm milk hit one, the animal leaped off its perch and fled out of the milking parlour.

'Sometimes, I can get both of them with one squirt,' she said, laughing, turning back to the cow.

Hannah kept her distance. She was just as fascinated and as terrified by the size of these animals as she had been of the shire horses and was glaring at the beasts suspiciously when she heard heavy footsteps.

'Here to cause trouble again, are you?' Jed said. He dragged his wooden leg behind him like a recalcitrant child and his other boot was held together with string. He stood by the door with his arms folded, looking at Hannah with disgust. She felt he could see through her uniform right to her inadequacy. She had only briefly met him the day before, when he had roughly handed her a bucket and told her go and feed the horses. He had been curt then and there was something about him that made her toes curl up in her stiff new wellington boots.

'You're even more useless than the other one,' he said, eyeing Hannah up and down as if he was seeing her properly for the first time. His prejudice against these girls was in-built, but then he smirked as he took in her fresh complexion and the dark hair that framed her face and Hannah shuffled her feet uncomfortably under his piercing gaze.

'Well, I've got too much to do to nursemaid you girls, just make sure you fill in those milk records,' he said, turning on his heels.

'Hann, be a love, will you, and go and get that sheet from over there?' Dotty said. 'That's the one, and there's a pencil next to it. Can you fill in the amounts as I milk?'

'Yes, of course,' Hannah said, relieved to be given something she could cope with doing. 'But didn't you want me to start the feeding?'

'Um, no, it'll be quicker if we do it together,' Dotty muttered into the cow's flank.

The task made the girls late for supper. Hannah's muscles were so sore from the physical work on the farm she could hardly walk but Dotty skipped in, looking eagerly to see what the cook, Mrs Hill, had prepared for them. When she had arrived at the farm, a thin, almost emaciated figure, Mrs Hill had taken one look at her and sworn to Rachel in the farmhouse kitchen that she would put a bit of flesh on that young mite if it was the last thing she did. Dotty talked in a matter-of-fact way about her life in the large house near Stratford, where rationing had been used as an excuse to cut the servants' meals to a bare minimum. She mentioned beatings and being locked in the cellar for any slight misdemeanour and was embracing her new life as a Land Army girl with enthusiasm. This farm, particularly, had won her approval when fresh milk was put on the long table each morning and she had raised her eyes to the heavens in grateful thanks. There was even occasionally some fresh butter that they could spread on their bread.

Hannah was not feeling quite so grateful. Everything that Dotty accepted without question seemed so strange to her. She asked herself twenty-four times a day: what the hell had she done?

Dotty spoke with her mouth full of cheese pie, her eyes closed in delight. 'I've never eaten like this. It's heaven.' Hannah, meantime, was longing for her cosy little home in Manchester. Even her mother's suffocating reliance on her seemed a small price to pay for the comforts she had given up to join the Land Army and, yet again, a feeling of homesickness engulfed her.

* * *

Later, when Hannah was counting up her ailments from her prone position on the bed, she heard voices and then the door opened. It was a tall woman in a grey dress. Hannah recognised her as the sister-in-law of Andrew Hollis, Miss Agnes Clarke, who had greeted her when she first arrived. Then, she had briefly welcomed the newcomer before marching into the large barn off the main yard, through a latched door in the corner and up the staircase, with Hannah scampering behind her. The young Land Army girl watched the figure going up the stairs in front of her, all the while reciting the mealtimes, the laundry arrangements and the shift hours with a warning that the girls needed to be in bed by ten o'clock. She remembered thinking that the woman's collar was so stiffly starched, it looked as though it was holding her head up, and as she listed the rules, her grey bun wobbled. Hannah had repressed the urge to giggle but then the woman had turned sharply round at the top of the stairs to face her, looked with suspicion at the girl's slim frame and said: 'I don't know what you're used to, but this won't be it,' and with that, she turned on her heel and went back down the stairs.

Now, Miss Clarke was followed by a long-legged, beautiful girl in a red pillbox hat with a black veil that dipped over her eyes, a pair of black high heels and a fox fur around her shoulders over a pale cream-coloured suit. Instead of scuttling like a frightened rabbit as Hannah had done, this girl swept elegantly into the room as if she owned it.

'This is Lavinia. She'll be joining you,' Miss Clarke said, looking dubiously at the apparition standing next to her. 'One of the farmhands is bringing up a mattress for her now. It'll go under the window there.' She pointed to the space on the floor beneath the skylight, handed Lavinia some bedding and went back down the stairs, closing the door behind her. Hannah and Dotty sat up straight in astonishment. The girl looked as if she had got off the wrong bus in the wrong part of town – if this vision had ever been on a bus.

'Good evening,' the girl said in a posh voice, sounding like a presenter on the BBC. 'I believe I am to sleep somewhere in here.' She looked around her, trying to envisage such an amazing occurrence. 'What japes hey?' She looked at the two girls expecting a reaction, but they were both staring open-mouthed at her.

'Do you two share?' she went on. 'Oh how cosy. Wouldn't it be a giggle if we were all in together?'

Dotty murmured something, but the girl continued to look around, prodding the piles of clothes and peering to look out of the window, lifting one tapered heel behind her.

She turned back to face them, took one look at their scandalised faces and winked. 'Don't be fooled by the voice or the posh clothes. I was a dancer at The Windmill Theatre and there, to be honest, I hardly wore clothes at all!'

Chapter 6

Hannah found it hard to sleep that night. She was only just getting used to having Dotty's gentle snoring next to her and now there was another stranger in the room. She lay awake, processing the information that Lavinia had just shared with them.

As soon as the young farmhand had embarrassedly manhandled the mattress into the room, trying not to look at the three girls, Lavinia had made herself at home, arranging her clothes in a pile at one end of the mattress while she explained that she had been forced to leave The Windmill in a bit of a hurry. She gave another wink, but Hannah was completely bemused.

'What's the Windmill?' she said, glancing nervously at Dotty, who looked as if she was following every word of this bizarre conversation.'Oh darling,' Lavinia said with a lavish wave of her hand, 'it's the most wonderful theatre in London and we have the most spectacular shows and, do you know, all the way through the war so far, we've never closed . . . not in the Blitz or anything.

Bombs would fall all over London, but we kept going,' she proudly finished.

Dotty looked knowingly at Hannah and added: 'And they have nude dancers.'

'Not exactly dancers, although I do dance as well,' Lavinia put in. 'We just sort of stood there like statues, holding a strategically placed fan or something.' She struck a pose with an imaginary fan.

'Nude?' Hannah said weakly.

'Yes, darling, it's all very tasteful, I can assure you, but we do pack the audience in . . . they come from far and wide to see us. Such a shame I can't get you tickets but . . .' Her voice faded and she looked wistfully into the distance. 'Ah well, can't be helped. Things change and I had to leave.'

'Why haven't you got your uniform?' Dotty asked.

'It's on its way, apparently. Should be here in the morning. As I say, there wasn't much time.'

'Why, what happened?' Dotty asked her.

'That, my little dumpling, will have to wait. I'm absolutely bushed and I simply must get some sleep.'

And with that, she unceremoniously stripped off her bra and pants, flung her silk nightgown over her head and climbed into her hastily made bed.

Dotty giggled and got in her side of the double bed while Hannah fumbled with the bedclothes in embarrassment, trying not to transpose the vision of the naked body she had just glimpsed onto a stage watched by hundreds of people.

* * *

The next morning, there was no time for chatting and Hannah and Dotty quickly got dressed, leaving Lavinia to wait for her uniform.

It was as they were on their way out to the yard – Hannah to muck out and Dotty to get the cows that were lined up patiently, ready for milking – that Hannah got up the courage to ask the question that had been plaguing her.

'Do they really stand on stage without any clothes on?'

'Oh yes, it's quite the rage.' Dotty stopped and looked at Hannah with a shake of her head. 'Where have you been all your life, Hannah Compton? Under a rock?'

Hannah nodded slowly. 'Yes, I rather think I have.'

'Well, I'm younger than you, but I can see I'm going to have to take you in hand and educate you. But first, get that muck shifted while I move this lot so I can get at those udders.'

Hannah grabbed the pitchfork, her hands weak.

'What time do you call this?' Jed appeared behind her. 'You're two minutes late.'

Dotty muttered into the cow's flank and carried on pushing the animal towards the milking parlour.

'What was that?' the foreman said, angrily.

'Nothing, Jed. I just said Maisie has a lot of milk this morning.'

'Well, don't let it happen again. Get those cows indoors. Oh, for God's sake, this is ridiculous. Now I've got another of you useless girls to deal with. Where the hell is she?'

He looked straight at Hannah who mumbled and looked down at the ground. Dotty came to her rescue.

'She's just waiting for her uniform and then she'll be over.'

'Another one who doesn't know one end of a cow from the other. You, girl, put that fork down a minute.' He pointed his gnarled finger at Hannah and pushed her towards the milking parlour. 'You get yourself that stool and come over here, it's about time you got to grips with milking. Don't think I haven't noticed you've been avoiding it.'

Hannah looked around frantically before spotting another stool in the corner. This was the moment she had been dreading.

'Get it over here, these cows can't wait all day and neither can I.'

He took the stool from her and banged it down under the cow, making it jump. Hannah stepped back quickly, noticing how large the animal's hooves were. These cows were so big and powerful, she felt tiny next to it, even at five foot six inches tall.

'Oh, for crying out loud, come here,' Jed said. He was a man whose face crumpled into a constant growling frown and his overalls were filthy dirty, but he reached up to put a white coat over the top of them and washed his hands with the soap on a bit of rope next to a bucket of water before motioning to Hannah to do the same.

Hannah went over to him and took down a third white coat from the peg before washing her hands thoroughly. She didn't want to be the cause of any problems with the milk.

Jed grabbed hold of Hannah's arm and pushed her down on the stool. The cow backed up slightly and Hannah nearly fell over.

'Take hold of this teat, here,' Jed said roughly, and he took Hannah's hand and put it on the udder. Hannah flinched. She was not sure which was worse, the soft pink udder or Jed's rough hand when he held on to hers for longer than necessary.

'And then lean one shoulder, then your head in.' His breath smelt stale and Hannah flinched as he leaned nearer to her. 'That's it, girl.' His head almost touched hers and she felt his warm breath on her neck and shuddered. 'Ahh, that's it, you've got a lovely hold of that, now pull it gently up and down, up and down like this.' His hand covered hers then he closed his eyes and his panting got quicker as he guided her fingers slowly.

'I can take over with Hannah now, Jed,' Dotty said sharply from behind him. 'You've got much more important things to do.'

Jed looked around and was about to give Dotty a dressing-down for speaking to him that way, but when she looked back at him, her eyes blazed with such a fury, he found himself backing away. Hannah's hands fell from the teats of the cow and she breathed a sigh of relief. She was not sure what had just happened, but it sent a shiver through her.

Jed reluctantly shuffled out of the barn as Dotty turned to Hannah and whispered: 'Do keep him at arm's length, Hannah. Here, let me help you.'

The cow had become twitchy, as if sensing the tension under its stomach and was straining on its tether. Dotty came up behind Hannah and guided her hands back to the teats with a professional hold.

'Here you are, now don't be too gentle but go with her, she's ready to give up this milk.'

Hannah's heart was racing, both from terror at the beast above her and from Jed's proximity to her just moments before. She nervously pulled at the teats and was astonished to see a creamy white liquid emerge and flow unaided into the pail beneath. To begin with there was just a trickle, but as she tugged with more confidence, the stream of milk increased. She leaned her head against the animal's side and felt it breathing steadily. When she concentrated, she could hear its heartbeat. It was like the metronome that ticked on her grandmother's piano, rhythmically keeping time with Hannah's increasingly confident tugs. A feeling of calm engulfed her and she looked up gratefully at the cow above her. It was a partnership she'd never experienced before and, for the first time, she appreciated what her grandfather had said when he told her about the animals he worked with on a farm as a young lad. The cow needed her and she could help it to be more comfortable.

* * *

By the time it was twelve o'clock, Hannah was starving. She had milked three cows, getting quicker and more efficient with each one, mucked out the cowshed and prepared the whitewash for one of the barns for the afternoon.

'Look at me!' Lavinia arrived in the doorway to the cowshed just as Hannah and Dotty sat down on a hay bale to have their beetroot sandwiches. Like a vision from a magazine advertisement, Lavinia twirled in front of them with delight.

Dotty nearly choked on her bread. 'You look like one of them Land Army posters!' she squealed. It was true, Lavinia had tied her hair up in a gorgeous pink silk scarf, her uniform was pristine and her nails were long and tapered and painted pink to match the scarf.

Hannah looked down at her own uniform. Her green jumper smelt of stale milk, her breeches were stained with cow excrement from when she had failed to jump out of the way in time and her wellington boots were covered in mud and straw. She glanced at her hands; they were red raw with blisters.

'Well, I have to admit, you two look a sight,' Lavinia said with a laugh. 'I do hope you're going to clean yourselves up before you enter our boudoir.'

'It's all right,' Dotty laughed, 'tonight is bath night. Although,' she said, glancing at her watch, 'Lavinia, *you'll* hardly even have time to get dirty.' Getting clean was a major problem for Land Army girls and they were only allowed five inches of water between them once a week which, Dotty informed Hannah, was an absolute luxury. Tonight, she explained, the same shy farmhand who had brought in Lavinia's mattress, would carry a tin bath into the barn and then bring over just one pail of used warm water from the washhouse. Before the other girls had arrived, she had teased him by pretending to start to undress in front of him, making him almost run out of the door in embarrassment.

'I suppose I'll have to share the water with you both, now,' Dotty said with a shrug. 'Ah well, I knew it was too good to last.'

'What do we do on other nights?' Lavinia asked, fascinated.

'We have to use that pump over there at the trough,' Dotty said, jerking her head towards the other side of the yard. 'But be careful, Jed's always lurking around, hoping we'll take something off and he'll get an eyeful.'

At that moment, Jed came from around the corner and Hannah bristled. She felt nervous but he ignored her, his eyes lighting on Lavinia. His lascivious glance turned into a sneer when he took in her glamorous appearance.

'Don't tell me you're the latest new girl?' He looked Lavinia up and down with disdain.

'Yes, my darling, I am, and aren't you just the proper farmer with straw in your hair and everything?' Lavinia went over to him and picked out the pale, yellow piece of grass with her carefully manicured fingers.

Jed looked completely taken aback and for a moment his mouth twitched into a leering smile, but then he coughed to collect himself.

'Yes, well we'll see how long you last. I give you three days. Here, take this pitchfork and start moving that muck over to the wheelbarrow, the other two'll show yer where to stash it.' And with that, he stalked out into the cold, winter day.

Dotty and Hannah looked askance at Lavinia. Eventually, Dotty spoke. 'I can't believe how brazen you were with him. I can't stand him, and Hannah—' she looked towards Hannah, who was staring down in embarrassment at her boots '—well, she's already had some dealings with him.'

'Oh, we used to have much worse on the front row,' Lavinia replied. 'I can deal with him, don't you worry.' And with that, she started to attack the wet straw with more gusto than either Dotty or Hannah would have suspected she was capable of.

* * *

The girls had little time to talk during the rest of the afternoon but every now and then, Hannah and Dotty would glance over at Lavinia to see how she was coping. They had to admit, she was tackling each job with equanimity and surprising strength.

That evening, when they finally sat at the long refectory table to eat their evening meal, Dotty tackled her head-on.

'You're either putting on a brave front or you've got a secret past as a labourer,' she said, tucking greedily into the potato pie that Rachel had brought across.

'Well, I *was* in a circus where I did some wrestling,' Lavinia replied, daintily putting a small forkful of food into her mouth.

Hannah's mouth dropped open. Was there anything this girl hadn't done?

Chapter 7

As the weeks went by, Hannah hardly had time to think about the life she had left behind in Stretford. Her mother wrote long letters, weakly claiming she and her dad were doing just fine. Hannah doubted the truth of this. She could not shake off the feeling of guilt that she had abandoned them.

Her father had come back from the Great War as a shadowy figure who would talk in monosyllables and sit for hours staring out of the window, letting life unfold around him like a swirling mist. He worked as a postman, content to walk the streets of Stretford in the early hours of the morning, avoiding interaction with as many people as possible. Unable to get through the blank wall that was her husband, Margaret Compton had come to rely on Hannah for company as well as for practical help and moral support and Hannah had gradually felt the brick walls of the terraced house closing in on her.

'You're miles away,' Lavinia said to Hannah, blowing on her newly painted nails. The three girls were curled up on their beds, almost too tired to talk.

'Sorry,' Hannah said, emerging from her reverie. 'I was thinking about how I got into this.'

'I just went along and volunteered,' Dotty said, looking up from the pictures in the magazine she was flicking through. 'I thought I might have had to do some training, but it looks like we all got away with that one. I soon learned on the job.'

'Yes, straight in at the deep end,' Lavinia chuckled. 'Did you have an interview, Hannah? Mine was a breeze. Well, to be honest, they had little choice, my aunt was on the board and she would have done anything to get me away from The Windmill.'

Hannah's interview had been brief and whether she had flat feet and varicose veins seemed more important than whether she could wield a scythe, but when she was asked about why she wanted to join the Land Army, Hannah had floundered. She muttered something about how she'd helped her grandfather in his market garden and that the posters of girls in fields made the Land Army look fun, but that prompted scathing looks from the panel in front of her, so she blurted out that she had to get away from home before her mother suffocated her. Taken aback, the woman in the tweed suit with the clipboard suddenly nodded in understanding. The daughter of a domineering mother, she recognised a plea for help and immediately stamped the word 'Accepted' on Hannah's form. She didn't mention that she was delighted to be accepting at least one girl that day with size five feet – the only size they had left in wellington boots.

Hannah looked up to see the girls waiting expectantly so turned the conversation back to Lavinia.

'Umm, why did you have to leave The Windmill so quickly, Lavinia?'

Lavinia gave a lopsided grin and shrugged her shoulders.

'Married . . . rich and completely unsuitable. Do I have to say more?'

Hannah and Dotty stared at Lavinia, who was lying on her mattress like an artist's model, her arms casually lain behind her head, her silken dressing gown gaping over her long, slim thighs.

'Well, it was his wife, actually,' Lavinia acknowledged. 'She complained to the manager, so, et voilà, my aunt immediately took action to save the family from a dreadful scandal . . . well, an even worse one than when I joined the circus.'

She looked up and laughed at the stricken faces of the other two girls.

'Oh, you are a pair of innocents. What am I going to do with you? Anyway, enough of me, what about you two? Come on, Hannah, you've obviously led a very sheltered life, how did you persuade your parents to let you join? Dotty's been her own mistress for years, I think, but you . . . you look like a girl who's scared to say boo to a goose, let alone tell your parents you've joined up.'

Hannah gave a slow nod and hesitated before she spoke. She wasn't used to sharing her feelings like this.

'You're right. Um, actually, it was really difficult.' She paused but the other girls seemed genuinely interested in what she had to say. She went on: 'In fact, once I'd been accepted, my mum cried for three days and I was almost on the point of telling the LA I couldn't come after all when I had some help from my grandparents. They wrote to my parents and, you know, I've no idea what was in that letter, but it did the trick.' She exhaled, exhausted by the effort and sank back.

'I just told my dad where to sign, well, put his cross, actually,' Dotty said with embarrassment. 'I don't think he had any idea what he was signing but I just told him I was joining the Land Army and that was that.' She didn't mention how much she longed to never again hear his footsteps behind her every time she went to the privy. She raised her chin and said proudly: 'I've been left to my own devices since the age of eight.'

Lavinia gave Dotty a sympathetic look.

Dotty banged open her magazine again, anxious to avoid any further questioning.

'Do you think my hair would look good like this?' she asked, turning the page towards Hannah and Lavinia.

* * *

February was a punishingly cold month. The girls had no idea that Tripoli had been taken by the British or that the RAF had started bombing Berlin; they had no access to radios or newspapers and the farmhands certainly weren't going to deign to discuss war matters with girls. Hannah had been used to gathering around the wireless every night with her parents or devouring the morning papers and was desperate for some news. Without siblings, she had always absorbed books like a sponge, reading widely and extensively. Her homework was always done on time, much to Lily's chagrin, and her marks were usually excellent. One night, when Rachel came over with their supper, she plucked up the courage to speak.

'Have you heard any news, Rachel?'

'Why yes, miss,' said Rachel, too interested in what was happening on her own doorstep to consider there might be any news from elsewhere. 'Those POWs are coming here every day now. The boss tried to refuse but he's been told he's got to have 'em.'

The 'boss' was a distant figure who was rarely seen around the barn, overseeing operations more usually from his study in the farmhouse. Andrew Hollis ignored the Land Army girls and only spoke to the men about the practical needs of the farm. Hannah had seen the same haunted look in his eyes as she had seen in her own father and it made her wonder how many more secrets were being kept by these Great War veterans.

Rachel doled out the meal but her lips had tightened into a thin line. She went on: 'But none of us wants them Germans here. I certainly don't, I don't care if they all get caught under the tractor and die,' and with that she banged the spam fritters down on the table and hurried out.

A chill pervaded the air.

'I wonder if she's Jewish,' Hannah ventured. 'I heard they're being really badly treated in Germany,' she added in a whisper.

'Where did you hear that?' Dotty sounded almost challenging. Some disturbing memories were coming back to her of when she stood to one side while the boys next door to her taunted two Jewish children as they scuttled down the street. Her mother had told her it served them right. She had not questioned it at the time but seeing Rachel's sweet smile that night made her wish she had asked the question: *Why?*

Lavinia, too, was deep in thought. An older admirer of hers had come to the theatre every Saturday for months with a bouquet of red roses for her. He always wore a smart trilby and overcoat and the shiniest gold watch she had ever seen. He had a tiny gold tiepin with the Star of David on it. She suggested once that they should go for a drink after the show, but he refused, saying he was too old for her but that it gave him pleasure to admire her and bring her roses. Then, one week, she heard he had gone back to Germany to try to find his mother. She never saw him again but she kept one of the roses from his last visit in her pocketbook. She still had it and was keeping it upstairs with her things, dried and faded now, but every time she looked at it, for some reason, it made her cry.

Hannah had tried in vain to dismiss the uncomfortable reports she had read about how the Jewish people had been rounded up and killed, first in Poland, then in other parts of Europe. The haunting images were impossible to erase, but, then again, her whole life had been a testament to the damage war could do. As a little girl, she had spent her childhood longing for a father who would play with her rather than the shadow who talked little, always absorbed in his memories. Her mother, from being a calm woman Hannah could turn to every time she fell over and grazed her knee or when someone was mean to her at school, had gradually stepped back to let Hannah take control. There were some days when Hannah felt she had turned from being an only child in the family to being the only adult.

Chapter 8

The whole farm seemed tense waiting to hear whether the POWs were going to be sent back to the farm or whether the boss's arguments against them had prevailed. The prospect of any of these workers coming face to face with the enemy seemed like a bad joke. Jed never ate with his workmates, preferring to huddle up over a small fire in his quarters above the pigsty, fulminating against the injustice of the world that had taken his leg at the age of eighteen, and slurping as much alcohol as he could legally or illegally find. William Handforth, however, would use mealtimes to spout hatred towards anyone who wasn't English, the Land Army girls and especially POWs, from the other end of the table, encouraging resentment in the other men. William was the oldest of the farmhands and had worked there the longest. His bitterness when Archie was made foreman over him had soured his expression and his attitude to the world in general and he never missed an opportunity to spread his hostility.

Lavinia, however, had begun to think a few new faces around the place could be an interesting development and if those faces happened to be young, good-looking ones, then she saw it as a welcome change from Jed and William's sour expressions.

'I remember some Germans who came into the theatre one night, before the war,' she said to Dotty and Hannah. 'Students, they were and, oh, they looked so smart, we were all quite taken with them. And so polite . . .' She tailed off, remembering with a smile how they had clamoured to take the girls out after the show. She had met a particularly good-looking blond boy called Gunther, she told them, dragging herself back to the present.

'He was so gorgeous, just divine,' Lavinia gushed. 'Pure blue eyes and . . . he had money. They'd come over with a German professor and had escaped his clutches one night. They heard about our shows and couldn't wait to come.'

She laughed, but Hannah looked warily at her and stroked her arms as she had suddenly developed goosebumps.

'They don't have horns, you know, Hannah. They're just young lads like any others.'

Hannah kept quiet. In her book, Germans were more than the enemy and she blamed them for the way her father was.

The older men ignored the girls as usual, but then the young one that Dotty always teased looked over. He glanced at the older men around him nervously but then scraped his chair back to stand up, unfolding his long, thin body and spoke directly to Dotty, stuttering slightly.

'Ev-en i-if these Germans are going to be working again on the farm, d-don't you girls worry, we won't let them h-harm you.'

Exhausted by his courage, he shuffled away to the teacups but Dotty called after him.

'I'd love a cup of tea, George, as you're there?'

He nodded and turned towards the tea urn to hide his bright red cheeks.

'Oh, and it's Saint George to the rescue!' Albert, one of the other men, said with a chuckle. He was in his midfifties and his two sons were in the army, somewhere in Italy, he thought. He had developed a soft spot for George, who reminded him of his younger son. For the past few days, Albert had been watching the girls from afar, reluctantly acknowledging their dedication and determination. They were a long way from being farmhands, but, he had to admit, they were trying hard. He knew George to be a shy lad who minded his elders, and he watched with paternal amusement as the young man looked at Dotty out of the corner of his eye.

'You won't be allowed to speak to them,' another man, called John, was saying. With a crop of greying hair and sinewy forearms, he leaned forward to tell the girls: 'Fraternising is strictly forbidden.'

Lavinia looked disappointed, but Hannah breathed a sigh of relief. Hopefully she would not have to speak to any of the German POWs ever again. Dotty was too busy looking at George in a new light. She had seen his gentle concern and it had given her a warm glow. It had been a long time since anyone had wanted to protect her, certainly her dad never had. She shivered at the memory of the dark washhouse behind her home in Lozells in Birmingham and the door creaking open, and turned back to her fritters, hiding her face.

George blushed, feeling her appraisal. He had initially been wary of even speaking to the fiery Dotty, but a new role was giving him an increasing confidence. He'd started work on Salhouse Farm at the age of fourteen and, when war broke out four years later, he'd planned to join the army but, infuriatingly, he was firmly told he'd be part of the reserved occupation workers on the farm. Then two things had happened: firstly, the lovely Dotty had appeared on the scene and the second was that, not long after that, he'd been approached by a friend from the Civil Defence who took him to one side to ask if he would like to join the local auxiliary forces, a secret organisation working to defend Britain against invaders. From the moment the quiet, shy George signed the Official Secrets Act, he lost his hangdog expression and his stuttering stopped – until he was standing next to Dotty, who reduced him to a nervous young lad again. Several nights a week, he was learning about explosives, handling a gun and responding to covert instructions that were left for him in the old oak tree in the copse. In the daytime, he got on with the hard, physical work of being the youngest farmhand at Salhouse, while, at night, he pursued the shadowy and dangerous existence of a secret operative. Although he could never tell anyone, even a girl he wanted to impress, the satisfaction that he was a key part of Britain's defence was enough to make him think he might ask Dotty to one of the dances in Norwich.

* * *

Lavinia, however, was concentrating on the prospect of the new arrivals. A girl who inevitably found a social life in the most unlikely corners of life, she saw no problem in the fact that these prisoners were from the enemy country . . . they were men and that was all that mattered.

'So, these Germans. I know they're the enemy, but they have to be better than this lot,' she whispered to Dotty and Hannah, jerking her head towards the men at the other end of the table. 'I can't wait to see what they're like. At least they'll be young, and if those students were anything to go by, they'll be good-looking too.'

Dotty sat upright, her face ablaze. 'Our lads are being killed over there by people like them. They're dirt, no, worse than dirt. I can't believe you'd say that, Lavinia!'

Hannah felt a chill seep up her shoulders and hugged her arms around herself. Lavinia simply shrugged.

* * *

Two days later, Dotty was about to drive the tractor out onto the water-logged fields when a little troop of men in uniform, with black patches on their backs and legs, moved in formation towards the north field. She stopped the engine and, standing up, she put her hand over the top of her eyes like a peak to a cap to see if she could make out their faces, but they were too far away.

'Get that tractor moving,' Jed's voice called from behind her and she jumped down to crank up the motor again before hopping back on, glancing over every now and again to try to see more of the new arrivals.

She drove up to the top field where Hannah and Lavinia were waiting for her. They were about to start harvesting turnips, a job which Dotty warned them they were going to hate. It was back-breaking work, and looking at the rows and rows of plants in front of them, it was going to be a long day.

'I've just seen the Germans,' Dotty said, spitting the words out like a bad taste, as they all moved forward to start to pluck the turnips out of the ground. Hannah lurched forward and tripped over the plant in front of her. Lavinia reached over and caught her just in time.

'Careful, Hannah,' she said, 'you'll injure yourself before you begin. We haven't got time to be looking after you with a broken ankle. Come on, concentrate, girl, you'll get your chance with them.'

Hannah's face looked so stricken that Lavinia frowned. There was more to this than just a lack of concentration, she thought. She wondered about the experiences they'd all had before ending up on this farm and suspected they all had their secrets. Time for more questions later, she thought, and turned to Dotty:

'Are they gorgeous?' she asked.

'No idea, couldn't see them; don't want to see them. I just wish they weren't here,' Dotty replied, turning her back on Lavinia's interested expression.

'Come on, let's get this picking done,' Hannah said, supressing the panic that had risen in her throat. 'There's two more fields and we've only got today.'

John Whitworth was watching the girls from afar. In his pocket was a letter from his favourite niece, Milly. He had been surprised to learn she had joined the Land Army in Yorkshire and her honest appraisal of the harsh physicality of the work had elicited a strong feeling of sympathy. It was only as he looked at the bent backs in the distance that it occurred to him that these girls were someone's niece, someone's daughter, and he suddenly found himself hoping Milly was getting more support than he was giving these girls on his own farm and felt ashamed.

* * *

Before supper, Hannah was downstairs writing a letter of her own. She always struggled with what to say to her parents and needed peace and quiet to get her thoughts together. Huffing with frustration, she went to the door to get some fresh air. It was freezing cold, but she walked briskly towards the fields, breathing deeply to get some perspective. Above her, the bombers were heading out to do whatever they could to win the war. As usual, the noise was deafening and Hannah gazed upwards, wondering how many of those young men would see the next morning's dawn. It was as she rounded the corner of the last barn that she saw a figure leaning on the corner of the wall in the late-afternoon February gloom and stopped dead. Her heart was thumping and she immediately looked around for a place to run, fearing the figure was Jed.

Instead, a German accent spoke gently to her.

'It is all right, Fräulein. I will not harm you.'

For a brief moment, Hannah almost wished it had been Jed and started to turn on her heel. It was her rescuer from the stable. Her head was engulfed with mixed visions of the haunted faces of Great War veterans like her father and the huge, snorting head of Hercules. She could not, would not, speak to this German.

'Please, Fräulein, don't go. I promise I will not hurt you. I am just having ein moment of fresh air before we go back to the camp. I am not supposed to be out here, but . . .' He shrugged and moved forwards to see her more clearly, but she instinctively stepped back, tripping on a pallet that had been stacked up against the barn wall.

The man reached out his hand to steady her and Hannah felt an electric shock shoot up to her elbow. She looked up in alarm.

'You are the young lady who was having a terrible time with the very big horse, yes?' he said, releasing her slowly.

She nodded. He had saved her life, and even if he was her enemy, she felt she really should thank him, but no words came out of her mouth.

He went on, sounding relaxed and in control, two things that Hannah certainly was not.

'It is very frightening when an enormous animal like that rears up, *nicht wahr?*'

She nodded again.

'But they are just like a little puppy,' he said, 'they will react to anything they do not understand.'

Hannah could not resist: 'But what did I do wrong?'

He glanced at her watch shining in the twilight and pointed at it.

'It is these things that will make him scared,' he said. 'On that day, the sunshine reflected from it. He could not see and was very frightened.'

Hannah gave a huge sigh of understanding. She vaguely remembered he had said something about her watch on that day in the barn, but she had been so traumatised, it hadn't really registered. Now, finally, it made sense.

'Thank you,' she said, feeling very stupid.

'That's OK,' he said with a smile and held out his hand.

'My name is Karl.'

Hannah felt her hand move forward without her telling it to. It clasped his hand and she was surprised how warm it was.

'Hannah Compton,' she finally said, looking for the first time into his face. There was no animosity. All she saw was concern.

'Hello, Hannah Compton.' He smiled, his blue eyes lighting up with humour. 'I know we must seem as frightening as the big horse to you, but, believe me, I am not normally frightening at all, at least, that is what my patients tell me.'

She did not mean to speak but she was intrigued. 'You're a doctor?'

'Yes, well, I was training to be one, until I was told I must fight for the Fatherland.' There was a bitterness in his voice.

'You didn't want to?'

'No, I did not.' His voice had hardened but then his face became gentle again. 'I think you, like me, did not want this war, English Hannah. We are just young people caught up in something terrible we cannot control.'

With that, he heard Peter's voice call from behind him.

'Karl, *komm schnell rein, er kommt zurück.*'

'I must go, goodnight, Fräulein English Hannah. Please do not think we are all bad people.' He looked with interest at the pretty girl in front of him. It was hard to turn away from her but, hearing Peter calling him again, he moved towards the compound, looking wistfully over his shoulder.

Hannah stood in the yard, feeling some warmth had just gone from the spot where she was.

Chapter 9

In the girls' bedroom, Lavinia and Dotty were putting their heads together.

'We have to do something with Miss Horrified Hannah downstairs,' Lavinia said. 'She's terrified of everything.'

'I know,' Dotty replied, 'she's so shy and scared. What can we do to bring her out of herself?'

Lavinia immediately said: 'Well, I for one, am not spending the next however long it is, with someone who reminds me of a scared rabbit. We need to show her how to have some fun.'

'Agreed, but how?'

They both lapsed into silence but then Dotty sat up straight. 'I know, I've got it, there's a dance on in Norwich soon.' She did not mention that George had shyly asked whether she was going.

'Oh, that's it! We'll make her come dancing!' Lavinia said, already planning her outfit.

* * *

As the girls got ready for bed, Hannah seemed distracted, but Dotty nudged Lavinia who took the hint and said, casually, 'We're all going to a dance in Norwich in a couple of weeks. What are you going to wear, Hannah?'

Hannah was shaken out of her thoughts and taken back to the Boys' Brigade dances in Manchester with Ros and Lily, where she had perfected the art of sitting on the sidelines with a fixed smile on her face. She was a hopeless dancer and had always dreaded being asked onto the dance floor.

'But I can't dance,' she stuttered, leaning down to remove her socks and examine the latest hole.

'Nonsense,' Lavinia replied. 'Everyone can dance, and anyway, I'm an excellent dancer and can teach you. On your feet.'

She grabbed Hannah by the arms and pulled her into the middle of the floor, ignoring the fact that she was trailing one sock behind her.

'I'm too tired,' Hannah said plaintively.

'Of course you are, we all are, but you haven't got long to learn so we need to start now.'

Lavinia grabbed Hannah's hand and started to swirl her round. Before long, Hannah was dizzy and fell back onto the bed puffing, but Dotty got her up again, saying:

'Come on, Hannah, let your hair down a bit. It'll be fun.'

Hannah suddenly heard Lily and Ros's voices pleading something similar with her. She had never really learned how to let go like other girls but then Lavinia said, 'If you don't start to take control of your life, you'll end up with some horrible man like a Jed Junior, and believe me, that's not the future you want for yourself.'

Rather than a disturbing picture of Jed, Hannah's arm seemed to tingle where Karl had touched her and she stroked it as if to re-establish that connection, but then Lavinia grabbed her other arm and she had to concentrate on the complicated new jitterbug steps that Lavinia had learned in London.

After about half an hour of falling over her own feet and then Dotty or Lavinia's feet, Hannah looked down in surprise as her legs seemed to know where to go next. She was astonished to find she was getting the hang of dancing and did a rather effective twirl while the others stepped back in admiration to watch. Lavinia looked triumphantly at Dotty, who gave a slow, approving nod.

* * *

In the morning chill a few days later, Hannah was whistling 'Little Brown Jug' while she was whitewashing the south barn. As her arm swished the brush backwards and forwards, her feet were performing dainty yet precise steps.

She heard clapping and turned round to find three of the farmhands watching her, including John Whitworth.

'I . . . I . . .' She did not know what to say.

John's expression softened, smiling at Hannah's oblivion of anything around her. 'It's all right, love,' he said, remembering the dances with his lovely Flo before she became stricken with arthritis. Since Milly's letter, he had been seeing these girls in a new light and he felt a need to make up for his behaviour towards them.`

'Well, she may have a lot to learn about whitewashing,' he said to Albert behind him, 'but she's certainly not got two left feet.'

John laughed and reluctantly Albert joined in, to be rewarded with a beaming smile from Hannah. As they walked away, John started to speak.

'You know, we've been pretty rough on these girls. You've seen how hard they're working. I think we should give them a chance. They're very young.'

Albert glanced back to see Hannah swaying to an imaginary tune in her head, her brush moving up and down the barn wall in time with her hips. He gave a rueful smile.

'I suppose you might be right, John, they are just young lasses, and I have to admit, they stuck at those turnips even though the weather would've frozen the bollocks off a bull.'

George looked pleased; he was already a big fan of one of the girls in particular.

When the men came into the barn that night, Albert, John and George got their plates and moved nearer to the girls to sit down.

John coughed and looked meaningfully at William Handforth, who was still sitting at the far end of the large table.

William looked grumpily at the girls and determinedly tucked into his meal, staying exactly where he was. John gave him an irritated look and started to speak.

'I think we owe you girls an apology. It's not your fault you know nowt about farming, I s'pose. We'll say this for you . . .' at this he looked round for support from Albert next to him ' . . . you're making an effort and that's probably all we can expect.'

William Handforth scowled and stored up information to discuss with Jed the next morning. He looked at the turncoats with disgust.

Lavinia was the first to speak. 'Well, that's just wonderful, gentlemen. We'd so love to learn from your expertise, so any help you can give us, we'd be really grateful.'

She looked up through her long eyelashes and delightedly watched fifty-five-year-old John's face as he struggled with being both completely charmed and horrified that such a young lass should flirt so outrageously with him. He had forgotten what it was like to have a woman smile at him like that and he could not decide whether it felt good or whether it made him feel like a dirty old man.

He decided the latter, as a disturbing vision of Jed came into his mind.

'You just stop your flirting, young lady. You're young enough to be my daughter,' he told her gruffly.

'I know, I know,' Lavinia said, slightly embarrassed at the telling-off. These were men of the land, not used to the parlour games of the aristocracy and his expression scorned the shallow world she came from. She looked suitably apologetic. 'I'm only joking with you, but it's so nice to see you all smiling for a change and it would be lovely to be friends.'

George, who was sitting on the other side of John, was concentrating fiercely on the mashed potato in front of him. His face was burning and he knew he was blushing. He looked shyly at Dotty; she had her head back and was laughing. It was a tinkling sound like a fingernail on a glass and made him catch his breath.

Her dark hair was glistening in the kerosene lamplight and her brown eyes were sparkling. He wondered whether he was falling in love.

'So, who's seen these Germans then?' Dotty asked. Hannah shifted uncomfortably in her seat but said nothing.

George tore his eyes away from her hair and mumbled.

'Speak up, lad, she won't eat you!' John laughed.

He blushed a deep red colour and looked at the floor planks, hoping they would swallow him up.

Dotty said gently, 'Come on, George, tell us what you know. We won't tell anyone.'

Everyone else at the table faded into the distance in the young lad's mind and he spoke for her and her alone.

'Th-they look n-normal. Well, you know, German, but, well, just like us really.'

Lavinia butted in: 'Come on, lad, we need more information. Are they good-looking?'

'Um, I've no idea. I s-suppose so. Most of them are b-blond and, yes-s, maybe they did have blue eyes, m-most of them.' George was struggling with fighting a faceless enemy at night on manoeuvres and then seeing the real thing on his very own farm during the day. They looked so harmless, laughing and joking, as they mended fences in the next field to him and yet, a few hours later, he was being taught to throw grenades at their countrymen. He shook his head. None of this made sense.

Hannah was thinking the same thing and crossly dismissed the vision of the attractive young man in the twilight.

'They sound divine!' Lavinia gushed. 'How do we get to meet them?'

John leaned forward. He was having none of this.

'You keep well away, girls. I've heard terrible tales of what these Germans do to young women. And if the boss catches you talking to them, you'll be for it. He hates the Hun. And you'll be fined,' he finished triumphantly.

Dotty muttered under her breath that they already had Jed, they didn't need a group of Germans as well, but the men's conversation had already moved on to something they'd heard the boss discussing with the man from the Ministry that morning.

'He said at those Casablanca talks, Stalin didn't turn up,' John was telling Albert, 'I'm not sure what to think of that Stalin, I'm not sure I trust 'im.'

Hannah listened in silence as the men debated the value of the latest talks and what they all thought of Stalin. She was cross that she was falling behind on world affairs. She'd always had a keen interest in what was happening in the wider war while Lavinia and Dotty seemed to have no such concerns and were playing with their forks in a bored manner.

Eventually, as the men argued about how America had increased the bombing of Germany, she could keep quiet no longer.

'I think it's a wise decision to transfer resources to the Far East,' she said quietly. 'If we don't, that's the war that's going to take the longest time to finally settle.'

The men looked at her in surprise. They had heard the other two girls chattering on many occasions but this one was known for hardly uttering a word – let alone being able to express an opinion on world affairs.

Dotty and Lavinia, too, looked at Hannah with wide eyes.

'How do you know about all that?' Lavinia asked.

'Oh, I just heard something on the wireless before I joined up,' Hannah replied, retreating back into her shell, where she felt safe.

John Whitworth stared at Hannah. *This girl has got more depth than we know,* he thought.

* * *

It was as the girls were getting ready for bed that Dotty turned to Hannah.

'Hannah, you're really clever, aren't you? I wish I'd had an education like you.'

'No, I'm not,' Hannah replied, deflecting any interest in herself as usual. 'I just listen to the wireless a lot, and, well, I read the papers when I can.'

Dotty looked impressed. She had made hasty judgements about Hannah and was beginning to think she might have to revise them. The Land Army was providing her, a girl from the back streets of Birmingham, with more opportunities than she had ever imagined – to mix with girls from very different backgrounds to her and she determined she would soak up their knowledge.

'I left school at fourteen,' she said pathetically, 'I never learned nothing. But oh, I want to. Maybe you can help me?'

Hannah had always followed others, never the one to lead, and, for the first time, someone was asking for her help.

'Well, if you want, maybe I could,' she said, climbing onto the bed and curling up under the covers. 'We'll start as soon as we get a minute."

Chapter 10

A hectic schedule and punishing physical work did not give the girls much free time and Hannah explained ruefully that Dotty's education was going to have to wait as early spring crops had to be harvested, the fields needed turning over and the weeding had to be done in preparation for the summer crops. Every meal was rushed. Breakfast, in particular, was a matter of getting the hot porridge down their throats as fast as they could, but, one morning, their meal was interrupted by the arrival of a woman in full Land Army uniform striding into the barn.

Lavinia almost choked on her porridge, groaned and put her spoon down. She dropped her head onto her arms on the table.

'There's no hiding, Doris Braithwaite,' the woman said, tapping her on the head sharply.

From the depths of her armpits, Lavinia muttered, 'Hello, Aunt Deborah. What took you so long?'

The woman stepped back and sized all the girls up.

'I'm here officially to check on my girls. Now, how are you all? Being treated well? Got all your uniform? Any problems?'

Dotty and Hannah were unable to speak. This woman exuded authority and her expression was so formidable that they were stuck for words.

Lavinia, however, finally stood up to her full height and faced her relative.

'I'm fine, thank you, Aunt Deborah. I've got sore muscles, my hands are red raw and I've got blisters on the backs of my heels. Isn't that what you wanted?'

'Good,' the woman replied. 'About time you did some hard work. But first I need to check on these real Land Army girls.'

Her voice softened. 'Now, young ladies, I'm your welfare officer and I'm here to look after you and make sure you're being treated all right. Any problems, you need to confide in me.'

Hannah looked askance at the terrifying figure in front of them. Anyone less like a confidante, she could not imagine, but Dotty immediately interjected.

'My greatcoat hasn't arrived, miss, um, madam, um . . .'

'Ah yes,' the woman said, looking somewhat embarrassed. 'We, er, don't issue the greatcoats until we know that people are staying. So many leave in the first few weeks.'

Dotty tutted in disgust. 'I'm not going anywhere. I've been here ages now and, anyway, what do you think I'm going to do? Go back to that scullery? Not on your life.'

The woman got out a notebook and scribbled something with an elegant tortoiseshell fountain pen.

'And what about you?' she said, looking at Hannah.

'I, um, think I'm fine. I could maybe do with some plasters,' she said, holding out her blistered hands.

'Ah yes, the hands of a gentlewoman,' Aunt Deborah said approvingly. 'What did you do before you joined up, dear?'

'Nothing,' Hannah replied, looking shamefaced. 'My mum needed me at home, you see. Although I did help out with fire duty, obviously. We all had to something . . .' She tailed off, feeling as always as if she had to justify her existence.

'They're not on the list, but I'll see if I can get some sent to you,' the woman said, making another note. 'Now, Doris will undoubtedly refer to me as Aunt Deborah, but you may call me Lady Parker. I will be calling in from time to time to check up on you.

'And,' she said, with a warning look, 'I will be checking with your foreman to make sure you're all behaving.'

Dotty caught Hannah's eye, thinking that anything Jed said about them would hardly be complimentary. She was so desperate to stay in the Land Army, she didn't want anything to jeopardise it – and she did not trust Jed one bit.

'I'll give your mother the good news that you haven't run away to Outer Mongolia or anything yet, Doris.'

With that, Lady Parker swept out of the barn, banging the door behind her.

Dotty turned immediately to Lavinia.

'Doris?' she said, giggling. 'Doris?'

Lavinia shrugged. 'Well, Lavinia's my second name and it is a lot more glam, you must admit.' She grinned, but then the memory of her aunt turned her cheeky smile into a frown. 'I know she was on my interview panel, but I thought I'd be saved this. She'll be watching me like a hawk.'

'Do you really come from the aristocracy, then?' Hannah said. Lavinia had given away so little about her background up to now.

'Oh yes, shields, mottos, stately pile, the lot,' Lavinia said with a pout. 'I tried to break out but, as you can see, I've been recaptured and am supposed to go back into the fold. 'Well, they've had that,' she said, suddenly drawing herself up. 'I'm the black sheep of the family and that's how I'm going to stay, and if that means I'm not welcome in Oxfordshire, then so be it.'

Hannah looked enviously at the tall, blonde girl opposite her. With only one tiny rebellion against her parents to her name, she already spent every night tossing and turning, wondering what she had done to them and how they were surviving. Lavinia's priority seemed to be Lavinia and it gave her a freedom Hannah could only envy.

* * *

Margaret Compton was staring at the back kitchen wall. The supper needed to be prepared, but for a moment she had to hold on to the edges of the cold Belfast sink to steady herself. She felt the rising panic in her chest and her heart begin to pound. This had happened so many times since Hannah had gone and always after a night like last night when the house was shaken as huge RAF four-engine bombers flew directly over their chimney pots. A few hours later, the sirens went to warn them of possible retaliatory action by the Luftwaffe. It reminded her too much of the Blitz and, without Hannah, she'd been unable to think amidst the ominous drone of the planes above and had started scrabbling around for the torch, believing the bombing was starting all over again. Alf was standing uselessly behind her, a blank expression on his face. She had shouted at him, she remembered with shame. But it had taken anger to get him to finally move his body and follow her into the cupboard under the stairs, once again waiting in that purgatory between safety and oblivion.

They had sat there for hours until the 'all-clear' told them the Luftwaffe weren't coming and they'd returned to their bed, shivering with cold. This morning, in a fit of shame at her actions, she'd rushed to take extra blankets to the Red Cross centre nearby. The woman behind the trestle table thanked her, but confided that they needed far more than blankets for the thousands of people who were still homeless and Margaret had walked home in a daze, feeling close to despair.

The inability to think rationally was happening more and more and she was starting to be unable to tackle even the simplest of tasks. She grasped the sides of the sink even more firmly, as if its ceramic surface could protect her, and shivered in terror. The house seemed so empty and quiet, it was hard to bear. She couldn't fathom what was going on in her husband's mind; his face would contort with memories as he sat in his armchair after work and it was almost impossible to remember the man with the dancing eyes who had flirted so outrageously with her at the local church dance all those years ago. It was if he was trying to process something that he had locked away for so many years. She watched him, a shadow of the man he used to be, looking vacantly into an abyss and she wanted to scream. Margaret was trying, really trying, not to express her anguish in her letters to Hannah but it was hard. She realised how much she had come to rely on her daughter, and without her, she felt all her strength ebbing away.

Margaret clutched her chest and felt behind her for the wooden stool before her wobbly legs gave way but then she heard the doorbell go. She knew Alf wouldn't move so she made herself stand up again and make her way to the front door.

Opening the door she saw Ros, Hannah's school friend, standing there. She looked so familiar that Margaret grabbed hold of her shoulders and fell against her sobbing. Ros gently led Margaret indoors. She had been visiting the house since she was five and recognised a woman at the end of her tether. She had seen the same wide-eyed look in women on her way to work, wandering the bombed-out streets searching for something solid, something familiar that would make them feel safe.

'There now, Mrs Compton,' she said, gently, 'you sit down, I'll get us a nice cup of tea.' She looked around at last night's dishes, still not washed, at Hannah's dad in the corner, barely lifting his head in recognition of a visitor, and the ashes not cleared from the grate.

This is worse than I thought, she said to herself, wondering how on earth she was going to reply to Hannah's worried letter in which she had asked her friend to 'just pop in if you've got a minute'. The scene in front of Ros was so much more desperate than she had ever imagined.

Ros, who was the smallest of the three friends, had shoulder-length wavy brown hair and green eyes, which twinkled with fun at every opportunity, but the scene in front of her made her dancing eyes frown. She was a practical girl and had gone into a munitions factory to be close to her widowed mother and two younger brothers, but she was now being put forward for a position where she would be testing explosives thanks to a rudimentary year in physics at school and was justifiably proud at the prospect of moving on from grey overalls to a white coat. As the only one of the three school friends still at home, she felt a responsibility to keep an eye on Lily and Hannah's families.

Taking a gentle hold of the shaking woman's shoulders, she sat a grateful Mrs Compton down in an armchair in the morning room opposite her husband.

'I'm guessing you heard the bombers last night?' Ros said.

Margaret Compton nodded.

'Did you hear that . . . ? Well, never mind that, at least you're all right.' Ros changed tack realising Mrs Compton did not need to hear any more bad news about what had happened to so many of those young RAF pilots.

'Have you heard from Hannah?' she asked.

At that, Mrs Compton perked up a little and reached up to the mantelpiece above the range to pick up a letter that was propped up between the Toby jug and the little carriage clock.

'Yes,' she said, glancing for the hundredth time at the quickly penned letter. 'She's doing ever so well, learning to milk cows and everything . . . oh, and next week, she's been told she's going to learn to drive the tractor. Fancy that?'

Ros spent the next half-hour trying to raise Mrs Compton's spirits, talking about what a wonderful time Hannah seemed to be having and how she'd heard how good the food was at the farm. She didn't mention how homesick Hannah had admitted to being. She tried repeatedly to engage Mr Compton in conversation, but he just nodded blankly at her.

Ros decided she needed to bring in reinforcements and, as she left, she told Mrs Compton that she was going to call on the Mullinses soon, keeping to herself the hope that Lily's sensible parents might be able to help. As she turned to go, Margaret grabbed her arm and gave it a hard squeeze.

'I wish I was stronger,' the woman said pathetically, 'but with Alf, well, it's so lonely.'

Ros felt tears prick her eyes and gave the diminutive woman a strong hug.

'We're all just getting through, Mrs Compton, that's all we can do.'

Chapter 11

Hannah was trying to write regular letters to her parents, but it was hard to keep up an enthusiastic tone when she was feeling so miserable. The homesickness had developed into a dark cloud that seemed to engulf her each morning when she pulled herself out of bed. Every bit of her body hurt and she was struggling to keep up a cheerful face while spending each day terrified of a future where Jed would find her alone, that the cows would trample her to death and that her first attempts at driving the tractor would end in disaster. The only thing that took her mind off her misery was scanning the horizon for any German prisoners of war to see if she could spot that doctor – it was disturbing how his gentle voice kept coming back to her and it made her shiver. Fraternising with the enemy was not just forbidden, it was the ultimate betrayal of her country, the servicemen who were dying and family and neighbours who were living in such hardship they could barely function. She tried really hard to listen to that voice of reason in her head, but she still found her eyes darting from left to right over the farm to see if she could spot the good-looking German.

She turned her attention to watching and trying to learn from Dotty and Lavinia, who both managed to tackle each task with enthusiasm, or, in Lavinia's case, if not with enthusiasm, at least with determination. The dancing lessons had been put on hold, abandoned after long hours of getting the sowing done, the feedstock stacked and the fencing mended, leaving the girls with hardly any energy to eat their supper before falling asleep. However, in the time between, their little bedroom was becoming their own private haven and it was there that by swapping embrocation for their tired limbs, sharing the darning needle for their socks and talking endlessly about the dance that was going to be held that Saturday, a friendship began to develop.

Finally, the night of the dance arrived along with the prospect of a day off on Sunday. The three girls piled onto the bus into Norwich; Lavinia and Dotty falling against each other and giggling, squashing the new handbag that Lavinia had had sent from London. It cleverly disguised the obligatory gas masks they all had to carry but Dotty joked that it looked as if she had a secret camera in the bottom. Hannah followed, worrying whether her cream-coloured dress was going to be appropriate for a dance in the big city. She wished Lily and Ros were with her. When they arrived at the venue, Dotty burst out laughing.

'This is the perfect place for you Hannah. It's called the Samson and Hercules!'

For a moment she had forgotten her promise to Hannah that they would not tell Lavinia about the altercation with the horse. Hannah had been worried that Lavinia's characteristic sarcasm would make fun of her stupidity.

Hannah glared at Dotty, then cast a stricken glance at the huge white sculptures holding up the entrance porch to the dance hall, prompting Lavinia to give them both a puzzled look.

'It's all right, Lavinia,' Dotty said, 'we'll tell you about it one day,' and determinedly marched on through the front door leaving the other two to follow.

The room was packed and many of the people there were in uniform. Dotty had told them how it had been a swimming pool in the summer and a dance hall in the winter, but there was no sign of the pool beneath now with just over a hundred people, searching for an opportunity to forget the war for a few hours. The band was playing at one end, fronted by a sea of uniforms and Hannah immediately felt out of place, wishing she had put on her best Land Army clothes so no one could accuse her of not being part of the war effort. She had a need to blend in and looked sorrowfully at her cream dress that stood out among the sea of uniforms.

Lavinia, however, swept straight into the middle of the dance floor and gave a very impressive twirl, her blue silk dress swirling around her. The crowd parted, and while half of them smiled indulgently at the pure joy of her movement, the rest frowned at her brazen attitude.

Lavinia called out to Hannah and Dotty, who were standing on the side of the crowd.

'Come on, you two, let's show them what the Land Army's made of!'

At that, some of the faces softened and they looked on the three newcomers indulgently. It was a country area and many of them came from farming backgrounds; the rest were service men and women from nearby RAF stations, and some were in American uniforms. From another corner came about six other girls – some dressed in the familiar Land Army brown and green colours and others in their best frocks like the Salhouse Farm girls. They immediately made a beeline for Lavinia.

'Are you LA too? Oh, it's so great to see you here, we've been the only ones,' one gushed. 'Which farm are you on? What are the meals like? Is there any hot water?'

These questions were crucial to a Land Army girl's life and Lavinia immediately started chatting enthusiastically, swapping experiences.

She vanished into a group of excited chatter but Dotty spotted her arm waving high above the crowd, beckoning them over, so she grabbed Hannah's hand and dragged her into the middle to join in.

By this time, the band had struck up and there were a group of RAF men edging their way past the GIs as well as some burly farmers, who felt this was their territory and no 'fly boys' were going to take the best bunch of girls they had seen in the dance hall for ages. There was a certain amount of jostling and shoving but the end result was that all the girls found themselves surrounded by men clamouring for a dance.

Lavinia took the lead. 'Well, the first of you lovely men who can get me a cider will be the first to dance with me. Oh, and my friends will have the same.'

It did not take long for Hannah to be handed a glass with cider in it. She looked up at the young RAF man who had thrust it into her hands. He was quite good-looking and she immediately felt the shyness that had overwhelmed her since she had first been asked to dance at the Boys' Brigade, but once she had taken a sip of her drink, he gently removed the glass from her grasp and put it on a nearby table, edging her towards the dance floor.

The band was playing 'Boogie Woogie Bugle Boy' and the music was so fast Hannah's feet got in a muddle. She had forgotten everything Lavinia had taught her and wanted to crawl away to the powder room.

'Is this your first dance in Norfolk?' her partner was shouting in her ear. She nodded. 'Well, we'd better make sure you have a good time then,' he said, taking her hand and propelling her into a complicated sideways step.

Hannah tried to concentrate but her feet would not go where she wanted them to and she kept tripping him up. By the end of the dance, she was feeling quite exhausted.

'Well, I think my feet survived that,' her partner said, laughing. 'What's your name?'

'Hannah.'

'I'm Reg,' he told her. 'Based at Coltishall. I'm a navigator. So, which bit of the cow's your favourite?'

He only meant it as a joke but Hannah immediately remembered Jed's hand on hers and stepped back. She made a feeble comment about needing the ladies' room and made her escape, leaving Reg standing alone in the middle of the floor.

Dotty saw her leave, jerked her head to notify Lavinia and they both made their excuses and followed Hannah's retreating steps to the toilets.

'What are you doing, Hannah?' Dotty asked impatiently.

'I . . . I'm just not comfortable with dances like this,' Hannah said, looking down at the floor.

'Oh, that does it,' Lavinia replied with frustration, taking hold of her head with both hands and making her look up, 'this has to stop. You are not going to spoil all our fun, now get back out there or I'll tell Aunt Deborah on you and she'll move you to somewhere boring like . . . oh, I don't know, but somewhere in the middle of nowhere with no dances!'

With that, she pushed Hannah back out into the hall and went to whisper to the young man she had last danced with. He was also in the RAF but was an older man with a kind smile. He listened intently to Lavinia, nodded and went over to Hannah.

'Come along, young lady. Let's take this slowly and see whether we can't find those twinkle toes of yours.' With that, he put his arm around her waist and gently led her around the floor to the strains of 'You Always Hurt the One You Love'. He kept up a constant chatter, telling her about his wife and two children and she started to relax.

'That's better,' he said. 'You're really getting the hang of it,' and with that he twirled her so that her feet left the ground. It was as if she was flying and Hannah beamed with delight.

Once the dance ended, she gasped for breath, but her partner stood back and clapped. Behind him, Dotty and Lavinia joined in. Hannah expected to feel embarrassed, but, instead, she felt jubilant. She had never felt so free.

Before she had the chance to recover, another young man presented himself in front of her and stretched his hand out questioningly.

She nodded and they took off around the dance floor. This time it was a quickstep, and although Hannah made mistakes, the young man's steadying hand on her back led her in the directions she needed to go. He was trying to speak to her, but she shook her head; she really needed to concentrate. He laughed and did three little steps that made her fall over her feet.

'Never mind,' he said, 'you'll get it next time. You're a real natural.'

Hannah glowed with delight, and when he tried that move again, she let her feet follow his and was delighted to find she had reached the other side of the floor in no time.

Four dances with four different partners later, Hannah stepped back from the dance floor and told the disappointed farmer waiting for his turn that she needed to join her friends.

She found Dotty and Lavinia near the bar. They both looked very smug, she thought.

Dotty handed her a cider and she gulped it down too quickly, almost spluttering over her dress.

'Calm down,' Lavinia laughed, 'just because you've become the Ginger Rogers of the night, it doesn't mean you have to go to pieces.'

They all started to giggle and Hannah looked gratefully at the other girls.

'Thank you so much,' she said. 'The Boys' Brigade dances were never like this and I was usually a wallflower anyway. I never knew dancing like that could be so much fun, or . . .' she hesitated, unwilling to sound big-headed '. . . that I'd be able to do it.'

'Do it?' Lavinia scoffed. 'They'll be signing you up at The Windmill next. If you ever learn to get undressed in daylight, that is.'

Hannah always found it difficult to gauge when Lavinia was joking and gave a nervous laugh. She dismissed the scandalous image of herself with an ostrich fan that had come to mind with a guilty smile, thinking what Stretford would make of quiet, shy Hannah Compton on The Windmill stage.

'That's better,' Dotty said, grinning. 'We were about to give up on you but if you're going to be interesting and fun after all, then we'll definitely keep you.'

Lavinia looked at her watch, it was just after nine and they faced a fine if they were not back at their farm by ten. 'We need to go, I don't want to give anyone an excuse to complain to Aunt Deborah about me.'

Dotty and Lavinia each took hold of one of Hannah's arms and led her out of the room to several calls of 'Shame,' and 'Don't go, girls,' from a group of men standing at the bar waiting for the next dance to strike up.

Hannah felt her friends' arms move around her waist and, with the effects of the cider giving her a feeling of joy, joined in the banter that accompanied their trip home. They had missed the bus and had to hitch a lift with a passing truck, risking life and limb to step out into the pitch-black road to attract the driver's attention. They all piled into the truck, giggling, and by the time they were dropped off at the farm gates, Hannah's stomach ached from laughing. The anonymity of the darkness, as they made their way up the drive, made Hannah open up a bit more. She tentatively explained to Lavinia why the name Hercules held such horrors for her.

Lavinia grabbed her arm tightly and whispered fiercely, 'The next time that horse comes near you, just shout for me and I'll terrify him with my best impression of Aunt Deborah.'

The three girls doubled over in laughter, made worse when Lavinia did an impression of her aunt quelling a huge shire horse, sending it scurrying in fear to the back of its stable. For the first time since she had said goodbye to Lily and Ros, Hannah felt the warm glow of proper friends.

* * *

Karl too was beginning to feel more at home in the compound at Mousehold Heath. His bunk was in the corner of the room and above him was Peter, a sound sleeper but one who snored loudly. Karl started off by jabbing at the thin mattress above him, but Peter would turn over and, five minutes later, be snoring again. Karl gave up and stuffed some wool in his ears that he had begged from Hans, whose bed was in the opposite corner and who liked to make cloth figures for Christmas toys. While Karl was becoming accustomed to life as a prisoner of war and knew he was being treated well, he guiltily suspected English prisoners in his own country were not. As he mulled over the disturbing reports that were coming out of Germany, he concentrated instead on the appealing image of the little dark Land Army girl in those scruffy breeches, and the thought calmed him. He had only glimpsed her occasionally in recent weeks, but he was desperately trying to convince himself that her eyes lit up when she spotted him. He cursed the war that put such a divide between them, but then reluctantly admitted that, without it, they would probably not have met. He just had to work out how he could wangle a chance to speak to her again.

Chapter 12

Ros sat with her pen poised over the blank sheet of paper. She had no idea what she was going to write to Hannah. Three screwed-up pieces of paper on the floor bore witness to her frustrations over the last half-hour. She started again:

Dear Hannah . . .

She gave a loud sigh; this was even more difficult than she had thought. The Comptons were hanging on by a fingernail she felt, with Mr Compton unable to engage with the world around him and Mrs Compton reminding her of those people she had seen sitting on piles of rubble on street corners, clutching a blanket or a toy or a shoe, with blank faces as grey as the dust around them.

She couldn't discuss her concerns with her own mother. As a widow with three children, she had enough on her plate trying to get through every day. Ros made a decision and grabbed her coat.

'Mum, I'm just going to call round to the Mullinses,' she yelled from the front door. 'Won't be long.'

Lily's parents' home was the one all the girls loved to gather in, knowing they would be welcomed with a piece of cake and a pot of tea. The Mullinses were a couple who were always happy to give advice, help and sometimes just an understanding silence that both Ros and Hannah appreciated. Lily took it for granted and simply shrugged her shoulders, only vaguely aware that her home always felt warmer than the other two girls', not realising that the warmth came from more than just the cosy range fire.

* * *

An hour later, Ros was feeling much better. She sat in the familiar morning room of her favourite adopted parents as Mrs Mullins handed her a welcome cup of tea and a carrot biscuit while Mr Mullins was sitting puffing on his pipe, exuding calmness and control.

'I don't know what to do, Mrs Mullins,' she said, stirring Carnation milk into the china cup with a little silver spoon. 'I can't tell Hannah too much. She doesn't get leave like Lily and it will only worry her to death.'

'Don't you worry,' Mrs Mullins said, 'I'll call round and see how I can help.'

'You could take her one of your potato pies,' her husband said, adding with a chuckle: 'If that doesn't make her feel better, nothing will.'

Mrs Mullins looked doubtful. She worked three times a week at the Red Cross and she knew there were people all over the country who were crumbling under the strain of being at war and, as the years were passing, the stresses were increasing, leaving people feeling they had no resources left to draw on. She wasn't sure a potato pie would help.

It was all very well those politicians telling us we'll get through this, she thought, *but how much more can we take?*

John Mullins was staring into the meagre fire. During the Great War he had been a Tommy in Europe, too occupied with trying to survive to have time to think; now he was beginning to understand what it was like being on the home front and he could not believe how useless he felt.

Once Ros had been waved off down the road with a reassuring hug and clutching three baking apples from the cold pantry in the back kitchen at Rusholme, he turned to his wife.

'Is there anything I can do, love?'

Ginny said down opposite him and thought. 'Make the war stop, maybe?'

John Mullins nodded sadly. 'If only I could, Ginny, if only I could.'

* * *

97

In Norfolk, Hannah's triumphant night out at the dance hall was soon obliterated from her memory by the increasing numbers of chores that were being thrust upon the girls. Today was the day she was going to have to drive the tractor. As a child, Hannah had never even managed to learn how to ride a bike. The attempts had resulted in her being taken to the doctor with badly grazed knees and a bumped head and she had never tried again, leaving the second-hand bike her mother had got from the jumble sale to rust next to the garden fence. A large vehicle with an engine seemed to pose an impossible challenge.

John Whitworth, had taken a shine to Hannah, a sentiment that grew every day that he worked alongside her; she seemed to have a natural affinity with the land and no matter how difficult the task, he would watch her bite her lip in an effort to build herself up to tackle it. He began to make encouraging comments to help her to gain more confidence, but knew the tractor was going to be a new obstacle she was going to have to overcome, a belief endorsed by the anxious look on Hannah's face as she stood next to the John Deere tractor. It was one of the smallest on the farm, but Hannah was looking up at it as if were the Eiffel Tower. He stepped forward.

'Come on, lass, put your foot on that plate there and swing yourself up. That's it. Don't be nervous of it, it's not as hard as it looks.'

Hannah climbed up and peered down at the ground. It seemed a very long way away. She was glad it was John and not Jed who had been told to show her how to drive one as she knew she would have been a gibbering wreck if it had been Jed.

She got into the seat, moulded to fit her backside, and John climbed up to stand on the flat platform behind her. He showed her the hand-operated clutch and explained to her how the two-cylinder machine worked, then he told her to get down again while he showed her how to 'start her up', by turning the fly wheel.

Hannah was so nervous it took her several goes until the engine sparked into life. She jumped back on to try to jerk the machine forward, but each time she did, it stalled so she had to hop on and off a few times, until she got the hang of it, managing to get the machine to shudderingly make its way across the yard. John told her to start with circles, so she held her shoulders taut as she slowly turned the wheel, making the tension pulse up her neck. She could feel the engine purring under her as she made her way around the concrete. Little by little, her mouth formed a smile. Then she yelped.

'The handle's so hot, it's burning me!' As she said it, she took her hand off the lever and the machine started to race towards the barn. Hannah looked with horror as the brick building seemed to be moving towards her at a terrifyingly fast speed.

John was almost sent backwards from his perch at the back but regained his balance in time to quickly lean over and turn the machine off before jumping down to examine the tractor from the side.

'Ah, that's what you're doing, young miss,' he said. 'You're slipping the clutch and it's got that hot it's sent the heat up the lever. You need to push the lever all the way forward, then it'll lock in position.'

'I don't want to do it again,' Hannah said plaintively.

John looked at her worried face and went round to the front of the tractor to look directly at her.

He leaned on the radiator grill and gave her a stern look. This was reminding him too much of his niece, Milly, who had spent her young life being too scared to try new experiences and had needed hours of encouragement to get her to even consider joining the Land Army.

'Now listen to me, Hannah Compton. I've got a niece like you and I've just heard she won't even look at driving the tractor but look at you! You've been milking cows, you've mended fences and you're becoming an expert at so many jobs. You've been doing really well and we're not going to let a little thing like a tractor beat us, now, are we?'

Hannah slowly shook her head. He reminded her of her grandfather with his patience and understanding and it made her not want to let him down.

He jumped back up on the back of the machine and said gently, 'Right, now let's take it slower this time and see if you can take her out of the yard and over to that field over there.'

He helped Hannah start the tractor up again, and when she pushed the lever all the way this time, it clicked neatly into place and the tractor moved forward. She tried moving the wheel from side to side and couldn't resist a little squeal of satisfaction when it turned with her. She felt immensely powerful and in control and turned to beam at John, causing the tractor to veer to one side.

'Steady, girl,' he laughed, leaning forward to grab the wheel to straighten it. 'Let's not get ahead of ourselves.'

Lavinia and Dotty were waiting by the farm gate and cheered as the tractor drew up next to them. Lavinia had taken off her scarf and was waving it like the chequered flag at a racing track.

'Oh, my little darling,' she drawled, 'you are so very clever. Look at you up there. You look as if you could win Le Mans. I really should have a laurel wreath to put round your neck.' With that, she reached up and put the scarf triumphantly around Hannah's shoulders.

'Oh no, you don't,' John said, taking it immediately off again. 'Don't you remember that dancer, Isadora Duncan? She died when her scarf caught in a car wheel. Don't ever mix your fancy ideas with farming, young lady.'

Lavinia shrugged, but quickly tied her scarf tightly around her head again, chastened for once.

Meanwhile, Hannah Compton was grinning from ear to ear. She stood up, flung her arms out and flapped them like a bird.

'I'm a tractor driver, I'm a tractor driver!' she shouted to the empty field.

The other three burst out laughing.

Chapter 13

After her debut, nothing could keep Hannah off the tractor. She felt giddy. First there was the dancing, and now, here she was, able to drive an enormous piece of machinery. Her mother would not believe it. From the first time Hannah had tried to ride that two-wheeler bike, her anxious mother had stood on the sidelines telling her daughter she would not be able to do it – and Hannah had believed her. Now, every time she climbed up onto the tractor, she raised her head high and smiled. Never again would her mother be able to tell her she was too scared to try something new. She knew now that it was her mother who had that fear, not her.

'I'll do it,' she told Albert when he was looking for a volunteer to plough the furrows on a chilly May day. He smiled. He and John had had many a discussion about these young lasses and how they were beginning to get to grips with the physicality that farming demanded of them. From looking like frail little creatures, they were all beginning to develop muscles and a surprising strength and aptitude for every job the men put in front of them. He had to admit, they were a welcome help on the over-stretched farm and it occurred to him that he was beginning to look forward to working alongside them, listening to their chatter. They made each day a little brighter. Albert and John were watching with particular interest as this shy one, Hannah, was starting to come out of her shell.

'OK,' Albert said, with a mischievous grin, 'but first let me show you one of the best things about a tractor.' He opened the engine cover. On the radiator were about ten dandelion leaves which he added to the hot water in the flask he was carrying. 'Here you are,' he said, 'now you'll be able to make a hot drink when you're out driving it and in the winter you can even warm your hands on this here radiator.'

Hannah was delighted: it seemed these vehicles had a great deal to offer a young Land Army girl.

'You know, if you're going to drive this thing, then you'd better learn to mend it,' he went on.

Hannah hesitated for a brief second but then, buoyed by her recent achievements, looked him in the eye and said: 'OK. Show me how.'

From that moment, Albert took the time and trouble to explain to Hannah how to use the wrench, the spanners and the screwdrivers. To begin with, it was incredibly complicated and Hannah was constantly reaching for the wrench when she needed a spanner, but gradually, she learned which tool did each job and she happily walked around with her overall pockets stuffed with them, ready to have them to hand whenever she needed them.

It became a familiar sight to see Hannah's legs protruding from under the tractor, now affectionately known as 'Deery' by the girls, as she lovingly tinkered with the mechanics and oiled it to perfection before driving it out onto the fields. Jed still complained that her furrows were not straight enough but John confided to her that Jed always hated everyone who drove the tractor because his wooden leg wouldn't let him operate it.

'What happened to Jed's leg?' Hannah asked one day.

John shrugged. He had heard something about Jed hurting his leg as he ran away from the police. He had fallen into a ditch and had to hide there in the mud until after dark. It was after that an infection had set in and he had to have it amputated. John felt it was not up to him to pass on the unsavoury rumours without being aware of the full facts, so he said nothing, but he was beginning to have his own doubts about Jed. He noticed how the foreman would lurk around the yard when the girls were about to wash down and how, in particular, Jed would sidle up to Hannah to get as near as possible to her. John knew the man wouldn't risk anything with the other two – they were quite capable of looking after themselves, but John felt a sudden shiver as he thought of Jed taking advantage of innocent Hannah.

One day, when he and Hannah were working the top field with the tractor, he tentatively asked her, 'Have you ever had any trouble with Jed, Hannah?'

He watched the blood drain from the girl's face and took a sharp intake of breath. He felt a sudden loathing for the man he had worked with for several years.

'You can tell me, Hannah,' he said softly, watching as she stared down at the ground, waiting for a fissure that would allow her to slip through and out of sight.

John put his forefinger gently under her chin and raised her head, then looked questioningly into her eyes.

'He . . . I . . . Dotty saved me,' she blurted out.

'I see,' he said slowly. 'Well, you listen to me, young Hannah, don't you ever put yourself in a situation where you're on your own with him again, do you hear me? I don't trust that man one bit.'

Hannah nodded and gave him a weak smile.

Later that evening, when all the farmhands were washing down at the end of their shift, John coughed. Jed had already vanished into his rooms above the barn.

Albert, William and George looked up expectantly.

'I think Jed's been trying to interfere with Hannah,' he said.

George gasped, but Albert's mouth tightened into a hard line. William shuffled uncomfortably from foot to foot. He met Jed regularly in the local pub, The Bell, and felt a strong need to defend his friend, but couldn't quite bring himself to say the words.

'I think we should try to make sure the girls aren't left alone with him if we can,' John went on. 'And I tell you now, if I ever find he's tried anything ever again, I'll be straight on to the boss, make no mistake.'

With that, he stormed furiously off towards the drive to go home to his little cottage in the village. Every time he saw Hannah's sweet face, he saw his own niece and the thought of anyone trying to harm either of them filled him with a deep anger he was in danger of not being able to control.

William sidled off, trying to avoid the other two, who had huddled together in solidarity. Albert had had his suspicions about Jed, but George was too busy trying to impress Dotty to notice. Now, however, he felt a deep unease and he turned to Albert.

'What can I do?' he asked, thinking that his new skills as a secret operative might come in handy.

'It's all right, lad, there are more of us than there are of him,' Albert told him, 'don't you worry, we'll keep an eye on things but you let me know if you see anything. That man needs watching.' And with that, he gathered up his overalls and went off into the darkness to go to his small house on the edge of the village, his step resounding with an angry thud.

* * *

More determined than ever to keep Hannah out of Jed's path, John decided to tackle another issue that he knew was haunting her and, a few days later, he addressed it before she had even had breakfast.

'Now you can drive the tractor, you need to learn to drive the large cart,' he said, as he passed her on his way to the privy.

She stopped in her tracks.

'What? With . . . a horse and everything?' she said in panic, picturing the huge shire horse.

'Yep. You're not going to be beaten by a big softy like Hercules, are you?'

Hannah's eyes widened. She was still having nightmares about that animal.

'Wait until I've been to the bog, then I'll show you how to do it,' he said, putting a kindly hand on her shoulder. 'He's not nearly as scary as "Deery". For one, he's got less horsepower,' and he wandered off, chuckling at his own joke.

Hannah paced up and down the yard impatiently, glancing every so often towards the privy. *Why did men have to take so long?* she wondered. The privy had been a revelation when Dotty had shown it to her. With a wicked grin, she had carefully watched Hannah's face as she prised open one of the two doors. Inside was a long drop toilet but, Hannah's eyes widened as she realised, that right next to it was another, exactly the same.

'Are you supposed to . . . I mean, there are two of them . . .' Hannah spluttered, 'side by side.'

'Yep, it's ever so cosy,' Dotty said, laughing at her friend's discomposure.

Closing the door quickly on the stench, Dotty had warned her: 'Just try to avoid going immediately after breakfast . . . it's a male thing.'

Right now, Hannah wished John would just get a move on, she still had so much to do. Eventually, he came out, pulling the belt on his trousers tight.

He beamed at her. 'Come along, young lady, let's put those demons to bed once and for all.' And with that, he marched off towards the stables, Hannah following meekly behind.

The confidence that she had felt recently was ebbing away with every step she took towards the stables. She remembered what the German had told her – she still found it difficult to say his name – and quietly took her watch off and put it in her pocket.

John walked straight up to Hercules with Hannah trailing behind. All the time, he was murmuring calming words of assurance and the horse's ears pricked back to listen.

Hannah looked up . . . and up . . . and up; she could not believe how big these animals were. She avoided looking him straight in the eye in case he recognised her – and her fear.

'Come over here,' John said in a low voice to her. 'Don't make any sudden movements. See, he's curious.'

Hercules was bobbing his head in Hannah's direction.

'Her name is Hannah,' he murmured in the horse's ear. 'She wants to be friends with you, but she's frightened. You have to be nice to her, she's a bit of a scaredy-cat.'

'I am not,' Hannah whispered indignantly, terrified she prompt a reaction from the enormous beast. 'But he did try to kill me.'

'No, he didn't. He was just being a scaredy-cat too. See how calm he is now. He's just a big softy really.'

Hannah approached cautiously. The huge animal, with a white streak through his mane and tail, looked nothing like a big softy. But then as she got nearer and felt his breath on her face, she looked again into the horse's eyes. They were such a deep brown and had so much feeling in them, she was taken by surprise.

'Here, give me your hand,' John said, and he gently placed it on the horse's nose. 'Stroke it,' he said, standing back to let her get nearer.

Tentatively, Hannah reached up with her other hand and felt the coarse hair on the side of the animal's face. She moved her hand slowly down towards his mouth and felt a moment of dread when he turned towards her so that her hand touched the soft part on the front of his nose. She had never felt anything so smooth, and as she stroked, the horse made a low whinnying sound.

'He likes that. He likes you,' John told her approvingly. 'Now, I'll just get this harness here and put it on him. Yes, boy, you know you're going out, don't you? You like going out, don't you?'

He went to one side of the flank and passed the harness over to Hannah, nodding at her to take it.

'Just do everything slowly and gently and keep talking to him; he's listening.'

Hannah followed what John did and fastened the huge brass buckles, taking care not to pinch the horse's skin and murmuring to him as she did it. She could not believe how patiently he was standing, letting the two of them fuss around him.

Finally, they had him ready to lead out. John took the reins and headed out towards the cart in the yard. He fastened the horse to the harness and then told Hannah to climb up into the wooden seat. It felt so high, Hannah sat with her back up straight, worried that the horse would sense her nerves, but he seemed to know he was off on an outing and contentedly waited for John to adjust the reins.

John clicked his teeth and flicked the leather reins against Hercules's huge back. The horse set off, his long strides almost making Hannah fall back against the rails. John steadied her and then slowly took Hannah on a tour of the farm. Once he felt her relax, he helped her hold the reins, showing her how to guide Hercules to the left or the right, how to start him off and, most importantly, how to stop.

Towards the end of the ride, Hannah started to enjoy herself. It was like milking the cow – a partnership of man and beast – and when they worked as a team, she suddenly realised there was no feeling like it in the world. She turned round and beamed at John.

'Thank you, John, thank you so much.'

'Just read his mood before you set off,' John told her, watching her bring the cart and horse back into the yard. 'Always give him respect but make sure he respects you, too.'

Hannah jumped down and went round to the front of the horse and looked him squarely in the eye.

'You, Hercules, are no longer going to haunt my dreams. Instead, I'll learn how to handle you properly, and just like all the other things I'm learning on this farm, I'm going to be good at it and you're going to help me.'

And with that, she gave him a confident pat and led him back into the stable.

John watched her with satisfaction.

Chapter 14

The prospect of the weekly dances had been keeping the girls' spirits up through the relentless days, giving them something to chat excitedly about whenever they had the chance, and the energy, but recently Lavinia had seemed quieter and Hannah felt her sense of humour had turned more sarcastic than usual. She shrugged, putting it down to the exhaustion they were all feeling and concentrated on practising the more complicated steps with Dotty, ensuring that men were queueing up to dance with them whenever they arrived at the Samson and Hercules dance hall.

Hannah, in particular, had taken to dancing like a professional and, one night, after one particularly complicated quickstep, she looked up to see a good-looking American pilot standing in front of her with his hand outstretched.

'OK, little lady,' he said in a deep Southern drawl, 'let's see how those dainty little feet of yours cope with a bit of jitterbugging.' Lavinia had tried to teach both her friends the incredibly fast moves involved in the latest American dance craze, but in their crowded bedroom, there was little room for more than just the basics, so with the whole dance floor at their disposal, Hannah had the chance to experiment.

'Left foot, right foot, now tap behind,' he said, grinning as she bit her bottom lip in concentration. 'Great, now mirror what I'm doing. That's it. One, two, three, four, again. That's just dandy, you've got the basic step. Just keep repeating that, getting faster.'

Hannah looked up at him; he did have rather nice blue eyes – a bit like that German, it occurred to her. She tried to focus on the face in front of her rather than the image of the POW that kept popping into her head.

'Right, before we go any further, 'cos this bit gets a bit more touchy-feely, I think you should know my name is Benjamin.'

'Hannah,' she replied shyly, making herself concentrate on her feet.

'All righty, Miss Hannah, put your palms against mine and I'm just going to gently push your shoulder round, yes, that's it. Don't let your hips follow for a sec otherwise you'll look like one of those penguins in a "tux". Push off your back foot and then I'll steer you round.'

Hannah relaxed into the movement, and as he turned her, she dipped under his arm and emerged on the other side. She had never felt so exhilarated. The band was playing 'Minnie's in the Money', and as the tune progressed, her partner became more ambitious. He grabbed hold of her and pulled her through his legs, she jumped up behind him, disorientated for a moment but then grinned as he pulled her back round to the front and then she jumped up onto his hips before he thrust her away again. The dancing got more frenetic but every move her partner made, Hannah mirrored and matched his speed and dexterity. As the last notes died out, she noticed a crowd had gathered around them and was cheering and clapping. Benjamin took a bow and nudged her to do the same. She did, but with a bright, red face, unable to believe the undignified moves she had just performed. She was sure the whole room had glimpsed her knickers.

A crowd of young men gathered around Hannah, anxious to be the first to take her for the next dance, but Hannah shook her head with a grin and looked around for Dotty and Lavinia. Dotty was nowhere to be seen, but Lavinia was leaning on the bar, her long, tapering fingers wrapped around a half-empty glass. She had one eye on Hannah on the dance floor and the other very firmly on the good-looking flight lieutenant in front of her.

Hannah went up to her.

'I'm exhausted,' she said, unnecessarily, as Lavinia took in the dark patches under her armpits and the sweat on her brow.

'I can see that, my darling. Well, what a little star you're becoming. You'll be taking all the men off us at this rate.'

There was an unusual tinge of bitterness in Lavinia's tone and Hannah looked sharply at her face. She was not quite sure whether Lavinia meant it or not, but doubt took the excitement of the moment away from her.

'Perhaps we should go,' she said quietly.

'Yes, probably, I'll meet you by the door, when I've just said goodbye to this darling man. I think we'll find Dotty outside.'

Hannah crept off to get her bag and gas mask and went to the door. Outside, to the left of the huge statues of Samson and Hercules, she spotted Dotty in an embrace with a tall, young man. Hannah gave a little cough. Dotty immediately looked up and stepped back and Hannah, with a smile, realised it was George she was with. She was pleased; she liked George.

'Time to go?' Hannah called over.

'OK, I'm coming,' Dotty's muffled voice replied. 'George is going to come back with us.'

The little group just made it to the bus stop in time and jumped on-board the bus. Hannah watched Lavinia out of the corner of her eye, but she was making a point of using her compact mirror to put some lipstick on.

'Are you OK, Lavinia?' she asked nervously.

'Of course, darling, what an absolutely wonderful night, reminded me of The Ritz. Well, maybe it's not quite up to The Ritz . . . Obviously, you girls from the provinces wouldn't understand how much I miss the real glamour of the West End.'

Hannah's elation popped like a balloon. The dance hall had seemed so exotic to her and she had loved the glitz of it all. The fact that Lavinia seemed to be looking down her nose at it made her feel like an uneducated girl in the presence of a high society heiress. Dotty was still looking adoringly at Lavinia as if she were a heroine of a Hollywood Land Army film.

* * *

After that night, Hannah began to notice the tiny barbs that were thinly disguised by Lavinia's breezy comments and wondered whether something had happened to make her lose her joyous zest for life. She decided she would watch her friend closely. A clue came one morning when Lavinia seemed quite cheerful at breakfast, but as soon as the postman's bicycle was heard in the yard, her face fell and her mouth tightened. It was if Lavinia was hoping for – and dreading – a letter.

The postman dropped a small pile of letters by the barn door with a cheery wave. John, on his way into the room for breakfast, called over.

'Here you go, girls, here's your post – checked and marked as usual. Pass 'em over, Dotty.' He handed two letters to her, but she just stared at the names on them blankly.

It suddenly dawned on Hannah: Dotty could not read! She gasped. Now she understood why she flicked through magazines, why others had to fill in the milk forms and why she always hung back at the bus stop until one of the other two recognised the destination on the front of the bus. She felt guilty that she had forgotten about Dotty's request for help to improve her education and went over to gently relieve Dotty of the two letters. The young girl gave them up as if they were hot coals.

'Here's one for you, Lavinia,' Hannah said, trying to draw attention away from Dotty. She looked closely at the envelope. 'Oh, it looks posh. The letters are embossed.'

Lavinia raced up from the table and grabbed the letter from Hannah. She stuffed it in her pocket and sat back down again, refusing to meet Hannah's curious gaze.

The other letter was for Hannah. It was from Ros. It was the second one that week and her face showed her alarm before she ripped it open.

Oh, I wish I could get home, she thought with a frown, reading between Ros's determinedly reassuring lines.

The Land Army girls were supposed to have a week's holiday a year, but they all knew that was not always possible. They worked fifty hours a week, more, they had been told, in harvest time and it seemed the needs of the farm were always too pressing for them to take any time off.

118

They did get one day off, usually Sunday, and, very occasionally, an extra, luxurious half-day.

The post was the highlight of the day for Hannah; Dotty never got any, a fact that finally made sense. Looking across at Lavinia's blank expression, Hannah thought, sadly, that she knew even less about this strange girl than when she had walked into the bedroom that first night, her eyes hidden behind the net of her pillbox hat.

Hannah scanned her letter, her eyes alighting on the words 'struggling' and 'worried'. Before she knew it, she had blurted out:

'My mum's going to pieces ... and my dad ...' She faltered, not knowing where to begin.

Dotty looked at her watch. They had to do rat-catching that morning and there was no time for a cosy chat.

'Let's make sure we have some time tonight to talk,' she said. 'Now, let's go and sort those bloody rats out.' Dotty hated rats and dreaded this particular job. She shivered as she stood up to go out to the barn, remembering the long list of facts about rats Hannah had insisted on reading out to them from *The Land Girl* magazine. Knowing that there were fifty million of them and that they devoured a total of two and a half million tons of food a year had not made her feel any better about having to root them out, but every grain was valuable and to lose so many to 'Hitler's little helpers' meant it was a job that had to be done.

Hannah was surprised that vermin did not bother her at all, and Lavinia normally tackled the task with enthusiasm, but today she was subdued and whacked the grain store bales without any fervour.

'Are you feeling all right, Lavinia?' she asked.

'Hmm? Yes, course I am,' Lavinia snapped.

Dotty was too absorbed in watching the corners of the barn in terror for long tails that might appear but Hannah took a step back, surprised at the sharpness of Lavinia's tone.

The girls had to check all the traps and then retrieve the dead, bloodied corpses. If the rats weren't dead, they were supposed to finish them off with a stick. Without gloves, they were constantly washing their hands to get rid of the lice that covered the animals' bodies, doing them twice before eating their sandwiches.

'Gotcha,' Dotty suddenly shouted, using her stick to flick an astonished mouse into the air to be caught by a waiting cat, sitting in the corner expectantly. It gulped down its prey then licked its lips.

'I did it, I did it, I got one; well, not a rat but . . .' Dotty said triumphantly.

Hannah gave her a grin and took up her position again on the other side of the bales.

Lavinia's strange mood was going to have to wait.

Chapter 15

'You girl, come here.'

Hannah froze. The boss, Mr Hollis, had never spoken to her before.

'Yes, you.'

She hurried over to the other side of the yard, near the farmhouse. He looked at her sternly.

'You're a Roman Catholic, I believe.'

Hannah was perplexed. It was the last question she had expected to be asked. She mumbled, 'Yes Boss,' and waited.

'Next Sunday, apparently I need to allow one of the prisoners—' he spat out the word '—to go to church. You're the only Catholic so you'll need to accompany him. You'll need to get a bus to their camp at Mousehold Heath and pick him up from there. Then you'll have to walk into Norwich; he's not allowed on public transport.'

He walked off. But then he stopped and turned.

'Oh, and he can't be left without an armed escort so Stanley'll go with you but, just in case, you'll need to learn how to use a pistol as well. I don't trust these bastards.

Sorry, young lady, I shouldn't have sworn, but you understand what I mean?'

Hannah nodded bleakly. She had only heard the bit about having to learn how to use a pistol.

The boss was still talking. 'Get Jed to teach you how to use it, but in the meantime, here's the Small Arms Training manual. Read it and learn it.

'Be here at half past seven Sunday morning,' he called over his shoulder.

'What did he want?' Dotty had come up behind her.

'He . . . I . . . a German . . .'

'Oh, do get your words out, Hannah,' she said, exasperated.

'He . . . said . . . I have to accompany a German to church.'

'No!' Dotty almost squealed, then lowered her voice. 'You have to be kidding, Hannah? Why?'

'I presume because he's a Catholic,' she said, wishing for the first time in her life that she had been a Protestant. 'And,' she went on, 'I have to learn how to shoot a gun.'

'Why?'

Hannah's face was glum. 'Because if he suddenly makes a run for it during the Offertory or the Gospel, I have to shoot him. We've got that horrible guard, Stanley, with us the rest of the time, but in church, he's my responsibility.'

* * *

Hannah crawled into her bed that night. She didn't need this; she had been so pleased with herself recently and had actually begun to relax into her new role, but learning how to shoot a pistol with creepy Jed and then spending time with one of the German prisoners was enough to start off the familiar butterflies in her stomach that she had had since the age of five.

I haven't changed one bit, she thought with regret. *It's all a front, this, I'll never be anything except a girl who is terrified of everything.*

She gave up analysing, sighed and opened page one of the manual.

* * *

The following morning, Hannah reluctantly got dressed. As soon as she entered the yard, Jed was waiting for her, a sly smile on his face.

'Come on, you, let's go to the far field. We've got some target practice to do.' And with that, he marched off, followed by Hannah, who shot a glance at Dotty behind her. Dotty held up two crossed fingers at her and gave her an encouraging smile.

At the entrance to the field, Jed had set up four tin cans on the fence. He took out a Webley Mark 6 pistol that he had borrowed from the Home Guard and handed it over to Hannah, who took hold of it gingerly.

'Oh, get hold of it, girl,' he said, with irritation. 'It's not loaded . . . yet.'

She held the gun out in front of her, looking at it as if it were going to bite her, but then thought back to the times when she had played darts at the youth club. She had been rather good at it, she remembered, and tried to convince herself that shooting a gun could not be so very different from throwing a dart.

Jed came up behind her and put his arms around each of her shoulders. This was what he had been waiting for.

'Stop shaking,' he whispered into her ear. She could feel his breath on her neck and pulled sharply away, taking control of herself. She decided dealing with gun was preferable to dealing with Jed.

'Just show me how to use it, Jed. There's no need to come that close.' She was astonished to hear a strong, clear voice come out of her mouth. Her revulsion was so intense, it gave her a strength she didn't know she had.

He turned away, grumbling and refixed the cans in staggered formation to make it as difficult as possible for her. This one was not going to be as compliant as he'd first thought.

He begrudgingly talked her through how to hold the gun at a forty-five degree angle until she was ready to shoot it; how to load it and how to gently squeeze the trigger. He was dying to find an excuse get nearer to the tempting little minx, but she followed every instruction perfectly, giving him no reason to get any closer.

Dammit, he thought. *She's a clever one.*

He got out a box of ammunition. This was where she would lose that confident air, he thought. He handed the bullets to her, but Hannah saw the instructions from the manual in her head and casually placed them in the barrel of the gun. She pointed the gun up, momentarily getting Jed in her sights. She smiled to herself as he hopped sharply to the left.

Hannah lined the sight up on the first tin and fired. It missed. She noticed there was a slight kick to the barrel when she fired, so on her next shot, she went a little lower with the sight. As she pulled the trigger, the end of the gun jerked up just enough to hit the edge of the can. She felt a little thrill as it pinged off the corner of the top of it making it fly off at an angle and hit the gate to the side. Without stopping, she moved along to the third and pulled again. This time, she missed, and Jed gave a triumphant 'Hah!' She turned towards the fourth one and concentrated. Holding the gun with both hands to make it steadier, she fired. The can jumped into the air and fell off the other side. She couldn't help it, she turned round to grin at the scowling Jed and then walked towards the fence to set the cans up again.

She reloaded and this time she hit the cans every time, not always in the middle but somewhere on their round exterior, leaving them pitted and bent. She looked round triumphantly at Jed's scowling face. He moved towards her, his face contorted and threatening. Hannah grasped the gun more tightly.

'You OK, Hannah?' George's voice came from behind them. He had spotted the two figures in the distance and had run across two fields towards them.

Hannah turned gratefully to him.

'Yes,' she said with relief, 'I am, George. Jed's just leaving.'

'Well, you seem to have got the hang of that,' Jed said, walking away, disconcerted. 'Let's see how you do when you have to shoot a German.'

Hannah's smile abruptly faded.

* * *

Sunday morning came around all too quickly. Whenever they had time, Dotty attended All Saints Church in the village, but Hannah had been getting the bus into Norwich to attend the beautiful Catholic church there. She loved its huge columns and vaulted ceilings and the hymns seemed to float effortlessly towards the heavens. Lavinia, however, usually pleaded a headache or period pain and stayed exactly where she was – under the blankets.

Hannah shakily tucked the gun into her leather shoulder bag and, equally nervously, headed down the drive to make her way to the bus stop. Archie came up behind her, leading Hercules towards the fields to do some tree-branch shifting.

She gave Hercules a stroke, almost affectionately, feeling the need for an ally, but Archie simply gave her a smile and took her champion away from her. She looked wistfully after him and then moved her feet in the direction of the drive.

By the time she got to Mousehold Heath camp, she was feeling sick. Walking up to the gatehouse, which had barbed wire everywhere, she looked around her with suspicion, wishing herself anywhere but there on that Sunday morning. She loved her trips to mass and was resentful that she should share them with anyone, let alone some German prisoner. She took a sharp intake of breath; in front of her was that miserable guard, Stanley, and standing next to him was a tall figure in the distinctive POW overalls. It was the German from that first day, Karl. She felt a quiver of delight that shocked her and she quickly masked her expression in case Stanley saw her blush.

'*Morgen*, Fräulein,' the German said, turning to give her a grin. 'Please excuse the state of my uniform. It is the best one I could find. I believe you are to escort me to mass this morning.'

The 'Fräulein' turned abruptly on her heel to hide her red cheeks and left both men with no alternative but to follow in her footsteps. Her heart was thumping; the effect this man had on her was like nothing she had ever experienced before, and it unnerved her completely.

Stanley shouted at her back: 'Not so fast, you. I've got to keep this prisoner in my sights. You two walk in front.' He hated all Germans but the memory of being told off by the boss at Salhouse Farm was a particular thorn in his side and he glared at the man who had prompted the scolding. He would never forget and would wait for a chance to get his revenge.

He hung back, wanting to keep enough distance between himself and the Kraut to be able to get a clean shot at him if necessary. He kept his gun close to him, looking warily at the trees all around. It was the perfect place for a prisoner to escape, but Karl was exactly where he wanted to be and had no intention of going anywhere.

'We have about two miles to do, I believe, and it might be nice to talk?' the German said quietly so that Stanley couldn't hear. His English was excellent but he spoke with quite a strong German accent.

'No.'

Hannah picked up her pace but almost tripped over a tree root in front of her.

'Ah, it seems we will have to slow down,' the man said, laughing.

Ignoring her determined efforts to pretend she was not with him, he began to talk about his farm at home, the animals there and how he loved the spring when he would disappear for hours, foraging for food from the hedgerows. He talked about his love for the land, the animals and his family. He spoke with such affection that Hannah sneaked a sideways look at him. He was looking ahead and his expression was gentle.

She shook herself and concentrated on walking in a straight line. She had been so cross with herself after their clandestine meeting and had sworn never to talk to him again and here she was, facing a long walk then a whole religious service listening to how the congregation needed to live a Christian life. It had never occurred to her the phrase 'love thine enemy' actually meant it, and Hannah felt a momentary irritation with the Catholic Church's doctrine.

By the time they had walked up Grapes Hill towards the Church of St John the Baptist, Hannah's cheeks were a deep pink colour and her breathing was shallow from concentrating on both walking quickly uphill and embarrassment at the proximity of the man who had caught up to walk next to her. She almost felt the warmth of his body and the hairs on her forearms were tingling with the possibility that his arm might brush hers. She waited for Stanley outside the entrance to the church and he beckoned her.

'You'll have to take him from here,' he said, 'I'm C. of E. and can't go in. Have you got your pistol?'

'Yes,' she said, weakly.

'I'll meet you here at quarter to then, and . . . don't let him out of your sight, not for a minute,' he warned, glaring at the bland expression on the German's face.

Hannah walked stiffly into the honey-coloured stone building, immediately feeling the still calm that engulfed her every time she entered this church. She loved St John's, its imposing facade seemed to stand in defiance of a war that was tearing the congregation inside apart and even a bomb in 1942 on the buildings across the road had failed to destroy its landmark status in the city. But this week, her sanctuary seemed threatened by the enemy who was following her down the aisle. Everyone she passed stood aside to glare at her and at the man in uniform behind her. She walked with her head in the air, noting with dismay that there were some personnel from Coltishall RAF station in the pews. For them to see a German officer in their midst stunned them into silence for a minute and then, as Hannah and Karl genu-flected to enter the pews, there were hissed whisperings from the row behind.

'You know those black patches on his back and trou-sers, they're so's we can use them for targets if they try to escape,' one said in Hannah's direction, making a noise like a gun cocking.

'Don't know what he's doing in a church, God won't listen to *his* prayers,' said another.

'And I thought a Land Army girl would know better.'

At that, Hannah spun round and said through clenched teeth, 'I've been made to bring him, he's a POW on our farm. Believe me, it wasn't my choice.'

At that, the whisperings ceased and Hannah tried to concentrate on the priest, who had his back to the congregation at the altar underneath the the boarding-up where the stained glass windows had been, before they were removed for safe-keeping. She let the Latin flow over her as usual, the familiar words being uttered from her mouth. She noticed the German doing the same and for a moment wondered at a religion that was practised by so many people in so many countries. It seemed ridiculous that they could be sharing the same Christian prayers while shooting the hell out of each other.

At the end of mass, Hannah hung back, avoiding the crowds gathering in the foyer and pretending to say her prayers on her knees. The German sat patiently waiting for her. Once the congregation had filed out, she went to stand up, but then spotted the priest coming down the aisle towards them. She hesitated, not wanting to speak to him, but not wanting to seem rude either. However, the priest went past her and straight up to her companion and held out his hand.

'I'm Father Patrick,' he said, with a warm smile. 'Welcome to our church. Outside, you may be our enemy, but in here, you are our friend and I am delighted to see you.'

Karl Schneider looked gratefully into the priest's eyes. A man of about sixty, who had obviously experienced two world wars, Karl saw the same world-weariness he had seen in his own father and grasped the priest's hand firmly.

'I am sorry for what is happening,' he said. 'We . . . none of us, can control any of it. But today, I heard your wise words and I will pray for a better world, and I thank you for your welcome, it means a lot to me – a stranger and an enemy in your land.'

With that, the priest made the sign of the cross over Karl, tucked his hands into the front of his robes and walked slowly back towards the altar, wondering how long it would be before young people like that prisoner would be able to face the world without the dark clouds that threatened to engulf them all.

Hannah stared after the receding figure and then looked across at the German, his face bathed in gratitude for the kindness he had just received. Divided between the knowledge that this man was the enemy and the strong attraction she felt towards him, she fingered the little silver cross she wore around her neck and felt completely conflicted.

In silence, Hannah and Karl made their way out into the weak March sunshine to meet Stanley, but the guard was nowhere to be seen. He had lost track of time due to the paid-for caresses of a young woman at a well-known establishment. Hannah stood looking around her with no idea what to do. Karl leaned against the side wall of the church, relishing more time on his own with this delightful creature. He searched round for a topic of conversation and fixed on the weather, which his sister had told him was a constant obsession with the English.

'It is a lovely day, *nicht wahr?*'

Hannah looked surprised but then smiled. It was true, the skies above were blue and the sun was actually shining. It seemed so incongruous that the pair of them were being bathed in warm sunlight outside a church in Norwich when the world beyond them was at war.

'Yes, it is.'

The sun caught her hair and Karl couldn't resist leaning forward to tuck a stray piece back for her.

'Oi, you, what the hell do you think you're doing?'

Stanley's voice shouted at them from the other side of the road. He had run all the way up the hill, and after the exertions of the morning, he was out of breath.

Karl thought quickly. 'There was a little of the incense . . . it was on her face.'

Stanley knew nothing about the strange rituals of the Roman Catholic Church but gave the German a threatening look. 'Well, we need to get back now,' he said, indicating that the prisoner should walk in front of him back down the hill.

Karl caught Hannah's eye and gave her a smile that made her go weak, as the little trio set off back to Mousehold Camp.

Chapter 16

The next morning, Hannah refused to answer any questions about her Sunday morning trip to church. She simply dismissed Dotty's probing questions with a curt: 'I do what I have to do, I take him to mass. That's all. You know it's forbidden to fraternise with them and he's not worth a shilling fine. I mean, what do you expect? That we have a cosy little chat?'

It had been easy to fend them off. Firstly, Lavinia was still distracted and Dotty just assumed she would have nothing but a natural abhorrence of the occasion, but Hannah felt guilty at how much she was already beginning to look forward to her next trip to Norwich.

She went over every word Karl had said to her, imagining what she might have said in reply if the circumstances had been different. Hannah had only had one boyfriend, a lad from Stretford Grammar School called Wilf, but he had been as shy as she was, so their relationship had been a matter of convenience to keep Ros and Lily quiet. She remembered some rather unsatisfactory kisses and embarrassed fumbling behind the Boys' Brigade hut. When she was close to Karl, she felt a frisson of excitement that frightened her. It was as if every time his arm had brushed hers, a shaft of lightning went through her and she got an urge to reach out to him. Hannah had endless conversations with herself, reasoning the hopelessness of any relationship between them. She was on the point of convincing herself that it didn't matter anyway because he felt nothing for her, when she heard loud noises from downstairs.

'Lavinia Braithwaite, Lavinia Braithwaite? Where *is* that strumpet?' A piercing voice called up the stairs as the girls were dressing for the day.

Lavinia froze in the middle of putting her shirt on. Dotty and Hannah dashed over to peer down the stairs.

At the bottom was a smartly dressed woman in a tweed suit and a maroon hat with a diamond hatpin holding it in place. She had one hand on the bannister and one foot on the bottom step.

'Hey, you girls, is that Jezebel up there?'

Hannah felt a dig in her ribs from behind. She looked round and Lavinia was shaking her head vigorously behind her.

'Don't let her up here,' she pleaded.

Dotty marched down the stairs, followed by a wary Hannah. When she got to the bottom, forcing the woman to retreat to the dining room, Dotty stood with her arms folded.

'I don't know what you want or who you are, but you can't just come in here demanding things,' she told the woman, who stepped backwards even further.

Hannah was impressed. Dotty was only tiny but she was formidable and, it seemed, a match for anyone.

The woman faltered a little. 'I'm here to see that floozie, Lavinia.' Her mouth turned into a sneer.

'Well, you can't,' Dotty told her. 'She's out in the fields and won't be back until very late tonight. Maybe I can give her a message?'

The woman looked around her at the humble room with disdain, moving her feet as if they were stepping in animal dung. 'Well, you can just tell her from me, as she's ignoring my letters, that my husband is not for sale and no amount of money, titles or fancy clothes will take him away from me. I know how to control him and if she messes with me, she'll regret it.'

With that, she tilted her chin upwards and looked down her nose at Dotty and Hannah.

'You Land Army girls are all the same: dirty, low and without any morals.' And with that, she turned on her high heels and stalked out of the barn.

After a couple of minutes of stunned silence, wary footsteps were heard on the wooden treads of the stairs and Lavinia appeared behind them.

'Has she gone?'

'Yes,' Dotty replied. 'But who is she?'

'She's his wife,' Lavinia said with a sob and then she ran back up the stairs.

* * *

Lavinia was uncharacteristically quiet after her unwelcome visitor and spent the whole day with her head down, examining the turnips she was harvesting. Dotty pushed Hannah forward with a meaningful nod as the girls washed by the trough at the end of their shift.

Lavinia was giving herself a very cursory rinse. Normally, she would use a scrubbing brush she kept next to the stone trough, but tonight, it was as if she could not be bothered.

'What's wrong, Lavinia?' Hannah finally said.

'I'm fine,' she said tersely.

Dotty edged her way in. She could not bear atmospheres.

'Come on, Lav, you have to tell us what's wrong.'

Lavinia looked down her nose at both of them. 'You may have chosen this godforsaken life, but I didn't and I'm going to get out of it just as soon as I can. I've got a man waiting for me. His name is Jeremy.. He loves me and he's going to save me from all this.'

And with that, she looked from one to the other, challenging Dotty or Hannah to disagree with her.

She missed supper that night and was already tucked under the covers when Dotty and Hannah went downstairs to eat. They spent the mealtime whispering over the table about Lavinia's revelations, speculating about how a man who was married, was apparently going to come to Lavinia's rescue. They ignored the banter from the men when they came in to join them, causing John and Albert to exchange a concerned glance. The two men had frequently talked about the confined existence these girls were living and John had already expressed an opinion that the bubble they were creating in that small room upstairs could burst at any time. Lavinia's absence and the tense whisperings of the other, two only served to increase those concerns.

* * *

The next morning, the girls had a visit from Aunt Deborah, prompting a silent Lavinia to drop her porridge spoon with a clatter onto the floor before standing up, almost to attention.

'Doris,' her aunt said, 'follow me. This minute. I want a private word with you.'

Lavinia followed her out of the door, watched by the other two girls.

They finished their breakfast and were about to head out to clean the yard when Lavinia ran through the door from outside, fled past them and raced up the stairs.

They were tempted to follow her, but then Jed came in and looked threateningly at them, so they meekly went out to start scrubbing down and scooping up the muck from the corner of the stables. They glanced across to see the old black Bentley and Lady Parker standing leaning on it with her arms folded.

Five minutes later, they saw Lavinia, no longer in uniform but in her coat and red hat, emerge from the barn and climb into the back of the car without looking up at them. Hannah was pushing the wheelbarrow but stopped in her tracks. She tried to wave to get Lavinia's attention, but the car drove off quickly and disappeared around the corner.

'Well, what on earth prompted that?' Dotty said from behind her.

'I've no idea,' Hannah replied, 'maybe she's left us a note or something.'

But all the girls found when they raced up to the bedroom at the end of their shift was Lavinia's bedding piled up in a ruck on the mattress on the floor and her uniform flung carelessly on top. Apart from that, all sign of Lavinia had been erased. It was August, so not a chilly night but, for the first time, the two girls huddled up for warmth together, needing the comfort of the proximity of another human being in the sudden emptiness of the room.

Chapter 17

The atmosphere was subdued after Lavinia's departure, despite the demands of the harvest, which was normally a time for a great deal of laughing and joking. It was as if the little trio needed each other to function. The only time Hannah came to life was on the Sundays when she was able to go to church. She was uncomfortably aware that the mass itself meant little compared with the journey to and from St John's. Stanley, for once, had no complaints, as those mornings allowed him to have liaisons with a rather brash blonde and he always walked behind the pair, engrossed in anticipating the delights of the prostitute's soft, warm body to come.

Karl talked guardedly, aware that one word or gesture out of place would alert Stanley, so he did everything he could to look as uninterested as possible in the beautiful girl next to him, but as the weeks went on, it was Hannah who took the lead, unable to bear the stilted silence between them. She began to relax and made the odd comment about the woodlands or the flowers they were passing, which prompted looks of such pleasure from him that her heart melted.

Karl felt a quiver inside every time he glanced across at Hannah's dark curls. He was having dreams about this girl, imagining walking with her in the hills near his home in another summer, in another time. He tried to hide his feelings behind a mask of indifference, believing it would be impossible to expect an English girl to feel anything for a German POW but, one day, by the entrance to St John's, as he put his hand into the stoup to cross himself, hers was already there. They both reeled back as if they had been bitten. Karl felt such a shiver up his spine, he felt almost giddy, but then was immediately crushed with disappointment when he saw her look of shock and panic. In embarrassment, Karl stepped back, coughed, and then stepped quickly out onto the steps of the north entrance. He had seen the horror on her face, which reminded him that he was the enemy. She must hate him, he thought, as a representative of everything her country was fighting against. The shame was overwhelming and Karl felt a deep depression engulf him. In the silent journey back through the streets of Norwich, over the river and back up to the camp, Karl cursed the war, Hitler and the fates that had put him and the lovely young woman on opposing sides. He knew he was captivated by her, but this was a dangerous situation and could not possibly lead anywhere, he told himself crossly, never wanting to see that look on her face again.

* * *

Back at the farm, Hannah examined her hand, as if it would still bear some mark, some evidence of that moment between them. She turned every second of that particular morning over and over in her mind, analysing in forensic detail what he had said, how he had acted and, finally, how she felt about that casual touch.

Without a war, it could have been a very promising outing with a man who set her heart thumping, but the silence between them was overshadowed by a great big swastika and, like a spider, it spread its web over them both, so much so that she felt she like a fly, struggling to escape. She was trapped in August 1943, and there was no way out.

Every time she recalled a look or a smile, instead of seeing Karl's kind face, she saw the Pathé films she had watched at the cinema showing gaunt British prisoners being dealt blows by German soldiers. She had two conversations with herself. One was that Karl Schneider was charming, and incidentally, very good-looking, and the other was that he was the enemy and therefore an evil person.

She argued with the two combatants, one on each shoulder, so much so that every night, Dotty accused her of tossing and turning deliberately just to keep her awake.

In the German compound, Karl was doing no better. He sat at the breakfast table, idly stirring the strange concoction the British called porridge. He was glad there were extra supplies of cheese allocated to German prisoners, it was the only thing that made breakfast palatable. From the first moment he'd spotted Hannah, cornered by Hercules, he'd been completely entranced by her. He was not, for one moment, taken in by her seemingly shy persona. The fury and frustration that had burst from her mouth in the stable that day demonstrated a spirit that intrigued him and reminded him of the fierce loyalty of his dog, Britta. A cross-breed black bitch with short, curly hair, the dog was a calm and loyal companion, but on the day when her master was threatened by a gang of lads from the Hitler Youth, furious that Karl was trying to get out of joining them, he'd seen the dog turn into a ferocious animal who bared her teeth at the assailants, making them run off into the woods. Karl had turned round to tell Britta off but she sat, looking up innocently at him. He had laughed and ruffled her neck.

Hannah reminded him of that dog. There was something in the Land Army girl's eyes that told him she would jump to the defence of anyone who was being badly treated, but his hopes that she might also be able to look beyond a POW's uniform to get to know the man beneath seemed destined to be dashed. The situation was impossible. He had to forget her and turned his thoughts back to Britta, realising he hadn't thought of his faithful dog in years. He remembered how she used to follow him around the family farm and that memory, in itself, filled his heart with anguish. When he had first been taken prisoner, he had been given a postcard to send to his widowed mother, stamped with the words 'Transit Camp'. The pre-written words simply said: 'I have fallen into English captivity. I am well. Permanent address follows.' He knew the cards were sent via neutral Switzerland and could take an age to arrive, so once he arrived in Norfolk, he had sent another letter but had not heard anything back. He didn't even know whether his letters were reaching her. His brothers were both in the army – on the front line somewhere in Italy – and he lived in fear that they would be killed and that he would not know. The POWs were allowed to write home through the assiduously checked camp system but, while other prisoners were beginning to get letters back, Karl waited in vain for any reassuring post to reach him.

'*Komm doch*,' Peter said from behind him. They were supposed to be working on the bottom fields today, clearing the ditches, and Stanley was in a bad mood after a night drinking too many beers in The Bell with Jed.

'Move it,' Stanley said sharply, and the men shuffled forward.

'*Ist alles in Ordnung?*' Peter asked Karl, noting his thoughtful expression.

'ENGLISH!' came the cry from behind.

'*Ja*,' Karl replied, but then felt Stanley's breath on his shoulder.

'I would like to hear from my family, that is all,' he told Peter.

Peter nodded. He had regular letters from his wife, Helga, and he knew how important those words from home were to a prisoner of war in another country.

'Save your breath,' Stanley shouted. 'You'll need it, those ditches won't drain themselves. Here, you,' he shouted to Karl, 'you can be the one in the ditch with the shovel.' He loved picking on this particular German.

Karl found the physical work distracting and attacked the ditches with gusto.

* * *

That evening, after supper, Karl sat down to write yet another letter to his mother, but then paused and wondered whether he should try his Onkel Gerhard, who lived on the other side of the valley from Tübingen. The problem was that when he was shot down, he had no record of anyone's address with him and he knew the Feldpost would not be impressed by a less than exact postal code. The new coding system was only two years old but already it was an essential element in getting post to the right recipient in a country torn apart by war. Before he left Germany, his mother had told him that the farm had been taken over by the Reichsnährstand, desperate to use their control to combat the food shortages that were crippling the country. A widow, whose sons had been conscripted, his mother was left with no alternative but to agree to an amalgamation with the farm on the other side of the valley. Her last letter to him before the ill-fated plane trip, had sadly informed him that she was living in one room in the back of the farmhouse. The rest of the building was now being used to house strangers, drafted in to plough the fields, but he was not even sure whether she was still there, or, indeed, whether she knew that her youngest son had been taken prisoner. He was all too aware that the German authorities had been watching the family carefully, ever since his sister, Greta, had chosen to move to England just before the war, and he ran his fingers through his hair in despair.

It was the not knowing that was driving him to distraction; the other distraction was a dark-haired Catholic Land Army girl with the deepest blue eyes he had ever seen.

Of course, he suddenly thought, der Priester. Pastor Bonifaz of the local Catholic church would know. He put his pen to his paper and began to write, sending a mental thank you to the convent girl who helped him come up with the idea. He loved the idea that Hannah had been sent to him for divine intervention. That thought made him smile for the first time that day.

Chapter 18

The disappearance of Lavinia was the main topic of conversation at the farm and prompted a great deal of speculation amongst all the different factions. The two girls missed her lively chatter and their bedroom seemed eerily empty without her. There was more room, that was certain, but the other two decided that having enough room to hang up their clothes on the back of the door somehow did not compensate for Lavinia's lively chatter, caustic comments or her irreverent attitude to life, and both of them felt deflated. They had no idea what had happened to their room-mate and, as the days passed, they were getting increasingly concerned.

It was Rachel who gave them a clue one evening when she brought over their macaroni cheese.

'Miss Braithwaite left in a hurry, didn't she? I heard she's been summoned to her parents' house.'

Dotty stopped eating, her fork halfway to her mouth. 'What have you heard, Rachel?'

'Oh it's not up to me to say, miss, but . . .' She paused and leaned in to whisper: 'Her family's worth a bob or two, I bet it's to do with money.'

At that moment, the men came into the dining room, and Rachel scuttled off back to the farmhouse to get the rest of the meals.

Dotty gave a tiny shake of her head and Hannah took the hint and said nothing more until they were alone in their room later that evening.

'So, what do we think?' Hannah leaned forward on the bed, hugging her knees. 'Do you think she'll ever come back?'

'I don't know,' Dotty replied, 'all I do know is that now there are only two of us to do the work three of us were struggling to get done.'

'That's true,' Hannah agreed, gloomily looking at the empty mattress, 'but it's not just 'cos she was so good at her job. I miss *her*.'

Dotty nodded in sad agreement.

Lavinia's disappearance was also the topic of conversation in The Bell that night, when Jed and William met Stanley for their pint. They were already cross because their normal table had been commandeered by American airmen from nearby Rackheath. The local boys were all making a row outside as they guarded their bicycles for a few pennies. Grumbling about the noise, the crowds and the US in general, the three now had the Land Army girls and the German POWs to add to their list of complaints.

'Bloody useless, they are, all those girls are,' Jed was saying, 'but now, there's the muck that needs spreading as well as the sowing of sugar beet, not to mention the calving, and I've no idea whether that Lavinia's coming back or not. We've just been completely left in the lurch.'

Stanley took a sip of his beer. 'I think those Germans could be made to do more. They're treated better than bloody guests because of that Geneva Convention. One told me the other day that he wanted a better coat as his leaked. Can you believe it? They're already allowed to go inside when it rains and they get a day off a week when they can wander round all over the place without anyone watching 'em. They should never have taken their shackles off. Some of our lads in their bloody camps are still in 'em. It's a disgrace. If it were left to me, I'd have 'em all tied up in chains all day.'

William nodded. His nephew had been taken prisoner and was somewhere in a camp in Poland and his family spent hours imagining the hardships he was suffering.

'I've heard they get more coal than we're allowed, delivered straight to their camp,' he said, pleased to have something to add to the list of grievances.

'I think Churchill got it right,' Stanley said. 'Do you remember, he said: "A prisoner of war is a man who tries to kill you and fails, and then asks you not to kill him." Couldn't agree more . . . Bastards, I'd love to take a potshot at them. They all deserve to die.'

'How are the turncoats doing?' Jed turned to William.

'Oh, they're all charmed by those girls. John's almost adopted that Hannah one and George is in love with Dotty. I give up with 'em all.'

Jed then added after a pause: 'I never trusted that hoity-toity one, Lavinia, though. She was like Lady Muck. I gave her muck!' he ended with a guffaw. 'You should have seen her with her painted nails, shovelling dung around. It was quite a sight.'

He did not mention that he had been taken aback by the skill and strength that Lavinia had applied to the job. It was so much easier to make fun of the girls than give them any credit.

'Let's get another drink,' he said, standing up.

* * *

Karl waited every morning for a letter from home but, while the postman delivered a small pile to Stanley's desk for checking, there were no reassuring letters for him. He was beginning to think his whole family had disappeared and he would never see any of them again.

Finally, in early September, Stanley threw a letter onto Karl's bunk as if it were infected.

'Seems like you haven't been forgotten after all,' he sneered.

Karl raced to open it, his heart thumping. He sat on his bunk and tried to breathe deeply to calm himself. The writing was unfamiliar and it had been stamped with several examiner numbers. It had obviously been thoroughly scrutinised by the authorities.

He scanned the signature first of all. It was from an official in the town of Tübingen, not the church or Pastor Bonifaz. It informed him that the Catholic church had been 'requisitioned' as it had been found guilty of smuggling currency and that 'his friend' had been sent to Dachau for 're-education'. There were other bits of the letter that had been blackened out by the censor. He would never know what those words had said.

Karl frowned. He knew the Nazi regime hated the Catholic Church and had done everything in their power to suppress its influence in Germany, sending priests to concentration camps on fabricated charges.

How could I have been so naive? he thought. He had written the letter to Pastor Bonifaz without thinking of the consequences for either the priest or his own family. Had that letter been used in evidence against the priest? he wondered. Karl cursed the injury to his head. He knew it sometimes clouded his judgement.

'*Was ist los?*' Peter came up behind him. He was rubbing his itchy hands together. They were burning after spreading ammonia pellets on the soil for the potatoes.

Karl looked around at the rest of the prisoners; they were within hearing and he didn't want to discuss his concerns with them. There were some he really did not trust, he thought, knowing any sign of disloyalty to their comrades or the German Reich could be reported back to their commandant.

'Let's speak English,' he whispered to Peter. They both had a better grasp of the English language than any of the others so when Stanley wasn't around to use it as a tool to eavesdrop, they welcomed the privacy it gave them. Karl had learned it from the priests at the local school, including Pastor Bonifaz, and Peter had worked alongside a Dutch farmhand who spoke it fluently and they were secretly enjoying the chance to practise their skills.

Peter sat down and put his hand on Karl's arm, seeing his friend's distress. Like him, Peter had been designated as a category 'A' white prisoner by the British authorities after he told them of his affiliations with a resistance group, led by the Catholic priest, Heinrich Maier. The group had been set up after the Anschluss was signed in 1939, annexing Austria into Nazi Germany and, like many Austrians, he hated the fact that his beloved country had been bullied into the fascist way of thinking. After a particularly close escape from detection, he'd had no choice but to join the Luftwaffe and proclaim his allegiance to the Fatherland to deflect their suspicions. However, as soon as he was captured by the British, he felt as if a weight had been lifted from his shoulders, knowing he would no longer have to spend every day living a lie. The two men kept their distance from the rest of the group and, little by little, with the

English Channel between themselves and the oppressive Nazi regime, they had started to discuss their deep concerns about how Germany was conducting the war. Even so, they still checked the room for any unseen listeners, never sure how the war would end and whether their dislike of Hitler would work against them if the Germans did win.

'I think I may have done a terrible thing,' Karl said, dropping his head into his hands.

Chapter 19

George couldn't feel his leg, it had gone numb and his fingers were showing white in the moonlight. He had been expecting the 'German' patrol an hour ago, and according to the note from Agent T, which had been left in the oak tree as usual, there would be ten of them, and he just hoped his carefully lain fireworks would work or the whole evening had been a waste of time. George had worked a long day in the fields and it was now gone seven. He was supposed to meet Dotty an hour ago to go dancing but, with an increasing threat of invasion, this assignment had come in at the last minute. He knew she would be furious and he would have to think up an excuse – again. The dummy grenades had been set, the booby traps half hidden in the ground; all he needed now was the 'enemy'.

The instructions in the Auxiliary Unit Manual on how to carry out an ambush like this one had been studied by George and his cohorts in detail. The frontage of the book suggested it was an instruction book on how to mend a tractor, but the intricate drawings inside depicted a more deadly pastime. The government had learned from the mistakes made by the countries already invaded by the Nazis and had set up an intricate network of trained agents who would close the net behind any encroaching enemy. Every one of the Auxiliary Units took the training seriously.

At that moment, there was a noise behind George and he sprang to his feet, shaking his legs to get some feeling into them. He was surprised how hard his heart was thumping. His foe was not supposed to be coming from that direction.

He pulled his trigger back and fired into the air. The blast lit up the trees and he saw five figures running towards the ridge of the hill. He ran towards them, firing wide of them so that they were funnelled towards the grenades which were set with a toy gun cap to go off as soon as the first one stepped on the pin. His associates ran out from the trees ahead of them and started to fire their dummy rounds as well. There were no explosives involved but the effect was far more real than George had anticipated.

A shout came from the top of the ridge. 'Well done, lads, you've got 'em. You did a great job, young lad. We're proud of you.'

George stood up to his full height and grinned.

* * *

Dotty was pacing around outside the barn and constantly checking her watch. George was nowhere to be seen and she was losing patience.

'He's late again,' she complained to Hannah when she came to join her. 'He said he'd be here in time to go to the Samson. Anyway, never mind, it's his loss. We'd better go or we'll miss the bus.'

The two of them linked arms to go down the drive. They welcomed the chance to dance their cares away but now they wore their uniform to fit in, like the other Land Army girls, and even though they'd removed the steel bits for dancing, their shoes still crunched on the gravel drive.

As soon as they arrived at the Samson, they were both claimed for the next dance. Many of the men were Americans, stationed at nearby RAF stations, and their arrival on British soil had become known as 'the friendly invasion'. Their 'friendliness' was well known by the English girls and they all had a battle to make sure wandering hands stayed firmly in an appropriate place, but the men were certainly good at dancing and Hannah, in particular, was not allowed to stand still for a moment, being recognised as the best dancer to step onto the dance floor in years. At every opportunity, she was thrown over shoulders, slid between feet and rocked backwards and forwards. It was the only time she forgot the war and she loved every minute of it.

It was while she was in the middle of a particularly complex step that a vision of Hollywood swept through the room, causing everyone to stop and stare. The familiar blonde was dressed in a flowing pink silk dress that folded into perfect pleats down her long legs, her hair had been cut and elegantly arranged into a fashionable roll and her lips were a rosy red, pursed into a determined pout.

Behind her was Dotty, who had abandoned her partner to catch her up. Hannah stopped mid-twirl, leaving her own partner with his hand outstretched to an empty space.

'Lavinia. Where the hell have you been?' Dotty said, grabbing her arm.

'Having my hair cut,' Lavinia said with a grin. She took hold of Dotty's shoulder and reached out her hand towards Hannah. 'I've come to dance,' she said, 'let's just do that for now,' and she leaned in to them. 'We can talk later. Lovely to see you, girls, I've so missed you.' She turned, almost pushing the two girls away to look round at the crowd of admirers who had gathered round the glamorous young woman.

'Now, which one of you gorgeous men is going to lead me into this next little number?'

* * *

'So, come on, Lavinia, spill the beans.' Dotty closed the bedroom door behind her and stood with her arms folded.

'Oh, you know, a little holiday, that's all,' Lavinia said, unceremoniously stripping off for bed. Her leather suitcase was back on the stool next to her mattress, but it looked deflated on the top as if there were hardly any clothes in it.

Hannah and Dotty looked suspiciously at her. Dotty coughed, refolded her arms and waited.

'Oh, well, if you must know, I've been disinherited,' Lavinia said with a dismissive sweep of her arm. 'So, what you see before you, is an orphan with no parents, no home and certainly no income.'

She suddenly looked dramatically pathetic and clasped her hands to her chest before flopping down on the bed.

Dotty sat down next to her. 'Are you serious, Lav? What happened?'

'It seems I've let down the family name, I'm a disgrace and must never darken my parents' door – and, my darlin' girls, that's a pure oak, sculptured ancient front door to a beautiful stately home.'

With that, she flounced down under the covers and put her head under the pillow. It was obvious the conversation was at an end.

* * *

Nothing more was to be gleaned about Lavinia's situation. Jed's sarcastic comments the next morning received nothing but a stubborn pout, which left him in no doubt that, firstly, it was none of his business and, secondly, she very much resented his order for them to get up at dawn to get through the workload delayed by the late-summer thunderstorms. He admitted to no one that he was in awe of the terrifying Lavinia. She seemed to see straight through him to his twisted mind. He finally gave up and issued all three girls a long list of instructions for the day. Lavinia gave him a final look of disdain and turned her back on him.

No sooner had she started to make her way across the yard than George came running across from the other side.

'Take cover, take cover,' he yelled in a commanding voice, running towards Dotty.

At that moment, two planes appeared overhead. George recognised one as a Messerschmitt Me 410, one of the new fast bombers. It was being tailed by a Spitfire, which was doing its best to bring it down. Watching the bomber's manoeuvrability, George's expert eye concluded that the bomber had already dropped its payload during a night raid. These German attacks were being timed to coincide with the return of British bombers from Europe, but a mix of bad marksmanship and flawed navigation had meant recent strikes on Lincoln and Norwich had failed to hit their targets. German airmen, like the two in the Messerschmitt, were getting desperate.

The three girls stood, transfixed, looking upwards. George grabbed Hannah and Dotty's arms and signalled for Lavinia to follow, propelling them towards the barn.

The girls gathered their wits and ran, as fast as they could, to safety. Planes flying above them were a familiar sight, but ones engaged in a battle right over their heads was terrifying.

George quickly ushered them into the strongest part of the structure, under the big beam behind the doorway, just as gunfire strafed the stone slabs in the yard. It ran like a firecracker along the ground, making popping noises and Dotty jumped back in terror. The Messerschmitt was flying really low, almost touching the tops of the buildings, determined to take some of the enemy on the ground if it was going to be hit in the air; behind it, the Spitfire was pitching and turning to try to get it in its sights. The girls cowered behind the door and Dotty clung on to George, who was using his body to shield the girls.

On the other side of the farm, the Germans were standing watching. Some of them were inwardly cheering the German plane on, others, like Peter and Karl, were standing silently, not knowing which of the young airmen to pray for.

The two planes dipped and dived. The Messerschmitt disappeared for a moment and there was a communal holding of breath below before it reappeared out of the clouds to take up prime position behind the Spitfire. George bit his lip while Dotty hid her face in her hands.

'I can't watch,' she said. George pulled her towards him and held her close.

The British pilot hauled his aircraft into a steep, spiral-ling climb, hanging in the air by the sheer power of the propeller whilst skipping and slipping to make himself a hard target to follow, but his tail began buffeting vio-lently and he had to cut his speed to regain control. Then he seemed to get a second wind and accelerated into the white mass above the village, but the German pilot was not letting go and looped behind him, his guns firing. This was no cumbersome bomber aircraft; it was manoeuvring like a Mosquito. With pale faces upturned, the group on the ground watched in horror as the two planes emerged from the clouds to come down in a thunderous dive. The noise was deafening and Hannah put her hands over her ears to try, unsuccessfully, to block out the horrendous sound. Her own fear of what would happen if they plum-meted to the ground next to her was overtaken by her prayers for the airmen that she was frantically muttering under her breath. She could almost see their faces in the Perspex turret, only partially hidden by helmets and gog-gles as they levelled and swooped up again, reminding her of the swing boats at the fairground. Every time the Spitfire lurched in one direction or the other, the Mess-erschmitt was there. He was clinging on like a limpet and while the Spitfire had the edge for manoeuvrability, the German's grim resolve was helping him to match every move. The group watched as the Spitfire pilot threw his plane into a vicious starboard turn too late to avoid the pepper spray of bullets that were being fired towards him. Then, suddenly, the RAF Spitfire lurched in the other direction, determined that if he was going down, he was not going to take the terrified faces below with him. The Messerschmitt followed, going in for the kill, but the ground was coming up towards him at a terrifyingly rapid rate. They both veered towards the copse, skimming the tops of the trees, scattering branches in all directions and finally disappeared from view. There was an agonising silence for a split second and then a huge explosion made the ground beneath the girls' feet shudder. An ominous plume of smoke spiralled from the other side of the wood before they all heard the clanging of the bell from the volunteer firemen who had been standing by in Salhouse from the moment the aerial battle began. The girls crept out of the barn to see the boss, Andrew Hollis, and his foreman, Archie, racing past the end of the barn towards the commotion, with Jed trailing behind, cursing his leg.

George yelled to the girls: 'Get the buckets and some water and follow me.'

Dotty had a moment of pride watching the gangly youth spring into action to follow the older men. Leading the way to the pump, she noticed he looked nothing like the shy boy from her early days on the farm.

They all quickly filled two buckets each, their hands shaking and then Hannah spotted the wheelbarrow. *That's watertight*, she thought, and started yanking the pump up and down as fast as she could to fill it with water before following the other two girls on the path to the field, trying desperately not to spill her load.

But when she arrived at the site of the crash, she stopped in stunned silence. The two planes had crashed and were on fire. The crumpled aircraft were half the size they had been two minutes before and their noses were buried in the wheat drills the girls had prepared just that morning. The flames were swirling up towards the sky, their sparks raining down on the surrounding field. Hannah suddenly thought of the November the 5th bonfire at Platt Fields, but this bonfire had a deadly origin; no cheerful scout leader had led an excited countdown to ignition here. She started to shake. There was no hope any of the three men in those planes could have survived. Dotty and Lavinia stood holding their useless buckets; Hannah slowly tipped the water from the wheelbarrow onto the ground beneath and watched it ebb away, trying not to think about how it resembled blood seeping into the dark fathoms of the earth. There was a dreadful smell emanating from the burning planes; she realised it was not just the smell of the fuel.

George turned back and took hold of Dotty's shoulders. His training had prepared him for action, but this was the first time he had seen such drama close at hand. He realised with satisfaction that he felt calm and hugged Dotty to him, who was anything but calm. Lavinia and Hannah looked on enviously. They, too, could have done with a hug.

The dejected group started to make its way back to the farm, leaving the fire watch to do what they could. Their efforts had been in vain, and they were all processing the fact that they had, finally, seen the war up close – far too close.

As they walked past the German compound, the prisoners were standing in respectful silence, most of them acknowledging the deaths of three airmen, all paying the ultimate price for doing their duty. For some, it brought back horrific memories and more than one of them was trembling. Hannah caught Karl's eye and felt an undeniable connection between them. It took her by surprise and she felt her stomach lurch. She had an unexpected urge to run towards him, but made her feet follow Dotty and Lavinia instead.

Karl would have given anything to be able to hurdle the fence in front of him to hold Hannah, but he knew that would open up a Pandora's box that, once opened, could never be closed again. He forced himself to look beyond her at the blazing wreckage to wonder what use a doctor's skills were when war was nothing but total annihilation.

Chapter 20

In Manchester, Ros was feeling beleaguered. She cursed both her friends, who had sent her letters about their new lives. Lily's were full of gossip, and with every sentence, Ros could hear the excited voice of the young WAAF. Hannah's were more measured, but her descriptions of driving the tractor and learning to jitterbug made her smile. *It was about time that girl started to have some fun,* she thought. But none of that helped her in dealing with the situation in Stretford.

She was feeling so guilty that she'd had no time to visit the Comptons recently, but extra responsibility was being piled on her at work as demands for more effective explosives grew. In between times, she was trying take some of the load off her mother by being the one to join the long queues outside the butcher and greengrocer for the rationed food that was diminishing day by day. She decided war was a personal battle to fit thirty-six hours into twenty-four with days of thorough testing at the factory followed by a race home in the autumn evening to plant as many vegetables as she could in the backyard, putting cabbages in pots and digging up the flagstones to make soil patches for potatoes. The 'Dig for Victory' campaign was leaving no one in any doubt that it was their duty to provide for themselves as much as possible.

Clothes were the last priority for a government trying to feed a nation and now the 'Make-Do and Mend' scheme had taken hold with Mrs Sew-and-Sew's tips on how to remake old dresses into something more fashionable, but with a limit on buttonholes and a ban on wasteful pleats, Ros despaired of making anything that would look half decent. Every night, she sewed luminous buttons onto the family's clothes so they could be seen in the blackout and then she would search in old copies of *The People's Friend* magazine for inventive ways to use spam. She sometimes envied Hannah and Lily, who at least had their meals cooked for them and uniforms to wear. And every night, as she went to sleep, she had that nagging feeling, telling her she had, yet again, not been to see the Comptons.

Finally, one Saturday afternoon, she got on her bicycle and raced around to Colley Street to knock on their door. She was surprised but delighted when the door was opened not by Mrs Compton, but by Mrs Mullins, who ushered her inside. She whispered to Ros that she and her husband had been there for a couple of hours, trying to cheer the Comptons up.

'I'm not sure I'm getting anywhere with Margaret, but I do think Alf is beginning to realise what a state his wife is in,' she confided. 'I don't know, he just seems a bit more engaged, you'll see what I mean. It's very gradual but there has been a slight change.'

The morning room actually had a small fire lit in the grate and Mrs Mullins had set the tea table with a faded white linen cloth she had found in the cupboard. She immediately got another cup and saucer and told Ros to sit down opposite Mrs Compton who, for once, had taken her pinny off. Even Mr Compton looked as if he had brushed his hair. On the other side of the room was Mr Mullins, puffing on his pipe as usual. Ros thought that Mr Compton was making an effort because he had a male visitor.

Ros smiled at them both and Mrs Compton gave a brave smile back.

'How are you, Ros?' she asked politely.

'I'm well, Mrs Compton, and can I say, you're looking a bit better?' she lied.

With that, Margaret Compton shifted in her seat and glanced at her husband, who was being informed of the latest news about John Mullins's beloved Manchester United, excitedly telling Alf that they were searching for new players to help them in their War League matches. Suddenly, John stood up. 'Come on, Alf, show me your veg patch. I want to have a look at your beans. Mine aren't doing so well.' And, with that, he ushered his friend out towards the scullery and the back door.

Mrs Compton gazed at the retreating back of her husband as if he was a stranger she was trying to place. She tried to remember the funny young man who had stolen her heart all those years ago when they met at the local dance. The one who had always made her laugh but had also made her feel safe. It was so long since she'd felt his arms around her; she was sure he could have protected her against all this noise, anger and destruction. She unconsciously wrapped her thin arms around her frail body, as if trying to remember the warmth of that embrace. Without Alf and without Hannah she had no defence against any of it. Ros reached over and covered the woman's gnarled hand. 'It's all right, Mrs Compton, it's all right.'

Margaret's eyes were darting around the room like a frightened rabbit and she didn't seem able to focus on anything. Ros was searching for something to say when Mrs Mullins bustled back in, carrying a tray with a large brown earthenware teapot, a jug of Carnation milk and a plate of home-made carrot biscuits.

'Those two'll be out there for ages, John's a gardening addict and will want to know everything about Alf's planting plans. Well, isn't this nice?' Lily's mum said, beaming around the room. She had dragged her husband with her on this mercy visit for moral support and was pleased to see the figures of the two men actually talking in the garden.

* * *

'So, Alf,' John was saying, 'how are you doing?' He then waited patiently as the man who had been his friend for so many years struggled to find the words to reply.

Finally, Alf spoke. 'I'm not good, John. I can't seem to blot out the images of . . . well, you know. It was just so awful.'

His face seemed to crumple from within. John took hold of his shoulders.

'Now, listen to me, Alf. That wife of yours is falling to pieces in there, you're going to have to pull yourself together. We all saw terrible things, but this is here and now and you can't let your family down. That woman needs your help.'

Alf gave a slight nod and tried to pull his body up as if a piece of thin string was pulling him from above.

'I know, John, I know. I'm trying, I really am, but, to be honest, I just don't know how.'

'See that bean plant there?' John said, pointing. 'It's been rained on, the pigeons have tried to eat it and the slugs are having a go as well. But it's fighting and it's trying to stand up and do what it's supposed to do. You need to do the same.'

With that, he patted Alf on the arm and said, 'Now, show me your taters. I think mine have got blight,' and he wandered off to the bottom of the small yard that had been planted up by Hannah at the beginning of the war, forcing Alf to follow him thoughtfully.

* * *

The afternoon went slowly as Mrs Mullins and Ros tried to keep the conversation going. Ros chattered on about her work at the factory and how she was getting involved in the explosives side of the business. Mrs Mullins looked impressed and, in reply, told them all about how Lily was now on a proper RAF station in East Kirby dealing with Lancaster crews. She started to share her concerns at a recent letter from her daughter which hinted at lost crews, but when she saw the alarm that suddenly appeared on Mrs Compton's face, she hurriedly changed the subject. This woman did not need to hear her worries.

'How's Hannah doing?' she asked.

Mrs Compton frowned as if trying to remember who Hannah was and then said blandly, 'All right, I think. She's on a farm, isn't she? Oh yes, of course she is.'

As Ros got her coat to leave, she paused in the doorway to the morning room and turned towards Mrs Compton. 'I'm here if either you or Mr Compton need me,' she said to her and made her way to the front door.

Mrs Mullins followed her, squeezed her arm and whispered, 'It'll be all right, lass, don't you worry. They'll come round, but it'll take time.'

She reached out and folded Ros in her strong arms and the young girl felt less alone than she had done in months.

Chapter 21

The farm had been subdued after the crash. Every time anyone went past the field, they bowed their heads, remembering the three men whose blood would forever taint the ground there. The police had come to sombrely remove the bodies in the hope there would be something they could send on to their families, but the charred ground bore witness to the complete destruction of that fateful day. The fascinating wreckage of the valuable Messerschmitt was taken carefully away by the RAF, keen to pore over every nut and bolt to see what the Germans had developed. Mr Hollis said initially that the wheat was not to be harvested from that field, but he suspected the Ministry of Food would have other ideas – every part of the production process was precious and nothing could be wasted.

* * *

On the following Sunday, Hannah put on her best uniform and placed her hat on her head, tilting it first one way then the other. For Land Army girls, the hat was the most despised item of uniform. It never looked right whichever way she put it on. She gave up and pushed it to the back, curling her hair around the front of it. That would have to do, she thought, and headed out to the stables to see Hercules as she now did every morning.

She looked with glee at the new pile of dung on the floor. Animal excrement was becoming like gold dust on British farms and every bit was scooped up to spread on the fields to make up for the lack of nutrients in the soil – the result of four years of intensive farming. Hannah bent down with a shovel to gather the telltale little piles under Hercules's backside, then put it proudly to the side, ready to be collected later. She patted Hercules in gratitude and brushed down the jacket of her parade uniform. Hannah was anxious about this trip into Norwich with Karl – with so much to do to prepare for the next winter, it had been a while since they had been able to go, and not seeing him had sent all her negative thoughts into free fall. Finally she had a Sunday off when she felt a need to say a special prayer for the three airmen who had lost their lives in the crash, especially the RAF pilot who had so bravely led his pursuer away from the farm. The whole ghastly scenario had been replaying in her mind, and every time she thought about Karl, all she could see was that brave British pilot's plane disappearing over the horizon, pursued by a Luftwaffe pilot, and she was forced to think about Karl being in the Luftwaffe too.

As she left the farm to get the bus to the German camp, it also occurred to her that she and the rest of the farm's residents had come perilously close to being collateral damage in a battle that, actually, Hannah thought sorrowfully, achieved nothing and cost three young lives.

'*Guten Tag*,' Karl said to her, turning as she stepped up to the entrance barrier. Hannah's gaze was drawn to the smiling face of the man in front of her, but then she glimpsed the Luftwaffe insignia on the jacket he had borrowed to try to look a little smarter for the occasion. She immediately looked away to make conversation with the guard on the gate, ignoring Stanley, who was standing sulkily, as usual, to one side. The POW guard was not a religious man and the irony of a German wanting to go to church irritated him every time he had to do this. He was almost grateful to the Land Army girl that she took the initiative and was content to walk behind, absorbed in his own thoughts of Cynthia's voluptuous body, which would be waiting for him.

Karl had been longing for the chance to talk to Hannah again, feeling the start of a very gradual thaw in her attitude towards him, but one look at her face today told him that the crash had reversed all that and now he was back to square one. He clenched his fists at his sides.

'You ready?' she asked.

'*Ja*,' Karl replied, increasing his step to catch up with her as she turned down the hill to walk to the church, with Stanley behind as usual. They didn't speak all the way to

Norwich and Hannah kept her chin determinedly high. The farmworkers were taking every opportunity to retell the heroics of the young British pilot who had sacrificed his life to take down the Germans and she had spent hours trying to separate Karl from the conflict that had been played out right above their heads, but every time, when she tried to convince herself that he was different, she would glimpse that uniform which confirmed he was, undeniably, her enemy. By the time they left Stanley to scurry off down the road outside St John's, Hannah had almost convinced herself that she was perfectly able to deal with this and that she had no feelings for the prisoner of war beside her.

Feeling a weight had been lifted off her, Hannah moved towards the back rows as usual. Karl followed her but, standing back to let her enter first, he put his hand on the end of the wooden pew. At that moment, Hannah went to genuflect and inadvertently put her hand on top of his. They both jumped back and their eyes connected. She stumbled into the pew, sure that the whole church had felt the electricity between them and, after that, struggled to concentrate on any prayers at all.

When they came out into the bright morning, Karl checked Stanley was nowhere to be seen and said quietly to her, 'Perhaps we could take a moment around the corner, in the little garden?'

She nodded, unable to resist. Her breath caught half-way up her chest and she gasped for air. Reason flew out of the window when she felt him near her and she was about to break every rule, jeopardise her job, her reputation and alienate her friends. She could also be in real trouble with the authorities, but she could no longer resist the chance to be alone with this man.

It was as they made their way around towards the little garden area at the back of St John's that they both breathed deeply, as if they had been in a room without oxygen.

'So, Fräulein Hannah, tell me about you,' Karl said. There was an urgency to his voice. Judging by previous weeks, he knew he only had about fifteen minutes before the guard came back.

'I don't know what to say,' she murmured, trying not to look at his face.

'Well, maybe you tell me about your family. That would be a good beginning.'

She hesitated. This felt so wrong, but he was looking expectantly at her.

'I am an only child,' she started, 'I live in Manchester. My father ...' She stopped, hearing her father's voice saying how much he hated the Germans.

'Yes,' Karl prompted; he did not want to waste this moment.

'He is not well, after the Great War, you know. There are memories he doesn't seem able to leave behind.'

'I do know.' He nodded. 'My father too, he was in the Queen Olga Grenadiers based in Stuttgart. It changed him.'

A grim expression had come over Hannah's face, so Karl quickly went on to try to distract her.

'He had to leave the farm and *meine Mutter* had to take over, but it was so hard with all the men gone. You know Deutschland has always had a big problem feeding its people, and the farms were given too many things to do. In Britain, you manage to provide more than double the amount of food from your farms. I am learning so much here.'

Karl had been watching with a farmer's son's interest how British agriculture maximised every inch of land, every resource and every grain, and he was longing to tell his brothers how to improve their yields, but he also knew Britain was in danger of doing things that had cost his own country so dearly. He cast his mind back to stories he had heard as a child.

'You know, your country is making the same mistake as mine. *Meine Mutter* – she tell me how we had killed all the pigs so they did not have to feed them in the Schweinemord, but that made it worse because you know how pig manure ... it is good for the fields, so the soil turned bad. You killed the sheep so you did not have to feed them and now you have no animal waste to feed the soil.'

Hannah wanted to giggle; she couldn't believe she was wasting precious time having a discussion with this gorgeous man about manure ... and even worse, finding it fascinating.

But Karl was still reminiscing: 'And then they made people eat ... Oh I do not know what it was, it was supposed to be a substitute for meat but she said it was horrible and the bread ... it was mostly sawdust. So many people died. But then *mein Vater* came home and it was so difficult, he was not the same.'

'Is your father still alive?' Hannah asked before she could help herself. She had to know more about this man.

'*Nein*, he became so weak from the bad air in the trenches. He died twelve years ago ... of tuber ... tuberc—'

'Tuberculosis,' she provided.

'*Ja*, that,' he finished. 'I'm sorry, my English is not so good.'

'Your English is excellent,' she told him, shyly. 'Where did you learn it?'

'The local priest, he teach me. Taught me ... he did a good job, *ja*?' he said, looking very pleased with himself.

She laughed reluctantly. 'Yes, he did. But how did your mother survive after your father died?'

He told her of his childhood, hiding all emotion. His mother struggled on to keep the farm going, and when the three sons were still at home, it was just about manageable, despite increasing food shortages, but, as Karl was growing up, everything suddenly got harder. He talked of how the government printed money to pay back its debts and how when he was very small, a loaf of bread cost two billion marks.

'Our money had no meaning,' he told her. 'Farms like ours, we learned nothing and were struggling to provide enough food for the country. We could not pay our workers, so we all had to work, even me, a little boy – almost as much as you girls do.' He smiled at her. Despite the chill she felt listening to his determinedly bland words, she could not resist smiling back.

'It was so sad,' he went on, 'we were just getting better, but the American crash, it put us back to the bottom again.'

Hannah felt an unexpected affinity with the man standing opposite her. His father had come back from the war a different person and his mother had struggled to cope. She had never thought about how war affected ordinary Germans too. She slowed up and turned to look at him, wishing she could make the morning pass in slow motion. She could not believe how easy it was to talk to this man.

'I remember that,' she said. 'They called it the Wall Street Crash. My parents raced to the bank to get their savings out and hid the money under the mattress.' It had been a scary time, she recalled, even for a child.

She started to laugh and added, 'Do you know, I broke open my piggy bank and hid the pocket money I'd been saving up under the rug?'

'"Piggy bank"?' he asked.

'Ah yes, I had a little pig with a hole in the middle of its back. I used to earn money doing jobs and then put it in there to save for my holidays. Because it was called a "piggy bank" I thought they would come and take its money like they were doing from the banks in town, so I hid it where no one would find it.'

Karl saw a glimpse of the little girl in the woman opposite him and reached across to take her hand. He loved the way she laughed. Hannah looked down at their fingers entwined. She neither wanted to nor could pull away. For a brief second, they stared into each other's eyes. It was like disappearing into a parallel universe where it was quite normal for a British Land Army girl to be holding hands with a German prisoner of war while they stood at the back of a church in Norwich.

Karl forced himself to concentrate. 'Oh yes, the days when we had holidays. I used to go to my aunt's house on the Bodensee. That water was so blue.' He paused, it almost hurt to think of a different time.

Hannah thought of the weeks during the school holidays spent at her grandparents' house in Old Colwyn, when she used to help out in Grandad Ted's market garden.

She told Karl how it had been her grandfather who had persuaded her to join the Land Army. She had frequently weighed out the potatoes, carrots and swedes onto the little iron weighing scales in the wooden hut halfway up the hillside behind her grandparents' house in Coed Coch Road.

'He had this area of land where he grew vegetables to sell,' she explained, adding wistfully, 'I had to cross the Fairy Glen to get there.'

He looked puzzled. 'The Fairy . . .?'

'Oh, it was the most magical place,' she said. 'With wood carvings, a stream running through the middle and trees and flowers everywhere. You'd love it . . .' She stopped, realising the ridiculousness of what she had just said.

'If only we had been born at another time,' he blurted out. 'We . . . you and I . . . well, maybe I would have travelled to England to see my sister, she lives here, you know, in King's Lynn, and you could have taken me to your . . . Fairy Glen is it? Who knows, perhaps you and I, we would have met by chance somewhere on a spring day . . .?'

Hannah found her mind actually trying to work out how she, a girl from Manchester, might have happened to have met a German somewhere between King's Lynn and North Wales and it occurred to her that the war had given them a chance in a million to meet and, in a strange way, she was grateful for it. She made herself come back to the words that he had uttered rather than concentrate on his blue eyes, which were threatening to engulf her.

'Your sister lives in King's Lynn? That's just north-west of here.'

'Yes, she works in a little shop for the bread. I think she may marry the man who owns it one day. She came over here to learn to make the white bread you have and met Albert, he teaches her to use the white flour. She seemed so happy, but now . . . I do not know,' he said with a plaintive expression. 'And I hear nothing from my mother or my brothers.'

Hannah looked down at their entwined hands. She could not afford to care so much about this German family. She suddenly pulled her hand away and the spell was broken.

'We need to go,' she said in an officious manner. There was so much more she wanted to know. Anything to prolong this magical afternoon, but then she looked at her watch. Stanley would be coming any moment now and he couldn't find them like this.

'We must hurry,' she told him and turned on her heels to make her way back to the front of the church. Karl stood for a moment, his hand still outstretched towards her, but then reluctantly followed. There would be more Sundays, he told himself. They had time.

Chapter 22

The conversation with Karl left Hannah in more turmoil than ever and she felt exhausted by the anguish that was engulfing her. She lurched to the end of the next week. She was due a half-day off and, desperate to find some normality, she spent the night before going through all of the things she could do: wash her hair, wash her clothes, write some letters or glumly, she thought, stay in bed and hide under the blankets, but then Rachel tentatively mentioned there was a jumble sale at the village school and Hannah saw it as a chance to try to sort out her own jumbled thoughts and offered to go with her.

Rachel was touchingly delighted that one of the Land Army girls wanted to accompany her on an outing and, feeling a little sheepish, Hannah took her arm to walk down the drive. Hannah gave a wave to an envious Lavinia and Dotty, who had taken their half-days the day before when it had poured with rain and they had both ended up doing some mending and washing, whereas today was a bright, crisp day. They waved at the two disappearing figures unenthusiastically.

Rachel chatted on happily. She just hoped everyone in the village would notice her being led along the pavement by one of the smart Land Army girls and she suddenly felt very grown up. Mrs Hill had given her a list of things to look out for – a new frying pan, a vase to replace the one broken by the cat when it jumped onto the windowsill and a ribbon for her Sunday hat. Hannah told her she had had an idea of buying some material to cheer up the barn with some money her grandfather had sent her. Her wages only amounted to twenty-eight shillings a week, and of that, fourteen shillings was deducted for board and lodging and she sent a regular amount home, so she never had much spare, but her grandfather would occasionally manage to send her a postal order for a small amount that she cashed at the local post office and then put in a jar, waiting until she could buy something really special. That little jar had been mounting up and Hannah had decided she would splash out at the sale if she spotted something she wanted.

There was already a large crowd outside the little school when they got there and the women, for there wasn't a man in sight, were chattering with excitement; these WVS jumble sales were always really popular during rationing and this one was raising money for the Spitfire Fund, so was especially well supported. Hannah looked up at the stone inlaid above the door, proclaiming 'Salhouse National School'. She really was beginning to like this village.

'Let's go in and see what we can find,' Rachel said, squeezing Hannah's arm tightly.

They pushed their way past the crowd and entered the room. All around the edges were trestle tables with an unusually impressive array of goods on them. The two girls split up and made their own way around, fingering the old clothes and turning over the bric-a-brac to inspect it thoroughly. Hannah spied some old curtains that were frayed and dirty, but she suspected with a good wash and a bit of a remake, they would make some covers for the dull, brown chairs in the dining room, and was examining them when she was accosted by a woman in a hat that looked like a tea cosy.

'Like to buy a raffle ticket, dearie?' she asked, rattling a tin in Hannah's direction. 'It's all in a good cause. We're trying to get a Spitfire named after this area.'

Hannah fumbled for her purse.

'Yes, of course, what do I win?' she said with a grin.

The woman leaned forward, her hat nearly falling over her eyes. She pushed it back and winked at Hannah.

'Never you mind, but it's come from the vicar so it'll be a good prize.'

Hannah handed over tuppence and took two tickets.

An hour later, Hannah was holding on to her curtains and Rachel had managed to get a nice, flowered vase that she placed in her wicker basket. They made their way to the tea stand where the urn was boiling away, sending steam with a regular hiss into the crowd, just as the raffle was called. They paused in the queue to hear the result.

The woman in the woolly hat, with a beaming smile, thanked everyone for their contributions, delved into a glass jar full of folded up tickets and held one up triumphantly. 'Number thirty-three,' she shouted.

Hannah delightedly waved her ticket in the air. 'That's me!' she said, turning to Rachel, who was clapping loudly.

The crowd parted for Hannah to make her way to the front where she was handed an old Alba wireless to an enthusiastic round of applause and a murmur of approval around the room. Hannah smiled broadly; she could not have been more thrilled.

'Does it work?' she asked fearfully.

'Well, not exactly, not yet, that is,' the woman replied, 'but if you know anyone handy, I'm sure they can fix it. And you'll just need to recharge one of those acid batteries.'

Hannah lovingly touched the radio with its brown leather casing and metal dials. It reminded her of the one they had at home and listened to, so faithfully, every night. If she could get it fixed, she would be able to hear all the latest news again, she thought. To have her very own radio was a link to the outside world and she could feel the excitement rising in her stomach.

Rachel admired the radio with her. 'Here, let me help you. Gosh, it's heavy. I'm sure one of the men can fix it, maybe Archie?' she said. 'He's very handy.'

'I could ask him,' Hannah said. 'If you think he wouldn't mind.'

'Not a bit, he's a lovely man,' Rachel reassured her.

It was as they were leaving, both grinning, thrilled with their successful morning, that a woman brushed roughly past Rachel.

'Oh sorry,' she said, with a sneer, 'I don't see Jews.'

Hannah reeled back in horror. She stepped forward to remonstrate with the woman, but she had already disappeared into the crowd.

Rachel touched Hannah's arm. 'Don't worry, I get it all the time. It doesn't bother me.'

But when Hannah looked at the young girl's face, she saw the cloud of hurt dispel all the happiness that had been there just a moment before.

She gave her friend a hug.

'One day, Rachel, this war will end and we will all learn not to judge people who aren't like us.'

Rachel looked doubtfully at her.

* * *

The wireless became the centre of attention when Hannah proudly showed it off to the little group at teatime. She carefully placed the battery Lavinia had given her in the back and closed it, reverently. Even William Handforth could not resist peering over to look at it.

John and Albert took turns to examine the wireless like surgeons examining a patient.

Albert took out a screwdriver and was about to insert it into the screws at the back.

'No, you don't,' John said, laughing. 'That electric fire you "fixed" was a death trap after you'd finished with it. We'll ask Archie.'

Dotty stepped forward. 'Do you mind if I have a go?'

'You, lass?' John asked. 'You surely don't know how to mend this, do you?'

'I might,' she replied, biting her lip in concentration as she fiddled with the dials. 'I used to help out in the repair shop at the end of my street after school.'

'Well, I never,' John said, handing it over reluctantly.

Dotty put her head down and studied the wireless, but at that moment Rachel came in with the meal and all the men immediately put their minds to the more important task of eating.

Lavinia and Hannah looked proudly over at Dotty, who ate her meal with one hand while dismantling the wireless with the other. After she had finished her spotted dick pudding, she triumphantly looked up and said, 'Done it ... I think.' Everyone crowded round and there was absolute silence as she turned the dial to switch it on.

There was a moment's crackle during which they all waited expectantly and then Dotty moved the dial across the squeaks and squelches until it settled on one station. The room went quiet as everyone listened intently. An announcer was saying that tonight's World Service would feature recordings of German prisoners of war who would be sending messages to let their families know they were alive. Hannah had read that no German could ever admit to having heard these messages because they were not allowed to listen to the BBC, but it ensured that Germans could receive received a balanced and accurate reporting of the war, rather than the propaganda that was being put out on German radio. The little group around the table shifted in their seats, unwilling to make the connection between the men in the compound and the fact that they had families, just like them. Hannah, in particular, was thinking of Karl and she felt her heart miss a beat as she registered how worried he must be about not hearing any news from home. Her own mother wrote regularly, and even though she suspected the forced cheerfulness of her letters was hiding her true feelings, at least she knew her mother and father were safe. She could not imagine what it would be like to have no word from them.

After supper, Hannah brought out the pieces of material she had managed to buy at the jumble sale and began to spread them over the armchairs at the end of the room to try them out before she washed them. They immediately gave a sense of homeliness to the sparse barn and Lavinia raced upstairs to get an old yellow scarf that she draped over the scratched wooden table. Not wanting to be left out, Dotty dashed out into the blackout and came back triumphantly with some hellebores, which gradually opened their dropped heads as if to celebrate their new status as the centrepiece of the room. The three girls stood back to survey their work and smiled in delight.

'Let's see – if we're allowed to have a bit of whitewash for that wall over there, and then in a few weeks, we can put some Christmas decorations up,' said Dotty, 'we'll have it looking more cosy in no time.'

Hannah put the wireless in pride of place on the long table at the side and moved the dial until they heard some big band music. It was Henry Hall and his orchestra, and at that point, John and Albert pushed back the chairs, grabbed hold of Lavinia and Hannah, while George reached for Dotty, and they all danced around the room, their heads tilted back in laughter, ignoring William Handforth, who made a point of roughly brushing the blackout curtain to one side before slamming the door on his way out.

Hannah looked round with pleasure. With all the turmoil going on in her head about Karl, an evening like this was a welcome release and she would remember it for the rest of her life. This was a long way from a dull sitting room in Stretford with her mother's chatter trying to compensate for her father's silence and, she realised, she was finally loving being a Land Army girl.

Chapter 23

As the weeks progressed after returning to the farm, Lavinia was becoming increasingly withdrawn and the other two girls started to wonder whether there was more to her misery than just the argument with her parents.

On a night when she refused to join them on a trip to the cinema to see the new film *Girl Crazy* with Mickey Rooney and Judy Garland, Hannah and Dotty put their heads together on the bus back to discuss the problem.

'It's really odd,' Dotty said. 'I can understand her being furious with her parents, but this . . . I don't know, it seems deeper somehow. Do you think there's something else?'

Hannah shrugged. She too had wondered whether there was another secret that Lavinia wasn't sharing.

'Do you think it's that man, the rich one she mentioned?' Hannah said. 'She seems to have gone very quiet about that.'

Dotty, with her worldly experience, nodded sagely. 'It could be,' she agreed, pointing to irrefutable evidence of a broken heart such as how Lavinia no longer painted her nails or put her lipstick on to move the muck, and that her clothes were getting more worn and holes were beginning to appear – a very suspicious sign in a girl as glamorous as Lavinia, she added conclusively.

'We'll have to talk to her,' Dotty said, when they arrived back at the farm and she flung open the bedroom door and bounced down on the bed. Hannah jumped on next to her and they lay down on their stomachs, feet up by the headboard and heads dropping over the edge to peer down sternly at the prone body hiding under the bedclothes on the mattress.

Hannah spoke first. 'So, come on, Lavinia, talk to us. Is it just the situation with your parents or is there more to it? You've really not been yourself since you came back. What's up? Is it that man you talked about?'

Brushing her blonde hair back, Lavinia peeped out from the navy-blue blanket, her eyes showing signs of tears. She was tormented by the fact that Jeremy hadn't written for weeks but, unwilling to give her room-mates the chance to say 'I told you so', came back sharply: 'No, of course not, he's history. I just hate being a disinherited heiress. It's so hard. I've only got my wages and, as you both know, they don't go very far and now it seems . . . well . . . that all the excitement's gone out of life.'

'What do you need, though?' Dotty asked her, not liking the fact that her heroine had lost her sparkle to become as grey as the rest of the world. 'We've got beds, we get fed and we can just about manage to get to the Samson or the flicks every now and again.'

'Darlings,' Lavinia said, retreating behind the mask she had perfected over the years, 'this war's bad enough, but do you know how hard it is to come down to this level when you've been used to having enough money to get taxis in London, buy the latest fashions and have your hair done every week?'

'No,' Dotty replied flatly from her prone position on the other side of the bed. She suddenly sat up and looked furiously at Lavinia. 'You have no idea, do you, Lav? Of how the other half live, I mean?'

'No, my little dumpling,' Lavinia replied, leaning over to tickle her. Dotty looked so fierce sometimes. 'You know we rich have never bothered our pretty little heads about that. We're too busy having parties and drinking champagne.'

Dotty looked cross. 'Then it'll do you the world of good to learn what it's like for the rest of us,' she said, and lay back down on her front with a frown, flicking her feet towards her bottom in rhythmical fury.

Lavinia tried to look repentant, knowing she was only telling the girls half of what was going on in her mind. Hannah peered at her. She didn't believe a word of her protestations about her Jeremy, but decided tonight was not the night for any more quizzing so changed the subject to fend off the increasingly tense atmosphere.

'Dotty, how are you doing reading those newspapers I gave you? You said you wanted to educate yourself. Are they helping?'

'Hmm,' Dotty said vaguely, sitting up to turn her back on Lavinia.

Hannah was determined to confirm what she already suspected so pushed the issue further. 'But did you read the article about the Resistance Movement starting up in France?'

'Uh-huh,' Dotty replied.

'What about the news that Churchill's to divorce Clemmy? Did you read that?'

'Yep,' Dotty replied.

Hannah took her by the shoulders and looked straight into her eyes. 'Aha! I knew it. You can't read, can you, Dotty?'

Dotty picked up a bit of tassel from the counterpane and twirled it in her fingers. She said nothing.

Lavinia sat forward. Dotty's admonishments had made her feel incredibly guilty and her voice was softer than normal. 'Come on, Dotty, you can tell us. It's nothing to be ashamed of.'

'How would you know? You've always had everything... money, an education, a big house and a daddy who looked after you?' Dotty sounded so bitter and then started to cry, tears glistening as they ran down her cheeks. She looked from one of her friends to the other. 'No one in our family can read.'

Hannah jumped up and yanked Dotty to her feet.

'Well, that's all going to change. Come on, Dot, I'll help you. You're going to be reading Shakespeare by the time I've finished. Let's get some paper – we've got work to do!'

'Who's Shakespeare?' Dotty replied, but Hannah was already rooting under the bed amongst her pile of books.

From that moment on, Hannah took her friend in hand and, starting with the alphabet, began to teach her to read. She grabbed every book, leaflet, advertising pamphlet and instruction book she could, and they worked through them a sentence at a time, their two heads huddled together.

* * *

The December weeks passed quickly with reading lessons and dealing with the winter crops, but Sundays had started to take on a special significance for Hannah and she would hum as she got ready to catch the bus to the camp and then walk to Norwich with Karl.

These days had become a highlight for her, and although she did not know it, for Karl too. As she was about to go out of the door, Dotty stopped her.

'Why don't you take my bicycle?' she said. 'It's just sitting there and it's much easier than getting the bus.'

'I can't ride one,' Hannah confessed. 'I somehow never learned.'

'OK, during the week, I'll teach you,' Dotty promised, heading off to the milking parlour. 'It'll be payment for the reading lessons.'

* * *

Hannah thought constantly about the conversations she was having on those precious Sundays with Karl. They had got into the habit of going round to the back of the church to make the most of Stanley's reliable lateness in meeting them. There, they luxuriated in learning about each other's past. Hannah found she could talk to Karl in a way she had never talked to anyone and, little by little, it occurred to her she might be falling in love with him.

She longed to talk to someone about her feelings for Karl but she worried that Dotty would judge her and she felt sure Lavinia would laugh at her for falling for a German after all her protestations. She thought of Lily and Ros, but every time she started to write to them, the words looked so bleak and dangerous there in black and white on the page, she would tear the paper up for fear they would incriminate her to some authority. Once she could hear Dotty's gentle snores next to her and Lavinia's regular breathing on the other side of the room, Hannah would lie awake, staring at the ceiling, trying to make sense of how she could possibly have fallen for someone her friends and family would automatically hate. It was always at that point that she would gulp in despair and turn over, finally falling asleep.

Work became a shield for her and she put her energies into picking up the sprouts behind the tractor and banging them to get the mud off them. She moved so fast that the other two accused her of raising Jed's expectations about their abilities. She would smile and laugh with them, acting out a part while, all the time, hiding the enormous emotions that were assaulting her like a battering ram. After work, she spent hours helping Dotty learn to read, welcoming the excuse to avoid cosy chats, and she was fortunate that luck was on her side: Dotty was enjoying her early relationship with George, taking any opportunity to nip out of the barn to meet him, then, later, when she was in the bedroom, she tackled reading in the same way she had approached everything else in her life, like a torpedo. Lavinia, too, was wrapped up in her own thoughts about where her relationship with Jeremy could have gone so wrong and, for once, failed to notice the nuances in her friend's behaviour that she would have pounced on earlier in the year.

The reading was slow progress; partly because the girls had so little spare time but also because Dotty had never had to apply herself academically, but Hannah found she had limitless patience and settled down calmly to a long winter of going through letters, syllables and, eventually, words.

As promised, Dotty took on the role of teaching Hannah how to ride a bike. The first time Hannah got on the bike, she wobbled, and memories of the little girl with grazed knees came back to her, but Dotty shouted from behind: 'Attack it with gusto, Hann. Ride it like you mean it, if you're not confident, you'll fall off.'

Two false starts later and Hannah suddenly took off across the yard, yelling and screaming with delight. To begin with, she had to stop at each end, turn the bike round and then ride back, but, gradually, she started to arch round until she found she could turn easily. To help her, Lavinia put four buckets out in a line and made her wind her way through them until she could do it without knocking them over.

'I can ride a bike!' Hannah exclaimed, her cheeks red with exertion. 'I'm thrilled. Thank you both so much. I can't believe I was frightened of it. Think of all those years I wasted when I could have been pedalling all over Stretford.'

The other two shared a satisfied glance. Another goal achieved.

* * *

Margaret Compton was feeling anything but thrilled. She was waking at night, hearing bombers, even when they weren't there. She shook every time a door banged, and at the slightest noise, she would jump.

One Tuesday night, the week before Christmas, her husband found his tea was not on the table at six as normal. Hunger eventually pushed him towards the kitchen. He started clanging around in the pantry. It was practically empty.

'Where are the eggs kept?' he called into the morning room.

There was no reply.

He went back in and looked properly for the first time in years at his wife. She was staring blankly into the empty grate. It reminded him of something. It took a moment before he became aware that it was the same stare he had used since 1918 and that realisation shook him to the core.

He coughed loudly, making her look up.

'Margaret,' he said gently, 'I'll cook tea tonight.' She didn't even look surprised and just went back to staring at the space in front of her.

He slowly walked out of the room into the back kitchen, searched the pantry for the eggs and got out a bowl and a fork. He was going to make an omelette, he decided. It was the first decision he had made in years and it felt good. He broke the precious eggs into the bowl.

* * *

Dear Hannah,

I hope you are well. I don't know whether you could get a couple of days to come home early for Christmas. Your mum's not doing too well and I think it would do her good to see you.

Love Dad x

Hannah stared at the letter in front of her. She had been perplexed when she had seen the unfamiliar writing on the envelope and had ripped it open in a panic, fearing the worst. To see her father's signature had made her gasp. She couldn't start to think what had happened to prompt him to put pen to paper and quickly scanned the letter, then immediately raced off down to the yard to find Jed, who was, unfortunately, the person she would have to ask for leave.

She breathed a sigh of relief when she saw him talking to Archie, who invariably had a cheery word and a smile for the girls. He always looked so approachable and she ran more quickly than she had intended towards the two men to catch Archie before he had the chance to leave.

'May I have a word please, Jed?' she said as confidently as she could.

Archie stepped back. 'I'll head off, Jed, and leave you to it.'

Jed's eyes lit up. If this girl wanted something from him, he'd certainly make sure he got something from her.

'Um, no, if you wouldn't mind staying, Mr ... umm, Archie, I think I need to talk to you too.'

Jed glowered but Archie stood patiently.

'I, um, have had some news from home and I really need to go back to Manchester early for Christmas ... my mother's not well and I just need a few days now.'

Before Jed could say anything, Archie said, 'I'm sure that won't be a problem, will it, Jed? Would you prefer to go home now and just tag it on to your Christmas leave, Hannah?'

Hannah nodded. She knew Dotty and Lavinia wouldn't mind. They'd already said they were both happy to stay at Salhouse instead of going home to their complicated families where they would face a miserable Christmas.

Archie went on, thinking of the family up at the farm-house who were facing their own problems, 'I think sometimes we're all needed at home.'

Jed scowled. His plans were scuppered by Archie's interference and he also hated being outranked, but it seemed he had no option.

'All right,' he said, begrudgingly. 'You can go on Saturday but make sure you're back here the day after Boxing Day.'

Hannah's first thought was that she wouldn't be able to take Karl to Christmas mass and felt a pang of disappointment, but her mother needed her and she really had no choice. The problem was, she would have no chance to tell him. She really hoped he would understand and not think she had deserted him. There was no chance she could risk writing him a note or ask anyone to give him a message. She sighed, any relationship with this man was impossible; she really needed to forget him.

On the train journey home that Saturday, seeing his face in every blond-haired man she passed, she realised that was not going to be easy.

Chapter 24

The foggy weather of Christmas 1943 meant Hannah's train home travelled at a painfully slow speed and then her bus to Stretford from the station was led by a young lad with a lantern to show the way. The whole journey took hours and, as she got off the bus, she guiltily realised that part of her welcomed the delay, unsure of what she would find when she opened the door to her house. She peered at a figure in the gloom in front of her. It was a small woman with a determined stride, and a basket over her arm.

'Mrs Mullins?' Hannah called into the murkiness. 'Is that you?'

The woman turned and her face, which had been compressed into a frown, beamed.

'Oh Hannah, you've come. I'm so pleased, we weren't sure you would be able to.'

Hannah ran to catch her up and gave her a hug. 'Are you on your way to ours?'

'Yes, Ros asked me to call in. She . . . well, she was a bit worried about your mum.'

'What's happened?' Hannah asked, feeling suddenly nauseous.

'I'm not sure, but let's get along now, and I'm sure we'll find out when we get there,' Ginny Mullins replied.

Her common sense gave Hannah strength and she fell in next to the diminutive, capable woman she had been so fond of since her childhood.

Hannah used her key to open the red front door that looked unusually dusty, even the front step, which was normally polished regularly with Cardinal Red, was a dull brown. Her father came up the hall to greet her.

'Oh, Hannah, it's so good to see you.' He reached forward and held her in a tight hug. Hannah could hardly breathe, it was so long since she had been held by her father, but, after a moment, she felt his body crumple and tightened her arms around him.

She was about to go forward to the morning room, but he pulled her into the cold front room, unused for years. Mrs Mullins followed.

'I don't know what's happened to her,' he said to both of them in a quiet voice. 'She's just, well, sort of gone into herself. It was after the last raid heading to Berlin. It was as if it was the last straw. I don't think she could take any more.'

'Has she seen a doctor?' Mrs Mullins asked.

'Yes, but he couldn't help. Said there was nothing physical so he couldn't treat her for anything. I think he's too busy with people with wounds you *can* see.' Looking at Hannah standing in front of him, so strong and healthy, it occurred to him his daughter might be able to take on the burdens of the family neither of her parents seemed able to cope with and his shoulders lowered in relief. The last few weeks had drained him of all his new-found resilience.

Mrs Mullins, too, took another look at Hannah. She was taken aback at the way the young woman in front of her was standing up, so straight and tall. She looked nothing like the shy, timid girl who used to trail around in Lily and Ros's wake and she gave a small nod of satisfaction. She couldn't wait to write and tell Lily.

'Let's go and see Mum,' Hannah was saying, gently propelling her father towards the door and the three of them went down the corridor towards the familiar morning room where Hannah had spent so many of her childhood days, running round in circles to try to make her parents' lives more comfortable.

When she walked in, she took a breath. There were no familiar decorations hung across the ceiling, no welcoming signs of the festive season that her mother normally loved to scatter all over the house and the cosy range fire was cold. Her mother was sitting on the armchair in the clothes that Hannah had helped her sew, but they hung on her thin frame like a dust sheet, their folds gathering uselessly at her sides. Hannah shivered; the room was freezing, but her mother did not seem to notice.

'Mum, Mum . . .' she said gently.

Margaret Compton looked up and slowly focused her watery eyes on her daughter, like a vision in a dream.

'Hannah' she muttered. 'Is it really you?'

'Yes, Mum, it is. I've come to see how you are. Dad said you hadn't been well.'

A single tear trickled down Margaret's cheek.

'Right, Alf, I suggest you get this fire lit while I make some tea,' Ginny Mullins said, heading towards the kitchen. It was her default suggestion when she did not know what to say and, like all Englishwomen, she believed tea was the panacea for all ills.

Hannah pulled a chair up towards her mum and enfolded her in her arms. Once Margaret felt the strong muscles of her daughter around her, she seemed to shrink into herself and started to sob. Hannah rocked her backwards and forwards until her mother ran out of tears, by which time, Ginny Mullins had put a cup and saucer and biscuit from the tin she had brought on the table in front of her. She also put one on the table next to Alf, who was holding a sheet of newspaper over a shovel in front of the range to try to get the flames up.

Hannah cradled her mother and looked over towards her father. She was pleased to see him making an effort with the fire. It seemed to be taking all his concentration. 'OK,' she said out loud. 'OK. I have just a week to fix this but I have no idea how.'

Mrs Mullins leaned over and patted her on the hand. 'It's just good you're here, lovely. It will do your mum good and,' she whispered in her ear, 'look at your dad, he's almost come to life, so that's something.'

Hannah nodded and peeled off her mother's tense arms, one, then the other, before folding them limply back into her lap. She stood up.

'You're right, Mrs Mullins. There's a lot I can do in a few days.' She looked around the room, taking in the dust and the pots left unwashed and rolled her sleeves up.

'You get on home, now, Mrs Mullins. This fog is worsening. I can't tell you how much I appreciate you coming over and it's wonderful to know you're keeping an eye on things while I'm away.'

'It makes me feel useful,' Ginny replied, putting on her coat. 'It's a strange war, Hannah. There's always so much to do, but so little of it seems to make a difference. So, if I can help here, then . . .'

Hannah leaned towards the older woman and gave her a hug before following her down the hallway.

'How's Lily?' she asked as she opened the door to let Mrs Mullins out.

'Oh, she's doing well. I'm sure you've heard that she's moved to East Kirby now, where she's in charge of Lancasters and everything. I think she's finding it a bit difficult after the training in Blackpool but she's doing a proper job now.

'And how's the Land Army?'

Hannah somehow couldn't equate being able to drive a tractor with bringing in huge bombers like Lancasters after raids so just smiled. No matter what she achieved, somehow Lily always managed to be more glamorous, she thought ruefully.

'It's actually good, Mrs Mullins. Hard work, but good.'

'Well, you take care of yourself, Hannah. And try not to worry,' Ginny finished, before tucking her handbag under her arm and setting off down the road. Hannah stared after her for a moment wondering why she couldn't have had uncomplicated parents like Mr and Mrs Mullins.

* * *

Her own worries were put into perspective the next morning, when gloomy details were printed in the *Manchester Guardian* about how a raid on Berlin by 480 Lancaster bombers had been blighted by the terrible fog that was engulfing the Eastern airfields. The raids were still going on and Hannah spent the next few days glued to the wireless to hear any news that was released, thinking of Lily dealing with silent headphones as her crews failed to return. It helped her to rationalise the tension in her own home while she determinedly tackled the dusting, polishing, cleaning and cooking that had been so badly neglected there.

After a couple of days, she was relieved to hear the doorbell ring. Hannah stood up from polishing the hearth and brushed her hair out of her eyes. She was exhausted but pleased to see the morning room looking cleaner and tidier. She had brushed her mother's hair and made some food for them all, persuading her mum to eat, one forkful at a time, and both her parents were sitting next to the radio. She suspected neither was listening to it, which, as they were estimating up to 300 airmen may have lost their lives, was probably a good thing, she decided. They had enough to deal with.

When she opened the door, she shrieked in delight. 'Ros! I can't tell you how pleased I am to see you.'

The two girls hugged and Hannah hung on for just a few seconds longer than Ros, which told Ros all she needed to know.

'Are you coming in?' she said, wondering why Ros was hovering on the front step in the December cold.

'Well, yes, but I really came to see whether you could come out for a bit . . . so we can have a proper natter,' she finished in a quiet voice.

'I'll just get my coat,' Hannah said.

They walked arm-in-arm towards Victoria Park. The fog had lifted slightly and the birds were making the most of quiet skies and the weak winter sunshine, twittering their insistent song from the bare trees.

As they entered the park, Hannah grinned in pure delight.

She looked around, taking in the archway, where trails of ivy were growing in defiance of a war that had destroyed so much of Manchester, and the familiar fountain and water feature. Behind her were holly bushes with clusters of red berries bringing a cheerfulness to the bareness of the foliage. It all looked so permanent and untouched. Since she had started on the farm, she had noticed nature so much more than she ever had before and she was surprised how much the birds, the crops and the animals were beginning to represent hope to her; a hope that one day the world would heal.

Ros was chattering away beside her, telling her all the latest gossip from the factory. Hannah felt she knew all the people Ros was talking about, their letters were so frequent, but she also knew there was also so much they had not had chance to talk about. She wondered for a brief moment whether she could tell her friend about Karl. There were so many things she wanted to say but where could she begin?

I think I'm in love with a German prisoner of war. She turned the words over silently in her mind.

No, she could never voice them. There was nobody who would condone such feelings, not one person in the whole of Britain, and she was not ready to share them, even with one of her best friends.

Ros's next words broke through her reverie.

'And what about your parents, Hann? What can be done there do you think?'

'I've no idea, my father seems ever so slightly better and I think he's managing to at least feed them both, but my mother's in quite a state. I don't know who to turn to.'

At that moment, Karl's face came to mind. He had told her he had a special interest in psychiatry. Maybe she could ask him, she thought.

'Hann? Are you listening to me? You're miles away.'

'Sorry, Ros, I was just wondering what to do about Mum. I've always had Dad haunted by heaven knows what demons but now I've got my mum as well. It seems people are so preoccupied with the external injuries, there's no one who's got any idea what's going on with the internal ones.'

Both girls were thinking of the blank expressions they came across every day in the street – the ones whose stories would probably never be told, the empty chairs, the telegrams kept in a jar on the mantelpiece, taken out at regular intervals to see if the bland words could possibly say something else that might offer hope not despair.

Ros grabbed hold of Hannah's arm and swung her around.

'Race you round the paddling pool,' she said. 'Like we used to. Let's see who can reach the other side first. Ready, steady, go!'

They both set off, laughing in relief at the pure physical exertion until they bumped into each other at the other side. They both grinned.

'I needed that,' Hannah said.

'I know,' Ros replied.

The rest of the afternoon was spent catching up on their daily lives, the ones they could never have envisaged just a few years before. They both had pride in their voices as they discussed the astonishing range of things they were being asked to do.

'Do you think we'll ever go back to being the three of us, going out on a night out in town in our glad rags with nothing else to worry about but whether we have enough money between us for a cider?' Ros asked wistfully.

Hannah stopped in her tracks.

'No,' she said, slowly, 'no, Ros, I don't think we ever will and, to be honest, I'm not sure we'll want to go. We've come such a long way. I for one don't want to go back to life as it was. I feel as if I've broken out of a chrysalis and am only just developing my wings.' She thought about the last year and barely recognised the young girl who had timidly battled her way along Norwich station platform, too scared to ask directions to Salhouse.

'Although a night out with you two . . . that *is* a night I'm looking forward to,' she laughed, grabbing Ros by the arm to march off down the path.

* * *

By the time Hannah got home, the house was in darkness. She called out, but there was no reply, so, believing both her parents had retired early to bed, she went to bank up the fire and lock the back door, but then she heard her father's voice emerging from the armchair in the corner.

'I can't take it anymore, Hannah.'

She froze, terrified by the chilling words and the bland tone in which they were uttered.

'What do you mean, Dad?' She leaned over to put the light on. He was slumped in the chair, an empty glass in his hand. On the table was a whisky bottle; that was empty too. She frowned; her father never drank.

'This.' He extended his arms to take in the dimly lit room with its blackout curtain. 'That.' He pointed through the walls to the skies outside where the bombers thundered through so regularly.

'Come on, Dad, we're all in this together,' Hannah told him, going to kneel next to this stranger who was her father, 'and we'll get some help for mum. Has she gone up by the way?'

Her father nodded then said: 'No, you don't understand. I can't look after anyone; I can't even look after myself.' He paused and then said in a whisper, 'I've seen things . . .' His voice faded.

She knew he had been a private in the Manchester Regiment and had fought in the Battle of the Somme, but, like many of his generation, he never spoke about his experiences. Until now.

She was not sure she wanted to hear what he was about to say next.

'I have to tell someone, Hannah, it's eating me up. You see, I watched them, those Germans . . . I watched them do it. I escaped from the battlefield, battered and bruised, but alive, and some Frenchies took me in. They hid me for a week in their barn – without them, I'd be one of those poppies that come up on those fields now.'

He looked up at his daughter and added, 'Do you know, Hannah, it's as if those flowers have been sent by nature to make something lovely out of all the blood that has been spilled.'

She put out her hand to stop him, but he could not.

'They were so kind. The Monsieur and his wife and . . .' he paused '. . . their little daughter. Her name was Josette, she was so beautiful with golden curls and a dimple in her cheek. She'd bring me warm milk every morning.'

He looked into Hannah's eyes but it was as if she wasn't there.

'They killed her. I saw it.'

He buried his head in his hands and sobbed. Hannah put her arms around his heaving shoulders and held tight while he let out more than twenty years of pain at his terrible secret.

After a few moments, the sobs subsided and she left him to regain his equilibrium by going to make a cup of tea for them both. By the time she came back to her kneeling position next to him, two cups and saucers in her shaking hands, he was ready to talk more. He spoke in a flat tone, staring at the wall.

'When the Monsieur heard them coming, he dashed out to tell me to hide in the woods. But he should have stayed, he should have got his wife and daughter out.' He looked at his daughter for help. She just shook her head and he continued, looking disappointed that she could not rewrite history.

'When he went back to the house, the Germans were marching his wife out through the front door. Four of them, there were, with their rifles poised to shoot. I could see them from the woods. Then little Josette appeared from behind. She screamed and ran towards her mother. A young soldier panicked and fired his gun. The bullet hit the little girl and she fell, bleeding against her mother's overalls. They had blue flowers on them,' he added, as if it were important.

'The monsieur lunged forward and the soldier fired again. Now there were two bodies on the ground. The Madame collapsed into a heap next to her dead husband and daughter, but the soldiers dragged her up and marched her off, all the time she was looking over her shoulder, trying to go back. But they would not let her. That is what I see every night in my dreams, Hannah, that woman's face contorted and grief-stricken and now I'm seeing your mum's face, just a blank registry of the pain of four years of war. I can't watch any more of it. I'm so eaten up with hatred for the Germans, I can't think. I can't live while those people . . . they saved me and now they're dead.'

He finally stopped. Hannah sat back on her heels in shock. For the first time, she saw the scene in her head that had changed her father's life. It was like seeing a horror film that she would never be able to forget.

'Have you told Mum?' she asked.

'No, I can't. It's taken that—' he pointed at the empty whisky bottle '—for me to tell you. I just couldn't hold it in any longer. It's too painful. Don't tell her, Hannah, she's not strong enough.'

I'm not sure I am, either, she thought, feeling the enormity of the responsibility her father had just thrust upon her.

Chapter 25

Christmas at the German prisoner of war camp at Mouse-hold split the prisoners. For some, it was a particularly poignant time and sniffling was heard at night as those men wrote letters to their wives, mothers or children, trying not to recall the cosy fireside meals when '*Stille Nacht*' was sung around candles and the *Weinachtsbaum* was still decorated with a star and not a sunburst as dictated by the authorities in an attempt to eradicate any connection with the Jewish religion. To compensate for not being with their own families some of them made wooden toys for the children in the village, knowing that parents would be hard-pressed to find any in the depleted local shops. It made them feel closer to their own children. But for others, the Nazi regime's propaganda that Christmas should be dismissed as a celebration of someone Jewish, resulted in them ridiculing the rest for their lack of commitment to the Führer. As a result, tensions in the huts were growing.

Karl, however, was walking around with a vague smile on his face. When he thought of Hannah, his head cleared and the haze that dulled his rational thinking processes lifted. It occurred to him that if he could blot out everything except that lovely dark-haired girl, he could be happy. He had spent his life feeling he needed to be serious – serious about becoming a doctor, serious about looking after his mother and serious about trying to prove a post-Great War Germany had more to offer the world than aggression. As every other aspect of his ambitions fell apart, some stolen moments with a young English girl had given him hope. He felt as if a big lead box he'd been carrying around all those years had opened up to reveal it was full of butterflies. A practical man, he laughed at the fanciful nature of his thoughts, but there was an undeniable bubble of joy that gurgled up from his stomach every time he thought of Hannah and he loved every moment of it. He was tempted to talk to Peter about these new feelings, but with so many rules and regulations about fraternising, he didn't want to put Hannah in any danger, so he hugged them to himself, knowing he had just a few days to wait until he saw her again for Christmas mass.

Peter watched Karl hanging up some paper decorations and wondered whether the head injury was prompting some long-term effects. The man was humming for heaven's sake!

Peter tried to talk to Karl but had received nothing but a mischievous grin in return, so he shrugged and passed over more paper chains for Karl to string up above their bunks.

Karl and Peter's separation from the rest was facilitated by their knowledge of English. They'd already been accused of being 'enemy lovers' and 'traitors' by the more right-wing members of the group, but there was one advantage they both had and they used it to the full. Neither of them smoked and cigarettes were the most valuable currency in a German POW camp. The farmer was paid four pounds ten shillings a week for each prisoner but by the time they deducted their bed and board, the final salary for the German men was just five shillings, which they could only spend within the prisoner of war camp. That meant cigarettes became a valuable currency and Karl and Peter had control of a 'black market' supply of them, which kept them safe from room-mates who would willingly barter bits of food, clothing or magazines for the tobacco products.

* * *

On Christmas morning, Karl had never been more grateful that he had 'currency' he could use to bargain with as twenty cigarettes 'bought' him a smarter jacket from a new prisoner. He brushed his hair carefully and wet his palm to flatten down the stubborn fringe that flopped into his eyes. He had bartered another few cigarettes to get a tortoiseshell slide that a fellow prisoner had been keeping as a memento of his girlfriend, until he got the letter telling him she was going to marry someone else. Karl fingered the slide lovingly, imagining Hannah's face when she saw it and checked the time to see how long he had to wait until he would see that guileless smile.

An hour later, Karl was pacing outside the guard's hut. There was no sign of Hannah or even of Stanley. A shiver of fear shot up his back. Something was wrong.

'Do you know where the guard, Stanley, is?' he politely asked the soldier standing in the doorway. Bad-tempered at having to work Christmas morning, the soldier shrugged. 'Or the young Fräulein?' Karl ventured nervously.

'Should think she's got better things to do at Christmas than take a Kraut like you to church,' he guffawed. 'Been stood up 'ave you? Better take you back to your 'ut then.'

Karl had no idea what 'stood up' meant but he knew what it felt like and after insisting he should wait another half an hour, he sadly walked back behind the guard and into the hut, glaring at the pathetic attempts to make it festive. He grabbed some of the paper chains he'd so patiently made and pulled them down towards him, crumpling them fiercely in his hand.

Karl looked around the fifty or so tiered bunks that surrounded him and swore at the incongruous way he was having to spend Christmas. In the middle were two stoves fed by the allowance of coal each man got, but the supplies always seemed to run out by Wednesday. Their beds were folded back, with one blanket folded inside the other, spare shoes were cleaned and placed sole up against the folded mattresses. The towels were folded on the mesh at the end with a plate and cutlery on top of each, and down the middle between the stoves were two tables and four benches. Damp washing was strung up next to the remaining paper chains and the two sixty watt bulbs they were permitted for the whole hut cast nothing more than a dim glow. Even with the strewn garlands, it looked nothing like his own home would have looked on a Christmas morning and he closed his eyes to try and imagine the red checked tablecloth, the holly in a vase and the tempting stollen that would be waiting on the sideboard for the festive feast. He frowned, the image of his family's farm was getting increasingly blurred around the edges and the familiar panic started to rise.

Peter was placing his socks on the line next to his bed. He looked up in surprise. 'No church?' Karl gave a curt, '*Nein*,' and Peter took the hint and very quickly changed the subject. 'I don't think these look like Christmas decorations,' he said retreating into speaking German to his friend, 'but at least we get socks. Do you remember those *Fußlappen?* Those bits of cloth were so bad, they moved on your feet and then, oh, the blisters.'

Karl opened his eyes to look at the dripping socks. They never managed to dry properly and there was a constant drip onto the wooden floor below that seemed to mesmerise him. He vaguely heard Peter determinedly talking about how strange it was that some members of the Wehrmacht were not issued with socks and how there were so many things to be grateful for as a prisoner of war. Peter's optimism was a thin mask for the homesickness he was feeling. That morning he had almost wished they had not been given the day off work; idleness left too much time for reflection and left him with a gnawing pain that he was so far away from his beloved Helga.

But Karl's brain was like a swirling eddy in a deep pool. Every worry that had been tormenting him since he was captured seemed to suddenly engulf him and he slumped down on his bunk. A German who loved his country, he was completely conflicted in his loyalties. The regular films that were shown to the POWs about the atrocities of the Nazis were dismissed by many of his fellow prisoners as fabricated propaganda, but he, like Peter, would bow his head in shame at the images that were put on the screen before him. His family had always had an enormous affection for England, encouraged by the priests in the town who had taught both him and his sister to speak the language. He thought back to the cosy evenings on the farm, when two of the priests had talked in glowing terms about the beautiful landscape of the countryside around their seminary at Oscott College near Birmingham, chuckling at the strange English sense of humour and the fact that nobody seemed to mind that the buses rarely came on time.

Karl clasped his head to block out the questions that were flooding into his brain. What had happened to

Hannah? Had he imagined she felt something for him? Why did he feel there was something terribly wrong? These led on to the other questions that he wrestled with every day: would he ever be able to hold his head up again as a German and lastly, and with crushing insistence, the one that had been haunting him for so long: were any of his family still alive?

He stood up, wobbled, and walked out of the damp hut where he breathed in the fresh morning air and meandered across the camp like a sleepwalker. Prisoners were not supposed to be out of their huts without a guard, but Karl had no idea what he was doing and he walked in a wavy line towards the perimeter fence.

'Halt!' a voice cried from the scaffolding around the water tower.

Karl looked up in surprise, suddenly coming to out of his reverie. *How had he got here?* He had no recollection of walking out of the hut and was astonished to see Peter running towards him, his hands in the air.

'Don't shoot, don't shoot, I take him back.'

He grabbed hold of Karl and yanked him back towards the dark hut at the end of the tarmac.

He pulled him inside the hut and turned round to face his friend. In a furious tirade of rapid German, he accused Karl of trying to get them both killed.

Karl looked confused and staggered towards his bunk. Sometimes his head ached so much it was hard to think.

He curled up on the bed and pulled the covers around himself and went immediately to sleep.

* * *

The next morning, Karl could not get out of bed. Peter gave up trying to get any sense out of him and went reluctantly to inform the Lagerführer, who was the commandant they all feared. The sharp footsteps of his boots resounded just a few minutes later, echoing throughout the Nissan hut. All the men stood to attention at the side to let him pass, looking straight ahead to avoid his piercing look, which scanned the lines of prisoners. He stopped at the end of Karl's bed with his arms folded. Karl tried to sit up, but his head swam and he had to lie back down again. The commandant looked down his nose at the prisoner in front of him, disgusted that here was another one who failed to live up to the high standards of health and resilience of the Wehrmacht. He had no time for weakness and stalked back out of the hut, deciding that the English guard could deal with this one; he had better things to do with his time. He found Stanley standing casually by the truck, having a cigarette, before he had to take those damned prisoners over to the farm. The German commandant curtly told him one of the men seemed a little ill and walked off. Stanley slowly went over to the hut, cursing the responsibility that had been laid at his door to take care of these POWs. He found Peter leaning over Karl with a concerned look on his face.

'Hmm, I suppose he does look a bit pale,' he said with a certain satisfaction. This German had already caused him so much trouble and if he fell ill, Stanley, for one, would be delighted.

'But there's no reason why he shouldn't work,' Stanley said. 'He'll be fine. He just needs some fresh air and a day fixing fences at the farm'll sort that out.'

He then turned towards Peter. 'Get him in the truck, we leave in five minutes.'

Peter gave a concerned glance at his friend and reluctantly gathered up both their coats to get Karl out to the truck. He helped his friend onto the back of the wagon, Karl's legs giving way like jelly while he looked around, as if trying to recognise where he was. Peter placed him next to the tailboard, making the others shuffle up to give him room, and was about to get in next to him when Stanley grabbed his arm, shoving him into the front nearside seat. 'You can watch the ditches at the side,' Stanley told him, 'I can't see a bloody thing in this.' Peter looked reluctantly back at his friend. He didn't like to leave him but he hoped the cold air would revive him.

Stanley got in the front and started the engine. He looked around and took a mental count to make sure they were all there and propped his gun up on the seat next to him. That Schneider at the back looked ghostly white, but Stanley didn't care. As far as he was concerned, if he dropped dead it would just mean one less Kraut to deal with.

The regular morning journey to the farm might as well have been a trip to the moon as far as Karl was concerned. He gazed out at the grey mist covering the familiar fields and roads but failed to register any of it. He had no recognition of where he was going and looked at the tarmac beneath the wheels as if the ground led to a precipice into the unknown. Stanley was swearing in the front. He was in a bad mood and was suffering from a severe hangover from Christmas celebrations and he didn't need this thick fog. His eyes narrowed as he tried to concentrate. Peter shouted instructions about how near the ditches were and, while clinging on to the side window frame, he nervously urged Stanley to drive very, very slowly. When the truck stopped at a junction, Karl stepped out over the back of the wagon and started walking. Just walking.

The truck full of German prisoners disappeared into the distance, leaving the men inside staring after Karl's retreating back, the driver unaware he had lost one passenger.

Chapter 26

There were no signs on the roads but even if there had been Karl would not have seen them. His mind felt like it was full of the smog that shrouded the countryside and not a single, rational thought was going through his brain. He simply put one foot in front of the other and walked towards the horizon.

A bicycle went past, ringing its bell in warning as he suddenly appeared out of the grey smog in the middle of the road. The young rider looked back over his shoulder at the strange man in a pair of brown overalls with round patches on them. The boy was only thirteen, but it gradually dawned on him that he might just have seen a German POW. His heart pounding, he started to pedal twice as fast, despite his inability to see more than fifty yards in front of him, his mind racing through the options. If he told his mum, she would panic, then he thought of the butcher, Mr Lewis; he was in the Home Guard and would know what to do. Young Walter suddenly sat higher in his saddle as his feet circled faster and faster. It occurred to him that he could become a hero. That would teach those bullies at school, he thought with satisfaction.

Karl walked on, oblivious, for about three miles but then it started to rain. Feeling the drips falling onto his head, he looked up at the heavens. Touching the drops of water that were dribbling down his collar, he tried desperately to concentrate. *Where the hell was he? What was he doing here? How did he get here?*

Karl sat down on a rock at the side of the road and put his head in his hands. He shook it from side to side in an attempt to clear it and then touched the rock next to him hoping it would connect him with reality. His fingers grasped the freezing cold stone and, slowly but surely, that grip helped to ground him back in the present. That was it! He had stepped out of the truck! But why?

The initial panic was gradually suppressed by the calm doctor in him and he tried to think rationally about what had just happened. He had a vague memory, like someone waking from a dream, of setting off for work in the truck but . . . he searched through his mind for something that might help him, but he couldn't remember anything after that. He shook himself. He hated these episodes, they left him feeling weak and foolish but, he realised, peering down the road, they put him in danger too.

Then it came to him; he had had it in his mind to try to get to King's Lynn to find his sister.

'What a ridiculous idea,' he said to himself but then thought for a moment. There were so many times since Hannah had unwittingly told him that King's Lynn was to the north-west of Salhouse that he had peered over the horizon working out which direction that was. Maybe this was his answer. He was already in dreadful trouble and was desperate to find out information about his family. Could he risk it? Could he find his way to King's Lynn in a German POW uniform, without any money, and on a cold December day?

A feeling of excitement bubbled up inside him and he suddenly felt better. These episodes were coming more frequently but, once they cleared, it was as if he had extra clarity. He had felt so powerless recently, in the control of others; he couldn't help it, he grinned broadly, becoming once again the young lad who would head off into the countryside around his home, with a piece of bread for dinner, with no idea where he was going.

He needed to think his plan through, but, hearing a vehicle in the distance, he raced behind a hedge into a field where in front of him he spotted a dark shadow looming out of the gloom. He felt his heart start to race, wondering if a farmer was about to put an end to his escapade but then, as the mist swirled, he realised the figure was actually an abandoned scarecrow wearing, if he wasn't mistaken, a very fetching plaid shirt and jacket, cord trousers and a tweed cap on its head.

Karl ducked down behind the hawthorn hedge to let the car go past. It was driving slowly, like Stanley had, nervously navigating the narrow lane and unaware that there was a POW hiding behind the hedge. Karl suddenly remembered the young cyclist and worked out that he had only about another half an hour before the boy would get to the town and potentially raise the alarm, so as soon as the car had vanished into the gloom, he ran towards the scarecrow and quickly relieved it of its clothes. He took off his telltale overalls and put the scarecrow's clothes on, then headed back to the hedge where he scooped out soil under the branches and buried the uniform in a hole. Thinking better of it, he dug the uniform out again. It was December and he was going to need every item of clothing to keep warm. Then he sat back on his heels, the soiled garments rolled up in his hands. This was premeditated escape. Did the Brits shoot escaped prisoners? he wondered. When he had just stepped off the truck he could have cited his illness as a reason, but once he had changed into different clothes, the escape seemed planned.

At that moment, he heard an old military vehicle approaching, rattling as it too travelled at a slow speed to avoid ending up in a ditch at the side of the road. He ducked down again, grateful for the driver's focus on the road. Behind the wheel was an older man in uniform, huddled against the cold in the open vehicle. Karl assumed he was a member of the Home Guard. He wondered whether the man could possibly have been alerted to Karl's presence so quickly and crouched down further to keep out of sight.

Once the road was clear, Karl looked around him. He knew he had come from the left so he peered into the distance to the right and tried desperately to remember where he was now in relation to Salhouse. Weighing up the terrain, he was glad to see a mixture of fields and woods, which would give him cover, but he would be visible in daylight. Following the inside edge of the field, Karl came across a pond and scooped some water up in his hands, realising how thirsty he was. He shivered; it was cold and the fog was penetrating the scarecrow's tweed jacket. He had to find some shelter while he worked out what he was going to do.

As the afternoon wore on, he felt overcome with weariness so headed towards some woods to his left. By the time the sun was going down, he was becoming increasingly hungry. Food was going to be his main problem; foraging in the woods in Germany in the summer was a very different proposition from scouring the land here in winter for anything to sustain him. He thought rationally; some sloes or, if he took the seeds out, rosehips would help. If only he had something to trap a rabbit or, he thought dejectedly, a knife to skin it. He ruefully wished he had thought about this a little more. In front of him were some pine trees and he bent to collect as many seeds as possible. Working on the principle that a little of each of these gifts from the land would not cause too many problems, he stuffed a few gratefully into his mouth, keeping the rest for later. He wished he had that book on survival he'd borrowed from the library as an obsessive twelve-year-old. It had been full of information that could save his life.

Karl scanned the horizon and almost jumped for joy when he spotted a field of turnips. He checked to make sure no one was watching and ran to the edge of the field where he pocketed a few of the bulbous roots. Now, all he needed were some shrivelled dandelion leaves and, with a bit of luck, he might survive a week.

He started to gather some branches, weaving the evergreen foliage between the twigs to make a shelter, then folded the POW uniform into a sort of pillow and lay back with his arms behind his head, listening to the crows above. He felt a strange peace and just before he fell asleep he decided that whatever happened next, it had been worth it to have this moment.

When he woke, it was night-time. He stood up, scattered the shelter then relieved himself in the hedge and headed off into the unknown.

* * *

Karl found he was rather good at being a fugitive. He walked by night and rested by day and, with a mental image of where King's Lynn was, he kept heading north-west, keeping a firm eye on any sun that might appear during daylight hours to allow him to plot his course for the following night. However, after yet another foggy day, he looked from right to left but had no idea which way to go. He thought back to his schooldays when he had watched his classmates pore over maps with compasses to prepare for Hitler Youth challenges. Intrigued, Karl had gone home and mithered his family until, on his fourteenth birthday, he was proudly presented with a cleaned-up old compass by his brother, Werner. After that Karl disappeared every Saturday with his faithful dog Britta by his side, roaming the countryside around his home, compass in hand. He would ask one of his brothers to pick a place about five miles away and would then set off to find it. How he wished he had that compass now.

'I know!' he said suddenly. 'All I need to do is find a needle.' He looked around him as if one was suddenly going to present itself to him out of thin air. Karl shook his head at his own stupidity, but then remembered his mother's wise words: there are no such things as problems, just solutions waiting to be found. He wracked his brains.

He needed to find somewhere to stay for the night so made a decision and turned left, but after walking for a few minutes, it did not feel right. In this relentless fog, Karl knew he could be going round in circles so he stopped to give his tired brain time to think, putting the tweed cap down next to him. Karl scrabbled in the earth and was delighted to find some withered leaves of sorrel that he chewed slowly to extract as much juice as he could, but they hardly touched the gnawing pangs in his stomach. He unearthed the squashed leaves of hairy bittercress he'd found earlier and stuffed those into his mouth too, but he knew he had to find some real food . . . and soon. He sighed and picked up the hat again, automatically turning it on his head so that the badge was at the front.

That was it! The badge, he thought excitedly. He peered at the back of it, and yes, it was fastened with a pin! He carefully wrenched the straight pin off the metal of the rim, noticing the insignia on the badge which proclaimed: For Home and Country. Unaware of the elderly woman who had smilingly enlisted the scarecrow into the Women's Institute, it did not occur to him how horrified she would have been to know her joke was going to help a German prisoner of war; he just hoped this badge could lead him to his sister. He fingered the yellow silk scarf all the Luftwaffe had been issued with that he still wore around his neck. It had been introduced to the uniform so that downed airmen could signal for help, but today it was going to save his life in another way.

He stood up, reasoned that he had a fifty-fifty chance of heading in the right direction and set off. Every hour he was on the loose, the danger increased and he found himself nervously checking behind him every few minutes. As he walked, he scanned the ditches for a receptacle and could not believe his luck when he found an old tin can, casually discarded in the hedgerow. Now he needed some water, and not just for his experiment, he thought; water was the only thing keeping him alive right now. He walked the edge of the fields but found nothing but dark, murky ditch water.

Just before dawn, he came across a small village. He normally avoided any signs of habitation, but he was getting desperate. The hamlet was still in darkness as all its good citizens obeyed the blackout regulations, but, at that moment, a milk cart and horse turned a corner at the top of the street. Karl felt a shiver of excitement; he hated the idea of stealing but the chances of him surviving on just seeds and a couple of turnips were frighteningly low, so he hid quickly in a doorway and waited until the whistling milkman had placed his deliveries on a few of the doorsteps. Karl watched until the cart had turned into the next street then ran to the nearest house and picked up the bottle of liquid gold. He drank the milk down quickly, feeling its goodness swish around in his empty stomach and put the empty bottle in his pocket, thinking it might be useful if he ever found any clean water. He turned around to see a dog in a wooden kennel outside the next house, watching him with envy.

'Shhh, *sei ruhig*, shhh, *es ist gut*.' He did not need this dog to bark.

The dog started to wag its tail, deciding a gently spoken visitor was a welcome change during a boring night in a kennel. Karl approached the animal slowly, murmuring reassuring noises and knelt down to reach through its little doorway to stroke it. The dog, which was tied with a rough piece of rope, immediately fell onto its back and rolled over in the hope of being tickled. Karl obliged, looking round the inside of the kennel as he did. He was delighted to spot a bowl of water and, squatting next to the dog, still rubbing its tummy, he used the milk bottle to scoop up as much as he could. With one last pat and a silent apology for taking all the dog's water, he started to slink as quietly as he could away from the houses. He looked back at the dog, who was following his new friend with wistful eyes. For a brief moment, Karl considered taking the dog with him for company but knew that it would be more of a liability, and he certainly wouldn't be able to find enough food for both of them. He blew a kiss back to his saviour, getting a wag of the dog's tail in response.

The taste of the milk had made his stomach rumble and he looked round desperately. Next to the last house was a shed. He made his way noiselessly towards it and gently lifted the latch. It was open. Breathing a sigh of relief, he peered inside. On the wooden racks were some apples from the previous autumn. Being careful to take just enough not to leave an obvious space, he crammed as many as he could into his pockets and peered into the darkness at the rest of the shelves. He could not believe his luck when he saw some walnuts stashed in a corner. He took some of those too and silently closed the door behind him, feeling like a pirate who had found treasure.

As dawn broke, Karl excitedly walked towards a spot in a field far from prying eyes and looked longingly at the last dregs of water in his milk bottle. He was going to have to save it for his 'compass' if he was ever going to make his way successfully to King's Lynn, but it was not easy to walk, holding the open-topped vessel with the sloshing liquid inside like a precious trophy in front of him. He found an upturned log that he nestled down behind and took hold of the pin with one hand and rubbed it vigorously with the silk scarf until he could almost feel the static electricity. He just hoped the pin wasn't too thick. He plucked a leaf from the ground beneath him and laid the pin carefully on some water he'd put in the bottom of the tin can. It swung round to point to his right. He looked up at the leaden sky to try to gauge where the sun might be hiding.

'*Verdammt!*' he exclaimed. He had walked all night towards the south when King's Lynn was to the north-west. He lay back in despair.

Chapter 27

Hannah arrived back at Norwich station after the quietest Christmas she had ever had. Despite her best efforts, she could only manage to provide a 'murkey' – a mix of sausage and onion with parsnips for legs – which was a sorry excuse for Christmas dinner and didn't come close to the plump turkeys of previous years. Her mother had hardly engaged at all with the Christmas jokes Hannah had read from *The People's Friend* and her father's valiant efforts to interest his wife in a game of Snap had received nothing but a blank stare.

Hannah felt guilty but was relieved when it was time to leave for Salhouse Farm. She fell asleep on the journey back, only to wake with a jolt when the train juddered to a halt at her stop. She was astonished to find the station swarming with police and military and pushed her way through the crowds, who were standing nervously on the platform, until her way was barred by a soldier with a gun.

'What's going on?' she asked the woman next to her.

The woman, who was carrying two shopping baskets, shrugged. 'Something about an escaped prisoner of war,' she said. 'But it's holding me up. I need to get home with this veg. My sister saved it special for me. I've even got a nice swede.'

Hannah edged her way past the woman, vaguely wondering which camp the prisoner had come from, but then she had to run to catch the bus, so quickly forgot all about the drama. As the bus rattled along, she was too preoccupied with thoughts of her parents to worry about a random POW. Her parents were like those figures on a Swiss clock she'd seen once, she thought, where one figure came out while the other one went back in. She had been extremely worried by the state of her mother, but the major shock had been her father's revelation. It had taken a few days after the devastating conversation but she started noticing a difference in him. It was strange, but once he had unburdened himself, it was as if he could start to reclaim the man he used to be. It started with him making his wife a cup of tea, which he tenderly placed in her hand, helping her to lift it to her mouth to drink. He stood back with pride, looking at Hannah for praise. She smiled at him approvingly and then beckoned to him to follow her into the kitchen, where she showed him how to make a potato stew and boil some scrag end to get them through the week.

Just before Hannah left, she wrote a letter to Mrs Mullins, telling her about how the situation in the house had changed and what had caused those changes. She knew she could rely on her to call round to keep an eye on things and, for the first time, she felt a growing confidence that she could depend on her father too. At teatime on the last day, Hannah had prepared some scones, and as she gathered up her bag, her father was smiling at his wife and buttering one for her. Hannah went over to give her mother a hug, but all she could feel were the bones of her ribcage and although she made a brave effort to smile, Hannah experienced a deep disquiet. Then she felt a pat on her arm from her dad. He was nodding reassuringly at her, and as she made her way towards the front door, he took her into the front room instead and closed the door.

'I've been a terrible father, and a terrible husband,' he said, his head hanging down. 'I was so bound up with my anger and guilt I failed to see what was happening to your mum. I don't know how I could have let this happen, Hannah.'

He looked so forlorn, she reached forward and wrapped her arms around him. For a second, his body felt frail too but then he raised his head, put his shoulders back and said, 'Don't you worry, lass, I'll deal with this. You get back to that farm. It sounds like you've got enough on your plate.'

He looked closely at his daughter, registering the bloom on her cheeks and how her young frame had developed a robustness and a strength.

'Ee, lass, I'm that proud of you,' he said, his eyes misting over. 'You've always been such a clever girl, but now you've got so many new skills, I'm almost in awe of you.'

Hannah broke the tension by laughing. 'I doubt that, Dad, but it's so good to see you getting strong again.'

'I make a promise to you here and now,' Alf Compton said solemnly, 'I will never let you or your mum down again and I'll do everything in my power to get her well again.'

Hannah leaned her head on his shoulder and tried not to cry.

* * *

When Hannah got back to Salhouse, it all looked reassuringly familiar. The butcher's, the Bell Inn, the post office. She walked casually back to the farm, but was alarmed to see two soldiers guarding the entrance. There were many other farms where POWs had been brought in to work, surely the escaped prisoner wasn't one of theirs? Her immediate thought was for Karl. She hoped he was all right.

She ran up the drive and straight up to the girls' bedroom, her heart in her mouth. Dotty and Lavinia jumped up when they saw her.

'Oh, you're back. How was Christmas?' Dotty asked, but then not waiting for an answer, she went on excitedly, 'Hannah, guess what? Your brave rescuer has done a runner.'

'What . . .' Hannah stammered, her chest constricting.

'That German, the one who rescued you from Hercules, he's vanished.'

Hannah's face looked stricken and Lavinia looked sharply at her. Dotty was chattering on enthusiastically. It was the most sensational thing to have happened in weeks.

'The boss is furious and Stanley's in terrible trouble,' she went on.

Hannah focused her attention. 'Stanley?' she asked.

'Yes, he was driving them all to work but apparently your hero was behaving oddly and then just jumped out of the truck and made a run f—'

Dotty didn't have time to finish as Hannah butted in, her heart thumping. 'Behaving oddly? Why, what was the matter with him?'

'Oh, I don't know. Apparently he was having some sort of blackout, so who knows. Everyone's saying the rest of the Germans in the truck managed to keep it quiet for hours and covered for him to give him a chance to get as far away as possible.'

Dotty looked at her watch.

'Bloody hell, the cows! I've got to go. Roll on that new milking machine. I can't wait for that to arrive.' And with that, she grabbed her overalls off the back of the door and raced out of the room.

There was silence for a moment then Lavinia said, 'OK, Hannah. Tell all.'

Hannah looked at her in horror. Surely she hadn't guessed? She looked at the knowing face of the tall blonde girl and crumpled in a heap on the bed. Of course she'd guessed. Hannah's face was an open book.

Lavinia came over and curled up next to her. She laid her hand on Hannah's.

'You can tell me, Hann. I have so many secrets locked up in here . . .' she patted her heart '. . . there's room for one more.'

Hannah burst into tears. The tension of holding in her feelings for all these weeks had been so intense, and although she had tried to concentrate on her tasks, her parents and Ros, the whole time there was a part of her that was thinking about Karl. His face haunted her dreams and she spent her days imagining a world when two young people from different countries could maybe be lovers, rather than enemies.

'I can't. I can't. I just can't.'

'Yes, you can. I'm not going to judge you. Are you in love with him?'

'Oh, I don't know, Lav. Maybe. I don't know. I can't be. He's a German.'

'I think you'll find he's an extremely attractive young man first,' Lavinia said, smiling.

'But it's forbidden,' Hannah said weakly.

'Everything's forbidden. I can't love a married man; you can't love a German. It seems we're a right pair.'

In a wave of solidarity, the two girls hugged each other.

Chapter 28

Hercules nuzzled Hannah as she tried to take his harness off after she had used him to help move some logs. She was all fingers and thumbs and the large horse seemed to sense her disquiet. She leaned her head into his flank, feeling his warmth and strength and put her arms around his neck.

'Oh Hercules, I'm in such a mess.'

The tears started to flow, and once she'd started, Hannah couldn't stop crying. She flopped against the reassuring solidity of the shire horse and, one by one, the thoughts that were swirling around like a maelstrom in her head came gushing out of her mouth. She needed to speak them out loud and the sympathetic gaze from the horse's big brown eyes was as comforting to her as any human listener . . . and a good deal safer.

'You see, Hercules, my mum's just not coping and although my dad's finally managing to face the world, I feel so guilty all the time. I should be there. I don't know what to do.'

The horse made a whinnying sound and Hannah looked up suspiciously. It was almost as if this animal understood every word she was saying.

She glanced around the empty stable and whispered, 'And there's another thing ... I think I've fallen for a German.'

To actually speak the words terrified her because they made the whole situation more real.

She'd felt unable to say any more to Lavinia, it was all too raw, but the situation had, for the first time, made her face up to the fact that she had feelings for Karl. But every time she thought about it, she just despaired at the impossibility of it all. For a British girl to fall in love with a German was the ultimate betrayal. Her father would be horrified, she knew all the men on the farm would condemn her and she suspected Dotty, with her forthright views, would hate her as well. And then there were the authorities ... She groaned. She knew the penalties for fraternising were bad enough, but they must be so much worse for having a romantic relationship with an escaped prisoner of war.

The sudden thought of Karl lying dead in a ditch came to her. Then a vision of him in front of a firing squad. She started to sob again and slid down the wall to the floor. She had no idea what they did with escaped prisoners, it was such a rare occurrence in Britain.

At that moment, Jed came into the stable.

'What the hell are you doing, girl?'

Hannah scrabbled to her feet and, after brushing her tear-stained face with her sleeve, she started to pull the straps from around Hercules's girth.

'NOTHING, Jed, I'm just unharnessing him to get him ready for grooming.'

Jed took one look at her distraught face and seized his opportunity. He moved in behind her and took hold of her hand on the harness.

'Here, let me.'

Hannah jumped as if she'd been burned, but Jed's arm was strong. He turned her to face him, putting his other hand on her breast. His eyes were bright with desire. This little miss was such a tasty morsel and she was such a quiet little thing, she wouldn't cause him any problems, he was sure.

Hannah tried to struggle free, but he held her fast, pinning her against the horse with his shoulder while his other hand went down to try to unfasten her breeches. She tried to use one leg to brush his large, hairy hand away but he held on, fiddling furiously with her buttons.

'Ah yes, you see, I knew you wanted it,' he said, beginning to pant, moving his other hand to unbuckle his belt. He pushed her down and she yelped as her head hit the ground. Jed was strong, the product of many years of farming, and she could hardly breathe. He started to pull at her trousers until they ripped, leaving her knickers exposed.

His excitement rose and he reached into his trousers with a grunt of triumph.

Hannah suddenly erupted into fury. She was no longer the timid little girl who needed to be saved.

'Get off me this minute or I'll tell the boss,' she said, and she brought her knee sharply up to Jed's crotch, making him fold in two in agony.

'Tell the boss what?' A voice came from the barn door.

Hannah looked over Jed's shoulder to see Andrew Hollis standing there, silhouetted against the light. He had his arms folded and his face was the colour of stone.

He quickly looked from Jed to Hannah and very quietly he said, 'Move away from her, Jed. *Now!*'

Jed staggered backwards, desperately trying to do up his fly buttons as Andrew Hollis moved forward towards Hannah. He held out his hand to help her up.

'Oh, my dear, are you all right?' Then he looked at Jed, whose face was purple from a mixture of pain and embarrassment.

Andrew caught sight of Hannah's fierce face as she pulled her breeches back into place. It contrasted sharply with Jed's and, despite the fury he felt, he almost smiled at the strength of character in this young girl. Jed, meantime, was struggling with intense discomfort as well as rage at being caught.

'Well, I'm glad to see you seem to be in better shape than your attacker,' Andrew said with relief. 'Jed, in my office in five minutes!' Once Jed had staggered out, Andrew gave his whole attention to Hannah, putting his hand on her shoulder to scan her face. 'Are you really all right?'

'Yes.' She thought for a moment; she should have been shaking after such a dreadful experience but she found she was completely calm, just incredibly indignant. 'Actually, do you know what, Boss, I am.'

'Well, good for you, Hannah.' He looked with admiration at the young woman in front of him, thinking back to the terrified girl who had joined his farm all those months ago. 'If you're sure you're OK, I'll go and see Jed Roberts.' His face clouded over into a frown and, patting Hannah on the arm, he walked with determiniation out of the barn.

Andrew Hollis had come back from the Great War with his feelings locked up very firmly in a drawer that he seemed unable to find the key to. His daughter, Bobby, who had joined the Air Transport Auxiliary, seemed determined to thwart him on every decision he made. Unable to let his guard down to reconnect with his daughter, he had felt a deep, protective anger when he saw Jed on top of Hannah. That righteous indignation had burst through his reserve and, for the first time since 1918, he saw a glimmer of the man he used to be. That vision gave him a little glow of pleasure and a hope that perhaps, one day, he might be able to let his wife and daughter back into his life.

Hannah went back to grooming Hercules, finding that the rhythmic stroking of his flank quelled her constricted breathing.

'That'll teach that horrible creep not to mess with Hannah Compton,' she told the horse. 'I'm no longer a pushover, and do you know what, Hercules, I *am* strong enough to deal with all this.'

She started to brush his gleaming coat with confident and purposeful strokes. The horse nodded his head as if agreeing with her.

* * *

Jed was livid. The boss had been unequivocal in his condemnation and disgust at the man standing with his head bowed in front of him. He didn't mince his words when telling Jed that, in normal times, he would have been out on his ear without a penny. Andrew Hollis was furious that he was unable to sack his under-foreman because the Ministry of Agriculture had demanded that British farmers should produce an extra 84,000 tons of wheat and he was struggling for farmhands. He'd battled to keep the men he had, especially George, who had fought so hard against being classified as a reserved occupation worker, anxious not to be seen as a 'shirker'. Like everyone else on the farm, he assumed George's affection for Dotty had diverted his attention, but he knew nothing of George's other work and his nocturnal escapades. Andrew weighed up the situation on the farm: the Land Army girls and, he hated to acknowledge, the prisoners too, were helping, but he needed every pair of hands. He had no choice but to keep Jed, however, he took great pleasure in demoting him.

He called the rest of the men into his office and, to Jed's squirming embarrassment, filled them in on the events in the stable, announcing: 'John will take over as under-foreman and will therefore now be in charge of the girls. This is as a result of Jed's appalling attack on Hannah,' he explained blandly. 'That means your pay is cut,' he said, turning to Jed and watching with delight as the man glowered at him. Andrew wished he had been able to do more to punish this odious man and looked down at his paperwork to indicate the discussion was at an end but then, as Jed started to slink out, he added, 'But if I ever see you anywhere near those girls again, make no mistake, I won't hesitate in getting the police involved.'

At that point, Jed bristled. He did not need the police to be involved, he had had enough of that ten years ago when he'd moved to Norfolk to escape the gossips, and he had no intention of having to move on again.

Chapter 29

That night, as the girls curled up on their beds, the room was quiet. Dotty had Enid Blyton's book, *The Enchanted Wood*, in front of her, which she was slowly reading, mouthing the words. Lavinia was pretending to write a letter to see if her grandmother would intervene in the stalemate between her and her parents, but the writing paper remained on her knee and she'd picked up some mending instead.

Hannah took a deep breath. 'Jed tried to rape me today,' she said as casually as she could.

Dotty fell off the other side of the bed where she had been perching, landing on the floor with a thump. Lavinia pricked her finger with the needle she was using to unsuccessfully darn her socks, and swore, putting the bloodied end of her finger in her mouth. Dotty's head appeared over the top of the bed.

'He tried to do what?' she stammered.

Hannah looked affectionately at the pale face that was peering over the bedclothes. Dotty was aghast. Hannah held out her hand to help Dotty climb back onto the bed.

'He thought he could get away with it, but the boss came in just after I'd kneed him in the groin.' Hannah gave a weak smile. She was putting a brave face on it, but after her initial feeling of triumph, her mind had constantly replayed the whole, horrendous episode and she had come to the conclusion that the only thing that had saved her had been the arrival of Andrew Hollis. The image that kept coming back to haunt her was of Jed's expression changing to one of pure venom when she fought back. The way he narrowed his eyes made her realise this man was capable of anything and that made her shiver to remember. It led her to the undeniable conclusion that, thanks to the boss, she had had a lucky escape.

Lavinia put her sewing down. Her face was a mixture of horror and understanding, and when she saw Hannah's brave little face, she felt like crying. She knew what men could be like and had learned early on in her chequered career that a few well-placed moves were more effective than any tears or pleading. Then she remembered something she had seen on her way back from the fields.

'That explains it,' she said.

The other two sat up, expectantly.

'I saw Jed coming out of the boss's office. He looked furious. Oh, I hope he's been given the sack. That would be real justice.'

Dotty fingered the edge of the green eiderdown. This was all too familiar to her.

Lavinia leaned forward and said to Hannah, 'Did you really get him in the nuts?'

Hannah blushed; she had never used such terms, but she nodded sheepishly. 'I . . . fought him but then the boss came in, thankfully.'

'Well good for you, Hann. Jed's a bastard and deserves to have more than just a knee in his groin. He obviously thought you were easy prey. That'll teach him. You're not the pushover you might once have been.' She clapped her hands together in delight.

Hannah looked up, registering the awe in Lavinia's voice. The old Hannah, she knew, would have retreated into her shell, but Lavinia's faith in her gave her the hope that she might actually have the strength to put the ordeal behind her.

'We've all changed so much since we first came here,' Lavinia went on. 'Don't you think, Dotty?'

Dotty gave a slight tilt of her head and continued to look down at the bedcover. She didn't know how to respond, but, fortunately, Lavinia didn't notice her reticence; she was in full flow.

'I'm so proud of you, Hann. You know when I first met you, I thought you were, well, to tell the truth, a bit of a wet blanket, but I've never seen anyone change as much as you have over the last few months.'

She paused for a moment and then addressed both Hannah and Dotty with a serious look on her face.

'You've both taught me so much. This life wasn't an choice for me, I was told it was either the Land Army or they would marry me off to an old colonel with bad breath. I was so furious, I can't tell you. I felt this life was, oh dear, Dotty, you're going to hate me for this, sort of beneath me, but you two have taught me that there's no dignity in being rich and superior but there is in working really hard with the land and the animals despite, let's be honest, the worst weather, the worst foreman and the worst pay.'

She burst out laughing and Hannah joined in, feeling slightly better, and, finally, Dotty started to grin too, relieved that the subject had been changed. Lavinia leaned over and tickled Dotty, who writhed and giggled, and, after a few seconds, the two of them were rolling around on the bed in hysterics.

As Dotty tried to get up, Lavinia somehow managed to topple her back down so that she was pinned with her arms behind her.

'Don't forget I was a wrestler,' she said from a position above Dotty's prone body.

A muffled voice from the bedclothes said, 'I'd like to learn that move.'

Lavinia got up, letting her victim go, and stood with her arms folded at the end of the bed.

'OK,' she said. 'I'll teach you. It won't do either of you any harm to know how to fend off an attacker. You, particularly, Hannah, pay attention.'

The girls spent the next hour learning how to do a sling-shot, a chokeslam and a monkey flip. They thumped and fell around the room causing the lightshade above the bed to wobble. Lavinia was surprisingly adept at the moves, contorting her elegant body so that she was always in the optimum position to suppress her opponent. Being careful not to hurt either of them, she then repeated the moves in slow motion, patiently explaining how each part of the body worked in harmony to create strength and dexterity. Her life in the circus had given her skills unknown to most deb-utantes. 'It's all about using the body in subtle ways rather than just flinging your opponent around,' she told them. 'As a woman, if you're attacked, you will naturally be weaker, but you can make up for it by being quicker.'

And with that, she took hold of Hannah's arm and twisted it round so that she was behind her and able to put her foot out to force the rest of Hannah's body to the floor. She stood with one foot on Hannah's back and raised her arm in triumph.

'See, that's how it's done. Now it's your turn.'

First, Hannah, then Dotty, slowly repeated the manoeu-vre and when the diminutive Dotty had managed to get Hannah onto the floor, she muttered with some bitterness, 'Oh, I wish I'd known that move years ago,' her face sud-denly darkening.

Hannah glanced at her. Her recent experience was opening her up to nuances she hadn't noticed before.

Did Dotty's words hold a deep significance that only people who had faced brutality would recognise? She wondered how many more secrets were being hidden in this bedroom.

After a while, Lavinia fell back on the bed.

'I'm exhausted,' she complained. 'I haven't done those moves for years.'

Hannah wanted to hold on to the lighter atmosphere and pleaded with her to tell them more about her life in the circus, but Lavinia shrugged.

'That's enough for one night. The circus was just one more escape route I tried. I ran away from home to join the circus, you know, as you do.'

Hannah giggled, enjoying every moment of this levity after her traumatic day.

'Anyway, girls,' Lavinia said, turning towards her mattress, 'I'm bushed and we've got to get those winter crops sorted so we're going to need every bit of strength we possess to get through the next few weeks.'

Each of the girls got into bed that night deep in their own thoughts. Lavinia realised that without money a huge burden had been lifted from her. All those expectations that she had battled to thwart had been taken away and she was left exposed, but calmer and happier than she had ever been in her life. She no longer had to fly in the face of every demand of her title and family. She had nothing to prove any more. It was as if she had finally broken away from the shackles of wealth and privilege to discover that she was just a girl after all.

Dotty was having darker thoughts. She still woke at night in a cold sweat, imagining her father's face over her, his expression a mix of lust and disgust. Any time she thought of physical contact with a man, her whole body froze and Hannah's story had brought every sweaty touch, every forced encounter back to her. She knew George was finding it hard to get any affection out of her apart from a warm kiss and while she was becoming increasingly fond of the young lad, his inexperience shone like a beacon against her unwilling knowledge of the carnal act. She was terrified that she would show evidence of the experienced woman she had been forced to become and she did not know how to explain it to him, bringing back all of the painful memories.

Once they had turned out the light, Hannah stared up at the blackout over the roof light above them, and through the dark material, she tried to imagine the moon shining its innocent benevolence down on a war-torn world. Had her journey really taken her so far? she wondered. When she arrived at the farm, she had been timid and, frankly, terrified of everything, but today she tried to tell herself she had fought off a man wanting to rape her without a moment's hesitation. Her mind went back over the past few months. It seemed so long ago that she had discovered she had a natural rhythm on the dance floor, faced her demons with an animal that threatened to kill her, and from not even being able to ride a bike, had learned how to do that and drive a tractor. Hannah felt her arm muscles. There were definite bumps there, she thought, and she knew her face had a healthy glow from working in the fields. And all this, because she had had a moment's rebellion at home and joined the Land Army. She had even . . . this was where her daydreaming ground to a halt . . . She was about to think, found someone to love, but the thoughts that replaced this had a more desperate tone to them: fallen in love with an enemy soldier in an army who was trained to kill her own countrymen. And now that man had disappeared without trace, and she began to wonder how he could have done that if he really cared for her at all. She moaned and turned over to bury her face in her pillow.

Chapter 30

The girls were working in the fields, starting the back-breaking job of digging up the turnip crop when three figures came through the gate. John was in the front followed by Albert and William. He waved jubilantly at them.

'I'm your boss now,' he shouted from afar.

All the girls looked up and shaded their eyes against the low winter sun to check who was bringing the news.

Hannah, in particular, looked delighted when she saw it was John. 'Has Jed been given the sack?' she asked hopefully.

'No, 'fraid not, but he has been demoted.'

John looked at Hannah's young, innocent expression and curled his fists. Albert and William came behind him with William dragging his feet. He had been very quiet since the boss's revelations and was struggling with a guilty suspicion that he may have backed the wrong side with Jed Roberts. For the first time, he noticed that Dotty had similar dimples in her cheeks to his own niece and it sent a shiver down his spine. He had never thought of these girls as anything but a damned nuisance, interfering in a man's world, and his natural resentment of them had blinded him to the possibility that they were, after all, just young women, trying to do their bit in a terrible war. He glowered at them all, mentally accusing them of having the nerve to challenge his convictions, which had been so firmly backed up by Jed, but he knew that somewhere, in the back of his mind, he was finding some sympathy with them, and even worse, he realised with a frown, some respect.

'Why couldn't they bloody sack him?' Dotty asked fiercely, butting in on William's thoughts.

'We need all hands,' John replied with regret. 'We've got all the winter crops to harvest and we've got to get that flax in. We're not going to manage as it is.

'But I tell you this, girls, I'm going to make sure you're nowhere near him and the boss has threatened him with the police if he does anything like it again, so I don't think you'll be hearing much out of Jed from now on.'

Dotty caught Hannah's eye. They both looked sceptical.

* * *

The hard, physical winter work left no time for anything else – between hedge laying, harvesting the turnips and sprouts and then clearing their remains for the next crop, the girls' hands were chapped, their backs ached and their lips were crusted dry from the biting winds. Dotty had recommended Vaseline but the moisturising effect was negated by the amount of dust and dirt that the grease attracted, leaving them with grit all over their faces.

'I'm not sure I don't prefer sunburn,' Lavinia said, rubbing her chapped cheeks on the first day of lifting the sprout tops. The girls had been at the farm for a year now and were experienced in all types of weather. The previous summer, she had burned badly and had walked around with calamine all over her cheeks, which made her look like a ghost, an image that was intensified when she walked into a door in the blackout and ended up with a black eye. She wistfully remembered the person who had first walked into the girls' bedroom, her immaculate makeup highlighted by a bright, cherry-coloured lipstick and looked down, almost in disbelief at the mud-encrusted boots on the ends of her slim tapered legs. She thumped the boots on the ground in a vain attempt to loosen the clay from the steel nails she'd put in to stop them slipping in the wet ground, but she was feeling particularly bad tempered as her monthly period was wreaking havoc with her equanimity. The girls hated that time of the month, especially in winter when their normal practice of nipping behind a gate or a hedge took on a new complication, taking away the option to use a small trowel to bury a used sanitary towel in the frozen ground. Dotty bore it better than the other two as she hardly seemed to suffer from the 'curse' as they called it, but Lavinia would talk longingly of the days when she'd been able to curl up on the sofa with a hot water bottle to her stomach. In a Norfolk field in winter, surrounded by men, she had no choice but to tuck one of her hands in the front pocket of her breeches to cushion the pain, while battling the frozen ground with the other.

Rachel usually brought them some welcome hot soup in a Thermos to add to their sandwiches when they stopped for a short break at dinner time. It was really too cold to stand still for long so they worked solidly. There seemed to be endless fields full of sprout tops to be lifted and the ground was solid. They raced to get along the rows, trying not to look over the horizon where there seemed to be endless little tufts left sticking out of the ground beckoning to the girls.

Hannah was quiet, too busy torturing herself with the fate that could have befallen Karl. It was the not knowing that was tearing her apart, she realised, taking her frustration out on a particularly stubborn stalk.

Within two days of working on the sprout tops, the backs of the girls' thighs were so pulled and stretched, they could hardly walk. The whole process was dominated by the weather and each one of them would constantly peer up at the sky to check for any change in the clouds that might suggest snow, hail or rain. John, who felt a pressure to get on top of the workload, listened intently every night to the BBC weather forecasts; these took longer than usual because they were in code, so the enemy didn't know where or when to bomb. As a result, he was much more irritable than usual, going up and down the lines of stalks to make sure none were missed.

On the fourth day of the same exhausting work, Dotty looked at the expressions of abject misery around her. They still had four hours to go before the long-awaited bath night. It was normally the highlight of the week, but there was not an ounce of cheerful anticipation in either of her friends. Dotty decided it was time for desperate action.

'OK . . .' She started to sing loudly, looking expectantly at the other two.

Hannah saw Dotty's waiting face and, without much gusto, joined in to sing the title track to the musical *Oklahoma!*

Lavinia raised her eyes to heaven and capitulated, her voice piercing the cold air.

They all started to laugh as they got louder and louder and then Hannah changed the words about glorious golden fields of waving wheat to include words like 'mud' and 'snow' and 'ice', prompting all three of them to double up with laughter. William Handforth glowered at them but could find no reason to criticise their work so forced himself to keep quiet, ignoring his foot as it would keep tapping in time with the tune. Jed kept well away from them at the far end of the field, muttering as he worked, dragging his false leg behind him.

The next few hours passed more quickly with a succession of musical tunes until the girls were finally able to link arms and head towards the barn with the thought of the shallow bath of, hopefully, warm water. Hannah glanced over to her left as they skipped over the furrows in the fading light. In the distance were the prisoners of war working on mending the fences. She found herself scanning the group for Karl before she remembered he was not there. The realisation was like a wet, cold flannel across her face and later, as she tried to sleep, all the cheerfulness they had conjured up with their singing had dissipated and instead her dreams were of a variety of disasters that might have befallen him, leaving her tossing and turning in anguish, convinced he was dead and she would never see him again.

Chapter 31

Karl pressed his fingers into his stomach. It was hollow and his ribs were poking through like the skinned rabbits he used to see hanging outside the butcher's shop at home. With the security of the compass to consult, he was pretty sure he was travelling in the right direction, but he had no idea how far away he was from King's Lynn, or indeed, whether his calculations might cause him to bypass it by accident. Each village he came to twinkled in the moonlight and he found himself entranced. He had had no idea that England was so beautiful and the houses with their dappled walls that looked as if pebbles had been stuck onto them were really pretty against the red bricks. He couldn't resist reaching out his hand to stroke them.

Every village, every landscape was different, each with an individual character, and if he could ever just fathom the English sense of humour, he felt he could be at home here. The irresistible vision of a life with Hannah in a little cottage in one of these villages made Karl sigh with frustration and he made himself concentrate on the task in hand, searching the fields for something to eat, but, so far, scrabbling in the earth had yielded nothing. There had been so many times over the last couple of weeks that he had almost given himself up, but that moment, on the outskirts of one of the villages, was the most intense of all of them. He sat on a large tree trunk with his head in his hands and wept. The calculations that whirred in his head told him it had been ten days since he had left the truck. He knew he could survive up to twenty-one days without food, maybe more with just water, but he was getting weaker and it was becoming harder to think logically. His thoughts jumbled in his head and in his hunger and misery, he almost fainted.

To send blood to his head, he laid his head onto his knees and breathed deeply, trying to make sense of his predicament.

He knew he was already in so much trouble that it made little difference how long he was on the run, as long as he could survive. Besides which, he couldn't bear the thought that all this had been in vain. His need to find out if his family was safe and he had decided that he would track them down or die in the attempt. Karl stood up and made himself do what he had been doing since he stepped off the truck . . . put one foot in front of the other.

Before dawn, Karl hid in a wood where he settled himself against a tree, poured some of his precious water out of the milk bottle into the old can and used his compass again to check his direction. He imagined what his sister would say when she saw him but stopped short of thinking what he would do after that. He just wanted to get to her front door and find out whether his family was alive. His stomach rumbled, reminding him that three walnuts and one apple a day was nowhere enough to keep a six-foot man strong and healthy. He looked longingly at a cheeky rabbit that scuttled past him, cocking his finger at it like a gun, but it tossed its back legs in his direction as if aware that a finger posed no threat at all. Karl's shoulders slumped and he fell asleep until, hours later, he was woken by the sound of twigs cracking over to his left. Karl crouched down as much as he could behind the oak tree and peered out from behind its reassuringly wide trunk. There were two scruffy children, one about ten years of age, the other slightly younger, coming towards him. They were filthy dirty, wore little more than rags, and were speaking a rough dialect he couldn't understand. He immediately registered that one of them was badly injured and was being supported by the older lad. Karl spotted an evil-looking steel trap clamped onto the boy's leg. It was pouring blood, but the metal was also very dirty, which alerted the young doctor. He could not help it, he stood up, ignoring the warnings in his head.

The boys looked up in surprise and then the older one tried to run, dragging the other one behind him. Karl put his hand up and said, 'Wait, I can help you.'

The boys hesitated but then the smaller one fell onto the ground with a cry. Karl dashed forward. He gently leaned over the boy while the older one hovered nervously above him. Karl used every last vestige of strength to prise the trap apart, finally releasing the boy's leg. He felt very gingerly along the bone to discover that yes, it was definitely broken, but also there was also a deep cut which was oozing blood. That wound had to be cleaned, and quickly, or there was a danger of the boy getting an infection.

Karl sighed to himself. This was going to be the end of the road for him, but if he did not help this boy, he could end up crippled or with gangrene and he could die. Karl had no choice.

'What are your names?' he asked quietly.

The boys glared suspiciously at him.

'You the police?'

'No,' Karl laughed. 'I'm an airman – and a doctor.' He hesitated; there was no need for the whole story. 'I'm Dutch and I'm making my way back to my unit.'

The boys accepted his explanation without question. They had watched the way this thin man had expertly felt his way along the wound and, so far from any help, they were prepared to put themselves in his hands.

'I'm Sylvester and this is Nathan, my brother,' the older one told him, gingerly picking up the trap from the ground and tying it to his belt.

'Where do you need to get to?' Karl asked.

They pointed to the clearing at the far edge of the wood.

'OK, let's get Nathan to somewhere where we can clean this up.' He went round to the other side of the injured boy to show Sylvester how they were going to lace their fingers together to provide a seat for Nathan.

After an agonising twenty minutes during which Karl realised how weak he had become, they arrived at the clearing and he looked up in astonishment. There were four round-topped wooden caravans – one was painted red and the other three were green with elaborate paint-ings on the doors. There were also a couple of tarpaulins strung across between bushes to make a shelter. To one side, several scrawny horses were tethered on rough ropes. In the middle was a fire with a black cauldron hanging on it, bubbling with something that smelt irresistibly delicious and made Karl feel lightheaded with hunger. Surrounding the fire were two older men and four women. The men had on corduroy trousers and old tweed jackets that looked just like the one Karl had taken off the scarecrow. The women all had shawls wrapped diagonally across them-selves and full skirts on. To one side, there was a group of young children playing with sticks. This, he realised, was a gypsy encampment.

Karl had seen the ruthless hunting down of the Roma by Himmler in the 1930s in Germany and, for a split sec-ond, recoiled at the little group in front of him. He shook himself; that revulsion was exactly the sort of brainwashing he had railed against for so many years. It shocked him to find there was a distrust of these people, deep inside of him, nurtured by his forced membership of the Hitler Youth. He had not realised just how thorough the Nazi regime had been in its determination to turn its people against anyone not of the Aryan race. He felt a profound disgust with himself.

One of the women spotted the little trio coming towards them and let out a scream. The oldest man reached for a gun that was propped up against the wheel of one of the vans and pointed it at Karl. The older boy shouted something in a strange language and the man tilted the gun down again, looking suspiciously at the intruder.

Karl went into professional mode and said in a loud voice, 'I am a doctor. Get something to lay this boy on and get me some water – quickly.'

The man looked from Karl to the two boys, who nodded. Nathan suddenly fell to the ground in a faint. Karl moved forward to raise his legs. He signalled to the woman to his left, who gave him a blanket and helped him move the boy across onto it. She looked panic-stricken and, he suspected, was the mother of the two boys. He smiled reassuringly at her. Meanwhile, another woman came up with a bucket of hot water that had been at the side of the fire.

'I must have some clean . . .' Karl couldn't think of the word and he was doubtful anyway whether such a thing could be found in this ramshackle camp, but, to his surprise, one of the men gave him a relatively white handkerchief that he had plucked from the clothes line hanging between two trees.

A dark-eyed older woman came up with a small dish of paste which Karl sniffed: turmeric. 'Perfect,' he said, nodding in approval and then carefully cleaned every bit of the wound, using the turmeric to stop infection.

He then looked around for a straight twig, which he found on the ground next to him, and set to work.

There was silence as he worked and even the younger children came over to watch in awe. Nathan had come round and was whimpering in pain. His mother went round to his head and cradled it in her lap. Sylvester produced the iron trap from behind him and showed the men where it had clamped over his brother's leg while Karl placed another hard twig between the boy's teeth to stop him biting his tongue.

At the moment when Karl straightened the broken bone, Nathan fainted again, but Karl had to concentrate on cleaning the wound, leaving his mother to bring him round. Binding the twig with another piece of clean rag, he worked fast to minimise the boy's pain.

Finally, Karl stood up and wobbled, the effort having exhausted him even further. Nathan was lying back with a relatively clean bandage and splint on his leg and Karl faced the group of people who were surrounding him with curiosity. Before he could speak, however, one of the women handed him a bowl of the stew he had smelt and a spoon. He looked gratefully at her and, putting the spoon to one side, slurped the delicious meal as fast as he could, not noticing the meaningful looks that were being passed between his audience.

The food fortified him within minutes and even though it sloshed around in his stomach, it gave him the warmest feeling he had had since he started this insane journey.

The oldest man motioned to Karl to sit on a rug next to the fire and Karl sank down in a heap. He fell back and closed his eyes. Explanations could come later. He just knew he had been saved by the most unlikely bunch of rescuers and the only thing that mattered to him was that, today, he wasn't going to starve to death after all.

Chapter 32

It was still light when Karl woke. He'd been covered by a blanket and another had been placed under his head. He struggled to sit up to see the two men and Sylvester sitting opposite him, waiting patiently.

'I, er, I um . . .'

He did not know what to say. Part of him was tempted to tell them the truth that was suffocating him, but when he looked closely at their swarthy faces, he thought better of it. The kindness he had been shown would vanish in a second if they discovered he was a German, a man whose country was sending their people to camps and killing them in their thousands.

In a thick accent, the oldest man said, 'So, here you are, wandering the woods in the month of Iveskero and not finding enough to eat by the look of you.' He tutted. 'My grandsons tell me you are a Dutch airman. Yes?'

Karl nodded. He hoped they had never met a Dutchman so would not be able to distinguish the accent.

'And you are a deserter?' the man went on. Karl looked fearful, but the man reached across and put his hand on his arm.

'We do not condemn people,' he told him. 'We have too much of that when we travel, so we'll make our own decisions about you, as a person, not for what you have done.'

Karl felt a tremor of guilt. He had been so quick to judge and now this man in front of him was being so much more tolerant than he had ever been. It occurred to him that it was possible that all his preconceptions were going to be challenged before the end of the war – if he managed to survive it.

Sylvester handed him something that looked like bread. He chomped on it gratefully. It tasted so good. He raised his eyes to the boy's mother, standing behind her son, and they misted over; he could not help it, he was over-whelmed with the kindness of these people. The woman leaned down and patted Karl on the shoulder.

'How is Nathan?' he asked her.

'The wound is clean and there is no sign of infection, thanks to you. Now, we need to repay you, but we have no money, so what is it we can do for you?'

Karl shook his head; his automatic reaction was that he should not have any more to do with these Romany people. His own uncomfortable prejudices combined with the fact that he could not risk them finding out his true nationality were enough to make him think he should leave now before things got even more complicated.

The man who'd pointed the gun intervened. 'Where are you going? Can we take you there?'

'I'm trying to get to King's Lynn, I have a sister there,' he confessed, wondering how on earth he would explain his German origins when they delivered him to her front door. But, if they could just see him a bit further along his journey, he thought, that would help a lot and the memory of that stew was a lure.

The men looked at each other and nodded. It mattered little which way they went as long as they could get a bit of work here and do a bit of poaching there, so they were happy to head towards King's Lynn. The weather was hardening and that meant more opportunities for itinerant workers, who were often a welcome source of casual labour to replace the young men who were being sent off to fight.

'Why not?' the taller man said. He leaned forward and held out his hand. 'As long as you're not in a rush, we have some work to do along the way. My name is Pyramus and this is Loverin.'

Karl clasped his hand, fighting the distrust he felt inside. He'd read the research by Dr Robert Ritter during his training, noting that these people were of such mixed race that they qualified as having 'degenerate blood'. Karl was shocked to realise that even though he had been taught to query everything, it had never occurred to him to question the findings of the study or the fact that thousands of Roma were incarcerated at a camp near the sewage dump in East Berlin; he'd scanned the reports without much interest. Staring across at the women now, laughing and joking over their cooking, the only negative feelings he had were for himself. This war had been caused by intolerance and here, he was horrified to find, he had been about to perpetuate the same bigotries. He reached out to shake the hand in front of him warmly.

'I think I need to take some time to recover my strength before I find my sister,' he told the two men. 'So, if you will have me, I would like to travel with you.'

'You need to be kept hidden' Pyramus said; it was not a question. 'But you need to earn your keep as well. What do you suggest?'

Karl cast his eyes around the camp. 'I could look for food, I know how to find food in nature,' he ventured.

The men looked unimpressed; their community had lived off the land all their lives and this extra guest would have to earn his keep with more than that. There was one compelling argument that the look between them acknowledged – now their own young men had been con-scripted, they could use a younger body to help with some of the heavy work and Karl could provide that – once they had put some meat on those bones, Pyramus thought.

'Well, I can trap animals but also, I know about medi-cine and perhaps I can help with that.' Karl looked up hopefully. He did not add that he was actually trained to use a gun; he thought that might be an admission too far and would lead to difficult questions.

'I'd like to learn from him,' the dark-eyed woman said, in that now familiar guttural accent, turning from the cauldron that was bubbling away on the fire, 'and Charity is due any day now but has problems. She's been separated from her husband's family and the pregnancy's not an easy one. He may be able to help.'

The men looked a little scornful. Such things were women's work, but Karl was looking at the woman enthu-siastically. 'I can do that,' he said, 'and more. I see one of your children has bowed legs. I may be able to improve that, and your skin, too,' he told Pyramus. 'It is, how you say, flaking? I know a way to help that also.'

'Come with me then,' the woman said, not waiting for Pyramus to reply. 'My name is Vadoma, that means the "knowing one", but,' she laughed, 'I always want to know more.'

Karl followed her and she showed him a space under one of the caravans, giving him a rough, grey blanket to use and a piece of tarpaulin that would stretch under him and over the wheel to give him cover.

'You are probably used to more comfortable sleep-ing,' she said, looking shamefacedly at the patch of earth beneath the van.

'Not, it seems, in recent days,' Karl replied, taking the blanket from her with a smile. He noticed she had bent over double and was clasping her side, her face contorted in agony.

'Do you have any pain? Here?' he asked her, pointing out where kidney stones might be causing problems. He thought if he could dig up some couch grass rhizomes, he might be able to help her.

'Yes,' she exclaimed, 'and increasing pain.'

'Well, we will see if I can help that with *dieses Gras*,' he told her, pointing to the bottom of the stems of some strands of couch grass that were just poking above ground near the caravan, 'and perhaps I will also help the skin of Pyramus if you have, I think it is called the cider vinegar of *Apfel*? It will also help you.'

She smiled in delight at him. To be able to swap ideas and remedies was a pastime she would relish.

'I can see we're going to be glad you came into our camp,' she said.

As evening fell, the little group gathered around the fire – flames were a welcome source of heat. Each night, when Karl had set off into the dark to try to find his way towards King's Lynn, he'd had to gird himself up to face yet another night without food, cover or company, unsure of the direction he was travelling. Watching the cosy scene in front of him, he felt a satisfied glow seeping up his body, unable to believe how pleased he was to share his time with people again. He looked around him – a couple of the women were leaning affectionately against each other, the children were tiredly rubbing their eyes and then, just as Karl was dropping off too, Loverin grabbed a small piece of wood that had been carved out to make a musical pipe. He played some joyful tunes, which pierced the quiet of the woodland. In the background, an orchestra of rooks, owls and bats added their sounds and, with the crackling fire, Karl felt a surge of pleasure he had not felt since before the war and suddenly felt an intense need to have Hannah curled up next to him. He shivered; if only life were that simple.

Chapter 33

'Hannah, the boss wants to see you,' John called across the field.

Hannah looked up in surprise. *What on earth could he want with me?* she thought.

'You're becoming quite the favourite,' Dotty laughed, nudging her on the arm.

'I doubt that,' Hannah replied. 'Oh, I do hope I haven't done anything wrong.' She put down the basket she was carrying and headed back towards John. 'Is everything OK?'

'I don't know,' he told her, not mentioning that he had seen a police car arriving on the drive. He didn't want to put her in a panic. 'But go up to the house, he's waiting for you there.'

Hannah brushed her hair out of her eyes as she arrived at the back door to the house. She had never stepped foot in the farmhouse before and she looked with curiosity through the window to the bustling kitchen. She saw Rachel carrying a pie with a cloth over it across the room, being watched by Mrs Hill. At that moment, Rachel spotted Hannah's face at the window and beamed, but then frowned, remembering the policeman who was in the boss's study. Hannah was alerted by the change in her expression. *What on earth was going on?*

Rachel came to the door and ushered her in. Mrs Hill looked at the girl in breeches and a green jumper, who was now standing in the doorway. She had mud all over her clothes and boots and her face was grubby.

'Hello, my dear, perhaps you should nip into the back scullery and wash up,' she said kindly.

Hannah smiled in thanks, took off her boots and followed Rachel through to where there was a large Belfast sink and a tap. Rachel passed her a tiny bit of precious soap and Hannah swilled her face down.

'That's better,' Mrs Hill said when she emerged from the scullery. 'Now, Rachel, show Hannah to the study. Mr Hollis and . . . is waiting for her there.'

Hannah walked through the hallway, marvelling at the oak staircase that wound its way up at least two flights. It was all so posh and she picked at her hair to try to push it into place. The large wooden door opened onto a study, with bookcases on each wall. Hannah looked around her and gasped in delight at the volumes on all sides. It was her perfect room and, despite the anxiety that had besieged her, she was distracted by the wealth of knowledge that was contained in all those wonderful books. Her eyes narrowed as she tried to read some of the titles, her hand clasped to her mouth in excitement. Andrew Hollis noted her interest with surprise but then gave a small cough to alert her to the presence of a policeman in the room.

Hannah jerked her head round to focus on the scene in front of her. The rather large inspector was standing next to Mr Hollis, clutching his notepad and pencil, looking somewhat grave. She immediately thought something had happened to her parents and clasped her hand to her chest.

'My mum . . . dad? . . .' she stammered.

Andrew Hollis came forward and took hold of her shoulders. 'No, they're fine, as far as we know,' he told her gently, 'but this policeman wants to ask you a few questions about our escaped prisoner, as you are the only one we can trust who has spent some time with him. We can't believe anything any of the other prisoners tell us.'

Hannah felt a new panic rising in her. She had no idea what she was going to say and immediately forced her face to take on an impassive look to hide the tumult of feelings that were engulfing her.

'I'm sorry, the escaped prisoner?' she stalled to give herself time to think.

The inspector stepped forward. He felt sorry for her. She looked so young and so frightened.

'I'm sorry, miss, but we do need to just go through a few things with you. Those Germans all covered for him so it was hours before we even realised he'd gone and here we are, weeks later, and we're still having no luck tracking him down. He's either very clever or dead, but, in any case, we need to find out a bit more about him. I believe you were assigned to take him to mass occasionally?'

'Yes,' she replied warily; that word 'dead' had sent a shiver down her spine. She was desperately trying to remember if Stanley might have noticed anything about their relationship, but she and Karl had been so careful that surely their secret chats were just that . . . still a secret.

Mr Hollis went to sit behind his desk. He consulted his diary.

'I think you took him several times to Norwich. Can you think of anything he said that might help us find him?'

'N . . .no,' Hannah stuttered. So many thoughts were whirling around her head but she made herself stop and think before she uttered anything.

'We're forbidden from fraternising, as you know, so we hardly spoke,' she lied. Hannah had always been the one to obey the rules when Lily was pushing the boundaries and she thought how horrified her friend would be at this conversation. What had she become? she wondered. Had she really turned into a traitor to her own country just because of a young man's kind blue eyes.

'May I sit down?' she asked, needing a moment.

'Yes, yes of course.' Andrew Hollis motioned towards a green leather-backed chair with brass studs on it. She sank gratefully into it.

'I knew you wouldn't have much to add,' Andrew went on and then turned to the policeman, 'You should have seen her lay into him when he rescued her from our shire horse. I've no doubt this young lady hates all Germans as much as any of us, don't you, my dear?'

Hannah nodded, unable to speak.

'I felt terrible, asking her to take him to church, but . . .' his mouth tightened into a sneer '. . . the regulations say I have to oblige and she's the only Catholic.'

'That's OK,' the inspector said. 'So, there's nothing you can tell us, miss?'

Hannah shook her head, looking at the floor.

'No hint that he was thinking of escape?'

Hannah took a deep breath. She could not put a German's safety before her own country, even if it was Karl.

'He did seem almost happy to be here,' she ventured. 'He seemed relieved to be out of it all, he spent a lot of time looking around at the countryside. I . . . think he's from the country and may know how to live off the land.' She was relieved to be telling the truth without incriminating Karl or herself.

The policeman nodded. 'We've got experts looking at how he could do that, but they believe he would struggle after a few weeks at this time of year. He's not seen as a risk and his answers at his interrogation when he was first captured were reassuring, but you never know, he is a German. No, even with knowledge of the countryside, he couldn't last this long. Anyway, miss, thank you for your help. We had to ask. It was worth a try.'

Hannah opened her mouth to speak again; she just had to tell them about his sister in King's Lynn even if it showed they had actually talked, proving she'd lied before. She breathed out her relief when the policeman beat her to it, speaking more to Mr Hollis than to her.

'His sister was in King's Lynn, you know, working in a bakery, so we're concentrating our efforts on that part of the country. Obviously, as an alien, she's been moved, but he won't know that.

'We just don't know how a POW could disappear like this,' he told Andrew. 'I think he must be dead somewhere; I just wish we could find his body and get on with important investigations.'

Fortunately, neither man was looking at Hannah or they would have seen her eyes widen as horrendous images were conjured up in her brain; she quickly put her head down again to examine her hands.

'But, if that's all you can tell us, young lady, then you may go,' the inspector said.

Hannah got up slowly, feeling as guilty as a condemned man. She hoped it didn't show.

'Although, wait a moment, Hannah,' Andrew said, 'let me see the inspector out, just wait there.'

Hannah was dying to escape from the room, but stopped in her tracks, letting the two men pass her, her heart thumping at the thought of more questions from Mr Hollis.

A few moments later, he came back into the room.

'I couldn't help but notice your face when you came in here,' he said. 'Do you like reading?'

Hannah's shoulders dropped in relief and she replied enthusiastically, 'Oh, I love it. I read everything I can get my hands on. I think I may want to be a teacher when all this is over.'

She ignored the thought that she could be in prison or even dead by firing squad by that time and forced her eyes to focus on the books in front of her.

'Well, you're welcome to come here and borrow some if you would like. Is there one you'd like to take with you now?'

Andrew Hollis was beginning to like this girl, she had so much more to her than most young women of her age. He also recognised that he found it easier to be kind to her than to his own daughter, the headstrong Bobby, who seemed to court fierce arguments every time she came home. He envied Hannah's father, who must, surely, he thought, have an easier time with this amenable girl than he was having with his daughter.

Despite the last uncomfortable half-hour, Hannah's eyes lit up with delight. To be offered access to a library like this made her feel like a child in a sweet shop.

She scanned the shelves to her left and immediately spotted *A Christmas Carol* by Charles Dickens.

Andrew Hollis smiled and reached up to get it down off the shelf for her.

'A perfect choice. We've been having some odd Christmases, but,' he said, with a kind smile, 'I always think this book reminds us what a proper Christmas should be like, no matter what's going on around us.'

She gasped her thanks and Mr Hollis smiled at her and showed her out through the front door.

Hannah's delight dissipated quickly on her walk back to the barn, clutching the leather-bound copy of her favourite book. She replayed the scene in her head and was aghast at her lies about her conversations with Karl, thinking how quickly Mr Hollis would rescind his invitation once he found out what a traitor she was.

Chapter 34

The second interrogation began as soon as Hannah got back to the dining area of the barn, and she had hardly curled up in the armchair when Dotty weighed in. Hannah just about managed to sound casual and unconcerned that she'd been interviewed by the police and, despite a sharp look from Lavinia, no more questions were asked. To turn the attention from herself, Hannah put her treasured book down and turned her concentration to Dotty, who was struggling with an article in 'Woman and Home' on how to make animal hair into wool. She had been making great strides with her reading, but she still struggled with words of more than two syllables. Hannah had been wracking her brain to find a way to help her and rapidly came up with a plan, which she hoped would have the added benefit of distracting Lavinia from any further probing. 'Dotty, let's write down the lyrics to some of your favourite songs from the musicals,' she said, curling up in the old armchair in the corner.

Dotty's face lit up. She loved musicals above all things and spent hours fantasising about being Judy Garland or Evelyn Laye.

'You sing, Dotty, in that lovely voice of yours,' she called across the room, 'and Lavinia and I will write the words down. Then you can read them back.'

The whole evening was spent with Dotty singing every song she could remember from their trips to the pictures in her tuneful voice. The men came in and sat quietly in the corner, George leaning forwards, trans-fixed, committing the scene to memory for when he was lying in mud in the woods, preparing to risk his life in case of invasion. He saw Dotty not as a Land Army girl in a threadbare, green jumper but as a dark, curly-haired Hollywood star to rival even Ginger Rogers. He thought if he could just spend the rest of his life listening to the pure sound coming from the girl in front of him, he would die a happy man.

* * *

Hannah had been avoiding Lavinia. She suspected the sly looks Lavinia had been giving her meant that her friend hadn't finished with her yet and had more questions about the police interview. Since the night after the attempted rape, it had become an unspoken agreement between them that their confessions would not be discussed in front of

Dotty, but Hannah suspected that as soon as an opportunity arose, Lavinia would have much more to say.

The three girls were so tired all the time that they would almost fall asleep over their evening meals, struggling to stay upright. The wireless news reported that British farmers were successfully producing far more than their German counterparts but that output was coming at a cost. The Ministry of Agriculture sent representatives regularly to check the systems were working to optimum levels and everyone felt as if they were being constantly appraised and tested and that nothing they did was enough. On top of the fatigue that began to settle in, their feelings of inadequacy made for a tense atmosphere and sharp words were exchanged between the men and the girls on a daily basis.

Dotty, in particular, was finding the constant observation unnerving. It reminded her of the sharp-tongued butler at the house in Stratford and the more William Handforth found fault with her, the more she made mistakes. One day, when she was rushing to pick up hedge cuttings alongside the tractor, William yelled abuse at her for not being quick enough and she looked round in fear. At that moment, her foot caught on a clump at the edge of the ditch and she fell against the metal strut next to the wheel of the trailer behind the tractor.

'Stop! Stop!' Lavinia shouted to John, who was driving the tractor. At the same time, Hannah ran up in front of the tractor, waving her arms frantically. John stopped the engine immediately and looked round, puzzled.

Both girls ran to Dotty, who was writhing on the floor. Her leg was badly gashed and blood was spurting out over the remaining stalks of last summer's crop, seeping into the stems, making them look like gruesome instruments of torture.

'Quick, get the boss . . . or Archie . . . anyone,' Hannah shouted to the men who were standing uselessly to one side. John immediately sprang into action and started running across the field.

Lavinia searched round for something clean to stop the bleeding, but Hannah had already torn the scarf from her head. She shook it to try to get rid of the dust and mud and then used the underside to wrap around Dotty's knee, just above the gaping wound, tying tightly to stem the flow of blood. Hannah cradled Dotty in her lap, rocking her slightly like a baby. Shock had not set in yet and Dotty was simply aware of how much the gash hurt.

'Damn, damn, damn,' she was saying through sobs. Her first thought was that she would be laid off and not have any money to live on, and her second, which filled her with even more dread, was that she'd be sent home.

Working on the line behind them, making sure furrows were stripped clean of old stems, were the German POWs. Peter looked over at the commotion and when he saw what had happened, thought immediately of how much he wished Karl had been there; he would have known what to do. Hannah was thinking the same thing.

Archie came running full pelt across the field, followed by John, who was holding some clean bandages and a flask of water.

'Let me see,' he said, kneeling next to Dotty, who was beginning to shake.

He started to very gently swab the wound with the water he had in his flask. He'd taken it directly from the pump next to the trough so it was cold, but it did the job, and although Dotty flinched at his every touch, he was able to clean away the blood and see beneath. There was a four-inch cut that looked very deep and he suspected would need stitches. Wrapping the bandage around the injured knee, he looked towards the men.

'Come and give me a hand to get her on the trailer,' he said, putting his hands under Dotty's arms to lift her up. William sprang forward, his face showing a guilty expression. He knew he had been the one to distract her so that she fell under the wheel. *She could have been killed*, he thought with a sharp pain in his chest.

Between them, the men got Dotty carefully onto the flat, wooden trailer and John set off on the tractor to gingerly take her over the fields to the farm. The other two girls stared after her, their brows furrowed in consternation.

Archie turned to them and put a hand on each of their shoulders.

'Don't worry, girls, she'll be all right, but she might be out of action for a bit.' His reassuring words were immediately followed by his own thoughts that her absence would leave them short-handed at a time when they were struggling to get the fields prepared and the crops in. They were already ploughing by night, as instructed by the Ministry of Agriculture, and even then, there were not enough hours to get the work done.

* * *

Later, as Lavinia and Hannah washed themselves under the pump, they were unusually quiet. There was no sign of Dotty and they were desperate for news. George came racing across the yard, his face a picture of anguish.

'I . . . I've I've just heard what happened.' He almost fell over his words. 'Oh, my poor Dotty, do you think she'll be all right? I was over mending the fences and only found out just now. Was she in pain? How bad is it?'

Hannah put her hand on his arm. 'Calm down, George, I'm sure she'll be fine,' but she didn't sound convinced.

At that moment, Rachel came running across the yard. They all looked up with trepidation.

'It's all right,' Rachel told them, 'but the boss has taken her to hospital and they're keeping her in overnight. They're worried about tetanus; I think because there was some rust on the bit of tractor that cut her. I heard the boss say that they've got some sort of toxoid, I think he said it was called, that they're about to use in America to treat it, but he wasn't sure if we've got it here yet, so I don't know what they'll use instead,' she finished in a rush.

George went pale and Lavinia grabbed hold of Hannah's hand. Her uncle had died of tetanus after being wounded in battle in the Great War.

It was a subdued little group who ate their meal that night and even the men had little to say. Lavinia and Hannah went straight up to their room as soon as they had finished their rice pudding.

'I do hope she's all right,' Hannah said, and Lavinia just nodded. When Hannah climbed into bed, she peered down at Lavinia on her mattress and said, 'I don't suppose you'd come and take Dot's place, would you? This bed feels so big and empty.'

Lavinia climbed in next to her and they snuggled up together, taking comfort from the other's warmth, but Hannah took a deep breath, dreading what was coming next. This time there would be no escape.

'So, Hannah, the interview with the policeman, did you tell him anything?'

Hannah shook her head. 'No, I didn't and I feel terrible. Oh Lav, I feel like a traitor.'

'What could you have told them that they didn't already know?' came the matter-of-fact reply.

'Well, that's true. I was so relieved that they already knew he had a sister in King's Lynn and were thinking that might be where he was heading, so I didn't even have to tell them that. And to be honest, Lavinia, all he told me was about his childhood and the farm where he grew up so I wasn't hiding anything, was I?' She looked at her friend for absolution.

'How are you coping, Hann?' Lavinia asked, putting her arm around her. 'You know, with Karl still missing.'

It was the last straw for Hannah and she gulped and then started to cry. It was all going so wrong now and when she had been so happy in her new life, feeling she was doing her bit to help win the war. It had just taken one man, who happened to be a German, to ruin it all.

'I just wake myself up with dreams of him dead somewhere, rotting in a ditch. I've become someone I don't even recognise and now Dotty's been so badly hurt—'

'Come on, Hann, pull yourself together', Lavinia butted in. 'There are people dying every day in this war while you're sitting here worrying about things you can't change.'

Her straight talking, as always, took Hannah by surprise, but Lavinia hadn't finished.

'Firstly, you've got to be grateful that these are your only problems, at least we're not on the front line and being shot at all the time. This Karl, he sounds like a resourceful man and . . .' here she paused '. . . in some ways, if he *has* vanished and maybe made it back to Germany, it saves all the agonising you've been putting yourself through. It could never have worked; you must know that.'

Hannah grudgingly conceded that she was probably right, but it really didn't help the ache in her heart. She looked sheepishly at Lavinia, leaned over and gave her a hug, and then turned over and tried to sleep.

Chapter 35

The next morning, a sharp knock came at the bedroom door and it opened to reveal the now familiar figure of Miss Clarke, who still struck the fear of God into Hannah. Her sister, Mrs Hollis, was sometimes spotted wandering aimlessly around the farmhouse garden and all the girls had commented how the two could not be more different. Mrs Hollis always looked nervous and hesitant whereas her sister's purposeful footsteps were enough to wake the dead. Both girls sat up in bed, almost to attention.

'Morning, girls. I thought I'd come and tell you that you'll be getting another girl to cover while Dotty is off,' Miss Clarke said, 'so please clear some space for her.'

She was about to leave the room when she turned around, trying not to grin at the two girls who were sitting up in bed, bleary-eyed and their hair dishevelled. They were both lovely girls, she had to admit, but they looked this morning as if they hadn't had any sleep and had been dragged through a hedge backwards. Lavinia's normally pristine bobbed hair was actually standing on end, she noticed.

Her voice softened. 'I've heard from the hospital and you'll be glad to know that Dotty's going to be OK, but she needs rest and is being sent home for a couple of weeks, so you'll need this extra pair of hands.' And with that, she turned on her heel and went back down the stairs.

Hannah felt a chill seep through her. She suspected a trip home was the last thing Dotty needed. She had started to feel there was something terribly wrong at Dotty's home

'Oh help,' Lavinia said. 'That's all we need, some rookie getting under our feet.' She was bad-tempered. This was their little world, the three of them, they didn't need – or want – someone new.

* * *

It was later that day that the familiar black Bentley rolled up into the yard. Lavinia had just finished Dotty's milking and she immediately dodged behind the pump to try and avoid being spotted.

'I can see you, Doris Braithwaite,' her aunt's voice thundered. 'You can't hide from me, now come over here and meet your new recruit.'

Lavinia walked reluctantly towards her aunt, dragging her feet.

Out of the other side of the car fell a tall, broad-shouldered girl with breeches that looked as if they had been worn by a whole battalion of Land Army girls before her. They were full of patches and her jumper had smears of goodness knows what all over it.

'Hello there,' she called loudly in a coarse voice. 'Bloody great to meet yer, I'm Bertha.' She marched over to Lavinia, grabbed her hand and shook it vigorously up and down. Her hands were huge and calloused and Lavinia slowly withdrew her own tapered fingers.

'Been up in Yorkshire, bloody cold up there, even in summer.' The girl looked around her appreciatively. 'Just been dragged down 'ere to 'elp you lot out. This looks a great set-up, proper posh and you,' she said peering at Lavinia's lipstick and makeup, 'you look as if you've come out of a fuckin' magazine.'

Lady Parker coughed and Bertha grinned at her. 'Oops, sorry, yer ladyship, got t'mind that tongue of mine.'

'Yes, well, we do expect standards in the Land Army. Right, well, I'll leave you to find your way around, but before I go, could I just have a word, Doris?'

Lavinia looked around to see if there was any escape. There wasn't.

Just then, Hannah came out of the stables and Bertha ran up to her to pump her hand too. Hannah reeled at the verbal assault as Bertha fired endless questions at her.

Lavinia turned to her aunt and folded her arms, waiting for her to speak.

'Your parents are passing through on their way to see the Cholmondeleys at Houghton,' Lady Parker said, 'and they would like to see you at eleven o'clock here on Sunday morning. I presume you'll be available.' It wasn't a question.

She moved towards the car but then turned back. 'And, Doris, this is your one chance to make amends. I've done everything I can to mediate but now it will be up to you. Don't mess it up.'

And with that, she swept into the car, which roared off down the drive.

'What was all that about?' Hannah asked from behind Lavinia's left shoulder.

'Mater and pater, they're coming this way on Sunday. I have to meet them.'

She shrugged and went over to move the full milk churns, but her mind was working at a fast rate. It seemed unlikely, but she began to suspect that her aunt had actually stepped in to try and rectify the situation between her and her parents.

Maybe the old goat isn't that bad after all, Lavinia thought, heaving the heavy aluminium churns onto the stone stand ready to be loaded onto the cart for delivery.

* * *

At teatime that night, Lavinia was thoughtful. She had heard nothing from Jeremy for several months and she was constantly replaying his last words to her when he said he was going to leave his wife and run away with her. As the weeks passed, the sincerity of his words seemed to diminish and she was left wondering whether she had been played for a fool. She was astonished to find that although she missed the excitement of her affair with Jeremy, she missed her parents more. Her father, for all his remoteness, had been the one to encourage her to be different. He just may not have meant her to be *that* different, she thought with a smile. And her mother, well, she spent her days trying to live up to the social heights that her marriage had encumbered her with. Lavinia thought about her mother with her unruly, wispy hair and her regular escapes into the boathouse where she spent hours with her paints, creating wild landscapes. She knew her parents had caused a scandal when they married, somewhere in Venice she had been told. Her mother was a free spirit, who defied all conventionality and lived a bohemian life. Her father was the epitome of respectability, but he threw all caution to the wind when he met the eccentric Cordelia.

Perhaps it was no surprise that their only daughter had turned out to be so rebellious, she reasoned.

Her attention was brought back into focus by the raucous laughter of Bertha, who was holding court over the semolina pudding. John, Albert and George were staring aghast at the girl in front of them. Her hair was matted and her nails were filthy and she was in full flow: 'So, an RAF pilot was telling the padre how some fokkers appeared from out of the sky. "They *are* formidable aircraft," the padre agreed.'

John looked embarrassed and tried to butt in before the punchline, which he knew, but she waved her hand to silence him and said, '"No," the pilot said, "these fokkers were flying Messerschmitts."'

She then collapsed into loud giggles, bending over the table.

'Get it?' she asked, taking in the stunned faces in front of her.

'Oh yes,' Lavinia said, 'we get it. Very funny. Now does anyone want my semolina? I can't face it; always reminds me of frogspawn.'

George looked up hopefully and she handed her bowl over; he remembered Dotty saying that he had hollow legs and always looked half starved. He felt a jolt thinking about her and said out loud, 'I miss Dotty.'

Missing Dotty intensified for the girls too, especially when they went up to their room after their meal. It looked so different; Bertha's clothes were everywhere – on the floor, strewn on the bed and crumpled in a heap on what had been Lavinia's mattress. Lavinia picked up one particularly dirty sock and held it away from her in disgust.

'Do you think you could tidy up a bit?'

Bertha looked surprised, scanning the room as if she could see nothing wrong with it. Lavinia was getting increasingly irritated. She had no patience this week with Sunday's visit constantly on her mind and the last thing she needed was a new room-mate who thought dirt was fashionable.

'Look, just pick up all your things and put them in the corner over there,' she said curtly. 'Hannah and I don't want to be falling over your knickers and socks.'

'All right, all right, keep your hair on, hoity-toity,' Bertha replied wearily. The last farm she had been on had been very basic, but no one there complained about her untidiness.

Hannah spoke up, seeing Lavinia's irritated expression. 'Maybe you could just keep your stuff together,' she suggested. 'It will be easier to find then when you leave.'

'Getting rid of me already, are you?' Bertha snapped. She couldn't believe how fussy these girls were, but to keep the peace she started to collect up the clothes, scratching her head as she did so.

'Hold it right there,' Lavinia said. 'Have you got nits?'

She retreated towards the door and even Hannah moved away to the other side of the room.

'Dunno,' Bertha replied then thought. 'Ha, you might be right.' With that, she studied her fingernails. She stretched her index figure out towards them both.

'Look, there's the little blighters? See 'em?'

Lavinia went behind Bertha and propelled her out of the room and down the stairs before she could object. She hurried her to the pump outside and yelled to Hannah, who was following, to go and get some DDT.

Lavinia pushed Bertha's head under the water and told her to rub, hard. Bertha's objections were drowned out by the noise of the gushing water, which Lavinia pumped out as vigorously as she could.

Hannah ran back across the yard, carrying the spray with the DDT in.

'OK, stand back and you, hold your breath, I'm never sure what's in this stuff,' Lavinia ordered Bertha, and then, turning her head away, sprayed so that a fine mist covered Bertha's head.

'Got them anywhere else?' Lavinia asked suspiciously.

Bertha covered her crotch with her hands. There was no way that girl was going anywhere near any other bits of her body.

'No, definitely no,' she answered, turning her back quickly to go upstairs, but Lavinia grabbed hold of her and, in no uncertain terms, commanded: 'Strip, now!'

Lavinia's muscles had been strong enough when she was a wrestler and now she had worked for so long doing manual labour on the farm, Bertha didn't stand a chance. She was unceremoniously divested of all her clothes before Lavinia thoroughly and remorselessly doused her in freezing cold water, leaving her gasping for breath.

Hannah whispered to Lavinia, 'I think we should spray all her clothes too.'

Before Hannah could finish, Lavinia ran up the stairs and, using an old towel, wrapped all Bertha's clothes and then took them back outside, past the astonished new girl who was hurriedly trying to get dressed. She tipped the clothes onto the ground and sprayed them scrupulously.

'Oh, bring back Dotty,' she said wistfully to Hannah.

Chapter 36

Karl suspected he was beginning to look like the Romany men around him. Over the past few weeks, he'd put on weight, been given some of their clothes and had grown a beard so as to look nothing like the smart Luftwaffe officer who had stepped onto that plane so many months before. In addition, he was no longer getting the mental blackouts that had landed him in this situation. Vadoma had searched through the herbs and potions she had under the bench bed in her van to find the best ones for calming the mind and Karl found that unless he was under extreme stress, his brain functioned as normal. In the relaxed atmosphere of the camp, he almost forgot he had had a problem. He spent many hours with Vadoma, sharing knowledge and skills, and with her older, quiet wisdom and a true ability to listen, he slowly began to confess his feelings about a certain young lady with dark curly hair and the bluest eyes he had ever seen. She patted him gently on the arm and gave him some Romany advice: 'A man must put grain in the ground before he can cut the harvest.'

Karl looked puzzled so Vadoma went on, 'You must tell her, show her, how you feel.'

Karl just hoped he would get that chance.

Life became a pleasant round of finding places to stop where the men could trap a few rabbits or do a bit of handiwork while the women offered trinkets and palm-reading to locals. Karl would keep out of sight until the evening, when he emerged to join the fireside conversations and listen to music. He developed a real affection for the gypsies, who lived life on a precipice of survival but somehow managed, every evening, to forget their troubles and dance and sing around that fire. Karl had not felt this relaxed since his childhood on the farm and it occurred to him how much the growth of the Third Reich had blighted his young life. The teaching of hatred, resentment and anger had been so thorough that boys like him had inevitably absorbed some of it. His resentment of that fact led him to one conclusion and one conclusion only . . . he was ashamed of the Nazism that had taken over his country. *I have no idea where I belong*, he thought one night as he prepared the herbs for an on-going supply of poultices, food supplements and remedies. Charity was in the corner, feeding her baby. She looked up at him with that grateful smile she reserved for the man who had saved her life when her baby was trying to come out backwards. He looked around at the children who were playing on some logs near the camp. They looked better and Motshan, the boy with the bow legs, was already walking a little straighter thanks to the strict regime of exercises Karl made him do. Karl was surprised how much he had missed practising medicine and making a difference to this little group made him feel that, at last, he was doing something worthwhile. He also acknowledged that it had been a two-way process.

Pyramus came over to tell him that they were nearing King's Lynn, but, as he said the words, the gypsy looked embarrassed.

'What is it?' Karl asked.

Pyramus shuffled his feet. 'We have heard stories. About people they do not know what to do with. They've been rounded up and taken to somewhere called the Isle of Man and put in detention camps. While we are working, helping farmers, they leave us be, but you might attract attention to us so perhaps, my friend, it's time for you to travel on alone.'

Karl smiled a reassuring smile he did not feel. He had begun to rely on these people and knew he would have been dead if they hadn't taken him in.

He suspected his hosts had never believed his story, but hoped they did not know the full truth. It suddenly dawned on him that he might be going to King's Lynn on a fool's errand. Logic told him the British authorities would not trust any Germans to wander freely and he wondered whether his sister had been shipped off to an internment camp already.

'What do you know about this island?' he asked sharply.

Pyramus looked surprised at Karl's tone, it was unlike this usually gentle man.

'I'm sorry,' Karl said, 'I just need to find my sister and I'm not sure if she's still going to be in King's Lynn.'

'Because she is German?' Pyramus asked quietly, as Loverin joined them.

Karl jerked his head up in surprise.

'Did you really think we did not know?' his host asked him.

'Yes, but I am the enemy, I do not understand . . . Why did you take me in?'

Loverin laughed bitterly. 'Everyone is our enemy,' he said. 'You, it turns out, are just a nicer – and more useful – enemy than we normally come across.'

And with that, the two gypsies laughed and turned back towards the caravans.

* * *

From the following day, Karl was on his own again. He had hugged each one of the little troupe and, in return, they had packed him up a blanket full of supplies, which he tied to a stick and carried over his shoulder.

To Pyramus, he said, 'I have never had such kindness and I am more grateful than you can ever know.'

Pyramus smiled and patted him on the shoulder. 'Be careful,' he said, 'trust no one. You think the war is out there, but for you and me, my friend, it is everywhere. And, if I may give you some advice; in future, make your own mind up about people – do not let others tell you how to think.'

Karl gave him a rueful smile. He was learning so much about tolerance on this journey.

* * *

Karl walked by night as he had done in the beginning, stopping during the day in a ditch or in a wood, if he could find one. Having spent many a day sharing skills with Vadoma, he had been delighted to help her find leaves and berries she did not know would work as medicines, and he, in his turn, had learned so much about survival on nothing but what nature had to offer. However, the provisions he'd been given by the gypsies were running low and foraging in an English February yielded little. He didn't want to think about where he was heading, he just wanted to give himself a few days before he made a decision.

On the fourth day, he was napping behind a ditch when he heard the noise of a car. It was approaching very fast and the road was wet. He got up to a crouching position to peer through the hedge and saw a police car racing down the road towards him. As it approached the bend, the driver lost control on some ice and the car careered towards the thicket. Karl jumped out of the way, just as the car toppled into the ditch, its windscreen smashing with the impact.

It took just one split second for Karl to dismiss the thought that his adventure would be over if he helped. As with young Nathan, there was really no choice in his mind and he leaped forward to see what he could do.

The driver was unconscious and had a nasty gash on his forehead and blood was pouring from his arm. Karl opened the car door and dragged him out. He was only young and, Karl thought, obviously an inexperienced driver. He was alone in the car and Karl laid him gently on the ground, raising his arm up and propping it against a tree. That head needed stitches, he realised, but the urgent thing was the arm, which was emitting a constant flow of deep red blood.

At that moment, a cyclist came down the lane. It was a tall, blonde young woman in a blue uniform with gold wings emblazoned on the front of her left shoulder. She was wearing a scarf on her head to hold her hair in place and screeched to a halt before she dropped the bicycle to run to Karl's side.

'What happened?' she asked.

'He took the corner *zu schn*—too fast,' he replied without thinking.

She looked sharply at the blond hair and blue eyes in front of her. 'You are . . . you are a . . . German?' Her voice was incredulous.

'*Ja*,' Karl weakly replied; it was too late, he would have to face whatever the future held.

'I must help him,' he said simply. 'Take off your scarf, I need it to stop the blood.'

She did not hesitate but tore off the scarf and handed it to him. 'What do you need me to do?'

'Find me a stick,' Karl told her. She searched around and handed him one of about six inches long to him. 'Will this do?'

He nodded and folded the scarf over the stick so it didn't cut into the man's skin. Then he placed the stick about two inches above the wound on the man's arm and then twisted it to tighten the fabric.

'A tourniquet,' the girl said approvingly.

Karl nodded, surprised at her calm voice. Now for the forehead. Searching in his pack for a small bottle of honey, he cursed the noble gesture he had made when he refused to take Vadoma's turmeric. Honey would have to do. He washed his finger in a trickle of water from the flask and smeared the honey thickly on the man's head.

'Now we need to get him to a hospital,' he told her, 'he has lost much blood.'

'I have to get to . . . somewhere near here; I was on my way there when I found you,' the girl said, putting her hand over the golden wings that would give away the fact that she was, in fact, a pilot for the Air Transport Auxiliary. She did not know how much a German would know about their organisation. She looked intently into his face, wondering what his story was and then looked down at the pale face of the young policeman. There were more important things to deal with first.

'I could cycle on there and get them to send an ambulance.' The words came out of her mouth but in her head she was frantically trying to remember something her friend, Bobby Hollis, had told her about an escaped German prisoner of war, wondering whether this could possibly be the same man. She wracked her brains, trying to recall the conversation when Bobby had told the rest room at Hamble that one of her father's POW workers had run away, but that was months ago. Surely he couldn't have survived on his own for this long? Sally Ravenscroft was a practical girl and, much as she was dying to ask the man a myriad of questions, her first duty was to get the injured man to hospital and her second was to tell the authorities – and quickly. The problem was that, as usual, she was not where she was supposed to be. Sally was an ATA pilot who loved flouting the rules and she'd borrowed the bike to sneak off to see a very attractive RAF officer. Although she didn't really want to admit she'd been on this road, this was serious. She shrugged her shoulders. *Ah well,* she thought, *I'll just have to talk my way out of it as usual.*

'I will still be here, I do not leaving him,' the German told her, thinking her hesitating was because she thought he would do a runner as soon as she left.

Sally was a good judge of character and she looked closely at him. She decided to trust him.

'It's only two miles down the road, I'll be as quick as I can,' she said, and pedalled off.

Chapter 37

Sunday morning dawned as if nature was in blissful igno-
rance of the torment that was going on in Lavinia's head.
At precisely eleven o'clock, a shiny black Daimler drove up
the drive into the yard. Lavinia took one last look at herself
in the mirror in the bedroom, turned to give Hannah a
hug, then checked her watch and went downstairs. She felt
like a criminal going out to her execution.

Hannah couldn't resist creeping down after her to catch
a sight of Lavinia's parents. She saw a tall man in a pin-
striped suit with a moustache and greying hair, who held
out his hand to his daughter for a formal handshake, and a
pretty woman, her wispy hair escaping from an ineffective
bun, who was wearing a fur coat over a blue, flowing dress.
She looked nervously at her husband before giving Lavinia
a tentative hug. Then the three of them got into the car and
drove off.

Hannah felt anxious for Lavinia, she knew what this
meeting meant to her, but it brought back all her worries about her own parents ... and Karl. As long as she

kept busy, she had no time to think, but, on days like this one when she was off work and left to her own devices, she had too much time on her hands and found she was bombarded with disturbing thoughts. She did her washing, mended her socks and scrubbed her nails, then she went off for a walk, setting off at a fast pace down the drive. She just needed to get away for a couple of hours.

She made her way round the lanes trying to rationalise the information she'd had from Ros recently. Her mother was still hardly functioning, and although her dad was trying to compensate, she knew he was struggling. Ros wrote reassuring letters that she and Mrs Mullins were keeping an eye on them but that didn't help Hannah, who was hundreds of miles away with little chance of being able to get home.

As the evening sun went down, Hannah was on her way back to the farm when she spotted Lavinia being dropped off by the gate. She ran over to meet her.

'What happened, Lav? Are you OK?'

'Well, they bought me luncheon,' Lavinia said, 'I had a very nice meat pi—'

'Don't be daft, I don't want to know the menu,' Hannah said, pushing her gently.

'Oh well, they told me that Jeremy's wife is having a baby, so that's that. I suppose I'll just have to marry one of the farmhands – maybe Jed'll have me.'

Lavinia's face had taken on that mask that Hannah recognised so well by now, so she chose to ignore the feeble joke.

'Oh Lav, I'm so sorry. I know how much you cared for Jeremy.'

'Ah well, there's no point crying over spilt milk, or in that bastard's case, spilt champagne.' Her expression became bitter. 'He thought he had everything, that man: a fast car, lots of money, oh, and he just forgot to mention that he had a wife he had no intention of leaving.'

Hannah gave her friend's hand a squeeze and the two girls linked arms and walked back towards the barn.

'No, do you know what, Hann, I'm not even sure I mind that much. Being with you and Dot, well, it's taught me what the important things are in life. Jeremy was like a film star – a glam fantasy. He somehow doesn't look as sparkly in the grey reality of wartime. My life of grease-paint and ostrich feathers seems so far from all this—' her arms waved over the fields '—and I feel I've taken off my makeup and lo and behold, what's underneath is the real me.'

Hannah examined her friend's face. 'Nope,' she said, grinning, 'the lipstick's still there and you look as gorgeous as ever . . . but maybe, let me look at you, yes, maybe you do look just a bit more like a real person.'

'And at least I'm back in the will,' Lavinia added with a wry smile. 'Come on, let's run, I can't wait for some of

Mrs Hill's rice pudding. You know what those five-shilling menus are like, they're not very big and the desserts in that restaurant were terrible.'

*　*　*

It was several weeks before Dotty limped off the bus. She looked thin and pale and her head was bowed. Her shoulders looked as if her body had imploded like a balloon and all her jauntiness had vanished. The girls had just finished their Saturday chores and were washing in the yard when they spotted her. They raced up to her and enfolded her in their arms. Lavinia stepped back, shocked at how much weight Dotty had lost.

'Are you all right?' she said urgently.

Dotty nodded, but her eyes told a different story. Hannah and Lavinia took hold of an arm each and gently led her across into the barn and up the stairs. Bertha was already there, rifling through Lavinia's things for a scarf she wanted to wear. After an inauspicious start, Lavinia and Hannah had made a real effort to include Bertha, but she did everything she could to alienate them both, including helping herself to all their things when it suited her.

'You could have asked me,' Lavinia said, offering the scarf to her. 'Is this the one you wanted?'

Bertha snatched it from her, looking coldly at the little trio.

She had ignored every offer of friendship from her room-mates, more concerned about getting her own way, whether it was borrowing their clothes without asking or getting to the table first to get the biggest helpings, but the final straw for the two girls had been when she made fun of George, who was totally miserable without Dotty. At that point, Lavinia had snapped at her and the atmosphere had been frosty ever since.

'This is Dotty, Bertha,' Hannah said. 'Could you possibly give us a minute?'

'Oh, bugger, I can tell when I'm not wanted,' Bertha retorted, leaving Lavinia's things in a muddle and grabbing her tin of precious chopped-up cigarettes. She took her time to search around under her piles of clothes for matches, throwing a bra and pants carelessly out of the way and then headed for the door. She paused to look back at the three heads, bowed together, shrugged and closed the door loudly behind her.

Dotty suddenly folded into a foetal pose and hugged her arms around herself. She was shaking. Catching Lavinia's eye, Hannah signalled that now was not the time to talk and that what she needed was a good night's sleep.

* * *

The following day was Sunday and the girls' day off. Bertha took herself off early in the morning to get the bus to Norwich. She had no interest in Dotty's return; she was more intent on tracking down a crowd of ground crew who regularly went to the city's Bell Hotel on a Sunday. The men's plan was to catch a glimpse of the American Women's Army Air Corps who'd taken over the top floor, but Bertha's plan was to get to the bar downstairs first to stake her claim on the best-looking man and she'd pinched a bit of Lavinia's Yardley lipstick to help her cause.

* * *

Dotty woke to find the other two sitting on the bed next to her, patiently waiting. Her eyes flitted from one to the other.

'It's all right, Dotty,' Hannah said quietly, 'you don't have to tell us if you don't want to, but . . .'

'No, I do,' Dotty said in a whisper. 'I have to tell someone.' She lay back on the pillow against the wall.

She closed her eyes, unable to look either of them in the face, and haltingly told them the secret she had been holding in for so many years. Having sworn never to go home again, she'd been distraught when the ambulance gave her no choice and, in any case, she knew she'd been in no fit state to argue.

'It's my dad,' she said finally. 'He . . . he . . .' But she couldn't speak any more and buried her head in her hands. Hannah shivered, feeling the next five minutes were finally

going to sweep away the remains of her youthful inno-
cence. She heard Dotty's words, but they seemed to be
coming from a long way away. Lavinia leaned forward.
She had seen that haunted look before in one of the young
dancers at The Windmill, who used to flinch if anyone
went near her.

'I think her dad's been ... interfering with her,' she
whispered to Hannah.

Hannah gasped. The suspicions she had been having
seemed too dreadful to be true and now here was Lavinia
confirming them. But a father touching his own daughter?
It was such a terrible concept that Hannah's toes curled up
in disgust. It was the same feeling she'd had when faced
with Jed, but she could not even contemplate how she
would feel if . . . No, she shook her head; that was not a scenario she could imagine for one single second. Her father
may have been distant, but he was such a good man and
would never, ever have hurt her. Meanwhile, Lavinia was
thinking about her own father too.

Over their luncheon, he'd explained gently how he'd
been so disappointed in her for having a love affair with a
married man, and as he talked that day, she had finally realised how callous she'd been towards him and her mother.
She remembered the day, over a year ago now, when she'd
faced them in the grand library at their family home. She'd
been furious at being told in no uncertain terms to leave
The Windmill and come home, but when they tried to

talk to her, begging her to walk away from Jeremy, she'd ignored her father's crushed expression and her mother's distraught face and had challenged them to such an extent that they eventually said the words she knew were coming: 'It's either him or us.' She felt a burning shame rise up in her – her parents had only ever wanted the best for their only daughter, going to great lengths to find her a place in the Land Army. She knew she had pushed their patience to the limit but still they came back to reach out to her. Now, here was Dotty, who would have given anything to have a caring father.

After about five minutes, Dotty opened her eyes.

'When I was thirteen, he got me pregnant,' she muttered, confessing something she thought she would never say out loud. 'He made me go to see this woman who . . . it was horrible, there was blood everywhere. I can never marry anyone. I can never have another child. How could I ever tell a husband that?'

'What about your mother?' Hannah asked, unable to believe that a woman would stand by and let such a thing happen to her child. 'And the others . . .' she added, recalling Dotty had two younger sisters.

Dotty looked completely defeated. 'My mum's terrified of him. He . . . he drinks too much and then becomes violent. But if she leaves, she'll be on the streets. The other two, he never seems to touch, maybe because my brothers are bigger now and he knows they will stand up to him.

But me, well, he seems to think I'm his property. I had to spend the whole time spending a penny in the piss pot so I didn't go outside where he could—'

'Does George know?' Lavinia interrupted, unable to bear hearing any more.

'*No!* And he must never know.' Dotty started to cry, rocking forwards and backwards, hugging her knees. 'How can I let him love me . . . touch me. . . m-marry me?'

She looked up with desperation in her eyes.

There was no answer and she knew it.

Chapter 38

Dotty was back at work at dawn the following morning as if nothing had happened, but she looked completely crushed, not even raising a smile when she was shown the brand-new automated milking machine that would save her hours of work. Bertha lasted one more week before she triumphantly told them that they would all have to manage without her as she was being transferred back to the farm she had come from. She cheerfully gathered up her clothes from all over the floor, bade the girls a cocky goodbye and said she would see them all in Yorkshire – or maybe not. Lavinia, in particular, gave a deep sigh of relief and immediately washed every bit of bedding Bertha had used, put all her rubbish in the dustbin and wiped her hands in satisfaction. 'At last, we have our room back to ourselves,' she told Hannah.

Dotty, meanwhile, determinedly got to grips with the new milking machine, cleaned out the sheds and moved the manure to the fields before the spring sowing, but she was uncharacteristically quiet for days on end. The other two tried to cheer her up and even suggested they should go to Samson and Hercules one Saturday – it had been so long since they had been, but Dotty just shook her head and fiercely carried on cleaning the milking equipment. She avoided George, who searched for her round every corner, looking as heartbroken as a Shakespearean tragic hero.

* * *

One day, just before Easter, a police car came up the drive and two bobbies got out, one holding his truncheon and a pair of handcuffs. Andrew Hollis went over to meet them.

'Can I help you, Officers?'

'We're looking for Jed Roberts,' the older one said, looking round the yard. At that moment, Jed appeared by the north gate. He saw the policemen and started to veer in the opposite direction. The policemen set off at a run after him. By now, everyone was watching, even the German POWs, who were gathered by the truck, ready to set off to clear some ditches. They craned their necks to see what was happening. Jed's one-legged run was no match for the younger policeman, who grabbed him from behind, pushed him to the ground and put some handcuffs on him. He then dragged him back to the yard, telling him his rights as he pulled him along,

The older one spoke. 'Jed Roberts, we are arresting you for the rape of a young girl in 1928. You will be taken—' He did not get any further as Dotty flew across the yard and flung herself at Jed's back, pummelling him with her fists.

'You bastard, you bastard,' she was shouting. 'How dare you? How could you? A young girl? Do you know what that will have done to her life? Do you know how you've destroyed her?' She collapsed onto the floor, weeping, and George ran up to gather her into his arms. She fell against him in a heap, her tiny body jerking with sobs.

'He . . . my dad . . . they're all the same,' she whispered.

George hugged her to him. Now he understood. All those times when she had drawn back from him, when she'd stopped before she told him she loved him. All he wanted in the whole world was to take her into his protection forever and never, ever, let anyone hurt her again. His back straightened and the young boy with the sheepish grin was gone forever. He was a man and this was his woman and God help anyone who came between them.

Hannah felt a searing anger rising from her stomach. This man, who had tried to rape her, had stolen a young girl's life – a young girl like Dotty. She wished she'd done more than kick him in the groin, she thought to herself.

Andrew Hollis stepped forward. He was shocked but almost relieved that Jed was being taken off his hands. He had had enough of the man's belligerence and defiance. Archie came up behind him. He put his hand on Andrew's shoulder. They stood together as they had done so many times before, as a team.

The younger policeman pushed Jed into the back of the Black Maria and his superior came forward to talk privately to Andrew as the owner of the farm. They had found a woman's body in Norwich, he confided; she had hanged herself, leaving a note accusing Jed of the terrible crime against her that had led her into a life of destitution. The older officer was a father of three girls and he found his disgust for prisoners like Jed Roberts threatened the professionalism he had prided himself on all his working life. He could hardly bear the fact that he was going to have to travel in the same car as him.

Andrew went white as the police officer relayed the evidence against Jed. He felt a huge guilt that he had not acted earlier, especially after the attack on Hannah. He realised he'd been so anxious to keep the farm going at all costs that he'd suppressed the nagging suspicions. He blamed his experiences in the Great War for making him hide his feelings, but hadn't realised how far that subterfuge had started to threaten his humanity and, by ignoring his instincts about this man, he had risked irreparable harm to the young women in his care. He felt ashamed and had a sudden desire to see his own daughter, Bobby. *Maybe it is time we found some common ground,* he thought. He wanted to be a real father to her.

One by one, the little group of bystanders backed off, leaving George kneeling on the stone slabs with Dotty crumpled in his arms; they looked like a biblical painting.

* * *

About fifty miles away, another policeman was also performing his duty. Jack Wilson was a young constable in his first year after training, who had been in the police station when Sally Ravenscroft came in, after propping her bike outside and brushing her hair out of her eyes. In a calm, controlled voice she introduced herself and then informed him that there was an escaped German prisoner who was tending to an injured policeman after his car had crashed on a bend just a couple of miles south of the town. She then told him she had to leave as she had a Tempest aircraft to deliver but would be available for interview if needed. As she turned to go, she added, 'I suspect he may be the one who went missing from Salhouse Farm, near Norwich, before Christmas.' As Jack Wilson ran to the pegs in the corner to get his helmet, she said, 'Your police officer will need an ambulance, he has a serious head and arm injuries.

'And one more thing,' she told him as an afterthought, 'I think the German has done an excellent job of taking care of him. He could have run off but I'm confident he'll still be there.' With those words, she was gone, leaving

Jack to stare after the most terrifyingly controlled young woman he had ever met in his life.

* * *

By the time Jack arrived at the site of the crash in a police car, the ambulance men he had alerted were already there, carefully manoeuvring the bloodied, pale young policeman into their vehicle. They turned to Jack and whispered that, quite frankly, if it hadn't been for the strange, foreign young man, who had successfully and professionally halted the bleeding, this copper would be dead by now. The German, as the girl had predicted, was still there, tucking his patient's blanket around the stretcher. Jack coughed and the German turned towards him, his arms outstretched. It took a moment for Jack to realise the prisoner was waiting to be handcuffed and that he had forgotten to bring any with him. In any case, he reasoned, he wasn't sure he was supposed to put them on these Germans – his superintendent had given them all a warning that any treatment of aliens had to be fair in case mistreatment was used as an excuse to abuse British lads over on the continent. He bundled Karl into the car with as much authority as he could muster, trying to hide his excitement. He knew his mum would be very proud of him and his dad would tell the whole bowls team, but in the meantime, he had an enemy escapee on his hands and he was watching his every move to make sure he did not escape again.

In fact, Karl was not going anywhere. He was almost relieved to be captured and was willing to face whatever came next. He was tired, hungry, wet and, frankly, fed up with being on the run.

By the time they made it to the local police station, all the major players of the county constabulary were there to greet him, anxious to get their names in the papers as being the ones to apprehend the famous villain. They pushed Karl roughly into a cell, leaving him there for hours until a man from the Home Office came up from London to take charge.

Archibald Prendergast strode in, bowler hat in hand, huffing and puffing at the effort it had taken to walk at a less than dignified pace from the station. He was not in a good mood and had not been from the first day this man had escaped. Prevented from using a radio to alert police forces across the country for fear of interception, one hundred and twenty individual telegrams had had to be sent on that occasion. Now, news of the POW's capture was being circulated by the same method and Archibald had left a harassed underling to take on the task, preferring to get out of the office and onto a train to see the escapee for himself. It was exactly the sort of bureaucracy that sent Archibald reaching for the whisky bottle hidden in his office.

'I'll take charge of the prisoner now,' he told the little group who were crowded into the police station. 'I need two men, that's all, to guard him. He'll be coming back with me to a secret location in London where he will be interrogated and then held in solitary confinement for twenty-eight days, as is the rule.

'And, I have to insist, I'm afraid,' he went on, 'that no word of this capture is spoken of outside these four walls. We will deal with everything from here. Now, please go back to your work.'

The disappointed faces around him prompted him to adopt his most officious expression. To have a German wandering the country for so long was exactly the sort of information Whitehall did not want to disseminate to an enemy desperate for opportunities for propaganda. They simply wanted the German to disappear for a bit before being quietly reinstated at the farm. He knew that after the interrogation, the prisoner, if he knew what was good for him, would not wish for any publicity about his time on the run, and as long as this lot kept their counsel, the story would die down without issue.

The young police officer, Jack, looked particularly crest-fallen. He had really wanted to impress his dad, who was always, to be honest, a bit sniffy about his son's job, making fun of his bicycle clips and truncheon, and he had already sketched out the conversation he would have that night in the White Lion. Jack wondered whether he would ever be able to tell anyone of the most exciting arrest he would probably ever make in the whole of his career. Probably not, he realised crossly, hanging his helmet back up on the peg.

Chapter 39

Karl was taken to London by three men, his second visit since his interrogation at The Cage. He tried to recognise landmarks as they drove through the city, the blue light flashing. Two things struck him; firstly, how beautiful London still was and, secondly, how much he regretted the Luftwaffe's part in trying to destroy it. At last, the car pulled up down a back street outside a dark stone building with few windows and he was bundled out and straight into an underground cell. There was only one small window in the top left of the room, which had a piece of blackout card over it, leaving no light coming through, so Karl had to blink until his eyes adjusted. He saw a truckle bed with a folded blanket on it in the corner, a bucket for slops and, as far as he could see in the gloom, very little else.

He shivered, partly from cold and partly from the realisation that this was it – the end of the road for him. He had no idea what happened to prisoners of war in Britain who escaped, but he knew what usually happened to them in Germany.

The policeman who pushed Karl into the freezing cold, damp cell took great pleasure in thinking that this prisoner was about to suffer deprivation and discomfort, but, in fact, the hard bed with springs poking through was the most comfortable place Karl had slept in months and he curled up on it, wrapping the rough blanket around himself, resigned to his fate. He closed his eyes with an almost grateful sigh and fell into a deep sleep.

It seemed only moments later that he was roughly awakened.

'Get up, you!' A large policeman was prodding him.

Karl rubbed his eyes and automatically stood to attention.

'Follow me,' the man barked at him and marched out of the room, up two flights of stairs and down several bland corridors.

A small room awaited him with a wooden table and three chairs in it. Sitting on one of the chairs was the large, red-faced man who had brought him there from Norwich. On another was a man in a police uniform, sitting stiffly and shuffling with impatience, and on the third chair was Andrew Hollis, looking furious at being dragged down to London just to identify a prisoner. He looked up with recognition when Karl walked into the room.

The rotund man spoke first. 'Is this him?'

Andrew nodded.

Turning to Karl, Archibald Prendergast said, 'You have caused us a great deal of inconvenience, but as prisoner of war, you will . . .' Here he hesitated. He hated giving these Germans any quarter at all, but he was bound by a higher authority, who insisted all prisoners had to be treated fairly. He coughed and continued, 'You will be taken from here to . . . somewhere else, for proper interrogation, then there will be a period of "re-education", after which you will be put in solitary confinement for twenty-eight days. Then it depends on Mr Hollis here whether he will have you back or not.' He raised his voice to counteract a telephone that was ringing loudly in the other room.

The constable who had brought Karl to the room put his head round the door. 'Sorry to interrupt, sir, but there's a very insistent young woman, who says she's an ATA pilot, on the telephone. She wants to speak to Mr Hollis.'

Andrew Hollis looked puzzled, but went out to take the call.

Archibald Prendergast was beginning to question Karl about his movements over the last few months, in preparation for the full interrogation that would take place later, when Andrew Hollis came back into the room.

'Um, that was my daughter. Apparently, her friend was the one who came upon the accident and saw this . . . prisoner . . . helping the police officer.' Here he shook his head in resignation. Why was it nothing surprised him about Bobby? Any sniff of drama and, somehow, she was always involved. He went on: 'Anyway, her friend is adamant that he was an example of kindness and skill and that his behaviour on this occasion should be taken into consideration going forwards. My daughter's understanding was that he could have ignored the accident and saved himself and says her friend is willing to testify on his behalf.'

Archibald made a huffing noise. This blurring of the evidence irritated the hell out of him. He had in front of him a German who had wilfully run away from his guard, managed to avoid capture for months doing God knows what mischief and now here was a witness who was prepared to defend him. There were times when he envied his brother in the RAF, who could just aim and shoot at the enemy.

'There'll be a full inquiry where witness statements will be taken into account,' he said after a moment, shuffling the papers in front of him. 'The prisoner will, naturally, have to undertake a full programme of re-education, but I believe, from his files, that this one's never been seen as a threat to us. His health will be checked by a doctor to make sure there are no more reoccurrences of the strange episodes he was experiencing when he went AWOL and it may even be that his mental health difficulties will help to mitigate his culpability. All I need to know now is whether, once all those checks are completed, you, Mr Hollis, would be prepared to take him back.'

Andrew looked across at Karl's face. It hid no guile, no rancour and no aggression. He remembered the man's kindness to Hannah and recognised that he was looking at the face of a good man caught up in a bad war.

'I will,' he said finally.

* * *

The farm was buzzing with rumours. Word had got around that the boss had been called to London to see if the police had really captured the German who'd given Stanley the slip all those months ago. The POWs were also desperate to find out the truth, Peter most of all. He'd really missed Karl during the months he'd been away and had begun to appreciate how much he needed his support. In the hut, which was usually full of divisions, Karl had become the hero and even the most ardent Third Reich enthusiasts were in awe of a prisoner who managed to escape. The mild-mannered doctor had really risen in their estimation and Peter, as his friend, looked set to benefit from their new-found respect.

But there was one person who avoided all gossip and could not find the words to express how she really felt, and that was Hannah. She'd experienced such huge relief when she'd found out that Karl was still alive, but his sudden disappearance had hurt her and had made her think he couldn't possibly care for her in the way she did him

Oh well, if he's sent back to Germany, I won't have to worry anymore, she told herself. Long conversations in her head had persuaded the young Land Army girl that, with such a distance between them, she would easily be able to forget him; her heart, however, had other ideas, and fantasies about the pair of them walking free amongst the summer flowers continued to disturb her sleep. The thought that he might, after all, turn up back on the farm, put her right back where she had been before Christmas – a woman hopelessly in love.

Unable to cope with the unspoken questions that were on Lavinia's lips, as soon as she finished work, Hannah took herself off for a walk and strode purposefully down the drive towards the Broad.

All the way, she muttered to herself, her head down, until she was jolted out of her reverie by the sound of a bicycle coming up behind her. It almost collided with her as it veered, out of control.

It was being inexpertly ridden by a young girl, about the age of eight, who dropped the bike at the side of the gravel path and looked crossly at it.

'Bah! Stupid machine. Ah, *bonjour*, I'm Elizé,' the child said, turning to look at Hannah. 'I am so sorry, I do not know how to ride this thing yet. Look at my poor knees, they are so sore, I keep falling off. I am fed up with this stupid thing. It is dangerous, but at least I did not knock you over, *n'est ce pas?* So far I have knocked over Tante Agnes, Archie and . . .' She paused to think. 'Ah yes, Mrs Hill too, but she is so fat, it was me who was knocked over that time.'

She looked up as if waiting for praise at her list of victims.

Hannah couldn't help but smile at the girl's gushing introduction.

'You're French?' she asked.

'Ah *oui*, but my father—' her face clouded over, the memories too painful to recall '—he is . . . was, English.'

'But what are you doing here?' Hannah asked.

'I . . .' The girl gave the famous French shrug. 'I have come to stay. Yes, that is correct. I stay here.' She nodded her head as if to agree with herself. The story was a long one and she did not want to share it with this stranger.

'But, bah, I will leave the bicycle here and walk with you instead. What is your name?' Elizé asked.

'I'm Hannah.'

'Do you work here?'

The directness of her questions was like a Gatling gun, firing one shot after another at the older girl.

'Yes, I am with the Land Army, I work on the land.'

'But you were going on a walk, so we can walk together.' And with that, she started to march towards the gate, leaving Hannah with no choice but to follow her, running to catch up.

Immediately, Elizé started to chatter about everyone up at the farmhouse. Firstly, there was Monsieur Hollis, who was always cross, but she believed he had a kind heart; he just had to find it. Then Madame Hollis, who was always so sad, and Tante Agnes who spent all her time making sure her sister did not hurt herself when she was in the garden with her pruning shears. Then her eyes lit up when she talked about 'Bobbee' Hollis, as she called her.

'She is wonderful,' she said, holding her hand to her heart in rapture. 'She flies aeroplanes and is very brave and very clever.'

Hannah finally managed to get a word in. 'But what are you doing here, Elizé?'

The little girl looked very mysterious and put her finger to her lips. 'I cannot tell you, but if you become my special friend then maybe we can share secrets, no?'

Hannah thought that sharing her own secrets was the last thing she would be able to do so said in a non-committal way: 'Uh-huh.'

To avoid more questioning, she headed towards the woods, which had just sprouted the magical carpet of May bluebells. Elizé followed her and delightedly clapped her hands as she took in the blue hue that covered the ground in front of her, completely entranced by the beautiful sight.

'Oh, I have never seen anything so lovely,' she said, hopping from one foot to another, but then she swung round. 'Do you think, Hannah, that when people die, they come back as flowers?'

Hannah stopped in her tracks. The question was like a cold slap to the face. *What horrors had this child seen?* she wondered.

She hesitated, looking at the earnest little face in front of her, aware that the next words she uttered could hold a special significance. 'I believe, Elizé, that nature has a way of taking the best of us all and recreating that every spring.'

Elizé put her head on one side while she considered this, but then dropped down to touch the flowers and closed her eyes. 'I hope so, Hannah, I hope so.'

* * *

After that day, Elizé searched out her new friend and every time Hannah had a spare moment to take herself off for a walk, she would turn around to find the little girl was there. Appearing at her side, she would tuck her little hand into Hannah's and babble on happily. Her lively conversation entranced Hannah but as soon as any mention was made of how she came to be in Norwich or what had brought her to the farm, Elizé would suddenly remember she had chores to do and race off. Hannah recognised a traumatised child when she saw one, having seen the same blank expression on Dotty's face. She, too, had become quite an expert in hiding emotions both as a daughter with a distant father and now as an adult with a guilty secret. She knew this child's inconsequential chatter was a front for a story she did not want to tell.

Chapter 40

Miles away in London, Karl was having a much easier time, unburdening himself willingly. The interrogators had started their investigations in an aggressive manner, but had been taken aback by the open answers that the prisoner in front of them gave, prompting them when they missed something out. Having started out with concerns that he might be a spy, they gradually gained more confidence that he was everything he said he was, and nothing more. They were impressed by the clinical detail that he provided about how his mental state prompted him to step off that truck in the first place and how he had survived those first days of escape. Having such a willing prisoner in their grasp allowed them to find out more about the brainwashing that he had been subjected to growing up in an emerging Nazi regime. The extent of the process could now be fully documented and the pen of the man recording the interview flew across the page. The one time Karl faltered was when he mentioned the gypsies, for fear of getting them into trouble but, once he told his interrogators that they believed him to be Dutch, his time with them seemed of little interest.

After a full interrogation, a re-education programme was started, which Karl undertook without objection, watching the films, reading the pamphlets and listening to the lectures with academic analysis. He was, in fact, traumatised by what had happened to his country, but he knew how constant indoctrination and fear had persuaded a whole nation into acquiescence. He only blamed the leaders and almost welcomed the opportunity to discuss how Hitler had persuaded so many to follow him, dissecting the evidence from a scientist's point of view of how fear had been used to quell any dissention. Karl's instructors made notes on his file, thinking what an asset a man like this would have been to those trying to gauge the German mindset earlier in the war. They wrote in the margins how he could still be useful in the future rehabilitation of Germany as well as in propaganda in the final months of the war. Karl, however, was not interested in being used as a mouthpiece for the British government, he was just impatient for the conflict to end so he could go back to finishing his training to become a doctor and find a way to claim the lovely Hannah for his wife – if she'd have him.

* * *

Hannah and Elizé were walking away from the village into the Norfolk countryside when a convoy of American jeeps, trucks and wagons passed them. The two girls had to step almost into the hedge to avoid them, but the trail of vehicles seemed to go on for ages. When it had finally passed, Elizé turned to Hannah questioningly. 'Where are they all going?'

The evening news bulletins on the radio had talked for so long about the 'big push' that Hannah found herself crossing her fingers that this was finally it.

She looked down at Elizé's trusting little face.

'I think we may be getting near to the end of the war,' she said.

The child's eyes filled with tears. 'Does that mean the world will go back to normal?'

'Maybe, for some, but for others, it will never be normal again,' Hannah said carefully.

'*Non*, you are correct. For some it will never be as it was.'

Hannah pulled the little girl to her, but Elizé froze, then stepped back, that familiar mask enshrouding her face.

'Come,' Elizé said. 'I've heard Mrs Hill is making her wonderful scones; maybe she'll send some over for you too.' And with that she ran off back up the drive leaving Hannah with the feeling that she had just witnessed a grown-up assessment of the effects of war from an eight-year-old's mouth.

* * *

The following night, the barn echoed with the tense silence as the Land Army girls and the farmhands listened intently to the first reports coming in of landings on the beaches of Normandy, fooling the enemy, who reacted too late to be able to repel the huge numbers of troops. The triumphant tones of the presenter disguised the reality that they all suspected, which was that the success had come at a terrible price. Nonetheless, they all sighed with relief that, finally, an invasion had taken place, and in the right direction – away from British shores.

As the news bulletin finished, the barn door opened and Archie came in, grinning broadly, carrying a cardboard box that he put down on the table.

'We've done it!' he pronounced proudly. 'We've got them on the run and the boss has sent over a few bottles of beer to celebrate.'

Dotty immediately jumped up, clapping her hands together. 'A celebration is exactly what we need,' she said.

William Handforth looked scornful. 'We haven't won yet.'

'No,' Archie said, grinning, 'but we're a lot nearer than we were yesterday. Come on, William, you can be the first to make a toast.'

Everyone grinned, looking with delight at William squirming in the corner. He hated optimism and celebration, but the bottle being offered to him was too good to refuse.

'Oh, very well then,' he said, banging the top of the bottle on a stone plinth on the wall to open it. 'I offer a toast: to all those brave men who have given us a chance, finally, to finish off Hitler and all his mates.'

The whole group cheered and, for once, the edges of William's mouth turned upwards.

* * *

On the last night of the re-education programme, before being locked up for twenty-eight days, Karl was given supper in the corner of an empty first-floor room and looked down at his last view of the world below. In the distance, he saw a newspaper seller standing next to a billboard. He squinted his eyes to read it. 'Our armies in N France,' it read. 'Four thousand invasion ships have crossed channel.' *So, this was the beginning of the end,* he thought, saying a quick prayer that the final stages would be quick with as few deaths on both sides as possible. Karl was also guiltily aware that he was hoping Hitler would not win.

He'd hardly finished his meal when he was ushered off downstairs to the windowless area that housed the cells. Resigned to a month of solitary confinement, Karl knew it was the lack of light he was going to find the hardest to deal with. Working the land had taught him how much the sky and landscape were etched into his whole being and, to counteract the gloom, he'd already planned to conjure up visions of the woods outside Tübingen, with blue skies, birds tweeting and children playing. He hoped that recalling such a joyful time would get him through.

The days were interminably long without a dawn or sunset and only a meagre breakfast to let him know it was morning, but Karl decided he would keep his mind busy by going through his studies in his head. He knew that the way to survive isolation was to keep boredom at bay by establishing a routine and, grinning at the fact he was using himself as a psychiatric case study, he systematically divided his day into a timetable of subjects, giving himself mental tasks to solve. Keeping fit and healthy was his other goal so he planned a regime of exercise starting with press-ups and running on the spot when he first woke up. Then, after the thin porridge he hated so much was pushed through the hatch and he had eaten it, he sat down for the first two hours for pathology, investigative medicine and clinical medicine. This was followed by jumping jacks and on-the-spot skipping. Chuckling, he then made himself stand up for ethics, pharmacology and psychiatry, pacing up and down as he mentally visualised the textbooks.

The guard, whose name was Tom, peered, puzzled, through the little sliding hatch in the door. He had never seen such an odd prisoner. Most started yelling or banging their heads on the walls by the end of the second week. As he opened the flap each evening with a weak vegetable stew or spam fritters, he was surprised to find he was smiling back at the gentle, slightly odd man on the other side of the door.

The only time that Karl did struggle was during the night, when the jail went quiet. He would toss and turn with nightmares of Hannah being dragged away from him, or his mother, homeless and begging on the streets in Germany, or even his sister, trapped behind barbed wire. He woke most mornings feeling as if he had not slept at all and it was then that he banged the brick wall with his fist, imagining breaking through to the daylight beyond.

After twenty-seven days, Karl recounted the scratches he had made on the stone wall behind his bed. He had tried not to think too much of his release, knowing that living in the present was the only way to keep his equanimity, but he allowed himself a little thrill of excitement as he pulled the rough blanket around him for the last time to go to sleep.

* * *

'Time to go,' Tom said, giving him a shake the next morning. Karl shook himself and then leaped out of bed. He couldn't help it, he hugged the guard, who immediately stepped backwards, trying to keep his professionalism.

'I'm sorry,' Karl said with a smile, 'but you 'ave been my only friend for twenty-eight days, but now I must leave you.'

Tom's mouth reluctantly turned into a smile. This prisoner was like none he had ever come across before.

'Follow me,' he said, turning to make his way out of the door. Karl blinked at the natural light that flooded the corridor. It was a beautiful July day and he breathed deeply. He was still alive.

Chapter 41

It was a hot summer's day that Karl was returned to the farm and the activity was centred around haymaking. There had been strict instructions issued to the prisoners of war that he was not to be made a fuss of and, to be honest, since the D Day landings, the more ardent Hitler supporters had gone a little quiet, sensing defeat. Their main focus now was on working out their best strategies for keeping clear of the British authorities' radars, so they might get home sooner rather than later.

Karl walked out to the fields, looking painfully thin and with hollowed cheeks, but his eyes were bright as they searched out the one person he'd been longing to see. Hannah was forking the hay onto a cart where it was piled up neatly, ready to be taken back to the barn for spreading out and treading down. She stopped in her tracks when she spotted Karl, but then hurriedly buried her burning face in the armful of hay. Her heart was thumping and she knew if she allowed her gaze to find Karl's, there would be no disguising

the emotion she was feeling. She went over to Lavinia
for help.

'Talk to me, quickly, Lavinia. Say anything.'

Lavinia needed no further information and started
an in-depth conversation about how the rest of the field
needed to be done before nightfall. The fact that she
expanded her arms to encompass the whole field, meant
that Hannah was able to glimpse the look of longing in
Karl's eyes, while she pretended to scan the acreage in
front of her without rousing suspicions.

She had forgotten how impossible this all was but then,
when she saw Karl's face light up with love, none of that
seemed to matter anymore. She looked around to make
sure no one was watching and gave him a warm smile
back, knowing that look would have to last him until they
were able to meet up again. Finally, she knew that the feelings she had been struggling with for so long were recip-
rocated and she was loved by the man she adored. It was
the best feeling in the world and she hugged the hay to her.

* * *

Three days later, she heard words that gave her hope they
might actually be able to spend precious time together.

'Hannah, I'm really sorry, but can you take that prisoner to church again,' Andrew Hollis called over to her in
the yard.

He saw her bite her lip and misinterpreted her expression.

'You needn't worry, Hannah, the authorities are convinced he isn't a danger, so Stanley's been stood down, but make sure you've got your gun with you, just in case.'

Hannah had to stop her feet from skipping over to the pump to wash.

* * *

Sunday came and Hannah curled her hair specially and even borrowed some of Lavinia's lipstick, avoiding her friend's compassionate look.

She cycled to Mousehold Heath, her pulse racing. She could hardly keep still as Karl came out of the camp to join her. As he looked at her, her heart turned over, and then he moved to stand next to her to sign out, brushing against her arm as he did so and her knees almost buckled at the warmth of his body next to hers. The soldier on the gate motioned Hannah to move to one side and whispered, 'There's no guard needed with this one anymore apparently. He's been cleared by the authorities as safe. I think you should be OK, but be wary.'

Hannah felt a shiver of excitement; time alone was what she'd been dreaming of for so long, but she and Karl both maintained a tense silence until they got out of sight of the camp and into the woods. Then Karl turned towards her and said one word: 'Hannah.'

She checked all around them and fell into his arms, which encircled her with a strength and determination she knew reflected his feelings for her.

He looked straight into her eyes and then leaned in to kiss her. It was a gentle kiss to begin with but then it intensified, and Hannah felt her chest constricting. She clung to him, acknowledging that she had never felt like this before and suspected she would never feel it again with any other man.

'*Ich liebe dich*. I love you,' he said quietly.

She nodded and was about to reply when they heard some children coming from behind them. They sprang apart and started to walk briskly down into Norwich.

They were both angry; could they never have just five minutes to themselves?

* * *

During mass, Karl's hand kept brushing hers and she felt her fingers coil in to embrace it. Each tiny movement had such an enormous significance and seemed magnified a hundred times. In his sermon, the priest was talking about reconciliation and how, if, with God's help, the British won this war, then it would soon be time to forgive the enemy.

An expletive was released by the soldier in the pew behind Karl and his sharp finger jabbed into the prisoner's back. 'Not if I can help it,' he said through gritted teeth.

Hannah looked down, praying for a better world, a more forgiving world and one where she could be with the man she loved. She wasn't sure if God was listening.

On the way home, Hannah slowed her pace once they got into the cover of the woodland. Without a word, Karl swung round to face her and scooped her up in his arms.

'Oh, you don't know how much I've missed you,' she said into his neck. 'I thought you didn't care about me – you just vanished.'

'I am so sorry, my head, it was not good, I could not think, but I am better now and, oh, my lovely Hannah . . .' There was so little time for everything he wanted to say so he had to go straight to the issue that had been torturing him for so many months. 'How are we going to do this, Fräulein Hannah? Do you think the world will ever let us be together?'

She shook her head and turned up her face to be kissed before the two of them fell to the ground, clutching at each other's clothes, trying to tear them off. It was all so urgent and passionate that their legs were starting to entwine when Karl pulled back.

He was breathing deeply. 'No, Hannah, we must not.'

She frowned; she'd wanted this for so long.

He sat back on his heels and looked sorrowfully at the young woman lying so enticingly on the undergrowth in front of him.

'I want you more than anything in the world, but if we do this now, then we will want more and that is putting you in danger. Passion is powerful and is so hard to control and . . .' He paused here, it hurt so much to say the next sentence. 'When you and I make love, we have to be free and we must be able to walk together down the street, proud of what we have. I will not have you hated for being with me – a prisoner of war. I do not care how long we must wait, but I want you to be my wife.'

Hannah didn't know whether to laugh with delight at his declaration or cry with frustration. It seemed such an impossible scenario and her confusion unleashed a fierce hatred for the world that had created a war that was tearing her apart like this. She stamped her foot like a little girl, but Karl was already starting to walk away from her. He could no longer look at her without taking her back into his arms.

* * *

That Sunday was the last one for several weeks when any of the girls or farmhands were allowed to have any time off. The Ministry of Agriculture was putting impossible demands on farmers on one side of the farm gate and the

Ministry of Food, with responsibility for the produce that went through that gate, had equally unreasonable expectations. They were desperate to protect winter supplies for a country facing increasing ration restrictions, and with food convoys still being targeted, Britain was becoming worryingly dependent on what it could produce within its own shores.

Up at the farmhouse, Mrs Hill was tearing her hair out trying to produce interesting meals that had enough nutritional value in them for a family that had been augmented by too many visitors and now Bobby Hollis herself had come home, nursing a broken ankle. On top of that, the Germans had started to send their own little reminders across to Britain that they had not conceded victory yet and the first V1 flying bomb had dropped on Swanscombe in Kent a few weeks before. After that, the ominous drone of the lethal doodlebugs was beginning to be heard far too regularly overhead, with everyone holding their breath to see if the engine was about to cut out, signifying it was about to deliver a fatal payload to the earth beneath.

It was as the little group of workers were busy in the top field that they heard yet another telltale buzz above them. They paused and looked up, all silently counting from one to seven, waiting anxiously to see if the V1's engine kept running to eight or whether there would be the deathly hush they all dreaded. As they all mouthed the word 'Se—', the unmanned bomber seemed to stop in mid-air and then point directly at the farm below, freezing everyone in place. Then, like greyhounds in the starting blocks, each one of the workers in the field started to race away from the killing machine they could see plummeting towards them at 400 mph.

The bomber seared like a torpedo through the air, missing the field, to hit the barn on the north side of the yard. The noise as it crashed was in total contrast to the ominous silence seconds beforehand. There were shards of wood that exploded in all directions and a spiral of smoke rose almost immediately from the building that housed the hay for the animals, seed for the fields and, they all fervently hoped, no members of the little Salhouse community.

Running full pelt from the fields, the girls and farmhands went straight to the pump where Archie was already gathering buckets to fill, remembering with sinking hearts the last time they had done this. Mr Hollis ran across the yard, carrying a hosepipe, but when he arrived at the barn, he stood still, looking up at the enormous amount of destruction that had taken place. There was a huge, gaping hole in the middle of the barn and debris had scattered in all directions.

From the other side of the farm came the prisoners of war and from the farmhouse emerged the members of the Hollis family, looking shaken and covered in dust from the shattered windows. Andrew Hollis ran over to them, mentally counting them all. There was someone missing. Where was his sister-in-law, Agnes? He moved from face to face for an answer until Mrs Hill quietly said, 'Miss Clarke went into the barn to get some straw for the haybox.'

At that moment, Archie, who had been standing behind his boss, pushed past all of them, racing headlong into the barn, ignoring the flames and huge plumes of smoke that greeted him like the gates of hell. Andrew, John and even William tried to run after him, but were beaten back by the heat, coughing and spluttering.

No one said a word, they all just stood, holding on to the people next to them for support. There were fingernails pressed into arms and tense facial muscles clenched while they all waited, trying not to let their minds run ahead to what the next few moments might bring. Just yards from the flames in the barn, there was absolute silence, only broken by Elizé's whimpering.

Suddenly, there was the sound of debris being roughly kicked out of the way and a figure staggered out, covered in dust and with a blackened face. It was Archie, clutching the lifeless body of Miss Clarke in his arms, her head lolling backwards. He was choking, but knelt down to lay her tenderly on the ground saying urgently between coughs, 'Breathe, breathe. Oh, for God's sake, Agnes, breathe. Please.'

Through the crowd of prisoners of war, Karl elbowed his way to the front. 'I can help' he said simply.

Hannah stepped forward and spoke to the Hollis family. 'Let him help, he's a doctor.'

Elizé ran over to take Hannah's hand and told them all, 'This is my friend, Hannah, and the doctor is a friend too.' She looked challengingly at them all.

Andrew Hollis was distraught; he didn't register which German it was, but instead, all he saw was the familiar image from his dreams of a German soldier standing over him on a field in France with a bayonet. 'No, you bastard, you will not touch her!' he screamed.

Hannah watched as the tall woman with a mass of dark, auburn hair, moved forward to touch the furious man on the arm, nodding towards Karl for him to deal with the woman on the ground. She realised this must be Bobby Hollis, the ATA pilot and Andrew's daughter. Although hobbling with her ankle bandaged, this formidable figure still seemed in charge.

Archie looked up with a stricken expression at the man he had worked alongside for so many years and pleaded with him, 'Move away, boss, he's our only hope.'

Slowly, Andrew Hollis allowed himself to be pulled back by his daughter so that the trainee doctor could step forward to shift Agnes over onto her stomach. Karl signalled to Hannah to give him her jumper so that he could roll it into a tube to put under Agnes Clarke's stomach then moved her forearms to put her head on them; he started to pummel Agnes from the base of her spine. There was complete silence as he worked. Then Karl turned Agnes over and motioned to Archie to hold her hands above her head. Archie's face was lined with tears and there was now no doubt how much he loved the prone woman in front of him. Karl pushed forward with his thumbs from below Agnes's ribs and suddenly she began to cough and splutter. The whole group heaved a communal sigh of relief and started to cheer. Archie gathered the woman he had loved silently for so many years up in his arms, looked around to convince himself that he was not dreaming, and carried her triumphantly into the house.

Karl sat back on his heels in relief.

Andrew Hollis reached out his hand slowly, finally looking properly at the man who had just saved his sister-in-law's life. The two men shook hands firmly.

Chapter 42

Shaken by the events, the Land Girls and the farmhands huddled around the wireless each night to hear the disturbing news about the V1 flying bombs' destruction across the south-east of England. It was like a loudhailer announcement across the Channel from Hitler that he had not finished with Britain yet.

The girls stomped around the farm, angry that yet another year of their youth was passing them by as here they were, still stuck in a routine of milking, mucking out, haymaking and ploughing. Everyone was tired and tempers were short. It was later in the summer, when harvesting had begun, that the clatter of wheels was heard coming up the drive. The girls looked up expectantly.

'Oh, great, they've come,' John said with satisfaction.

'Who?' Lavinia asked.

'The gypsies, we heard they were in the area and the boss went to see them to book them in for some help.'

Delighted at the prospect of extra hands, there was a rush to make the newcomers welcome by the exhausted workers at Salhouse Farm. Rachel showed them where they could camp and brought them some freshly made lemonade, trying to get a look inside their caravans as she did. She had never seen a gypsy before but had been fascinated by children's books depicting their romantic lifestyle and was delighted to see their little homes decorated in the very patterns and pictures she had coloured in her drawing books when she was a child. She knew that gypsies were as badly treated as Jews by some and she felt a need to make them feel especially accepted, smiling broadly at the women as she handed over the jug.

Andrew, and his father before him, had previously used gypsies on the farm, so thought nothing of their arrival, but Karl looked across with interest when he saw them setting up their camp. He scanned the faces, then spotted one woman who looked familiar. It was Charity, the woman whose baby he had brought into the world.

At the first opportunity, he sidled up next to her. She had recognised him immediately but, noting his uniform, had decided to say nothing until he made the first move, to avoid incriminating him. She smiled warmly at him.

'It is so good to see you, Charity,' Karl whispered. 'How are you? What are you doing here?'

'I'm well and my little one—' she indicated the baby in a shawl on her front '—is growing well, thanks to you. You see that I have joined my husband's family at last,' she said, indicating the little group behind her.

'I am pleased. I hope the others were all well when you left them?'

'Yes,' she replied. 'They were all fine, we did miss you though.'

Karl smiled and then, spotting Stanley in the distance, had started to turn away to make his way to the tool shed for a scythe when she caught his arm.

'We asked questions for you, in King's Lynn. We heard some of your people were taken to the Isle of Man. There was one young woman, a German learning to be a baker?' she queried. 'We heard she'd been arrested and taken there.'

Karl swirled around and, unable to help himself, he put his hands on her shoulders to turn her towards him, his face glowing with excitement.

'Who told you this?'

Releasing his hold, he glanced around to check that no one had seen.

'We know some people there and Pyramus, he liked you, he made some enquiries. He'll be pleased that I've been able to tell you.'

'Do you know anything else, Charity?'

'I think there were others who were taken, an older woman who had travelled from Germany. She was staying with her daughter.'

Karl bit his lip to stop the tears that were prickling his eyes. That had to be his mother, surely. His first thought was relief that she was safe, his second was despair that she was a now a prisoner of sorts, like him, and he could not get to her.

'Move, Schneider,' Stanley said from behind him. 'Those fields won't cut themselves.' He scowled at the prisoner who had caused him so many problems. No one got Stanley Parish into trouble and got away with it.

Karl looked back at Charity as he walked away and mouthed a heartfelt 'Thank you.'

That night, he could not wait to talk to Peter about the new information. 'It was so wonderful to find out they're both safe, but how do I find out how to contact them?' he asked his friend, reverting to German.

Peter shrugged. 'You could try writing, I suppose, but I don't know who to.'

The two men sat in thought on their bunks and Karl ran his fingers through his hair in frustration. He felt cut off from the world, unable to make any headway, and Karl hated being out of control. A group of POWs came into the hut and some of them smiled at the two men. Karl did not realise it, but he was gaining the status of a legend. Already the subject of discussions about how he had shown the Brits a thing or two in evading capture, now, he was a miracle worker who could bring people back from the dead.

After nearly two years of being prisoners of war, the group had divided into those who had become resigned to an Allied victory and those who still believed German superiority would prevail. Some of the new, younger POWs who had been brought more recently to the camp, had known little of a Germany before Hitler and, victims of intense brainwashing, they had no concept that he may not be their country's answer to greatness. But to others, a resignation had set in. They knew they would get fed, they had work to keep them occupied and the authorities made sure their spare time was filled with lectures, crafts, films and even music and performances. The plan was to send prisoners home re-educated with an understanding of the fairness and compassion of Britain and no opportunity to offer them an alternative to the Aryan philosophy was wasted. The Allies needed these men to go home to rebuild their country in a way that would never again threaten the peace of the world.

* * *

Hannah had tried everything to see Karl but every time she was tantalisingly near to the long line of prisoners, the bad-tempered guard had used the butt of his rifle to move the Germans along and all she had been able to see was Karl's wan face looking back at her. The separation hurt more than she could bear, and she waited, desperately, for a chance to take him to church again, but none came.

Her days were as busy as ever, but she felt flat and listless. One day, she had been charged with telling the gypsies they would be needed on the flax field the following day and having delivered her message to their camp, was about to go, when she felt a hand on her sleeve.

Hannah examined the young woman in front of her. She had such a knowing look that Hannah felt she was looking deep into her soul.

'I can tell you your fortune if you like,' Charity said.

Hannah's first instinct was to refuse but then she remembered her mother rushing her past the woman with the hooped earrings who had offered the same thing at the fair on Platt Fields. This time, she was going to make her own decision, so she nodded. She had a strange compulsion to hear what this woman had to say.

The gypsy sat her on a stool next to the fire where a cauldron was bubbling and Hannah felt excitement rising inside her. She couldn't wait to tell Lavinia and Dotty about this.

The woman took hold of her hand, her long fingers pressing gently on Hannah's calloused ones and closed her eyes. There was a heavy silence for a moment as the woman's fingers traced Hannah's palm. Her eyes remained closed as she started to speak.

'You will find your future, but you have to overcome many obstacles. There will be many who do not like what you do.'

Hannah felt a chill creeping up her spine.

The gypsy was continuing: 'Your love is strong, but it will have to stronger than you know. Search across seas and hills to find what you are looking for.'

'Will I, will we . . . make it?' she asked tentatively.

'Yes,' the woman told her, opening her eyes and squeezing her arm. 'And it will be worth every sacrifice.'

Hannah stood up. This was one conversation she would not be sharing with Dotty and Lavinia after all. She reached into her pocket for money.

'No,' the gypsy said. 'I do not want your money.' And Charity walked away, smiling to herself that Vadoma would be proud of her.

Chapter 43

It was several days later when Hannah was in the milking parlour that she heard a noise behind her. She automatically flinched and turned, dreading seeing Jed's figure there waiting for her, but, instead she saw Karl standing in front of her.

He put his finger to his lips and ran towards her, enfolding her in his arms and holding on tightly as if he could somehow avoid ever having to let go again.

'I have five minutes,' he whispered. 'The guard has gone to the toilet. Oh, Hannah, I miss you so much, I love you so much.'

She mumbled into his collar and then looked up into his eyes.

'*Meine Leibe?*'

'I said, I love you too but oh, Karl, this is impossible.'

'One day, this will all end, I promise, and then we can be together. It will happen, I know it will. It must.'

Hannah looked less sure. She really wanted to believe him, but she always had a nagging doubt about any future beyond these precious moments when they were actually together. As soon as they were parted, all the fears came back to her.

At that moment, they heard Peter coughing loudly outside. He had spotted the way the two young people looked at each other when Karl returned to the farm and it hadn't taken long for him to extract the truth out of his friend. The loud warning was enough to make the two lovers spring apart and for Karl to turn on his heels, only turning back to blow a kiss towards the girl he loved. She put her hand up into the empty air and grasped at the sunbeams that were catching the light, then hugged her tightly closed fist to her heart.

* * *

Keeping busy seemed the only answer and the following evening, when the girls were curled up in the armchairs in the barn, Dotty came up with an idea that offered them all a distraction.

The Land Army girls were encouraged to get involved in local community events and Dotty, with her new-found reading skills, was always finding impossible directives that they were supposed to follow.

'Listen to this one,' she said, looking up from the Land Army Manual, 'it says we must be prepared to help with our own welfare and make our own lives happy by making others happy too. That's all very well,' she complained, putting down her threadbare socks that she was darning yet again. 'But how on earth do we find the energy – or the time?'

They were all missing going dancing and Hannah feared she had forgotten how to do those wonderfully liberating moves. She wondered whether Karl was a good dancer and then sighed, realising she might never know.

'Perhaps we should have something here?' Dotty suggested. 'A party or something. Maybe we should plan it for New Year. After all, it's going to be 1945. That has a good ring to it, don't you think?'

Lavinia jumped up. 'Yes, let's do that.' And, glancing at Hannah, added, 'We could ask some of the girls from that farm near Little Plumstead and some of the lads from nearby farms. I'm sure we'd be allowed to ask the POWs too, they seemed to enjoy that rounders match Archie organised in the summer.'

It was true that there was a gradual thawing of attitudes towards the prisoners who were being held in camps all over Britain. The emphasis had shifted towards rehabilitating them and any opportunity to include them in local activities was encouraged.

Dotty still found bumping into the prisoners an unnerving experience, but Lavinia had developed quite a rapport with some of them and was delighted at the idea of including them. Hannah knew Lavinia's plan to invite the POWs was a ploy to enable Hannah to see Karl, but it actually made things worse, as the closer she was to Karl, the harder it was for Hannah not to give their secret away by the touch of his arm or a look in his eyes.

But by now, Lavinia was in full flow. 'I'll talk to Archie and see what we can organise,' she said, happily. She missed a social life more than anything else, she thought wistfully, except possibly regular hot baths.

Archie was surprisingly compliant and, after a chat with the boss, agreed to support Lavinia's plans. For the locals on the farm in Norwich, appalled by the stories of brutality in Europe, inviting POWs to a New Year's Eve party was an ideal way of proving to the enemy that they were on the side of righteousness and now that the familiar faces of the prisoners had started to look less threatening, they had already been included in a few of the activities, under the watchful eye of Archie. He couldn't fault the Germans for their attitude to hard work; they had certainly pulled their weight over the past couple of years, he conceded, and at the first opportunity, he extended an invitation to the delighted prisoners. Stanley and William stood resentfully in the background – they conceded nothing.

Archie knew that having something to plan would give the exhausted girls a focus that would carry them through the relentlessly repetitive tasks such as planting winter beet, spreading silage and milking the cows. As far as the girls were concerned, Lavinia took them in hand and, reminding them they were still young, encouraged an 'Amami night' where they would polish their nails, put their hair in metal 'Dinkie' curlers under turbans made from first aid bandages and sew, or rather re-sew dresses, to give them new outfits to wear for the party. Even Hannah was drawn into the excitement of the preparations and was sorry when they all hugged to say goodbye the week before Christmas.

* * *

Feeling deflated, Dotty sat alone at the dining table. She had volunteered to stay on the farm and do the milking, knowing that, apart from Christmas Day when George would visit his mother, the two of them would have some time on their own. Dotty had a pang of sympathy for her own mother, left at home with that man, but, as a daughter, she had always been powerless, caught in the middle of a disastrous relationship. She suddenly jumped up from her chair and clapped her hands together in excitement. There *was* something she could do. Now she could write, she would pen a strong letter to the local curate, urging him to keep an eye on the family. It wasn't much, but at least it was something.

* * *

Hannah arrived in Manchester with the usual trepidation that came with stepping off the bus at Stretford, but she felt stronger than she had ever felt in her life and straightened her back, held her head up high and walked the short distance between the bus stop and her house.

'I'm home,' she called as she opened the door.

Her dad appeared immediately. His face lit up when he saw her. It had been a long year and he was unbelievably relieved to see her.

'Hannah!' he said, grabbing her coat and ushering her through to the morning room. 'Look who's here, Margaret. Isn't she a sight for sore eyes?'

His wife looked pale and thinner than ever, but tried to raise a smile. 'Yes, it's lovely,' she said, her voice flat. 'Get her a cup of tea, Alf.'

Hannah sat down next to her mum. 'Are you any better, Mum?'

'I'm fine, dear, just tired. I don't seem to have any energy these days.'

Hannah did everything she could to get the house ready for Christmas, but it was like decorating an empty shell. She did see a slight change in her mum spurred on by Hannah's bustling presence and even managed to get her to help a little in the kitchen, which gave her some satisfaction. The limited rations of 1944 were giving Hannah – and the rest of the country – endless challenges and she was glad she had visited Mrs Hill to ask for some recipes before heading home. She made some surprisingly delicious gingerbread men and actually made her mum laugh when they put the currants on their cheeky little faces for eyes. One recipe included adding potato and carrot to a pudding so that it was moist, and once she had prepared that, she tackled the Christmas cake. This was made without eggs, with less flour, less fruit and less fat but, tasting a little of the mixture before putting it in the oven, Hannah was pleased that that, too, tasted better than she could have thought. The marzipan was a mix of semolina, sugar, water and flavouring, but her crowning glory was the holly that she had dipped in Epsom salts to make the leaves look frosted. Even her mother's face lit up when she saw the pretty cake topping.

Worn out from her domestic achievements, on the Friday, Hannah told her parents she was off to see Ros and Lily, who was home from her posting in Oxfordshire. Hannah almost ran towards Rusholme, so excited to see her friends again, but she was also nervous about how she was going to deflect attention from her life in Norfolk, so as not to tell them of her secret love, when faced with Lily's penetrating questioning.

The first hour was spent giggling, just as the three had done before the war, and they were too giddy at just being together to have a sensible conversation, but then, Lily, noting Hannah's new confidence, leaned in to encourage her friend to spill the beans about where her healthy glow was coming from. Hannah braced herself, but was reprieved by a knock at the front door, which Lily ran down to answer.

From behind the door in Lily's bedroom, she and Ros eavesdropped and heard three American voices.

They clasped their hands over their mouths in delight. They had both met American GIs at dances, but to have some in your own home, this was something only their glamorous friend, Lily, would achieve. They quickly used Lily's silver, bevelled hairbrush from her walnut dressing table to make themselves look more respectable and sneaked downstairs. Opening the front room door, they peered around it to see three gorgeous airmen, looking like Hollywood film stars. One of them even had sunglasses propped up on his head – in December, for heaven's sake.

The men were introduced as Kit, Wally and Chuck and they were attempting to look enthusiastic about the brown liquid they had been presented with by Mrs Mullins, who was looking extremely flustered. They had been warned that tea was an essential element in international relations, so did their best to sip it gracefully while longing for coffee.

Kit was undoubtedly flirting with Lily and Ros and Hannah watched their friend closely to see she was obviously feeling very uncomfortable.

'We were about to go for a walk, while it's still sunny,' Lily was saying, in a blatant attempt to get Kit away from the interrogation her father was giving him.

Once out of the house, they walked along the pavement towards Crowcroft Park and Kit ostentatiously linked arms with Lily. Hannah saw her flinch with embarrassment so started to sing the Land Army song to break the tension.

'Back to the land, we must all lend a hand, to the farms and the fields we must go, there's a job to be done, though we can't fire a gun, we can still do our bit with the hoe,' she sang, repeating the refrain until they all joined in.

Ros and Lily exchanged glances; this was not the shy Hannah they knew and they both grinned to see the change in her. By the time they reached the park, the boys had started to organise races, Kit ensuring that he always caught Lily up at the finishing line to grab her round the waist, and he seemed glued to her side all the way back to the house for more cups of tea.

A myriad of questions were swirling around in Hannah's mind, but with Kit constantly by her friend's side, she had no time to ask them and once Kit had made a point of kissing Lily very firmly on the lips at the front door, the young WAAF was too flustered to discuss anything. Hannah mentally drafted a letter that she would send as soon as she got back to Norfolk, which would include all those questions about Lily's relationship with the American. She also realised it was probably time, finally, to confide in her two oldest friends about her own complicated love life.

Chapter 44

By the time Hannah arrived back at Salhouse Farm, Dotty had already started decorating the barn for the party. Her eyes were shining with excitement.

'Oh Hann, there you are,' she said, spotting Hannah in the doorway. 'Did you have a good Christmas?'

Hannah nodded. It had actually not been too bad and her mum had made a real effort to put a paper hat on and join in the merriment that Hannah tried to inject into Christmas Day.

'What about you?' she asked. 'Did you really go up to the farmhouse?'

'Yes, it was terrifying, but they tried to make me feel welcome. I was glad their daughter, Bobby, was there, otherwise it would have just been me and the older members of the family. She was quite good fun, actually, although a bit scary. I honestly would've preferred to help Rachel in the kitchen, but they insisted I should join them at the table.

'Anyway,' she said, handing Hannah some paper chains, 'grab these, let's get 'em up as we've only got a few hours before everyone arrives.'

Hannah turned to Lavinia, who was crouched in the corner, behind an armchair, trying to plug in the record player.

'What about you, Lavinia?'

A muffled voice came back and then Lavinia crawled out, brushing the dust from her trousers.

'Yeah, it was OK. They invited over some eligible men they thought might entice me, but—' she looked sadly at them both '—I'm not ready for that.'

'No more chatting,' Dotty said bossily. 'There's too much to do.' She checked her list. Only half the things were ticked off. Now she had discovered writing, she loved making extensive notes at every opportunity and a New Year's Eve party was an ideal chance to display her new organisational abilities. Tucking her pencil behind her ear, she looked proudly at the page of carefully crafted letters and wondered how she had ever managed before she had learned how to read and write. She'd even had a reassuring letter back from the curate saying that, following her concerns, he was contacting the welfare to make sure her mother and siblings were given support. He did not mention how shocked he had been to see the bruising on her mother's face and that he had alerted the police as well.

Hannah was now perched on the top of a ladder hanging up paper chains, trying not to worry about the evening ahead and how she was going to stop herself from clinging on to Karl during the dancing.

* * *

Before the party, the girls had invited Rachel to get ready with them. She could not have been more thrilled. These girls had brought some glamour into her life that had been sadly missing. Lavinia worked on her makeup, Hannah put sugar water on her hair to help it curl and Dotty did her nails. When they twirled her round towards the mirror, Rachel gasped. She almost did not recognise the film star she saw in front of her. Before she rushed off to help Mrs Hill prepare the New Year's supper, Lavinia sprayed her with Soir de Paris. Rachel giggled.

'Cook'll worry she's put too many spices in those famous gingerbread men of hers when she gets a whiff of me,' she said, and then hugged each of the girls in turn, too overcome to say any more.

Lavinia spent nearly an hour doing the other girls' hair and makeup and, when she'd finished, Dotty looked with surprise at herself.

'I'd forgotten what I looked like without a layer of mud,' she said. 'I look almost acceptable.'

'Almost,' Hannah said, handing her friend the new silk scarf she had found for her at the jumble sale. Dotty delightedly wrapped it around her neck. That was the cue for Dotty to give them both some gloves she had knitted out of an old jumper. Lavinia gave Dotty a re-covered hairband for her unruly hair, but mysteriously told Hannah she would have to wait for her present. The government had decreed that only children should get presents but, with ingenuity and resourcefulness, by the time they were ready to go downstairs, they all felt as if they had been given the best gifts ever.

Before anyone else arrived, the farmhands came in, wearing their Sunday best, which was, to be honest, looking a little tired and bedraggled, but, to the girls, they looked incredibly smart. Even Stanley had put on a new tie for the occasion. William Handforth was nowhere to be seen, preferring to sit in his room, hugging a bottle of whisky he'd got on the black market. John walked over to Hannah and Lavinia and took one on each arm. He beamed at Dotty.

'You girls look amazing and this barn . . . well, it almost looks as good as the Ritz – not that I've ever been there,' he laughed.

Albert stood in the background until Dotty ran over and gave him a glass of beer, then she beamed as George came through the doorway, pushing the blackout curtain to one side. He was looking unusually nervous but had put on his best shirt and braces. John stepped into the middle of the room and made a solemn toast to the end of 1944 and better things in 1945. As they chinked glasses, Lavinia's chin started to wobble. She had never felt camaraderie at a party like she did at this one. Hannah spotted the glistening in Lavinia's eye and immediately jumped up onto a chair.

'I want to make another toast,' she said, holding up her glass. 'I want to toast women . . . and yes, Albert and John, you two have to raise your glasses for this one too. Women who have found they can do things no one ever thought they could.'

They all got to their feet, John giving a wry smile in defeat. Stanley hovered in the background.

Lavinia ceremoniously handed up an old pinny to Hannah and some scissors.

'And finally, here's my present to you, Hannah, you can finally cut those apron strings tying you to your mum. They've held you back for too long. We were nearly taken in by that "Horrified Hannah" expression, but look at you now! Beware world, here comes the tractor engineer, horse handler and brilliant jitterbug expert . . . I give you Hannah Compton!'

Hannah held out the end of the apron strings and with great determination and a flourish, cut them. She held the scissors and the two ends up triumphantly, feeling a little tearful but like the person she was always meant to be for the first time in her life.

George suddenly banged his spoon on the table.

'I too have something to say,' he spluttered, noticing everyone's attention on him. George looked down at the floor, his courage failing him.

John nudged him. 'Go on lad, we're all listening.'

George took a deep breath and held his head up high. 'I was forced to come and work here, I didn't want to, I wanted to join the army, but if I had done that . . .' Here he paused and looked at Dotty, who looked so beautiful in a red woollen dress with that stylish scarf around her neck. 'I would never have met the woman I want to ask to be my wife.'

There was a gasp. Dotty was not sure whether it was from her or the others, but while she was still wondering, George was on one knee, holding up a small box towards her.

Lavinia and Hannah clapped their hands together excitedly. 'Open it, Dot, open it,' they cried in unison.

Dotty tentatively reached forward to take the box and, in slow motion, with shaking hands, opened the lid. Inside was a beautiful, tiny diamond on a gold band.

'It was my grandmother's, I picked it up when I went home at Christmas,' George was saying. 'She left it to me, for when I chose the woman I want to spend the rest of my life with.'

Dotty slowly put the ring on and stretched her finger out to examine it. In that movement, she knew she was free, free of her father, free of the dread that had followed her around since she was a young girl and, most importantly, free of all shame.

'I love you Dotty,' George said, no longer looking like a young, gauche boy, but like a man who had fought for, and won, the one thing he prized most in all the world. 'I love everything about you and I want to look after and protect you for the rest of your life,' he told her.

Dotty looked into George's eyes; they were full of understanding, acceptance and love, and she flung her arms around him, pulling him to his feet.

It was the moment when Dotty finally dared to believe her pain would stop.

Chapter 45

There was a pink tinge to all their cheeks by the time their guests arrived, both from the excitement of the occasion and the number of alcoholic toasts they'd made.

First to arrive were Land Army girls from the nearby farm, who were ushered in by Archie, then some other local lads came in, shuffling their farm boots in embarrassment. Finally, about ten prisoners of war arrived, excited that they might be able to forget their differences and enjoy the evening as ordinary young men. They had all been assessed to make sure they were not Nazi sympathisers – Karl was among them. He was trying to focus his gaze on anything but Hannah in her pretty blue dress and with her hair curled in a fashionable roll.

John frowned for a minute; he always had to make himself forget they were the enemy. After such a long time working alongside them, when he met them individually he could accept they were not the monsters he had originally thought, but in a group, they looked so . . . well, Germanic somehow. But, giving himself a shake, he conceded that most of them were nice enough men, and he went over to hand out beer from a large aluminium jug. Archie followed him and made a point of shaking Karl's hand. He had developed a deep respect for this prisoner in particular.

The local lads, however, looked suspiciously at the POWs and moved quickly to claim the girls for the first dance. George was in charge of the gramophone and had raided the Toc H's supply of records, which were a bit old but better than nothing. It was such a shame they couldn't have a live band, he thought, but then shrugged and put 'Putting on the Ritz' on the turntable in honour of John.

Hannah purposefully ignored Karl and grabbed John's arm.

'Come on, they're playing your song!' she said laughing and took him into the cleared space in the middle of the barn. It did not take long for the others to follow her lead and Dotty, in particular, took delight in placing her left hand strategically on George's shoulder so that everyone could see the sparkle from her ring reflect in the light from the kerosene lamps.

The party was going well, but for Hannah and Karl it was agony to keep their distance. Hannah could not help showing off her dancing skills a little bit, hoping he was watching, not realising that everyone else was watching her too. John was having the time of his life with his partner, who, he noticed, really did know how to twirl, move her feet and follow the rhythm of the music, and it was not long before the Germans were vying with the local lads to dance with her. Lavinia had her own retinue that she kept amused with anecdotes, which were getting louder as she drained each drink. It was only as it was approaching midnight that Karl finally moved across the room to approach Hannah.

'Would you like to dance, Fräulein?' he said formally, aware that he had dreamed of this moment for over a year now.

She nodded, unable to speak, and, keeping a careful distance between them, the strains of 'I'm in the Mood for Love' started up.

Karl whispered in her ear, 'I just want to dance with you forever.'

She noticed Stanley glance over so did not dare look at Karl, but said in a loud voice, 'Did you men manage to have any sort of Christmas in the hut? It must have been strange so far from home.'

Karl took the hint so replied in as vague and factual a way as possible. 'Yes, many of the men had heard from their families and even received packages. They were the lucky ones.'

'Didn't you get any?' she asked, recognising his pain. She longed to know whether he had heard any news of his family.

'I still haven't had any letters from home,' he said, and then added in a quieter voice, 'But, I did discover that my sister and mother are safe, but in some sort of camp.'

Hannah took in a sharp breath, knowing what this news would have meant to Karl. 'Is that the one on the Isle of Man?' she said, even more quietly. She had heard how wire fences had been constructed on the island, behind which were Germans – both Nazis and Jews, conscientious objectors and anyone else the authorities did not know what to do with.

'Yes.' But then he dropped his head to disguise the emotion in his face. This dance was testing all of the willpower he had.

'It's always a relief to know one's family is safe,' she said, giving him time to recover.

'Yes, but I just wish I knew how I could get a letter to them,' he said, almost to himself.

Neither of them could look at each other, but the pressure of Karl's fingers on her back told Hannah everything she needed to know. She responded with a tightening of pressure on his hand. They both felt sure everyone knew what was going on in their heads but, in fact, the only one who did was Lavinia, who was looking on at them protectively.

At the end of the dance, she went over to the couple, aware that they were transfixed, staring into each other's eyes and unable to move. 'My turn to dance with the doctor,' she said in a loud voice, breaking the spell.

Hannah jumped back as if she were too close to a flame.

'Of course,' she mumbled and walking off to the drinks table, helped herself to a large gin.

The alcohol had been paid for by Mr Hollis, who wanted to thank his workers, but the local lads were taking advantage of the free drinks and some of them were beginning to sway. One of them, a large, dark-haired lad wearing corduroy trousers held up with braces made his way over to Lavinia. He'd had his eye on her all night.

'You don't want to dance with this Kraut, you want a proper man, an Englishman,' he said, pushing Karl out of the way.

Unwilling to draw attention to himself, Karl backed off, but immediately the tension in the room started to rise and the local lads moved slowly to one side of the barn while the Germans edged their way to the other. Archie moved between them, followed by John, George and Albert, who provided a semicircle like pioneers on the Oregon Trail defending themselves against raiding parties. They twirled around looking fiercely at the two groups, who were clenching their fists. The silence was broken when Dotty ran to turn on the wireless in the corner. It was sounding the pre-war recording of Big Ben. She heaved a sigh of relief and moved in between the men and started singing – her sweet voice resounded up into the ceiling, the tuneful notes contrasting like golden sunbeams with the thunderous clouds below.

'Should auld acquaintance be forgot, and never brought to mind? Should auld acquaintance be forgot, and auld lang syne?' She waved her arms to indicate everyone should join in and slowly, reluctantly, they did.

As the strange group heralded in 1945, Dotty whispered to Hannah and Lavinia, 'Phew, saved by the bell. I wasn't letting a group of badly behaved men spoil my engagement evening.'

Hannah squeezed her arm as Archie hurriedly shepherded the visitors out of the barn to make their way home in the trucks that were waiting outside. Karl turned to catch Hannah's eye as he went through the door with the others; all his hopes and aspirations for a better year were in that look. They were both so absorbed in each other they failed to spot Stanley narrowing his eyes at their undisguised longing.

*　*　*

The following morning, Stanley did not bring the Germans to work at Salhouse. Archie casually told the girls that they had been moved to work on a farm about ten miles away. Hannah looked intently down at the wheelbarrow she was pushing and Lavinia stepped in front of her to make a point of shrugging her shoulders and sighing loudly.

'Ah well, it's back to the local farm lads then,' she said, taking Archie's attention away from Hannah, who had gone very pale. 'We might have missed our chance though, it was last year that was a leap year.' She laughed. 'At least Dotty's hitched up, otherwise we'd be like the Three Little Maids from *The Mikado*. Come on, Hannah, let's get this muck shifted and then we can plot how we two are going to find the men of our dreams.'

She pushed Hannah forwards and out of sight of Archie, and just about managed to get her round the corner before the distraught girl's knees buckled.

'Oh, Lavinia, what do I do now?' the crumpled figure said.

Lavinia twirled Hannah round, took hold of her shoulders and looked sternly into her eyes.

'I'll tell you what you'll do, young lady, you'll get this muck shifted, you'll put one foot in front of the other and you'll wait for this war to end, that's what you'll do.'

Hannah sniffed and nodded. There was no choice.

Chapter 46

Without Karl to look out for, Hannah found life on the farm had become very mundane and she dragged herself around, doing her chores without enthusiasm.

Archie noticed how down she was and one day, when he passed the boss in the yard, he decided to share his concerns. After a brief word, Andrew looked over towards Hannah, noting her rounded shoulders and glum expression.

'I know how to cheer her up,' he said suddenly. 'Hannah, come here a moment, will you?'

Hannah looked up, concerned, wondering if she had done something wrong.

Andrew went on, 'You haven't been up to the house recently. I was sure you'd be ready for more books by now.'

She nodded, guiltily aware that her reading had been replaced by miserable bouts of scribbling in her diary.

'Well, come over tonight and then you can choose some,' Andrew said, feeling satisfied that he had set a ball in motion that might solve the problem.

*   *   *

Hannah walked over to the farmhouse, dragging her feet. She knew she was going to have to be more cheerful than this before she bumped into the family, but, when she got to the library, the only person who was there was Andrew. He was sitting in the large leather armchair reading an embossed volume. He beamed when he saw her and put his own book down.

'I've been wanting to talk to you, Hannah,' he said, standing up to offer her a small, cut-glass of liquid. 'Try it, it's marrow brandy, but it actually tastes OK.'

She sipped the drink, grateful that it gave her something to do, but Andrew was too pleased with the plan he had hatched to notice her discomfort.

'I thought you might want to choose some books, but you also mentioned you wanted to be become a teacher. Is that right?'

She nodded, wondering where this was going.

'Well, I have a friend who might be able to help you. He's in the education department at the council, would you like to meet him?'

Hannah was so overcome, she burst into tears. His kindness was the last straw.

Andrew was not a man who dealt well with feminine emotions, but he had been trying hard recently to step out from behind the mask he'd perfected for himself over the years.

He reached across and put his hand on Hannah's shoulder. 'What is it? You can tell me.'

'No, I can't,' Hannah said, sobbing. 'I can't tell anyone.'

Andrew stood up and faced her.

'Yes, you can. I promise you, nothing you say will leave this room and I will never, could never, think badly of you.'

Before Hannah knew what she was doing she was opening her mouth to say the words that she should never have uttered to anyone, least of all her German-hating boss.

'I'm in love with one of the prisoners.'

Andrew took a deep breath; there were so many scenarios he had imagined, but that was certainly not one of them.

'Which one?' he asked tentatively, dreading her answer.

'Karl Schneider.'

Andrew experienced a feeling of relief. The doctor!

He weighed up his words carefully. 'He's a good man, Hannah, but this is not going to be easy.'

Hannah looked miserably at the Persian rug beneath her feet. She knew that better than anyone, but her boss's next words took her by surprise.

'What can I do to help?'

She jerked her head up. Had she just heard correctly?

'I mean it, I don't hate all Germans, just those who want to kill us,' he said with a smile. 'And the doctor, well, without him, I doubt my sister-in-law would be here.'

At that, Hannah started to pour out her heart. She could not help it. The relief of saying out loud what had been torturing her for so long to a sympathetic face was too overwhelming for her to resist. She told him how she had tried everything to resist the prisoner, how she felt so guilty to have betrayed her family, her friends and her nation. 'But,' she said, looking pathetically at the man in front of her, 'I just couldn't help it. You know what it's like, you don't choose who you fall in love with.'

Andrew thought back to the dimple-cheeked woman who had swept him off his feet as a young man. How could he have forgotten that feeling?

'No, you can't,' he admitted.

He pushed his own marriage to one side and tried to concentrate on the dilemma in front of him.

'But the Germans have gone and I don't know if they're coming back,' he said.

'I know, and I may never see him again,' Hannah said, starting to cry again, but then she raised her chin. 'But there is one thing I might be able to do before I forget him forever.' She looked up at Andrew's face. He seemed to be encouraging her, so she went on, thinking she now had nothing to lose, 'His mother and sister may have been interned in the Isle of Man. He desperately wants to contact them and I'd love to know how to track them down. Can you help?'

Andrew considered her appeal. He'd been so pleased with his plan to help Hannah with a career in teaching, and now, here she was asking him to do more for her.

He gave a wry smile. All these young women were the same, he thought, recalling a recent battle he had had with Bobby. This one might be more polite, but underneath she was just as stubborn, feisty and determined to make his life as difficult as possible.

'OK,' he found himself saying. 'I'll see what I can do.'

* * *

Stanley was standing, leaning on his rifle and watching the POW in front of him. He had been biding his time, waiting for the perfect opportunity to seek his revenge against this Kraut who had got him into trouble twice now. The moment he'd spotted the look between the German and the girl, he had realised what a powerful tool he now had at his disposal, and to Stanley, at the age of twenty-three and at the end of his tether, the revelation could not have come at a better time. He checked the yard at the new farm; there was only him and that German there. This was his chance.

'Think you've got an English girl to fall in love with you, Kraut?'

Karl swirled around, almost dropping the flax he had just taken off the back of the cart. He was on his way to the shed where the seeds were taken out for linseed and the stems used for fibres. He'd just been thinking it was a process his brothers might be able to use on their own farm after the war.

Stanley's face had a smug satisfied look that contrasted with Karl's shock as it dawned on him that his secret had been discovered.

'Tasty young thing, isn't she, that Hannah?'

Karl felt his fists curling. He refused to rise to the bait this man was casting his way.

Stanley saw the effect his words were having and went on gleefully, 'You know she'd get into terrible trouble if your little affair was discovered, don't you? A court fine, definitely, yes, and she'd probably lose her job, not to mention all her friends.'

Karl wanted to protect Hannah at all costs so tried to keep his face impassive but, inside, his stomach was churning. He had always known that this English guard had held a grudge against him since the day of the escape and had just been waiting for an opportunity to wreak his revenge.

He decided to come straight to the point. 'What do you want?'

Stanley shifted his rifle from one side to other, pretending to consider his options, when actually he'd decided days ago.

'You're a doctor, aren't you?'

Karl nearly burst out laughing. If this guard thought he had money because of his profession, he could not be more mistaken.

'My studies were halted by the war,' Karl told him, 'so I cannot actually earn any money until I get my qualifications, but I do have some cigarettes you could have.'

Stanley guffawed.

'Cigarettes? You have to be joking. No, you German scum, I want something more than that. I need you to see someone, as a doctor.'

Karl looked nonplussed. He had not been expecting this.

'I'll let you know,' Stanley said mysteriously, 'in the meantime, leave those cigarettes for me tonight under the hay bale on the left of the barn door as a deposit for my silence, but don't think I won't be having a cosy little chat with the boss if you fail to deliver on all my demands. I'm sure he'd be delighted to know about your affair.'

And with that, he pushed the butt of the rifle into Karl's side before walking off, leaving Karl standing with his sheaves of flax drooping at his side.

When Karl told Peter later about the conversation with Stanley, they both wracked their brains to think what the guard could possibly want from a doctor.

'Maybe he's got what the British call "the clap".' The two men digested this thought and then Peter burst out laughing, imagining what sort of girl would have sex with that dreadful man.

'You have to be joking,' he said. 'She'd need to close her eyes so she wouldn't see that ugly face on the pillow next to her.'

He started to laugh again and at that moment the tannoy went for lights out. They climbed into their bunks. Peter was still chuckling, but Karl was thinking about how the guard's vindictiveness could destroy Hannah's life.

* * *

Stanley, by that time, was sitting on his own in the local pub, nursing a pint, with the first feelings of optimism he had had in a while. It had never occurred to him that a German prisoner of war could help him out of this situation that had given him sleepless nights, and he was delighted that a chance glimpse of a love affair across the room had offered him a way out. He took a long slurp of his beer and smacked his lips.

Chapter 47

Two days later, Stanley was skulking around the new farm searching for an opportunity to get Karl on his own. Aware his time was running out, he needed to move his plan forwards. Karl, true to his word, had delivered the cigarettes and the guard took that act as an indicator that the doctor would comply with his next request.

Finally, he spotted him heading out to mend a fence, hammer and nails in hand.

'You, Kraut,' he hissed.

Karl stopped and turned round, checking that no one was watching. He did not trust this man one little bit. He looked Stanley squarely in the face, waiting to see what happened next.

'Tomorrow, your day off, meet me at the copse at the top of the compound by Mousehold Lane, the one where the old blacksmith's hut is. Bring whatever a doctor needs. Ten o'clock.'

Stanley started to move away but then halted, adding: 'Tell anyone and you and your girlfriend will be hearing from the authorities.'

*   *   *

Karl had no idea what was to be asked of him but thought it wise to be prepared, so the next morning he washed his hands thoroughly in the ablution block and took with him the limited medical supplies he had been allowed to keep for dealing with minor injuries of fellow prisoners.

He made his way to the copse and found a broken-down hut that had been abandoned for years. Pushing open the creaking door, he found Stanley standing nervously with a young girl behind him; she looked terrified.

Stanley went behind Karl and shut the door quietly, then he turned towards him, pointing at the girl. 'She's up the duff and you have to get rid of it.'

Karl had no idea what 'up the duff' meant but he could read the girl's tear-stained face and had a good idea.

'I cannot, it is illegal,' he said bluntly and turned towards the door. From behind him, he heard the click as a rifle was cocked. He stopped and waited.

Stanley moved to bar Karl's way out, holding his rifle in front of him. 'You must. She's only fifteen.'

'I will not. It is forbidden and it is also dangerous.' He glared at the grown man in front of him, his eyes full of disgust. 'How many months?'

The girl whispered something.

'*Vas?*' Karl said and then, more kindly this time. 'What did you say?'

'I think a little more than five months, the baby will be born at the end of the summer.'

Karl shook his head. '*Das ist* too late, she would bleed, she could die – or at least be hurt for life.'

The girl surprised Karl by running over to Stanley and taking his arm. She gazed up pathetically at him. Karl was even more surprised to see the guard's face softening with affection as he looked back at her. But then his expression changed back to the sullen one and his fingers tightened on the gun.

'You *will* help her or I will tell everyone your guilty little secret.'

Karl's fury could not be reined in. '*My* guilty secret? All I have done is fall in love with a beautiful girl. But you . . . you . . .' he could not finish his sentence. No wonder this man had been such good friends with Jed. They were two of a kind.

The two men faced each other, their anger almost palpable, but then the girl pushed between them.

'Please help me.' She put her hands on her swollen stomach.

Karl looked from the girl to Stanley and stepped forward; he had never known a rage like it.

'No, no, you don't understand,' the girl said, putting her arms out in front of Stanley to protect him. 'He's my brother. He's trying to help me.' She started to cry.

There was a long silence while Karl absorbed this information. He looked again at Stanley. Was it possible he had misjudged this man?

Stanley set his face in a menacing frown. 'You *will* do this or I'll go straight to Salhouse Farm and tell them your little story,' he said through gritted teeth.

Karl spoke softly but there was no room for negotiation in his tone. 'I will not and cannot do this. You must do whatever you must. It would be against everything a doctor says he will do and and *dieses Mädchen*—' he looked sorrowfully at her '—I cannot say she would not die.'

He spoke directly to her. 'I am sorry, there is nothing I can do. You must go to the police and tell them what happened to you. Who did this?'

The child looked completely forlorn. She'd been so in love with the boy who lived next door to their tiny house in Wroxham. Terence had always been her hero but they'd both been so innocent. He'd been packed off to war and now he was reported 'killed in action'. He'd never come back and marry her as he'd promised, she knew that now. Stanley, in a desperate bid to protect her reputation, had told her he could fix the problem and she hadn't questioned his methods. Her brother shook his head at her; there was no need for this doctor to know the details, but without his intervention, the girl would be thrown out of home by their father. This prisoner had to cooperate.

He pointed the gun at him, but Karl just shook his head. 'You will have to shoot me,' he said calmly. 'I will not be part of this.' And with that, he moved sideways past Stanley and walked out of the door.

Karl heard sobbing from the girl as he walked away, and it broke his heart. There had never been a choice, but he was all too aware of what his refusal might now unleash.

* * *

The wireless news that was broadcast every night was evidence of the struggle that was still going on in the war, and to the anxious British, crowded around their sets each evening, it seemed that for every step the Allies took forward, they also took one back. The Germans moved out of Belgium but then American planes bombed Prague by mistake; the US raised a triumphant flag on Iwo Jima but Dresden was obliterated by the Allies.

Hannah was the first to turn the radio on every night, desperate for a glimmer of hope that might mean she could start to think about her future, but with Karl nowhere in sight, no word from Mr Hollis and Lavinia questioning her at every available opportunity, she had less and less idea what that future might hold.

She was so distracted by her own thoughts, she didn't notice a figure marching up to the farmhouse.

Stanley banged on the front door of the Hollis family home. He had not really thought this through, but he was so furious with that bloody prisoner of war, he was desperate to take his revenge.

He was taken aback to see the strident figure of Bobby Hollis open the door. He'd forgotten that a broken ankle meant this terrifying woman hadn't been able to return to her job delivering aircraft for the ATA. She didn't look pleased to see the scruffy man on her doorstep.

'Yes?'

Stanley shuffled his feet.

'For God's sake, man, what is it you want?' the girl thundered in her commanding voice.

Stanley faltered. This was not going how he had planned. 'Your dad . . . father. Is he here?'

'And who exactly are you?'

'I'm Stanley Parish. I . . . guard . . . the prisoners,' he stuttered.

From behind her came the little face of the French child, Elizé.

'Oh, have you come about my friend, the doctor?' she said, cheerfully. Elizé had fortunately never associated the prisoners of war with the German soldiers in their buttoned-up uniforms who haunted her dreams and had innocently accepted anyone who was liked by her wonderful friend, Hannah. 'It's too late, he's already here,' Elizé said with a grin.

Stanley's face fell. The German was already here? How could that be?

While he hesitated, Bobby looked at him with distaste. She was a good judge of character and the fact this man did not look her in the eye made her distrust him immediately.

'I'm sorry, but is my father expecting you?'

'N-no . . . I just needed to talk to him but . . .'

'But what, for heaven's sake. Make your mind up, man, do you need to talk to him or not?'

By this time, Stanley had started shuffling backwards down the steps. He almost fell at one point, making Elizé giggle behind her hand. Bobby looked reprovingly at her and then, ignoring the retreating figure scurrying off back down the drive, stepped back inside the house and closed the door behind them both.

'I didn't like that man,' Elizé said.

'No, *ma petite*,' Bobby answered with a frown, 'neither did I.'

Inside her father's study, Karl Schneider didn't know what awaited him. He'd been summoned back to the farm by a telephone call to his commandant's office and had immediately feared the worst. But when he arrived, he had been surprised to find Mr Hollis in a good mood, asking

Karl to sit down on a straight-backed chair. Karl perched on the edge of it, like a man poised for flight.

'So, Schneider,' Mr Hollis was saying, 'I believe you've been looking for your mother and sister.'

Karl almost fell off the chair. 'Yes, sir.'

'Well, I've made enquiries and I think we know where they were taken,' Andrew Hollis was saying, looking rather pleased with himself.

'But how did you know . . .?' Karl began.

'Hannah told me,' was the bland reply.

Karl felt his stomach lurch. Surely this man could not know about them?

'It's all right. Well, to be honest, it probably isn't all right, it's strictly forbidden.' Andrew seemed to searching for the right words. He went on to explain that Hannah had appealed to him for help, which took Karl completely by surprise; he hadn't thought of the man in front of him as someone Hannah – or to be honest anyone – would confide in.

'She told me about you two,' Andrew was saying. 'I must say, I've heard of a lot of this happening now to chaps like you who've been here for a while and you're going to have your work cut out for you, but . . .' here he paused, unused to giving any credit to a German '. . . you're a good man and she's certainly a lovely girl and I want to help you.'

Andrew felt the enormity of what he had just said, and for the first time since his terrible experiences in the Great

War, he felt unburdened of the hatred and resentment of an entire race. It was as if the clouds had cleared. He reached for the sherry bottle.

'Let's have a drink and I'll tell you what I've found,' he said, passing a small cut-glass into Karl's shaking hand.

Chapter 48

'Hannah, Hannah!' Elizé shouted across the yard.

Hannah was on her way to the milking shed with Dotty but slowed down so the little girl could catch them up.

'Hannah, you'll never know *quoi*,' she burst out, muddling up her languages in her excitement, 'Monsieur Hollis has found your Karl's family, he thinks they were taken to somewhere called . . . *attend un instant* . . . Port Erin on an island, oh, somewhere near England, I know not, but he can now write to them, isn't that wonderful?'

Hannah normally laughed when Elizé's enthusiasm got the better of her near-perfect English, but on this occasion, she felt Dotty's cold hand grasp her arm.

'Karl?' Dotty asked meaningfully.

Hannah tried to drag the little girl away but Dotty grabbed her wrist.

'No, do stay, both of you. I'd like to hear this.'

'Have I said something naughty?' Elizé said, looking from Dotty's thunderous expression to Hannah's guilty one.

'No,' Hannah said slowly, and then bent down to take the child's face in her hands, 'but maybe you and I can talk about this later?'

Elizé nodded, looking at the stricken faces of the two women in front of her. She decided that perhaps it might be a good time to leave these grown-ups now and go back to playing hopscotch in the yard.

As soon as she'd skipped off, Dotty rounded on Hannah. 'Well?'

'It's true,' Hannah admitted, her head drooping, 'I've fallen in love with one of the POWs. It's Karl, the doctor. I'm sorry, Dotty, I should have told you, but I just couldn't. I knew how you'd feel about it.'

'Does Lavinia know?'

'Yes.'

'So, you two have been having cosy little chats while I . . . I've been left in the dark.' And with that, she stormed off to do the milking.

* * *

Dotty's wedding was in three weeks and the girls had been enjoying planning for the best possible wartime celebration they could manage. Dotty had written to the curate asking him to relay the news to her mother, knowing, though, it would be impossible for her to travel to be there, and she was just hoping her father wouldn't find out about the ceremony. An excited bride, she was busy making arrangements, which included talking to Mrs Hill about a wedding breakfast, arranging posies for her two bridesmaids, Hannah and Lavinia, and remaking a dress from one of Lavinia's old ones. To hear her best friends had left her out of something so important was more hurtful to Dotty than the concern that one of them had fallen for a German. Hannah, however, was convinced that her friend's reaction was prompted by pure disgust at her betrayal of her country.

The atmosphere in the bedroom became charged with tension as Dotty ignored the other two, sitting on her side of the bed ostentatiously making plans that did not include them. She had her own worries, which were gnawing away at her inside, and felt angry that, just when she needed them most, her two friends had let her down and left her out.

The previous week, George had talked excitedly about their future life together, the children they would have and the little cottage he was hoping they might be able to rent on the other side of the village. It was as he mentioned the word 'children' that Dotty had frozen. She knew she could never have any; her visit to that filthy outhouse all those years ago had been a disaster and she had been left in no doubt that she would never again be able to conceive. It was that thought that was tearing her apart, and every time she saw George, she took a deep breath to tell him, and each time, she could not.

'Can we help?' Lavinia asked, peering over Dotty's shoulder to see a long list of scribbles.

'No,' Dotty said sharply, hiding her sheet of paper against her chest. She abruptly got up. 'I'm going for a walk.'

* * *

Lavinia did everything she could to try to improve relations between the three girls over the next couple of weeks but Dotty was intransigent. She felt betrayed by both of them and the worry about how to broach the subject of children with George was overwhelming her. As the wedding approached, Hannah wasn't sure that Dotty still wanted her to be a bridesmaid. She tried to talk to Dotty, but it was like talking to the wall.

However, at the end of April, 1945, she had help from an unexpected source. After work, Dotty stalked out of the barn, leaving the other two to follow in her wake as usual, but nearly bumped headlong into Archie, who was running excitedly from the house towards the farmhands.

'Hitler's dead,' he shouted, raising his arms triumphantly in the air. Everyone stopped where they were, as if posing for a photograph that would record this moment for ever.

Finally, John said, 'Dead? How?'

'He's committed suicide. Isn't that wonderful? That should finish this war off.'

Hannah turned spontaneously to hug Dotty, who was now standing next to her, forgetting she hadn't spoken to her in days. It took a moment for Dotty to remember how cross she was with her room-mates, but the atmosphere was so ecstatic amongst the little trio, who had been through so much together, that she gave in and started to laugh along with everyone else. Their squabbles seemed so insignificant compared with the fact that six years of cruel war in Europe might finally be coming to an end.

'Do you hate me for loving a German?' Hannah said simply to Dotty.

'No, you ninny. Well, I think you're an idiot but I know we can't choose who we love.' Dotty looked down at her engagement ring. 'But, no, I'm just furious you left me out and thought you couldn't tell me.'

Hannah breathed a sigh of relief. 'I thought you'd condemn me.'

'I was more upset you didn't trust me,' Dotty replied, giving her friend a reluctant hug.

* * *

The next few days heralded one piece of good news after another and each night was spent listening, almost incredulously, to the news that first the Russians had taken Berlin and then the Germans had surrendered in Italy. It seemed unreal and, nervously, everyone started to think about their lives after the war with excitement. Everyone, that is, except Hannah.

'What's up, Hann?' Lavinia asked.

Hannah looked bleakly around the bedroom. 'I don't know if I have a future,' she said. 'It all seems so exciting in some ways, but now what the hell do I do?'

Dotty leaned forward. 'Do you really love him?'

Hannah shrugged her shoulders. 'I think so, but if an English girl marries a German, they lose their nationality. How could I not be British anymore? How could I tell my parents? My dad hates the Germans with a vengeance. Where would we live?'

She felt completely overwhelmed and her shoulders slumped.

Lavinia stood in front of her and folded her arms.

'If he is worth all that, then, yes, you must love him. But you're not going to be demobbed for ages and they're not going to rush to sort out sending the Germans home, so you may be able to take time to see how strong that love really is.'

* * *

A few miles away, Karl, too, was mulling over what the end of the war would mean for him and Hannah. He had no doubt how much he loved her, but he also knew how much he was asking of her to love him back.

The early months of 1945 had been particularly uncomfortable for the POWS as they were made to watch films of the atrocities that their countrymen had perpetrated. Many of them vomited at the scenes, others shouted loudly in denial. Tensions were high.

For many of the younger prisoners, they had known nothing but Hitler's regime and, without their leader, they felt lost and lashed out at anyone who besmirched their hero's name. Their oaths to lay down their lives for him at any time were deeply etched into their psyches and to be relieved of those promises left them feeling lost and abandoned and many of them reacted with anger.

A British officer was brought in to try to calm the situation down, sidelining their own Lagerführer, which actually divided the POWs further, but the British officer's plan was simple: to send those men who were resigned to a German defeat back to Salhouse Farm and leave the others where they were on the new farm. The officer hoped this would defuse the situation.

* * *

The familiar truckload of prisoners arrived back at the farm on the day when the country took a communal deep breath of relief to celebrate Victory in Europe Day. The vehicle turned into the drive just as the wedding party was walking towards All Saints Church, led by Archie, proudly walking with Dotty on his arm. Karl craned his neck to see Hannah, looking exceptionally beautiful in a floral dress, holding a little posy of spring flowers. She faltered as she saw him and wondered in that moment why she had ever had any doubts. Her heart was thumping and her face reddened into a deep blush. Lavinia took her arm to give her strength.

Dotty's eyes were shining with happiness. Her dark curls had been painstakingly put in rags the previous night and they bounced in the sunshine. As she arrived at the church gate, she delighted her soon-to-be mother-in-law, Mrs Price, by breaking away from Archie's arm to greet her respectfully. George was dressed in his Sunday best and was standing at the altar waiting for her with his head held high. He spoke clearly and firmly and then Dotty repeated the marriage vows fiercely, as if defying the vicar to challenge her. It was at that moment that the church door banged open and a man in an old tweed jacket and cord trousers stood in the archway.

'She'll not marry 'im,' he shouted, causing the whole congregation to spin round to see what was happening.

Dotty stepped forward, uttered the word 'Dad' and then fell in a faint.

The man marched forward, shouting at the vicar, 'I'll not allow it. She's my daughter. I'll not 'ave her marrying some cretin off a farm.'

Hannah and Lavinia knelt over Dotty, trying to fan her with their posies. George stood stunned for a moment, but then Mr Hollis stepped forward. He was about to speak when George gently moved him to one side. 'It's all right, Mr Hollis, thank you, but I'll deal with this.'

He walked up to face the man who was shaking with rage.

'Dotty is now twenty-one. She does not need, or want, your permission to marry. I suggest you turn around and walk straight back out of this church and never come back.'

The man started to move towards George, but George's training as an agent in the Auxiliary Unit stood him in good stead and he dodged to one side to deftly grab the man's arm and twist it around his back, rendering him incapable of moving. Andrew Hollis looked on with admiration.

Dotty was coming round and had started to cry, but immediately stopped when she saw her beloved George taking control of the situation. She had spent so many years being terrified of her father and now she had her very own champion to protect her. She and his mother shared a proud glance at the tall young man in front of them.

George was speaking quietly but with complete conviction. 'I know everything you've done to Dotty and if you don't leave this second, then I will call the police. 'Well?' he added sternly.

Dotty's father started to back up. The scene in Birmingham when his wife had finally confessed to the curate about the dark shadows that had always engulfed the house had resulted in his packed suitcase being thrown out onto the street, accompanied by the threat of the police. Forced to flee the city, he devised a plan to stop the wedding of the one person he had always been able to control. However, that control was built on a lifetime of Dotty's shame, terrified to tell anyone about their 'little secret'. Seeing George's fierce expression and the look of horror on the faces of the congregation, it dawned on him that he had no power over her anymore. He turned to go, heading for the door and a life on the run, but at the last moment, turned and said through sneering lips, 'Yes, you can have 'er. She's not worth 'avin. But don't think you'll ever have any children. Bet she ain't told yer that.'

And with that, he ran from the church, leaving a shocked silence behind him.

Chapter 49

Hannah waited for someone to move, but when they didn't, she stepped into the middle of the aisle.

'I think we ought to just take a few moments for Dotty to regain her composure and then,' she said, spreading her arms and smiling, 'I think we should get on with this very happy occasion.'

Her words broke the tension and she and Lavinia ushered Dotty into the vestry.

Dotty was shaking and had gone white.

Hannah took her by the shoulders. 'You stop this right now, Dotty. That man is out of your life forever and can never hurt you again. Out there, you have a man who loves you with all his heart, now you go out there and finish off marrying him.'

'Yes, but he won't want me now, now he knows. . .' Dotty said, her face crumpling again.

They heard a noise behind them. It was George. He went straight up to Dotty and, looking steadily into her eyes, said, 'I'm marrying you, no matter what, Dorothy

Taylor. You will be my wife and that's all I care about.'
Then he swept her up into his arms and marched out
of the vestry to put her back down in front of the
bemused vicar, who stalled for just a brief moment
before saying, 'As I was saying, I now pronounce you
man and wife.' The whole church erupted into cheers
and applause.

The wedding party made its way into the barn, which
had been decorated with banners and paper flags. Mrs
Hill had put on a very impressive wedding breakfast and
Rachel was happily handing out bottles of ale. Dotty was
still shaken so Lavinia immediately found her a very large
beer and made her drink it. Dotty was in a complete daze
and glugged the liquid straight down, looking at the gold
band on her finger in disbelief.

At three o'clock, the festivities were paused for them all
to crowd around the wireless to hear Churchill's speech.
The Prime Minister reminded them that although this
was the end for Europe, there was a bigger war out there
that still had to be won, but even those cautionary words
could not quell the atmosphere of celebration and relief.
Dotty's eyes took on a wide, glazed look as the alcohol
went straight to her head, and while she put on a brave
face, it was obvious she was as fragile as a cut-glass goblet.
It was only when she was alone with George in the little
lodgings he'd taken in the village that she faced the issue
she had been dreading.

'He was right, George, I can't have children. I know I should have told you but . . . Are you sure you still want to be married to me?'

George gently unbuttoned her dress and laid her on the thin mattress. He looked down at her with longing and said in a muffled voice, 'Oh yes, oh yes.'

* * *

Dotty went through the next few days in a haze of happiness. She had never known it could be like this. The violent act that had been forced on her was nothing like the caring passion that she found with George and the fact that every touch was made with love was like a balm to her troubled soul.

She had been given a few days off by a delighted Mr Hollis and she spent them humming to herself while sewing old bits of material for curtains and trying to make tasty suppers on the one-burner stove in the tiny kitchen of the lodgings. She was glad George liked Marmite, as it was one of the few foods that weren't rationed, and she would lovingly wrap his sandwiches in newspaper for him to have during his dinner break at work.

One day, Dotty decided she would walk into the woods to collect some flowers to put in the little vase her mother-in-law had given them as a wedding gift. She was almost skipping, her joy was so unconfined, and she was singing to herself. When she stopped to listen, she could hear a sound coming from behind the trees to her left. She cocked her head to one side – that was definitely crying she could hear.

As quietly as she could, she crept towards the sound. There was a young girl there, crouched against a tree. She had her knees bunched up and her head was bowed over them, her long hair spread out like soft tendrils. Her shoulders were heaving with the sobs that were emanating from deep inside her.

Dotty knelt down. 'What is it? Can I help?'

'No one can help,' the girl said, getting to her feet and preparing to run away. Looking closely at the girl as she got to her feet, Dotty had a flashback to herself as a young girl with that same rounded stomach and the same desperate look in her eyes.

'Don't go, please,' she said, looking into the girl's eyes. 'Tell me your name.'

'Dorothy,' was the sulky reply.

Dotty stepped back, stunned. It was as if fate was playing a cruel game with her.

'I'm Dorothy too and I know exactly how you're feeling.'

'How can you?' the girl said angrily, turning on her heel.

Dotty put out her arm to stop her. 'How old are you?'

'I know what you're thinking,' Dorothy said. 'That I'm a fallen woman that I deserve this,' and here she broke down again, tears flowing fast from her eyes.

Dotty took hold of her shoulders and took a deep breath. 'No, what I'm actually thinking is that you remind me, oh

far too much, of myself at your age. What are you, fifteen?'
And she looked down meaningfully at the child's stomach.

As the realisation dawned on the young girl, she crumpled into a heap on the ground. To find someone who really did know exactly how she felt was like being handed a warm blanket on a freezing night.

The two of them sat for an hour while they talked. Dotty listened with sympathy as the young girl confessed the passion she and her beloved Terence had given in to just hours before he was shipped out with the army. The shock she'd felt when she realised she was having his child was nothing to the horror of hearing the bicycle bell of the telegram boy outside next door. She'd heard his mother's shrieks of despair through the paper-thin walls and had fallen in a crumpled heap on the floor just as Stanley had walked through the door. Fortunately, Dorothy was too involved in her own misery to think of asking Dotty any questions about the older girl's story.

At the end of it, they both sat in silence until Dorothy said, 'What am I going to do?'

Dotty thought about it for a moment and then it came to her. It may have been coincidence that they had the same name, even that Dorothy faced such a familiar predicament, but surely this was a chance for them to be each other's saviour? She just had to talk to George first.

* * *

With all the drama of the wedding, it was several days before Karl had the chance to talk to Hannah. He spotted her going into the stables and, checking to make sure Stanley wasn't in the vicinity, he followed her. Watching her start to groom Hercules lovingly, Karl grinned; how she had changed from that first day.

He said her name quietly: 'Hannah.'

She swung round, dropping the brush. Hercules neighed in disgust at the interruption to his routine.

'Karl . . .'

He stepped forward and took her in his arms. She seemed to melt against him and his arms tightened around her.

He muttered into her hair, 'Oh Hannah, I've missed you so much.'

She murmured in response. These snatched moments were like liquid gold pouring into her soul.

'What?' he said with a smile.

'I can't speak,' she groaned. 'My words won't come out. I feel like Elizé, my heart's all jumbled up with my head.'

'OK,' he laughed, 'just kiss me instead.'

And she did.

They eventually parted and stood back to look at each other's loving faces.

'I have a plan,' Karl said eventually.

'Good, I'm glad you have, because I have no idea how we do this,' Hannah said with a disgruntled pout that was just like Elizé's when she was thwarted in one of her plans.

'We're not the only ones,' Karl told her. 'There are more people like us all over Britain. We just have to wait; wait until this war is finally completely over and, little by little, people will get used to the idea that young people can still fall in love, even in war. I will find my family, they will love you and you will introduce me to yours and we will all be happy.'

It was those last words that made Hannah's head jerk up. 'No, not my father . . . he will never . . .'

'Yes, he will, he will when he meets me,' Karl laughed. He was determined not to listen to any objections.

'He hates Germans,' she said slowly. And she told him the story her father had shared with her that had scarred his life for so many years. Karl frowned, remembering the films the POWs had been made to watch. Deep wounds were going to take time to heal.

'We will find a way,' he told her and drew her to him again. She relaxed against his shoulder; she so badly wanted to believe this man could perform miracles. It took just a brief moment for Karl to feel a quiver of doubt before he shook himself and tightened his grip around her.

* * *

Any thoughts that VE Day would change the routine on the farm were quickly dashed and the harvest, if anything, was more frantic than ever with farmers desperately trying to feed a nation whose rations had been cut once again. This time, cooking fat was the victim, leaving Mrs Hill at the end of her tether at the inability to make biscuits or cakes. She'd long ago given up using much fat in pastry and moaned every day about the potato pastry she was forced to create. Bread was sold by weight and was carefully weighed for each customer so that, in the fields, not one stalk of corn could be wasted, and the girls spent hours scouring the ground to make sure they had not left any behind. After the initial euphoria, the war seemed endless and British troops, instead of planning their demobilisation, lived in fear of being sent out to join the fierce struggle that was going on in the East. Dotty still worked with the girls during the day, but was too busy contentedly bustling around doing her housewifely duties to spend much of her time off with them. Unbeknown to everyone, she was also gradually preparing the cottage for a future she had never thought she could have.

The bedroom above the barn seemed empty and quiet without Dotty in it, and Lavinia, after three nights of carrying on sleeping on the mattress on the floor, gave in and snuggled into the bed next to Hannah. In the dark, they whispered their hopes and aspirations for the future. Hannah was trying to convince herself that, somehow, Karl had it all sorted and, to take her mind off the uncertainty, started to plan how she might train as a teacher, but Lavinia was at a complete loss and had no idea what her future held. She just knew she felt a huge weight in her stomach when she thought of the endless array of eligible young men described in boring detail in her parents' letters.

Finally, on 15th August, the newspaper headlines proclaimed that the Japanese had surrendered and the inhabitants of the barn were torn between horror at the use of the most destructive weapon and relief that there might be peace at last.

Now the end of the war was more real, ironically, the celebrations became more subdued. It was a time for reflection as everyone weighed up what the war had cost the country, their families and themselves. It also opened up a cavern of emptiness for so many people about what would happen next. The girls had spent the last three years existing in a bubble with a common purpose and the end of the war was going to sweep that away. It also occurred to them that they would have to part.

Dotty was the first to crack.

'I can't,' she said, bursting in the bedroom, 'I just can't do it. I love George to bits and I've got so much to look forward to.' She stopped, she hadn't yet told them of her plans with Dorothy. 'But I can't lose you two.' And she collapsed onto her side of the bed, which felt so familiar, and burst into tears.

Lavinia fell on top of her and Hannah followed. The three of them lay there, feeling the warmth and comfort they had taken for granted for so long.

Hannah started to speak, her voice muffled and emotional.

'We'll never lose each other. Just think what we've been through. And if you two think I'm going to manage to sort out this marriage to Karl without your help, you've got another think coming.'

Lavinia sat up. 'You're right, Hann. This isn't the end, it's only the beginning. I've got no idea what I do next. I need you.'

Dotty got up and brushed herself down. She pushed her unruly hair behind her ears. 'Good, that's sorted then. Friends for life. Agreed?'

Hannah bounded onto the bed and started to jump up and down.

'We are the invincible three.'

'What does invinc—mean?' Dotty piped up.

'It means we are so strong that no one, that's no one, can ever hurt us or split us up,' Hannah said, grabbing her hand. Lavinia took hold of the other one and the three of them jumped up and down on the mattress, making the faded lampshade above them shake.

They all chanted together, laughing and crying at the same time: 'We are the invincible three.'

Chapter 50

It was the week before Christmas 1945 and Elizé ran over to the yard. She was so excited she could hardly speak.

'Hannah, Hannah, they've said yes, I can come with you!'

Hannah stopped washing her hands in the freezing cold pump water and knelt down to take the child by the shoulders.

'Really? They don't mind? What about Bobby? Won't she be here?'

Elizé shook her head sadly. 'No, she can't be here. She's working. But Hannah,' she brightened, 'I can come to Manchester and you can ask Karl and I can meet your parents and, *et voilà*, it will be a proper Christmas.'

Hannah hoped she was right. In a gesture of conciliation, the government had given permission for prisoners of war to be allowed to join families for the festive period and she had written to her parents to ask if she could bring 'someone' home with her. She knew her mother had improved slightly but wondered whether she would ever again see the cheerful woman who had read her bedtime stories when she was little. However, the main thing that kept her awake at night was the varying scenarios of her father taking a gun to Karl, her neighbours shunning her and, worst of all, of Karl deciding she wasn't worth all the aggravation. They'd hardly had any time to themselves over the last few months, it was only a meaningful look here and there that gave her any confidence that he still loved her.

She needed to see Karl, but the opportunities were limited, so Hannah watched closely for her chance. She hung about by the area where the truck would pull in and, as the Germans piled out, ready for another day's work, she 'happened' to be passing and pushed a note into Karl's hand, not daring to glance back to see his surprised face. Karl fingered the note all morning, wondering what it would say, but it wasn't until the whistle went to denote dinner-time that he was able to sneak round a corner to read it. His face lit up with pleasure and he hugged the little note to his chest while he absorbed the information. He had dreaded another bleak Christmas in the hut, but to be able to spend a few days with Hannah, like a normal couple, was almost too much for his love-struck heart to bear, and he crouched down to lean against the wall to take it all in. He couldn't believe her parents had agreed to including a German in their festivities, but he knew, he just knew, they must be as kind and as non-judgemental as their wonderful daughter. He whistled as he worked all that day.

* * *

Just a few days later, Hannah, Karl and Elizé set off excitedly on a train to Manchester. Elizé was clutching her teddy bear and a bag of presents that the Hollis family had sent for them all. Rationing was as severe as ever and supplies were still scarce, but after so many years of deprivation, the little treats that were in those packages were a new experience for Elizé; she could hardly remember a Christmas without war. Karl was allowed to dress in a suit that Archie had lent him and he walked with his head held high, convinced he was blending in with the crowds that jostled on the platform. He failed to see the suspicious faces of the people he passed as they took in his blond hair and blue eyes, but Hannah saw them.

Karl took hold of Hannah's hand and she smiled nervously. She began to wonder whether this had been such a good idea after all, but the prospect of being with Karl away from any prying eyes at the farm had been too tempting to resist.

There was no chance for the young couple to talk much during the journey as Elizé kept up a constant stream of chatter, delighting everyone in the train compartment. Hannah was relieved that Karl didn't want to talk, his accent would surely give him away and she suddenly experienced a feeling of dread.

Once she got to Colley Street, a place that was so familiar, she stopped, panic overwhelming her. *I must be insane,* she thought. *This surely will be nothing but a total disaster.*

Karl looked at her quizzically, but Elizé was running ahead looking for the correct number on the front door. Without waiting, she ran up the steps to the house and banged the door knocker. Before she had had a chance to take her hand away, the door opened and the delighted face of a kind man greeted her. Behind the man, was a woman, peeping nervously around his shoulder. Her face lit up when Margaret Compton saw the three people on the doorstep. She gave a weak smile of relief to Hannah and then looked with curiosity at the little girl, whose innocent smile was irresistible. Meanwhile, her husband was looking with interest at the good-looking young man standing patiently to one side.

'Please, please come in,' Alf Compton was saying, giving Hannah a hug as she passed.

Karl stepped forward and held out his hand. 'Good afternoon, sir. It is a pleasure to meet you both.'

His accent made Alf's hand freeze mid-shake. He looked at Hannah in disbelief. This man could surely not be a . . . German. He could hardly say the word, even in his head.

Hannah breezed past her father into the morning room, ignoring the light from the fire that had been specially lit in the front parlour.

She started to prattle on, feeling the familiar nerves that she always had in this house. She talked about the journey, the train, the number of people – anything but the fact that she had just walked into her home with an officer of Hitler's forces. In less than two minutes, the strong, resourceful Land Army girl had shrunk back into the shy child who had left Stretford three years earlier.

Her father came up behind her, grabbed her arm and dragged her into the back kitchen, his face ablaze with fury.

'That . . . man . . . is not staying in my house,' he hissed.

'Dad, I . . .' Hannah was at a complete loss and had no idea what to say. On the farm where the German POWs were such a familiar part of life, they had become individuals everyone knew and even liked. Salhouse had become somewhere she could cope with her and Karl's secret. Here in Stretford, in her own home, it was a different story.

They stood opposite each other, her father's mouth grimly twisted into a determined expression and Hannah looking at her father, aghast. From the next room, they heard her mother's voice.

'Now you come with me, young man, I'll show you the spare room we've prepared for you. And you too, Elizé, is it? Come on, I'll show you the rest of the house. It's been so long since we've had visitors. It's wonderful.'

'Surely, all this—' Hannah jerked her head in the direction of the other room '—is a price worth paying. It's so good to see Mum showing some interest at last, isn't it?'

She was clutching at straws, but her words seemed to work and her dad stalked out of the room to take up his usual spot in his favourite armchair with a disgusted grunt. Elizé was gloriously oblivious and clasping Mrs Compton's hand, dragged her off for a tour of every corner of the house, Karl meekly following them.

'I'll make some tea, then,' Hannah said eventually, her shoulders drooping. This was never going to work.

As soon as the others left the room, her father looked up at his daughter, his face grim with dread.

'So, is this some kind of joke, Hannah?'

'No, Dad, I love him. He's a wonderful man.'

Her father's face did not change, it was as white as stone, but his cheek muscle twitched.

Hannah started to explain to her father everything she had spent the last month practising. The arguments that had sounded so reasonable to her in the bedroom at Salhouse now sounded hollow and unconvincing.

'He always hated Hitler, he never wanted to join up but was forced to. He's training to be a doctor ...' She trailed off.

Her father had folded his arms, his eyes dull with disappointment.

She sighed and turned into the back kitchen to put the kettle on.

* * *

Dinner that evening was torture for Hannah, but Karl seemed to be enjoying himself and charming her mother. He gently asked her all about Manchester, gradually drawing her out of herself.

Hannah welcomed the fact that Elizé was so exhausted it gave her an excuse to be out of the room while she settled her for bed. By the time she came back downstairs, Mr Compton had hidden himself behind a newspaper, leaving Karl to help Mrs Compton with the washing up. Hannah couldn't meet Karl's questioning gaze and stood nervously twiddling her fingers. She eventually gave up and went to bed, curling up next to the sleeping Elizé.

The following morning, her father had gone out to the shops and Karl went with Hannah into the back kitchen. She swung around to face him, her face smeared with tears.

'We can't do this,' she told him. 'My dad'll never accept it.'

Karl gathered her into his arms. He could not, would not, let this young woman go.

At that moment, Elizé walked in. She saw them together and put her hand over her mouth to suppress a giggle.

'I knew it,' she said, bouncing up and down on the spot. 'You're in love and you're going to get married.'

She started singing her little refrain, 'They're going to get married, they're going to get married,' just as Hannah's father came in through the back door.

'Over my dead body,' he said, putting his shopping bag on the floor and glaring at them both.

Hannah opened her mouth to object, but Elizé got in first.

'But why not?'

'Because he is a German and I hate Germans.'

Elizé's face clouded over and very solemnly she started to speak.

'Monsieur Compton, you are a nice man, I think, but you must listen to me. The war is over. I too hate the soldiers who shot my father, here, in front of my eyes.' She pointed down at the stone flag floor in front of her that suddenly seemed stained with the blood of her beloved father. 'And then they took my mother away onto a train. If anyone should hate Karl it is me . . . but I don't.'

And with these words, she ran up to Karl and put her arms around him. She could only reach up to his stomach. She looked up at him adoringly and then over to Hannah's father.

'You see, he too is a good man, a kind man, and he did not want to work for that horrid Hitler. He is a doctor and my friend, and I think he and Hannah will be very happy.'

She stood up as tall as her young body would allow and looked sternly at Mr Compton. 'So, Monsieur Compton, I think we, all of us, need to forget the horrible things we have seen, or else, how can we have a nice world?' Her face showed a wisdom and maturity that took Hannah's breath away.

There was complete silence as the three adults stood and stared at the little girl. It was only broken when Mrs Compton came in, looking bewildered.

'Shootings, soldiers ... no, please no. I can't take any more.' And she collapsed in a heap on the floor.

Karl immediately stepped forward to lift Hannah's mother's head off the hard tiles.

'Get me a blanket, please,' he said calmly to Mr Compton, and he gently held Mrs Compton's legs about a foot off the ground. Alf handed him the cream blanket they kept out of habit by the back door, unable to believe air raids were really over. Karl rolled it to place under Margaret Compton's feet before loosening the woman's top button as Mr Compton leaned forward to try to sit her up.

'No,' Karl told him quietly. 'She may faint again. Just give her a moment.'

Alf Compton backed off and started to edge his way back into the morning room. He felt a huge relief that his wife was in such good hands, but he was tormented that those hands were German ones. At the same time, the child's words kept haunting him, bringing back the image of the little girl in France who had lost her life because of him.

He sat in his armchair and put his head in his hands. Would he ever be able to leave these nightmares behind?

* * *

Karl spent the next few days concentrating on Mrs Compton, talking to her, reassuring her and expertly using his psychoanalytical skills to help her start to recover from her depression. After her fainting fit, her husband had called the doctor and, with Alf's permission, Karl had a quiet word with him in the hallway. It resulted in some new tablets that Karl promised would help. Slowly but surely, Mr Compton started to feel a reluctant trust for this gentle man, but it took a visit on Christmas Eve from Ginny and John Mullins to help him take those final steps – the ones that would allow the Compton family to move out of the fog that had shrouded the house for so long.

Mrs Compton had made a real effort to set the front parlour tea table and had even helped Hannah make a fruitcake. Alf Compton always enjoyed John Mullins's company so looked forward to a catch-up about the football, but he was extremely nervous as to what his friends would think of their visitor.

The Mullinses looked curiously at Karl. Ginny's face started to clear as the veiled references about Hannah's 'new blond man' in Lily's letters suddenly made sense. Her daughter had hinted that she'd heard Hannah had a new man in her life, but she hadn't mentioned to her parents he was German. She turned to Hannah to tell her about Lily's pending demob to try to distract from the tension that was hanging in the air. Hannah had heard nothing about her own release, but she knew she was not in the same rush as Lily to get back to her old life in Manchester.

As the afternoon went on, Alf was surprised to find that the conversation that went around the room felt relatively normal, even if John Mullins did try too hard to include Karl. The fact that Lily's parents could make such an effort to pretend it was an everyday occurrence to have a German in the front parlour made him feel uncomfortable. They were all chatting naturally – perhaps it was just him who had a problem with the situation, he thought

By the front door on their way out, John Mullins turned to Alf and whispered, 'He seems a good sort of chap. Not like some of his countrymen but there again,' he said with a grin, 'not all Brits are perfect and there's many of 'em I wouldn't like to spend an afternoon like that with.'

He put his hand on his friend's shoulder. 'It's hard for the likes of us, Alf, we've seen two wars against the Germans, but we're supposed to be at peace now and this is a new age. I suspect if we don't move with it, we'll be left behind. No, Alf, he seems all right.'

Alf Compton closed the front door, wondering whether he could learn to close the door on the memories that had haunted him for so long as easily.

* * *

Hannah was wakened on Christmas Day by an excited Elizé. Hannah rubbed her eyes, which had dark circles under them, testimony to her broken night's sleep. There had been a moment when she had sat watching Mr and Mrs Mullins trying to chat naturally to Karl that she envisaged Christmases to come. He would always be an outsider and she was planning to put herself out there in the wilderness with him. She was not sure she was brave enough.

The little girl's determination that every possible English Christmas tradition should be followed to the letter had added some unexpected magic to the Compton family and they had ceremoniously put out a carrot and a tot of whisky for any night visitors who might happen to fly over Colley Street.

'Come on, sleepy head,' Elizé said in frustration. 'I've been awake ages. Can we go down now . . . pleeeaaaase!'

Hannah smiled, grateful for the child's presence in the overwrought atmosphere of the house and grabbed the faded blue candlewick dressing gown from behind the door. Elizé was already halfway down the stairs. Margaret Compton was waiting at the bottom with a look of real delight on her face and her pale cheeks even had a glow of pink in them. She took Elizé's hand and led her gently into the front room where there were some fir branches that she and Alf had decorated with tinsel and baubles late the previous night. Under them, were some brown paper parcels with bits of holly tied onto them and even a little handmade red stocking for Elizé.

The child stood transfixed, her hands over her mouth. In a life dominated by war and tragedy, she had never had a Christmas like it.

She looked tentatively at Mrs Compton. 'May I . . . May I see if any are for me?' she whispered.

Hannah came in from behind her and pushed her towards the little pile.

'If you don't, I'm going to get in first.' She smiled, and they both knelt down to rip open the parcels. Margaret Compton felt a joy she thought had been banished forever and hugged her arms around herself.

Behind her, Karl came through the doorway, already dressed and his hair smartly combed. He looked at the little scene in front of him and had to step back into the doorway to disguise the tears that had come to his eyes.

Alf Compton, who came down the hall at the same time, saw how moved Karl was and reached forward to put his hand on his arm. 'There, lad, don't take on so.'

'I'm sorry, Mr Compton, but I can't tell you what it means to be here and to—' he waved his arms expansively '—for all this. It is the most wonderful Christmas I could ever have asked for.'

'I know, I know,' Alf replied, thoughtfully. He looked again at the embarrassed young man in front of him and saw the war through his eyes for the first time. He found his heart, unexpectedly, touched by it all.

* * *

Later, after the best Christmas dinner Hannah had been able to muster, she, Karl and Elizé went for a walk so that Hannah could proudly show Karl her home area. Walking alongside him with Elizé, wearing her new hat and gloves, between them, Hannah felt a pang for a future she longed to have but she couldn't help but notice the sly looks she was getting from people who'd known her from childhood. Word had obviously got around about the smart, blond-haired man next to her. Karl was very quiet but he gave her hand a reassuring squeeze.

They made their way to Manchester city centre and while Hannah was depressingly used to the devastated buildings and streets that had been so relentlessly blasted during the Blitz, Karl looked around him in horror. Norwich had been bombed, but not like this. He knew that German cities had been equally destroyed, but to see such damage, here in front of him, was a shock and, for the first time, he understood Hannah's concerns. It was going to be a long time before people on all sides would be able to forgive and forget. They turned silently for home.

'Hello, Hannah.' A voice came from behind them. It was Mr Edge from next door; his wife, Ida, was clinging on to his arm. She was almost jumping up and down with excitement, thrilled to be the first to corner Hannah and this German the milkman had told her about.

'Happy Christmas,' she said, scrutinising the Aryan face in front of her. 'And to your young man, sorry, we don't know your name . . .'

Karl held his hand out and made the fatal mistake of clicking his heels together. Mrs Edge's eyes widened.

'My name is Karl, it is an honour to meet you.'

'Hmm, likewise, I'm sure,' Mr Edge said, disapproval dripping from his words. He pulled his wife to him and made to go past the young couple, but Mrs Edge wanted more information for the knitting group.

'So, are you one of them prisoners of war, then?' she asked.

'Yes, I am. But now the war is over and we all move on as friends, no?' Karl ventured, feeling the distrust emanating from across the pavement.

Elizé had been eyeing up these two people with their bad-tempered expressions, but she now needed to speak. 'Karl is a doctor and a good man. He is *mon ami*.'

Her chin rose in a challenge and Mrs Edge was taken aback.

'It seems your household has become quite international, Hannah. Well, it's not what we're used to here in Stretford but I'm sure you know what you're doing,' she said, sceptically.

Hannah muttered something about being back for tea and started to walk away. Her stomach was churning. The world she and Karl had created had been a perfect, secret one that felt safe when it was just the two of them, but taking their place in the wider world was going to be another matter. On the farm, she was Hannah, the capable Land Army girl. Without her uniform, she felt her armour had disintegrated and she was as vulnerable as she had always been.

* * *

Back at the house, Mr and Mrs Compton were sitting quietly next to the range. Alf was prodding the specially saved-up coal thoughtfully.

They both started to speak at the same time, making Mrs Compton laugh nervously.

'What were you about to say?' she asked her husband.

Alf reached across and took hold of his wife's hand. 'We've been through such a lot, you and I, and I know I haven't made life easy for you, but we've got a good marriage, haven't we?'

Margaret's face was lined and her hair grey, but, in that second, she looked for all the world like the pretty young girl he had married before he set off to fight in the Great War. She drew herself up to face him.

'We have, Alf, but I think the best's yet to come. Our Hannah's young man seems ...' she paused to find the right words '... someone I think I can trust to look after our daughter and she deserves some happiness. Heaven knows, between us, we've made things difficult for her. I've got a long way to go, but these tablets are starting to work, and now the war's over, I do think we can finally start to look forward. I want Hannah to have a husband and a family and I think Karl is just the man for her ... no matter what nationality he is.'

After the longest speech his wife had made for years, Alf Compton leaned across and kissed her gently.

Chapter 51

It was a thoughtful little trio that got off the train at Norwich. Karl had to leave them immediately to go back to the hut at Mousehold Heath, his mind swirling with everything that had happened in the Compton household. He went to reach for Hannah's hand, but she shook him off, claiming the bus to Salhouse was about to leave and grabbed Elizé's arm to run into the road, almost into the path of a second bus.

'Oh, for heaven's sake, Hannah,' Elizé said with uncharacteristic impatience, pulling her out of harm's way. 'Do I have to take care of *you* now? You're supposed to be the adult.' She'd felt irritated ever since she'd spotted Mrs Compton's knitting that had translated into a lemon woolly hat. It was supposed to have been from Father Christmas but now disturbing doubts had set in. She was growing up and she wasn't sure she liked it. As they walked into the yard at Salhouse Farm, Dotty was there waiting for them. She was holding a little bundle in a pink blanket and George was standing behind her, his arm proudly draped across her shoulder.

'Hannah, meet your godchild,' she called across the yard.

Hannah looked completely perplexed.

'We're adopting her,' George told her, beaming. 'Her name is Maria, named after the patron saint of farming, don't you think that's perfect? She's only five months old and she can almost sit up on her own already.' The new parents were so engrossed with looking adoringly at the new member of their family it gave Lavinia time to come up behind Hannah and whisper the truth behind the sudden arrival of a baby in their midst. A feeling of surprise came over Hannah at the mention of Stanley's name, but when she looked at Dotty and George's faces, she felt their excitement and reached forward to be handed the child, whose little face was screwed up, unsure whether to laugh or cry. When the baby saw Hannah looking down at her, her face cleared and she broke into a gummy smile that made Hannah's heart melt and forget all her troubles.

Lavinia had more news for Hannah. The Land Army girls' release papers had arrived and they would soon be free to leave the farm, a pronouncement that made the three girls look at each other in alarm. Lavinia was in a complete tailspin; her future loomed like an empty page. She thought, remembering Hannah's face that had always softened every time she saw Karl and Dotty's constant beaming smile, that her two friends seemed to have found the next stage in their lives, but as far as she was concerned, she had no idea what to do next.

It was as Hannah and Lavinia got undressed that the questions started. Lavinia wanted to know every detail of Christmas at the Compton house and Hannah told Lavinia about how her mother had improved with Karl's help to the point where she had actually seen her father give her mother a quick hug on Christmas morning. What she didn't tell Lavinia was how much the visit had highlighted all the problems she and Karl would face in the future. She'd come back feeling overwhelmed with the hopelessness of it all.

* * *

The following day, the girls received a visit from Lady Parker. She strode into the barn where they were having their breakfast and stood in front of Lavinia with her arms folded. Lavinia gave a deep sigh. What bombshell did her aunt have in store now?

'So, Doris, what are you going to do with the rest of your life?' she demanded. 'You're not going back to the circus or the theatre, so tell me, young lady, do you want to be married off to some toff, like your father wants, or do you want to do something worthwhile?'

Lavinia looked suspiciously at her aunt. She was never sure whether she should trust her but, with no options in mind, she decided she might as well see what she had to say.

'Go on then . . . what do you suggest?'

Lady Parker pulled up a chair opposite Lavinia and leaned forward. She almost looked enthusiastic.

'Well, I've made some enquiries and there are agricultural courses you could go on. You could learn to be a proper farmer and then your father could sign over part of the land in Oxfordshire to you.'

Lavinia felt a bubble of excitement rising inside her. She examined her nails, the nail varnish was chipped, her lipstick was already smeared, but she felt more alive than she had ever done in her life.

'I'll do it!' she said, jumping up and turning to the other two. 'I've loved this life, it's more important than anything I've ever done and there's so much to learn and just think what a farmer I'll make.'

Dotty caught Hannah's eye and started to giggle. The prospect of their gorgeous friend up to her knees in muck for the rest of her life was just too hilarious to take seriously.

But Lavinia was already on her way around the table to give her aunt a hug. 'Aunt Deborah, you're a lifesaver.'

Lady Parker pulled herself back from the enthusiastic hug and said haughtily, 'Well, it's about time you did something meaningful and now, at least, you look the part.'

'You've got to be joking, Aunt Deborah, just think of all those gorgeous farming types who are just longing to be bossed around by a girl like me. Hmm, I'm going to have to rethink this look,' she said, brushing her hair out of her eyes and glancing at her nails. 'I need to have a think. Just because I'm going to be a farmer, I really don't see there's any necessity for me to look like one. I've been letting things slide here.

'Girls, you'll have to help me choose my outfit for the first day. I need to make an impression.'

'Of course, but maybe not that red hat with the black veil,' Dotty laughed.

* * *

Karl had returned buzzing with plans for the future. Ignorant of Hannah's turmoil, he was hoping he'd made a good enough impression in Manchester and was trying to concoct a way forward for them.

'Have you heard? We're moving again tomorrow,' Peter said from behind him, his voice reflecting his disappointment.

The news had been posted on the hut wall and had completely disheartened the POWs. They had hoped their next move would be on a ship to Germany, but, tomorrow morning, they were to be drafted onto a farm in Lincolnshire where they were struggling for farmhands, a result of so many local men having been killed. Karl's initial thought was that he needed to find Hannah and tell her. He hated the idea of them being parted, but then he tried to be philosophical. Rules were being relaxed and, he thought with a grin, a man in love will always find a way. He already suspected he would be unable to go home for several months yet, maybe another year, while the British government concentrated on bringing their own men home, which gave him plenty of time, he reasoned. Besides which, until he knew where his family was, he had nowhere else to go.

Without any news from Andrew Hollis, Karl had taken on the task of finding news about his brothers himself and had asked the Lagerführer for the standard postcard that all German servicemen were given, with the intention of sending one to the local police station in Tübingen. The postcard read: *'Ein Mitglied der geschlagenen Wermacht sucht seinen nächsten Angehörigen'* ('A member of the defeated German army seeks his next of kin').

He wrote the five lines he was allowed to put under the standard message and placed them on the Lagerführer's desk to be sent, with a feeling of hopelessness, and went to get the truck to work his last day at Salhouse. The chatter on the truck was all about the move and how desperate they were to get home to find their families. One POW reported he'd heard that people all over Europe were throwing simi-lar postcards out of trains, even leaving them on platforms and in shops in a bid to track down their relatives. It was a desperate situation and it seemed everyone in Germany was in the wrong place.

When they got out at the farm, the lines of men all walked with their heads down, feeling as defeated as they did when they were captured. Stanley came up behind him and Karl bristled. He wasn't in the mood for any more aggression.

'The boss wants to see you,' Stanley said, but then added begrudgingly: 'It's all right, I think he's got some good news for you.'

He then moved over to get the worksheet for the day, feeling those words went some way to repay his debt to this man. Since their altercation in the blacksmith's hut, Stanley had finally realised that the doctor had done him, and his little sister, a favour. He had never been an uncle before, and he was astonished at how a baby could change a man's view of life. After several months of struggling to cope with the newborn infant, the offer of a permanent arrangement with George and his bride meant both he and Dorothy could watch the child grow up and he was grateful for that. He still hated the Germans as a whole, but, he had to admit, that man hurriedly making his way to the farmhouse was all right.

Karl was perplexed. These British were very odd. First, there was Stanley being almost pleasant and now Andrew Hollis, another one set in his beliefs, was again singling him out to help him.

'You've had a letter,' Andrew told Karl, handing him an envelope. It was stamped with the Isle of Man Internment Camp lettering on the front but that had a black line through it and another, stamped over the top stated: 'Canon Park Alien Reception Centre, Middlesex'. Karl felt his hand shaking.

'I had some help from a friend of mine who was in my regiment. He lives over on the Isle of Man,' Andrew said with a certain amount of pride. He'd strangely enjoyed being able to help this man.

'The camps there have closed but he managed to forward my query and, I think, has tracked your family down. I hope it's good news. Here, take it and read it.'

Karl nodded gratefully and turned to go but Andrew stopped him. 'How are you and Hannah getting on?'

Under normal circumstances, Karl would have kept his own counsel but he was in such a state over the letter in front of him and Hannah's recent behaviour that he blurted out, 'I want to ask her to marry me but I don't know if I can ask her to do it. She'd have to give up so much.'

'I suspect Hannah knows that but how do you think her parents feel about it? Did you talk to them over Christmas?'

Karl thought back. 'Yes, well, I talked to her father. He left me in no doubt of all the problems we'd have to face, but, actually, I think he will come round to it. I just hope . . .'

'Yes?'

'Well, it's just that Hannah's been really quiet since we got back. I'm not sure she hasn't changed her mind.'

'Give her time,' Andrew said, but Karl's words made him think. Somehow, once he had come to terms with the German in front of him, he had sort of assumed the rest of the world would follow, but feelings were very raw and this young couple's romance was heading for some choppy waters.

'If it makes it any easier, I'd be honoured to have the wedding party here if you'd like,' he heard himself saying.

Karl gasped with delight. One of the things that had been keeping him awake at night was how he could ask Hannah to get married without the celebrations she deserved on her wedding day, but this offer from the very man who had held so much bitterness towards the Germans meant more to him than words could express and, with moist eyes, he thanked Andrew profusely.

Making his way back towards the yard, he looked at the letter in his hands. He dreaded opening it. What was the significance of Middlesex? What if his mother was dead? What of his brothers? Eventually, he pushed his fears to the back of his mind and ripped open the envelope.

The letter was in familiar writing. Karl leaned against the barn wall in relief. His mother's script was as strong as he'd always remembered it and her gentle face came back to him like a wave of warm seawater. It was only a short letter, as if she'd been in such a rush to finally make contact with her son before he vanished into thin air again. He traced his finger over the words, some of which were smeared, he suspected with tears, which told him that she had escaped to England after the farm was requisitioned and had managed to get to Greta in King's Lynn.

Karl paused, realising there was undoubtedly more to the story behind those few words.

He read on: she was writing from a transit camp in Middlesex, where they'd been taken between internment in the Isle of Man and getting back to King's Lynn so that Greta could be reunited with the man she loved.

'Your brothers are alive,' her letter went on, 'but Werner has been injured and I must get home to see how he is and to find out what's happened to the farm.'

She finished with a promise to write again soon, now she had found him, adding that the Manx ice creams were the best in the world but that the kipper fishes were a bit strange.

Karl knew he was due out to join the rest of the POWs digging out the bottom field but, feeling jubilant with his morning of good news, he wanted to share it all with Hannah and he grinned with delight when he spotted her coming out of the milking parlour, followed by Lavinia and Dotty. Her hair was ruffled and she had straw in her fringe. Her boots were covered in cow excrement, but to Karl, she had never looked more beautiful.

He made his way over to her but when she saw him, she stopped in her tracks and put her hand to her mouth. She looked terrified and Karl was puzzled.

'Is everything all right, Hannah?' he said slowly, not sure he wanted to hear her answer.

'No, no, it isn't,' she sobbed. 'I can't do it . . . I just can't.' And she ran into the barn and out of sight.

Lavinia and Dotty ran after her, leaving Karl like a tottering lone skittle in the middle of the yard.

* * *

Hannah was lying on the bed, her shoulders heaving. She was emitting loud wails of despair. Lavinia sat on one side of her and Dotty on the other. Lavinia spoke first.

'Hann, come on it's not that bad . . . you've just got cold feet.'

At this, Hannah sat upright, her eyes awash with tears. 'No, no, I haven't. I just can't do it. It's impossible. How can I lose my nationality, my friends, any respect, all of it? I just can't. It's too much,' she shouted at her and then collapsed back onto the bed, sobbing once more.

'But what about Karl?' Dotty said. 'You can't just leave him like this. He won't understand.'

Between sobs, Hannah tried to say she would write to him, explain, but, then, picturing his face, full of questions, hurt and disbelief, she buried her head in the pillow again, her shoulders heaving. So this is what it felt like to have a broken heart, she thought, knowing that Karl would be feeling so, oh so much worse. She felt she had a choice between betraying her country, her family, her friends or betraying Karl. She pummelled her fists into the mattress. How could life be so cruel? How could she be so cruel?

Dotty signalled to Lavinia that they should leave her to it, aware that John was waiting for them to do the hoeing. Reluctantly, they closed the door on the distraught girl.

Chapter 52

Two years later. August 1947 – Stuttgart, Germany

Karl Schneider fingered his certificate with pride. He was finally a fully trained doctor. His mother looked on proudly as he received his scroll from the chancellor of the university. Next to her was his brother, Werner, stooped as a result of his injuries sustained on the Russian front. His other brother, Horst, was standing proudly, pretending he was not wiping a tear from his eyes. Greta had sent the family a letter with photographs of his new niece, Hildegard, and Karl felt with satisfaction that he had finally reached the end of a long road. But it was a road he was travelling without Hannah and the horizon was still so very bleak.

He patted his pocket where he kept her last letter. It was torn at the edges, proof of how many times he had read it, desperate to understand where their relationship had gone wrong. Hannah had avoided him assiduously after her outburst, leaving him devastated at her sudden change of heart. He'd been left with so many questions, and when an envelope in her handwriting finally tracked him down at the new farm in Lincolnshire, he felt hope surging that there had been some terrible misunderstanding between them that he could resolve. However, when he'd read the letter, he had felt his heart break into tiny pieces. Every time he tortured himself by rereading it, he felt the pain surge through him again. He shook his head angrily – would he never heal?

The worst thing for Karl was that he understood. He could hear her torment in her words. He knew she loved him, but to be able to do that, she would spend a lifetime being snubbed by her fellow countrymen. Her British passport would have to be surrendered and they would live with the sort of comments she had suffered from her neighbour that last Christmas. She'd told him she didn't have the courage and his letters back to her after that had received no reply.

He took his mother back to the train so she could return to the farm in Tübingen. There was little of it left and, when he looked at his mother, he wasn't sure she had the energy to try to revive it. His brothers were doing their best, but post-war Germany was a desperate place. Karl was sending as much money home as he could to help them, but it was never enough.

By the time he arrived back outside his little apartment in Stuttgart, the euphoria of his degree ceremony had worn thin. There was so much his country had to do to regain its status in the world, rebuild its economy and generate a feeling of hope. He stood for a moment under the plane tree near his apartment, looking up at the tree above him. On a branch, a blackbird was singing. It made Karl smile and looking at the leaves coming out, ready for spring, he felt grateful as ever, to nature for reminding him there was always hope.

'Hello Karl.' A voice in front of him made him jump.

'Hannah!'

He stood and took in the vision in front of him. It really was her, here in Germany, looking as beautiful as ever and dressed in a pretty polka dot dress with a pale-blue silk ribbon carefully curled round her hair. She was biting her lip to stop it quivering, he noticed. All the rage he had felt when he had received her letter melted away, but it took him a few minutes to be able to find his voice.

'W . . . what are you doing here?'

'To be honest, I have no idea,' she said, picking at the hem of her sleeve.

'How did you find me?'

'I went to King's Lynn and found Greta. She told me where you lived. I just had to come and see you. Karl, I am so sorry. I don't know what to say.'

She looked so forlorn standing there, like a lost child. Karl moved forward. As far as he was concerned she didn't need to say anything. But she stepped back.

'I've met someone,' she blurted out. 'He's a good man and he wants to marry me.'

Those words hung in the air between them and Karl felt an anger rising.

'So, why did you come, then?'

Hannah looked as flustered as she had when she had been facing Hercules on that first day, her cheeks tinged with red as she struggled with her emotions.

'Is there somewhere we can go for a coffee?' she said, looking around desperately.

Karl started to march off towards the café on the corner, leaving Hannah to follow. He'd imagined this scene so many times but not like this.

* * *

Max, the waiter, looked with interest at the couple sitting stiffly at the front table in the window. He loved trying to imagine the lives of his customers but these two had him stumped. The girl, obviously English, looked in a terrible state and was stirring her coffee over and over again. The man, he originally thought, hated her, but then, occasionally, his eyes softened and Max had to rethink his assessment. He leaned forward on the counter in front of him to see how this scene would unfold, wishing his English was better.

'I'm sorry, Karl, it was terrible the way I left it,' the girl was saying.

'Yes, it was,' Karl agreed. 'We'd been doing so well. Mr Hollis had even said we could have the wedding there at the farm.'

Hannah looked up in surprise.

'Yes,' Karl went on, his voice breaking, 'I knew how you were feeling and if you had a proper wedding, I hoped you would not think you were, well, settling for something less than the best. But even that wasn't enough,' he ended bitterly. His English had improved so much but just because he could express himself better, did not mean it hurt any less.

'I love ... loved ... you, but everyone was so against us – my father, our neighbours, even the men in your camp. Everyone felt we were betraying them. I felt like *I* was betraying them.'

'I know,' Karl said quietly, 'but what we had, it was worth it. Or at least I thought it was, you obviously did not believe in us enough.'

At that, Hannah's blue eyes flashed. 'I did believe in us. How can you say that?'

'Well, why did you not fight for us then?' Karl asked her, challengingly.

'Lavinia and Dotty both tried. They spent days trying to convince me, but I'm just not strong enough.'

Max was leaning further and further forward to catch the conversation and knocked over a plate of biscuits, sending the contents clattering across the floor.

Karl and Hannah hardly noticed.

'So, who is this man, then?' Karl asked reluctantly. He didn't really want to know.

'I've been studying to become a teacher,' she told him, pride in her voice. 'He was one of the lecturers.'

'Do you love him?'

'I don't know, I think so . . . I thought so.' Hannah's face looked so distressed that Karl couldn't help it; he reached across and took her hand.

The electricity shot through both of them, making them jerk back in their seats. Max almost clapped his hands. Their body language was unmistakable.

He went over to the table to ask if they wanted more drinks. Somebody needed to intervene here. In his best broken English, he said with a smile, 'Would you and your wife want more coffee?'

They both stared at him for a moment and then Hannah looked across at Karl. Dotty and Lavinia had been right, she didn't need to hide behind the Land Army uniform any longer. She raised her chin and said:

'Yes, his wife-to-be would.'

Acknowledgements

It's always as I start to write these acknowledgements that I am reminded of how many people help me on my journey. Without them, these books wouldn't be nearly as authentic and I am hugely grateful to them for sharing their knowledge and experience with me.

I'm going to start with my Land Army girls, the wonderful Dorothy Taylor and Iris Newbould. They welcomed me into their homes several years ago to proudly show me their scrapbooks and tell me those wonderful golden nuggets of information that aren't found in the history books. Iris then took me on a tour of her garden which had been the subject of an Alan Titchmarsh programme where he had done a design based on her career with the Land Army. Like Dorothy, she was incredibly proud of her time in the LA and as they described the physical tasks they had to undertake, I looked at these two slim women in their 90s and saw the strength of character as well as the physical strength they had to develop to get through. I just want to say thank you so much to both of them and I hope I've done justice to their stories.

Next was the revelation of Enid Mabel Hibberd's diaries. She was the mother of Trish Tunnifcliffe and Howard Price and I am incredibly grateful to Howard and Trish for sharing these personal items with me. Her wartime diaries were an amazing insight into a young Land Army woman's life over six years. I think the entry for the day war broke out summed up her stoic approach to life- so typical of that generation- when she wrote: 'War declared at 11.15. Spent day at S. School with women and children.'

I have had huge support from Cherish Watton, who runs the Land Army website. Her dedication and admiration for the Land Army women has meant she has been unstinting in her willingness to provide help with this book. Likewise, the Luftwaffe expert and final year PhD student, Victoria Taylor took time away from her studies to give me a huge amount of assistance to make sure Karl was a correct depiction of a Luftwaffe officer. I am indebted to both of them.

Helen Mills, a WAAF plotter in the Battle of Britain bunker is, as always, my first port of call to find out the wonderful minutiae of everyday life for these young girls during the war and, particularly during Covid, her cheerful advice to, as Churchill said, KBO . . . keep buggering on.. has brought many a smile into my Lockdown blues.

I have to thank Bella Holmes, who provided information about working with explosives so I could develop Ros's character. I was in awe of her stories of being a 17-year-old with one year's experience of physics at school when she donned a white coat to test explosives.

Hildegard Wiesehöfer was my German expert and any mistakes are due to my incompetence, not her translations. She also helped me understand the effect of Nazi rule on ordinary Germans at that time and I hope I've done justice to the millions of her countryfolk who were forced to live under that oppressive regime.

As soon as travel restrictions eased, I hightailed it over to Norwich to spend time in Salhouse and Norwich itself. I accosted every local I came across and was overwhelmed with the support and help I had from the residents of the village itself. In particular, I must mention Jo and Jess Shepherd who led me to Joyce Newstead; her personal knowledge of the area in the 1940s was invaluable. I also met Dennis Lynn who lost no time in sending me information that I needed. It was wonderful to meet them all and made me so glad I had set my book in Salhouse- they are such a generous lot.

I spent a very moving afternoon with Esther Carr and her mum, Lydia Fairweather hearing about her father's story. It was a tragic tale and made me realise what it was like for German people who didn't conform. I will be using more experiences in my next book about the internment camps in the Isle of Man but wanted to mention them here too.

There are times when the internet leads an author down a path that would have been unnavigable in former times and I had the most wonderful 'conversations' with antique tractor experts in Arkansas. Their detailed knowledge of tractor levers has to be experienced to be believed! I also have had wonderful help from the website, Norwich Remembers, to help me describe the Samson and Hercules dance hall.

I'd like to also thank our lovely friend, Jane Prescott, whose knowledge of plants and herbs meant I could make Karl's journey into the unknown a plausible adventure. She lives on the Isle of Man, so I may well come back to her for my next book!

I can't write these books without Claire Johnson-Creek at Bonnier Books and Kate Barker, my agent. They encourage, cajole, nudge and praise me just enough to help me to make these books so much better than I ever could manage on my own. Kate's practical advice and support is unstinting and Claire's clear vision and eagle-eyed editing has improved this book and all my others, so much. They are both just brilliant and I am so lucky to have them. I'm also grateful to Eleanor Stammeijer for all her sterling work on the PR side of things, to Grace Brown who does magical things with social media and to Katie Meegan who saw me through the copyedit stage. The support structure at Bonnier Books is just fantastic. I also need to pay tribute to Sandra Ferguson, who provided the much-needed safety net for that final version. She was brilliant at spotting those timeline errors and little faults that would have threatened the book's credibility and flow.

Finally, as always, it's friends and family who get me through the ups and downs of writing my books. In some ways, lockdown was ideal for writing but to keep that motivation going took a ridiculous amount of WhatsApp calls to daughters, Sarah and Jayne and sister, Hilary, not to mention the support and restorative cups of tea – and maybe the occasional white wine – from my husband, Kevin. He was brought up on a farm in the '50s and '60s so his knowledge and help has been particularly valuable with this book. I could not do any of this without the help of him and the whole 'unit.'

My love and thanks to everyone who has seen me through this, my third book. Your patience and sense of humour have kept me going.

Welcome to the world of *Shirley Mann*!

Keep reading for more from Shirley Mann, to discover
a recipe that features in this novel and to find out
more about what Shirley is doing next . . .

We'd also like to introduce you to MEMORY LANE,
our special community for the very best of saga
writing from authors you know and love and new
ones we simply can't wait for you to meet.
Read on and join our club!

www.MemoryLane.club

f **/MemoryLane.club**

Hello dear reader,

It's so lovely that you're either joining me for the first time or have come back for more with *Hannah's War*. It means so much to have you with me on my journey.

This book was always waiting to be written. From the first time I met Iris Newbould and Dorothy Taylor and they proudly showed me their photographs from their days as Land Army girls, it sort of sat there until I was ready. When I was researching my first novel, *Lily's War*, I rushed to travel the country in search of women who had been in the services during the war. I have to admit that I did not have any real plan of where this writing journey might take me. However, I knew I had to be quick because many of these people, like my mum, were in their 90s and I realised these womens' legacies were about to be lost, so I widened my search to find as many people as possible who would remember those war years. Little did I know that I might need their wonderful stories for future novels. I just loved meeting these women and taking notes about their amazing experiences. When I casually mentioned in *Lily's War* that Hannah, Lily's friend, was in the Land Army, I didn't really expect she would end up with her own story. In a typical Hannah way, she stayed quietly in the background, waiting to see whether I would ever recognise her potential and once I did, I just wanted you all to meet her, too.

It took me a while to appreciate this incredible girl and to begin with, I kept comparing her with Lily and Bobby; two formidable women who dealt with every hurdle placed in their way. Their strength was immediately recognisable to readers of the twenty-first century. To be honest, I started off by wanting to shake Hannah! But then as her character developed, I realised that her story was, in many ways, even more impressive than Lily's and Bobby's as she represented so many women's experiences. Women like Hannah were hurled out of a small, domestic world into an alien one, where they had to grow up quickly, respond to ridiculous hardships and learn to thrive against all obstacles. I learned to respect Hannah hugely and found myself rooting for her over and over again. I hope you did, too.

This book also led me to learn so much about the struggles ordinary German people faced during the war. Since I was a little girl, my father, who had been in the 8th Army, would patiently explain that many Germans had also been victims of Nazism. He never confused the twisted ideology of Hitler and the Nazi party with the ordinary people. In the 1970s, I met some German teenagers on a student trip. We had many a late-night discussion about how the oppression had framed their parents' lives. They were discussions that left a deep impression on me, and I have returned to Germany on many occasions since.

As the book unfolded, I started to appreciate how hard it was for the people on both sides of the Channel to simply survive. Not necessarily because of the brutal conflict, but because they struggled to find enough to eat or the will to face another day. I've never wanted to write a book that would gloss over the real hardships that people like Hannah's parents faced, so to talk directly – and candidly – to so many older people was a privilege. Their honest admissions of how frightened they were most of the time reminds me constantly of how lucky my generation has been, thanks to their sacrifices. I was lucky to be able to get hold of the diaries of my friend's mother-in-law, who was a Land Army girl. I was stunned by the physicality of the job, the hardships in all weathers and the relentlessness of field after field that needed to be sown, harvested and re-sown – and they didn't even have a glam uniform! They all hated that hat!

I was about to start *Hannah's War* when Covid struck and, like all of us, I was unable to go anywhere. This was frustrating because I needed to travel for research, but I was so grateful for to be able to conduct some of my research online. However, as soon as things started to open up, I was off to Norfolk to check out the environs of my fictitious farm. Throughout the lockdowns, every time I felt sorry for myself, I would immerse myself in the field of frozen sprouts with Hannah, Dotty and Lavinia and count my blessings. The women who inspired these books have had a life changing effect on me and have made me feel so grateful for the time and place I was born. From the comments I receive, I know that many of you feel the same.

I went to the National Arboretum in Staffordshire and stood in awe next to the statue of two Land Army girls. It struck me that at the bottom of the Land Army plinth was a dead rat and a trap. I thought that was just a perfect depiction of how, while men, and some other women, were doing the glamorous film-worthy jobs, these women were dealing with the nitty-gritty that made a huge difference to the nation. Without them, Britain would have starved as food stores were particularly subjected to rats, who were nicknamed 'Hitler's little helpers.' These girls operated at

a level that is often unappreciated and by the time I was nearing the end of the book, I wanted Hannah to be put on a plinth of her own. She so deserves it. I hope you agree.

If you haven't had the chance yet, I'd love you to read my first two books, both available now. *Lily's War* is about Hannah's friend who works as a wireless operator in the Women's Auxiliary Air Force. *Bobby's* War follows the spirited Bobby Hollis, who becomes a pilot in the Air Transport Auxiliary. My next book, *Bridget's War*, follows another inspirational woman. A newly-graduated police officer, Bridget is sent from the bustling streets of London to work as an internment camp guard on the Isle of Man, where more than her training will be tested. Coming soon!

If you'd like to find out a little bit more about me, the books I write and upcoming news, do sign up to Memory Lane, Bonnier Books UK's community for lovers of heartwarming and moving stories about women's lives, featuring wartime, family and romance
🅵 MemoryLaneClub.

Best wishes,

Shirley

Mrs Hill's Vegetable Pie

It took me a while to realise that Mrs Hill's vegetable pie was very similar to the homity pie I had discovered at the café at Scarthins, the best independent book shop in the world. It's really close to where I live in the Derbyshire Dales and has three floors rammed with wonderful books. Oh, and they are so supportive to local authors like me. But all that aside, this pie is just yummy and appreciated by everyone from Dotty in the 1940s to my own husband today so I thought you might like to give it a try. I've merged a couple of recipes – one from the war when some ingredients wouldn't have been available and one from modern times when we are lucky enough to get whatever we need. So feel free to add cream and as much cheese as you want! Mrs Hill would have had an apoplexy at such flagrant indulgence but hey, we can thank goodness we don't live in wartimes, so enjoy it!

Ingredients:

For the pastry
6oz flour (you can mix plain and wholemeal)
3oz butter or margarine
Pinch of cayenne pepper (optional)
1 egg

For the filling
4–5 medium potatoes, quartered and thickly sliced
2–3 medium leeks
1 apple, cored and chopped into small cubes
3oz butter or margarine, plus more for frying

Fresh or dried thyme
2 cloves garlic, finely chopped
Salt and pepper (to taste)
1 egg
2 onions or spring onions, finely sliced
1 tbsp thyme leaves (optional)
150ml double cream
125g mature cheddar, grated

Method

1. Preheat the oven at 200°C. Make the shortcrust pastry using plain flour and 3oz butter/margarine and add a pinch of cayenne pepper. Rub the latter into the flour to make breadcrumbs and bind together with the egg and a little water to make a pliable dough.
2. Roll the dough into a greased pie dish, chill for 30 mins and then blind bake in the oven at 200°C/gas mark 6, for about 10 mins.
3. Chop potatoes into small cubes (skins on) and simmer in boiling water until tender.
4. Chop the leeks and onions and fry them along with the garlic in butter/margarine until tender. Add the apple and thyme.
5. Drain the potatoes and add to leeks. Stir in one whisked egg, more butter/margarine and 2oz of grated cheese and, turning off the heat, the cream. Season with salt and pepper.
6. Fill the pie dish with the mixture and add 4oz of grated cheese on top.
7. Bake at 220°C/gas mark 7 until the top is browned.

Coming soon from Shirley Mann . . .

Bridget's War

The Isle of Man, 1942

Manx born and bred, Bridget Quayle loves the island and knows every inch of it like the back of her hand. But that doesn't mean she wants to be there now, as World War II rages around the world.

As a newly trained police officer, living in the vibrant and bustling city of London, she had it all. A budding career, celebrity status as one of only a few female officers, and a busy social life. Then World War II strengthened its grip and she found herself posted back to the island – a stark contrast to the exciting streets of the capital.

But tasked with managing Rushen Camp, a women's internment camp, she realises that war can be just as dangerous on an island in the middle of the Irish Sea as in the centre of a big city. When the arrival of two women claiming to be Austrian Jews arouses Bridget's suspicions, she finds herself tested beyond anything she was taught in her training.

Coming in ebook in 2022 and paperback in 2023. Read on for an exclusive extract . . .

Chapter 1

Port Erin, Isle of Man, January 1942

Bridget's heavy policewoman's shoes resounded in the of Port Erin as she ran towards the beach below. The shop frontages were so familiar, but she hardly registered them, concentrating instead on getting down to the commotion she could hear at the bottom of the hill. The thud of her heart seemed to echo the noise of the leather soles of her shoes on the ground beneath her.

Ahead, she heard a scream and quickened her pace. She looked behind her to see if there was any sign of back-up, but apart from the woman who had run to the police station to sound the alarm and was now struggling to keep up behind her, the streets were depressingly empty.

'Bugger,' she hissed. Swearing was a new skill she had learned during her police officer training, but she was not sure the satisfying expletive was going to be enough to help her deal with this. She pushed her dark hair out of her eyes and hurried on.

Ahead of her she saw a group of people. They were crowded into the narrow path by Christian's Cottage, silhouetted in the last rays of winter sunlight reflected on the sand behind them. As usual, it was a mix of arrogant Nazi sympathisers, German Jews hanging back trying to avoid being noticed and some Oswald Mosely fascist supporters who looked as if they were on their way to a cocktail party. As Bridget neared the commotion, the crowd stepped back, looking at her with relief and expectation.

Feeling anything but the saviour they were all expecting, Bridget stepped forward.

'All right, all right, what's going on here?' she said in the same commanding voice she had used as Lady Bracknell in one of her school plays, but then she spotted the knife.

Glistening in the weak early January sun, the serrated kitchen knife was being held by a tall woman in her thirties with faded peroxide blonde hair and wearing a floral pinny. Bridget recognised her at once as one of the fierce Nazi supporters. She was standing over a smaller figure, coiled up on the floor like a snail squirming to try and retreat into its shell. The victim's hands were clasped protectively over her head with her knees pulled up over her body while the shadow of her assailant cast a dark mark, just like a blood stain, over the tarmac.

Bridget edged slowly forwards, catching sight of the terrified, pale face of Ursula Artz, the young, timid Jewish girl on the ground. The next few seconds could mean the difference between life and death.

'Now, Helga, hand me that knife,' she said gently, reaching out her hand towards the German woman. 'You don't want to end up in prison, now, do you? What you do in the next minute will make that decision for you.'

Helga's eyes darted around her as if trying to work out where the voice was coming from. They finally focused on Bridget.

'You do not understand,' she said in broken English. 'She is a Jew and . . . she . . . took my soap.'

For women in the internment camp on the Isle of Man, soap was a commodity as valuable as gold, and from some of the other Nazi supporters, there was a murmur that such a theft deserved retribution and after all, the thief belonged to that dreadful race of people.

'I know,' Bridget said in a quiet, calm voice, 'but it's not worth risking a long gaol sentence for. You've never been to prison but I can tell you, you won't like it and, Helga, what about your little girl?'

Seeing the woman hesitate gave Bridget confidence. With more twists and turns to her life than anyone on the Island suspected, Helga exuded a ferocity that terrified anyone weaker than her, but Bridget was not going to be cowed. She didn't know much about this woman, but she did know that her Achilles heel was her little girl, Kirstin, and Bridget felt if she was ever going to capitalise on that knowledge, now was the moment. She could see Helga weighing up the policewoman's words but without any idea of the real workings of this woman's mind, Bridget had to be poised for any eventuality. Not for the first time, she wished she knew more about all these women in her charge.

'I want you to think about this, Helga,' Bridget said, bringing the woman's attention back to the present. Threatening someone with a knife is very, very serious. You want to get out of here and have a new life with that little girl of yours when all this is over, don't you? Don't throw everything away by doing something you'll regret.'

Helga held out the knife in front of her as if it were a match that was burning down towards her fingers. Her eyes flicked from the knife to Bridget and back to the knife again. There was a tense silence that echoed eerily around the crowd and the women in the little group surrounding the drama held their breath.

For a brief second, Helga looked as if she was about to lunge forwards, and Bridget tensed herself like a cat waiting to pounce on a mouse. Her whole body was taut, and she was already assessing how she would get round to the back of the attacker to disarm her. 'Your daughter,' she whispered urgently to the woman. 'Think of her.'

The purple haze of anger suddenly faded and Helga dropped the knife onto the ground, prompting a communal sigh of relief from the crowd. The young girl on the floor peered through her fingers when she heard the clatter of the weapon hitting the ground and slowly uncurled and started to warily stand up.

'Good,' Bridget said, trying not to sound as thankful as she felt. She looked at the huge, solid frame in front of her and realised she would have had little chance of preventing a violent attack if she had failed to divert Helga's attention. Playing out the different outcomes was something she would agonise over after her shift, trying to learn from it to prepare herself for the next altercation.

'Now, Helga, I'm going to have to take you in, you know that. But the fact that you've relinquished the knife will help.' She bent down to pick it up, cross with herself that she hadn't done that straight away. Under pressure, it was so hard to remember each step in a situation like this.

Bridget got out her brown, leather-bound notebook and flicked it open, licking her pencil in readiness to record the essential details of the event. She automatically recited a caution to Helga who, realising the consequences of her hot temper, seemed to shrink in size. The young woman police officer glanced around the group and wrote down individual names to make sure she could get statements later and then marched Helga off towards the police station, prompting a murmur of approval from the crowd. Bridget knew it was only a matter of time before another incident happened that would take yet one more paltry argument to a flashpoint.

Rushen Camp on the south end of Isle of Man was like a cauldron that simmered until it bubbled over, fuelled by something as simple as who was next in the bathroom. Resentment, indignation, boredom and fights like this one were an inevitable result of putting so many women with opposing views. These people had all been on UK soil at the beginning of the war and in a moment of desperation and not knowing what to do with any of them, Prime Minister Winston Churchill had issued the order to 'collar the lot.' As a result, men and women perceived as being a threat to security found themselves being rounded up, sometimes in the middle of the night, to be carted off and then shipped off to live 'behind the wire' on the Isle of Man. The camps that were set up all over the island now included male and female German Nazi sympathisers, fascists, IRA activists, Jews, conscientious objectors and those with every possible extreme view that abounded in Britain in the 1940s. A series of female police officers had been brought in to keep the peace at Rushen, the women's camp, but in those first years, there had been as many as three thousand women herded together in an area only just over three miles wide. Now, those numbers were dwindling as the threat to the allies were assessed, meaning some were sent home to Germany and others back to their adopted home in England. To those left behind, a fight over something as valuable as a piece of soap was just as serious as the international conflicts being played out all over the world.

Bridget glanced at her watch. Booking this woman in was going to take time and poor old Greeba, her chocolate Labrador, was going to have to wait, once again, for her walk.

*   *   *

It was pitch dark by the time Bridget and Greeba finally got onto Bradda Head above Port Erin, but they both could have found their way blindfold. There was no help from the town below with its blacked-out windows disguising the fact that there was any life there at all, but she had been walking these paths since she was little and knew every rock and twist and turn. Bridget pulled up the collar of the old tweed coat against the icy blasts which took her breath away as soon as she rounded Milner's Tower. The moon peeped out from the clouds to reflect on the Irish Sea below, where white horses were being stirred up to dance like bunting at a washed-out fair. The bay inlet surrounding Port Erin was calmer, protected as always by the huge presence of Bradda Head.

Bridget sighed. She loved this island; it was her home, but she did not want to be there. Not now, not during the war. She wanted to be back in London, where she had done her training. There were so few policewomen being accepted by the force, she had been enjoying a celebrity status. It was easy to be caught up in the excitement of being in the capital where real crimes happened and with a busy social life, the appeal of the Peel local pubs of pale into insignificance. The war may have devastated London but to the newly-qualified WPC Quayle, there was nowhere else she wanted to be.

She had spent so many years careering across these paths, following in the wake of her two brothers, Aedan and Brendan and their friend, Kieran Moore. All three of them had joined the RAF and the last she had heard of Kieran, he was a hero in the Battle of Britian.

She sniffed in frustration. So many of the boys she had grown up with were in the thick of the war and she was back home, babysitting a pile of women. Bridget scuffed her wellington boots against the gravel path as if to wipe out her footsteps and erase her presence from the island.

'Come on, Greeba, I'm frozen,' she called to the dog, who ran back to her, wagging her tail at the prospect of a cosy bed. Turning one more time towards the sea, Bridget shouted into the wind: 'Bugger, damn and blast.'

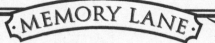

· MEMORY LANE ·

Don't miss Shirley Mann's inspiring
debut novel . . .

Lily's War

World War II is in full swing and Lily Mullins is determined
to do her bit for the war effort. Her friends and sweetheart
have all joined up and Lily's sure there must be a role for her
that goes further than knitting socks for the troops!

When she decides to volunteer for the Women's Auxiliary Air Force, Lily soon discovers that she has a talent as a
wireless operator. Helped along the way by a special gang of
girls, she finds strengths she didn't know she had and realises
that the safety of the country might just be in her hands . . .

Meanwhile, Danny is determined to marry Lily, but his
letters home become more and more distant. Will a long
separation mean the end of their love story?

Available now.

If you loved *Hannah's War*,
you'll love . . .

Bobby's War

It's World War II and Bobby Hollis has joined the Air Transport Auxiliary in a team known as the 'glamour girls' – amazing women who pilot aircraft all around the country.

Bobby always wanted to escape life on the family farm and the ATA seemed like the perfect opportunity for her. But there's always something standing in her way. Like a demanding father, who wants to marry her off to a rich man. And the family secrets that threaten to engulf everything.

As Bobby navigates her way through life, and love, she has to learn that controlling a huge, four-engined bomber might just be easier than controlling her own life . . .

Available now.